HOME GROWN TALENT

CREATIVE TYPES
BOOK TWO

JOANNA CHAMBERS
SALLY MALCOLM

Home Grown Talent

Cover art: Natasha Snow

Published by Joanna Chambers

ISBN: 978-1-914305-05-4

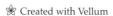 Created with Vellum

Home Grown Talent

Are you for real?

From the outside, it looks like model and influencer Mason Nash has it all—beauty, fame, and fortune. With his star rapidly rising, and a big contract up for grabs, Mason's on the verge of hitting the big time.

When an opportunity arises to co-host a gardening slot on daytime TV with his ex's brother, Owen Hunter, Mason is definitely on-board. And he intends to use every trick in the book to make the show a hit—including agreeing to his ruthless producer's demand to fake a 'will-they/won't-they' romance with his co-host...

Owen Hunter is a gardener with a huge heart and both feet planted firmly on the well-tilled ground. He's proud of the life he's built and has absolutely no desire to be on TV—yet somehow he finds himself agreeing to do the show.

It's definitely *not* because he's interested in Mason Nash. The guy might be beautiful—and yeah, his spoiled brat routine presses all Owen's buttons in the bedroom—but Owen has no interest in a short-term fling with a fame-hungry model.

As the two men get closer, though, Owen starts to believe there's more to Mason than his beautiful appearance and carefully-curated online persona—that beneath the glitz and glamour is a sweet, sensitive man longing to be loved.

A man Owen might be falling for. A man who might even feel the same.

But in a world of media spin and half-truths, Owen is dangerously out of his depth. And when a ridiculous scandal explodes online, with Owen at its heart, it starts to look as though everything he thought was real is built on lies—including his budding romance with Mason...

CHAPTER ONE

OWEN

February

Owen was hard-pruning the clematis that swarmed up the back wall of his garden when his doorbell rang. He knew immediately it was Lewis, his younger brother—no one else rang his doorbell so obnoxiously.

Owen's doorbell was a cheery little two-note bell. A proper little *ding-dong* of a bell. But Lewis had a way of leaning on it that made the *dings* run into the *dongs* and start to stutter, until it seemed like the whole contraption was having a nervous breakdown.

Which was… very Lewis. He had that effect on a lot of people too.

Owen unhurriedly closed his secateurs, crossed the garden, and went inside the house to answer the door. Sure enough, on the other side stood Lewis, and with him was Aaron, his boyfriend of the last few months.

"Could you not break my doorbell?" Owen asked mildly, stepping aside and waving them in.

"You were taking ages," Lewis said unapologetically, as he moved past him.

"I was in the garden."

"You're always in the garden."

Aaron flashed his cute smile at Owen as he stepped into the house and held up a be-ribboned cardboard box. "I brought cake."

Owen grinned. "See, this is why I like you more than Lewis."

"I heard that," Lewis called from halfway down the hallway, but he sounded a little bit pleased. The soppy sod.

Owen followed them down the hallway to the back of the house. When he'd bought the place, he'd knocked through a couple of walls to make one big kitchen and living area, adding some wide glass doors at the back that let in tons of natural light and gave him a nice view of his pride and joy: the garden.

"So, to what do I owe this pleasure?" he asked. "I wasn't expecting you today."

"Oh, just popping by on the off-chance you'd be in," Lewis said airily, which made Owen immediately suspicious, particularly given that Owen could now see that the cake box Aaron was holding looked very fancy indeed, with gold lettering and gold and blue ribbons.

"Any chance of a cuppa?" Lewis asked.

"Sure. Tea or coffee?"

"Hot chocolate?" Lewis said hopefully.

"Hot chocolate *and* cake?" Owen said, raising his brows. "You want to go into a sugar coma?"

"Can't think of a better way to die."

"Yeah, well, I don't have any hot chocolate, so pick a grown-up beverage."

Lewis made a face. "Tea then. Two sugars."

Owen rolled his eyes and turned to Aaron. "Coffee for you?"

Aaron nodded happily and held out the cake box. "I got a few different ones."

He certainly had, Owen saw when he opened it up in the kitchen. Six ridiculously pretty slices of French patisserie, each one constructed of an impressive number of layers and decorated with fancy chocolate and fruit. Owen grinned to himself, knowing that Lewis would prefer a cheap jam doughnut.

While he busied himself putting on the coffee machine and making tea, Lewis and Aaron made themselves comfy on his sofa. Lewis—always one to make himself at home— picked up the remote and turned on the TV, lazily scrolling through channels, pausing every now and again to make some acerbic comment that made Aaron laugh before moving on.

Owen loaded up a tray with their drinks and the patisserie Aaron had brought and carried it through. Lewis had just landed on a channel on which a good-looking silver fox was talking earnestly to two women in stretchy outfits standing on yoga mats.

"Hey, it's *Weekend Wellness*," Aaron said. "Leave it on."

Lewis groaned. "I hate magazine shows," he whined. "They're so inane."

"Yeah, well, anything's better than watching you channel-surf," Aaron said, wresting the remote out of his hand. "Besides, this is one of ours."

"One of yours?" Owen said, puzzled. Lewis and Aaron both used to work on Lewis's show, *Leeches*, a popular vampire drama series. Aaron had been Lewis's PA back then, but now he was a script writer in his own right, working on another show. Some historical thing.

"Not *ours*-ours," Aaron explained. "RPP's."

RPP—Reclined Pigeon Productions—was the company Lewis and Aaron both worked for.

On-screen, the silver fox began moving away from the two

yoga women, talking to camera as he walked. He was nattily dressed in tweed trousers held up by braces over a round-collared shirt.

"Male beauty and grooming is one of the fastest-growing markets out there," he said, his expression earnest, "with an increasing range of products, from hair and beard grooming to moisturisers and skincare solutions—even cosmetics for men. But what if you also want the products you buy to be ethical and sustainable?"

Lewis made a scoffing sound, and Aaron elbowed him. "Shh, I'm listening."

The silver fox emerged into another part of the studio where a young, handsome guy was waiting behind a table, blond hair gleaming under the studio lights, an array of bottles and jars set out in front of him.

Owen felt an immediate and shocking bolt of recognition, but it was Aaron who gave voice to that recognition, exclaiming, "Oh my God! It's *Mason*!"

Mason bloody Nash.

Mason, who had been Lewis's boyfriend for a while, before Aaron. For a blessedly short while, Owen thought darkly, even as his eyes greedily ate up every detail of Mason's appearance. He looked as gorgeous as ever. As gorgeous as he did in all his pictures—and since Mason was a model, there were plenty of those kicking about. There really was some truth in that old cliché about the camera loving some people.

Lewis glanced at Aaron. "Didn't I tell you he got a gig on *Weekend Wellness*?"

"No!" Aaron replied, a note of outrage in his tone. "Since when?"

"A few weeks ago?" Lewis guessed, shrugging a shoulder. "It's my fault actually. I was talking to Misty at the monthly budget meeting." He glanced at Owen, adding as an aside, "She's the producer of this show," before turning back to

4

Aaron. "She said she wanted to get someone on to talk about male beauty stuff, and I suggested Mason. His influencer thing is about all that sort of crap, and you know how much he wants to get on TV. It's probably the only reason he went out with me."

"You do have *some* other attractive features," Aaron murmured, shooting Lewis a heated look. "And I seem to remember him being pretty upset when you dumped him. He said you left 'quite a gap'."

Lewis snorted. "Yeah, on his Instagram. The truth is, the main reason he was upset was because *I* dumped *him* before he could line up teaser posts for his next boyfriend."

"Hmm. Well, it's true that he's a grandmaster at making the most of his love life on Insta."

"Yeah, the only thing Mason's ever been in love with is his follower count." Lewis huffed a laugh. "But at least you know where you are with him. He might be as deep as a puddle, but he doesn't pretend to be anything he's not."

Lewis's expression was amused but tolerant. His relationship with Mason had been as short-lived as all his relationships—until Aaron had come along. As short-lived as most of Mason's relationships too, apparently. Not that Owen followed what the guy got up to but… okay, he might have googled him once, a couple of months after he and Lewis broke up. Which had been a good thing. The results of that search had made him realise… Well, it had satisfied his curiosity. He'd spent an hour scrolling through endless celebrity photos featuring Mason on the arms of a bunch of other guys—all of them at least a little bit famous.

It had been enough to put paid to the idiotic idea he'd been formulating up until that point of maybe, possibly, asking Mason out for coffee. Which was good. It had saved him the bother of raising the topic with Lewis, which would have been excruciating, not to mention the inevitable rejection from Mason. Honestly, Owen didn't know why he'd even been considering such a thing. On the few occasions Owen had met him, Mason had been more interested in taking selfies than talking to Owen. He'd probably have been totally bewildered to get a call from Owen.

Christ, even thinking about that now made his neck heat with embarrassment.

"Anyway, after I mentioned Mason to Misty, she spoke to Mason's agent, and unsurprisingly, he was up for it," Lewis continued. "I think he might have already appeared on the show once before, a couple of weeks ago? It's not a weekly gig, but I think it is intended to be semi-regular."

On-screen, the silver fox was saying, "I'm joined today by Mason Nash, our favourite model, brand ambassador, and Instagram star." He sent Mason a flirtatious look. "Is there anything you don't do, Mason?"

Mason smiled, a practised tilt of his lush lips. "Oh, plenty. I don't do yoga for a start—you should see my downward dog, Marc. It's a *disaster*."

He gave a little shudder, and the presenter—Marc —laughed.

"But," Mason went on, with dramatic emphasis, "I *do* know the best ethical buys for male beauty products. So, let's start with skincare."

"Downward dog," Lewis said, chuckling. "Look at him flirt. He can't help himself. The viewers will love all this."

"He's actually coming across pretty well," Aaron said, sounding a little surprised. "He's a natural on camera, isn't he?"

Owen watched, mesmerised, as Mason squeezed a tiny amount of cream onto the back of his hand and rubbed it into his smooth skin, his forefinger moving in small circles as he blabbed on about the ingredients and the manufacturing process, and that this moisturiser was plant-based, cruelty-free, fair trade.

The details were pretty dull, and Owen found himself idly

imagining some fun ways to stop the flow of words from that pretty mouth. Unfortunately, that had the unwanted effect of making his cock begin to swell. Horrified, he shifted in his seat, leaning forward to disguise the bulge in his jeans as he selected a patisserie slice he didn't actually want, then hastily forked half of it into his mouth.

Aaron turned to him, smiling. "What do you think? Delicious, right?"

Owen hurriedly swallowed. "Um, yeah, amazing," he croaked, though he'd barely tasted the chunk of sponge and mousse and whatnot he'd just shoved down his throat.

He glanced back at the TV. At Mason, with his creamy skin, fair hair, and lean, elegant body. And those *eyes*—there weren't many people with eyes that intensely green, were there? Christ, he really was perfect.

Perfect on the outside, at least.

Inside was probably another story. Inside, Owen suspected that Mason was rather like one of those fancy chocolate Santas you got at Christmas. All colourful and glittery on the surface, but when you tore the foil off, it was just a boring chocolate shell underneath. Disappointingly hollow.

Silver-fox-Marc leaned his elbows on the bench and moved in closer to Mason. "Is sustainability important to you, Mason?" he asked. "Do you try to make sustainable choices in other areas too?"

"I do, yes," Mason said, pushing one hand through his hair and letting it fall artfully across one eye. "I'm pretty careful in my food choices, and I love to cook with home-grown produce when I can. Household products and clothing choices are important to me, too."

"For sure," Marc said earnestly, nodding. "The fashion industry is one of the major global polluters." He began droning on about the clothes he was wearing, inviting Mason to touch the fabric of his trousers, which was, he explained, locally woven and naturally dyed.

"Do you know what I call this fabric?" Mason said at last, stroking Marc's thigh suggestively.

"Tweed?" Marc asked, looking puzzled.

Mason shook his head, then winked. "Boyfriend material."

The studio erupted in laughter, and Owen gave a surprised chuckle too, unexpectedly charmed by Mason's sly humour.

Lewis grinned. "Great line."

"Cheesy line," Aaron said. "But yeah, a good one."

"Uh-oh," Lewis said then. "Aaron—look at Owen's face."

Owen glanced sharply at them to find them both staring at him with matching expressions of wonder. He scowled at them. "What?"

"You look like one of those cartoon characters that have love hearts bulging out of their eyeballs," Lewis said, clasping his hands together and making a goofy expression.

Owen's face heated. "I do *not* have love hearts bulging out of my eyeballs."

"Um, you kind of do," Aaron said.

Lewis waggled his eyebrows outrageously. "Or maybe something else is bulging?"

"Lewis!" Aaron swatted his arm, but there was amusement in his voice.

Owen straightened self-consciously. "Shut up," he said and turned his attention determinedly back to the screen. The presenter was smiling warmly at Mason, thanking him and starting the introduction for the next piece.

Lewis, who had already lost interest, pointed the remote at the TV and shut it off. "Seriously?" he said. "You fancy *Mason*? How did I miss that?"

Owen felt another wave of heat sweep over his already warm face. "For God's sake, Lew, he was your boyfriend!"

"What's that got to do with the price of fish?" Lewis said, looking genuinely puzzled. "We went out for, like, six weeks.

He was hardly the love of my life." He shot a sappy look at Aaron, which made Owen want to gag.

"Don't be obtuse," Owen said irritably. "You know what I mean."

Lewis frowned, seeming confused. "Um, no. You're going to have to explain."

"You *slept* together?" Owen pointed out.

"Okay," Lewis said slowly. "That's some very weird paternalistic bullshit, but whatever."

"It's not weird," Owen said. "Of course I feel awkward about it."

"About what?"

Owen threw up his hands in exasperation. "Finding him attractive!"

"Why would you feel awkward about that?" Lewis asked, seeming genuinely bewildered. "Mason's gorgeous—not as gorgeous as Aaron, of course—" He broke off when Aaron scoffed at this, diving at him and planting a noisy kiss on his lips.

"Oh my God, can you leave each other alone for *five* minutes," Owen begged, covering his eyes.

Eventually, Lewis came back up for air. "Sorry," he said, laughing. "What was I saying? Oh yeah, you fancy Mason—so what? I don't care. The reason I made the crack about love heart eyes wasn't because of my history with him. It's just… it's not often I see you look at someone, you know, like *that*."

"I didn't look at him like anything," Owen grumbled, but his face was hot.

Lewis shrugged. "Fine, have it your way," he said. "All I'm saying is I didn't think Mason Nash was your type."

"He's *not* my type." That much was certainly true.

Lewis bumped him with his shoulder, hard. "Then why have you gone bright red?"

Groaning, Owen sighed. "Look, okay, I'm *attracted* to him.

Strongly attracted, if you must know. But you're right. He really *isn't* my type."

"Your type being what? Very earnest eco-warriors capable of boring a man to death in five seconds flat?"

"Michelle was not an eco-warrior."

"She *was* boring, though. It's okay, you can admit it now. So was Eddie. In fact, he was worse."

Owen rolled his eyes. This was an old argument, but he was happy to be back on safer ground. "I happen to prefer partners who can hold an actual conversation and don't spend their whole life primping and preening in front of a mirror."

"In fairness, Mason doesn't do that as much as you might think." Lewis cocked his head. "He *is* obsessed with celebrity culture though. He'd go to the opening of a fucking envelope if he thought he'd get papped."

"Lewis," Aaron broke in patiently. "Do you think you should maybe leave Owen alone now? You've hounded him enough."

"Fine," Lewis said, holding up his hands. "I'll say no more." He frowned. "Except for one last thing—"

Aaron groaned, but Lewis turned determinedly to Owen. "For the record, I have zero problem with you going out with any of my exes. If you want to go on a date with any of them —or hell, have sex with them while hanging naked from a chandelier—just go for it." He shrugged. "It's no skin off my nose. I've got Aaron now."

Flatly, Aaron said, "How romantic. I feel positively swept off my feet."

Which prompted Lewis to dive at him again and Aaron to fall backward, shrieking with laughter.

As Owen eyed them, tussling, he turned over Lewis's words. The truth was, Mason was the only one of Lewis's exes that Owen had been attracted to this strongly. In a way that had him googling the guy and looking at his pictures online…

Ugh. Frankly, his own behaviour freaked him out. He still squirmed at the memory. But secretly? He *knew* why he'd done it. He knew what it was about Mason that had caught his eye. Because yeah, there was something Mason—and Michelle and a few other of Owen's exes—shared. Something that Owen saw behind those eyes as Mason postured in his bratty-charming way.

Yeah, there was something about that spoiled poutiness that punched every single one of Owen's buttons.

When Lewis finally sat up again, he said, "I'm not saying you should ask *Mason* out, by the way."

"I wasn't planning to," Owen replied drily. "Fancying him is not the same as wanting a relationship with him."

Lewis cocked a sceptical eyebrow. "Good, because Mason's a terrible bet for a relationship, but he could be good fun if you just wanted to scratch an itch one night, sow a wild oat…"

"Even if I wanted something like that, *which I don't*, it wouldn't be with Mason Nash—Jesus, Lew, it's not as though he'd be interested in me in a million years."

"Why wouldn't he be interested in you?" Lewis echoed disbelievingly. "You're good company, funny, kind, reliable, and handsome—what's not to like?" He grinned. "You're basically me without all the horrible personality traits."

Owen rolled his eyes. "Please," he said. "No one would call me handsome next to you."

Lewis rolled his eyes. "I wish you wouldn't do that."

"What?"

"Put yourself down, especially in comparison to me. Fucking hell, Owen, you're twice the human being I am—everyone loves you. Even Aaron keeps asking me why I can't be more like you."

"That's true," Aaron admitted, shrugging. "I do."

JOANNA CHAMBERS & SALLY MALCOLM

Lewis added cheerfully, "Most people think I'm a complete dick."

Owen frowned at that, his protective instincts surging. "Yeah, well, anyone who thinks that doesn't really see you."

Lewis chuckled. "You're literally making my point for me. You're such a fucking Disney princess that you can't see what a misanthrope I am."

But Owen wasn't buying that. He knew his brother. Sudden emotion made his throat swell and his eyes sting. He hid the reaction by hooking a big mitt round Lewis's shoulder and roughly pulling him in close, messing his hair with an affectionate one-handed scrub before planting a noisy kiss on top of his head.

"Ow," Lewis complained, extricating himself from the rough hug, and Owen grinned at him.

"Anyway," Owen said. "It's not like I'm ever going to run into Mason. We don't exactly move in the same circles."

"Actually," Aaron said, "you might see him sooner than you think." He turned to Lewis. "Are you going to ask him at some point?"

"Ask me what?" Owen said.

Lewis cleared his throat. "We kinda came round for a reason, actually. To ask you—" He broke off, clearing his throat.

"What?"

Lewis rubbed at the back of his neck. "There's this awards show next week. Awards *dinner*," he amended. "You know I hate shit like that—I was planning to avoid it—but the big bosses are saying I've got to go. They're taking an extra table."

"*Leeches* is up for an award," Aaron interjected. "The fact they're taking another table last minute probably means the organisers have given RPP the heads-up that we're going to win."

"That's great!" Owen enthused. Lewis did hate stuff like

that, but Owen loved to see his brother getting well-deserved praise for his work.

"Yeah, well," Lewis said, "don't get your hopes up. Aaron's a horrible optimist, but I do have four seats to fill, so" —he glanced at Owen uncertainly—"would you like to come?"

Owen's heart squeezed at Lewis's diffidence. "Come and see you get an *award*?" he said hoarsely. "Yeah, I'd love that."

"*Maybe* get an award," Lewis said, his cheeks a little pink. Then he grinned and added, "Mason will be there."

Owen's stomach sank. "Yeah? Why's that?"

"Jay Warren's bringing him," Aaron said.

"Jay Warren?"

"The guy who plays Skye?" Aaron supplied, naming the main character of *Leeches*. "RPP want Jay there for the photos —he's the face of the show, after all—but he's also a really nice guy. You'll like him."

"So who's getting the fourth seat?" Owen asked.

"Well, if there's someone you'd like to bring, feel free," Lewis said. "They'd technically be your plus-one."

"I can easily get someone to come, but there's no one I'm itching to bring," Owen said. "So if there's someone else you have in mind, I'm cool with that. It'll just be one big table, right? We wouldn't be going in couples. Maybe there's someone else from *Leeches* you'd like to ask?"

Aaron got a mischievous look on his face. "We should ask Tag," he said to Lewis, his eyes glinting with amusement.

"That would be kinda funny."

"Tag your actor pal?" Owen asked. "The one with the tattoos, who I met when I came to yours for brunch the other week?"

Aaron nodded.

Tag was currently an actor-slash-barista—he was a couple of years out of drama school, and he'd won a small part on

13

Aaron's show which he was hoping would prove to be his big break.

"What would be funny about asking Tag along?" Owen asked.

Lewis chuckled. "He has a… sort of *thing* with Mason and Jay."

"A thing?" Owen echoed, horrified. Why had Lewis been encouraging his attraction to Mason if—

"It's not what you're thinking," Aaron said, laughing. "Tag and Jay met Mason at the same party a few months back and they both asked him out. And now it's turned into this weird competitive fake-dating thing. According to Tag, Mason's in it for what he can post on his Insta—God only knows what the other two are getting out of it. They seem to see it as some sort of pissing contest though." He glanced at Lewis. "Jay will be so pissed to see Tag there."

Lewis grinned, then glanced at Owen. "What do you say? It's up to you. It's your plus-one. If you want to bring someone else—"

"Nah," Owen said. "I don't mind. Tag seems like a nice bloke." Besides, Owen was only going to see Lewis get his award. He didn't care who he'd be sitting next to, provided the guy wasn't a complete dick. And if Mason was there on the arm of a gorgeous, famous actor, that was a very good thing. It meant Owen wouldn't be tempted to act on his completely misguided attraction.

Aaron pulled out his phone. "I'll text Tag," he said and started typing.

Beside him, Lewis poked suspiciously at one of the slices of patisserie. "I don't see why we couldn't have brought jam doughnuts."

CHAPTER TWO

MASON

Carefully, Mason applied a last smudge of *Masculin* eyeliner and a final lick of mascara, before pulling back from the mirror to study the result.

Not bad. He wasn't actually that into cosmetics, but his contract with *Masculin* was lucrative, and he had to admit the mascara gave his light gold eyelashes some nice definition. Plus, the little bit of extra sparkle certainly worked with his outfit.

He'd eschewed a traditional tux in favour of a floral Simon Carter shirt and a cornflower-blue suit that fitted in all the right places. The whole point of the evening was to be seen, after all, so why dress like everyone else? Mason wanted to stand out, and stand out he would.

Picking up his phone, he took a couple of sultry selfies, eyes partly obscured behind a lock of hair that gleamed gold in the soft bedroom lamplight. He added a filter to deepen the green of his eyes and to ensure his makeup stood out, then posted it with the tags *#Masculin #BigNightOut #instagay #love #me*

Not in the mood to look at the likes and comments that immediately started flooding in, he flung his phone onto the bed and went in search of his shoes. Truth was, he was *not* in the mood for a Big Night Out. And even if he were, an evening at a tedious TV awards dinner was hardly his idea of fun. Especially after Jay had messaged him with the news that Mason's ex, Lewis Hunter, would be there with Aaron, his ridiculously wholesome boyfriend, and, even worse, his brother, Owen, who Lewis talked about as though he was a bloody living saint. Which, to be fair, he probably was to have put up with Lewis all these years.

In a fit of pique, Mason had messaged back to tell Jay that he'd changed his mind about going. He'd only relented after Jay promised to pick him up in a limo. That was a result, especially because Mason couldn't really afford *not* to go. Mason wanted—needed—to step his career up a gear, and the awards were a fantastic networking opportunity for him, not least because Misty Watson-King, the producer of *Weekend Wellness*, would be on their table.

Last time he'd spoken to her, Misty had hinted that there might be a permanent presenting role opening up on *Weekend Wellness*. Rumour had it that Marc, the current anchor, wasn't seeing eye-to-eye with Misty, and his contract was up at the end of the year. If Marc was on his way out, Mason wanted a chance at that anchor job, and it was crystal clear that schmoozing Misty was going to be key to making that happen.

Besides, arriving in a limo with Jay guaranteed a couple of decent snaps on the red carpet. Jay Warren was proper acting royalty—his mother, Dame Cordelia Warren, was a bona fide National Treasure for God's sake—and Mason's profile would get a nice boost if they were photographed together at the awards. Especially if *Leeches* won its category. They might even make it into the tabloids if Mason engineered a romantic 'moment' for the cameras. That alone would be worth a tedious evening watching Lewis drool over his new boyfriend while being judged by Saint bloody Owen.

Mason had met Owen a few times while he and Lewis were involved. Owen was an outdoorsy guy, strong and capable, and—annoyingly—pretty hot in a salt-of-the-earth kind of way. He'd also struck Mason as a holier-than-thou prick the first time they'd met, eyeing Mason disapprovingly when he'd walked in on him taking a selfie in Lewis's ridiculously huge bathtub—thankfully when the bath was empty and Mason was fully clothed. Then he'd made it worse by chuckling when Lewis had taken the piss out of Mason for, as he put it, 'plumbing new depths in shameless self-promotion' by posting the picture on Instagram. Whenever they'd met after that, Owen had seemed to make a point of keeping his distance, as if Mason wasn't worth getting to know. As if he wasn't good enough for Owen's precious little brother.

So, no, Mason was not relishing the idea of an evening with the Hunter brothers, even if he would have Jay Warren on his arm.

Talking of Jay, where the fuck was he?

Mason checked the time. Five minutes late already, which was typical. Mason really needed to be there for the drinks reception so he could talk to the right people before everyone was marooned at their tables for the evening. Jay never thought about things like that, though. People like Jay floated above the roiling sea of ambition that the rest of them had to swim in.

Pacing to the bedroom window of his basement flat, Mason looked up towards the road, but there was no sign of Jay's limo. The bastard better not have forgotten, or—

From the bed came the muffled sound of his phone ringing. Snatching it up, his heart sank at the sight of his mum's photo flashing up on the screen. For a moment, he dithered, watching it ring, tempted to let it go to voicemail. But no, then he'd just spend the evening worrying that something had happened, that the latest crisis was spiralling into something harder to handle. Something he'd have to deal with sooner or later anyway.

Biting back a sigh, he answered the call. "Hi Frieda. Everything okay?"

"Oh, hello," she said in that wobbly voice that heralded trouble. "I'm sorry to phone you. It's just I thought that I'd better keep you in the loop…"

Worry surged through Mason. Gazing out at the busy street beyond, he said in the steady voice he used when he needed to keep his mother calm, "In the loop about what?"

"Well, Kurt's payment hasn't gone through again this month…"

Mason closed his eyes. Kurt, his father, had left when Mason was thirteen and his sisters were toddlers, running off with the first in a series of women, all of whom, strangely enough, reminded Mason to some extent of his mother. Kurt was supposed to pay Frieda money at the start of every month, but he never had been the most reliable guy in the world.

"Okay," Mason said evenly, "don't worry. You know I'll make sure you're okay."

"I know, but I shouldn't have to keep asking you," Frieda said crossly. "It's *his* responsibility!"

"It's okay, though. You don't need to panic."

Please don't panic.

A sigh came down the line, part relief and part self-pity. "What would I do without you?"

Mason didn't answer that. *Couldn't* answer that because he honestly didn't know what she'd do without him, couldn't imagine her ever being able to cope without his support. Wearily, he sucked in a breath, his chest feeling tight. "Listen, I'm on my way out. Can we talk about this tomorrow?"

"Oh." She sounded disappointed, but then added, "Are you going out with Jay Warren?"

"Yes, we're going to the TV Best Awards," he said, knowing she'd like that.

Sure enough, she brightened. "Ooh, maybe you'll get into a magazine?"

"That's the idea, yeah."

Frieda loved it when he dated celebrities; she loved showing off his pictures to her friends. She'd be disappointed if she knew that he and Jay were just friends who fake-dated occasionally, so he let her think what she liked about that.

"Well," she said then, "why don't you come over for lunch this weekend? You can tell me all about it. And you could bring Jay. I'd love to meet him."

He would *not* be bringing Jay. Or anyone else, for that matter. He'd lived and breathed the consequences of a relationship gone sour when his parents broke up, and he had no interest in getting serious with anyone. So he just said, "I'll call you tomorrow and let you know when I'm free, yeah?"

Mollified, Frieda wittered on a little longer, but luckily— and at fucking last—the sleek black shape of Jay's limo pulled up in front of his building.

With guilty relief, Mason said goodbye and ended the call, took one last look at himself in the mirror, and headed out to the car.

The driver was already waiting. "Good evening, Mr. Nash," he said, holding open the rear passenger door. Mason gave him a polite nod and slid into the car, grateful for its warmth. The February night was cold and crisp, without a hint of spring in the air.

Inside, he found Jay relaxing on the back seat with all the self-assurance of a man who travelled around in limos all the time. Hell, he'd probably been travelling around in them since he was a kid.

"Mason," Jay said, smiling his actor's smile as the driver closed the door, "you look gorgeous. Quite ravishing."

Mason returned the smile with a dazzling one of his own.

"Thank you, I like to think so. You look rather ravishing yourself."

"Well." Jay glanced modestly down at his beautifully tailored tux. "Who doesn't look good in a penguin suit?"

"At least half the people there tonight, probably."

Jay laughed. "I see you're in one of *those* moods."

"Am I?" In fairness, he usually was after speaking to Frieda, and this was already the end of a long week full of too many people.

"Don't worry. I've come prepared," Jay said, reaching down for something near his feet. "You'll feel better after a glass of bubbly."

And, yes, Jay really did have a bottle of champagne on ice in the car—good stuff too. He held up the bottle in one hand and two glasses in the other. "I think we both need a little help getting through tonight, don't you?"

This time, when Mason smiled, it felt more genuine. He reached out to take the glasses from Jay, holding them while Jay expertly popped the cork. "You read my mind."

"Hardly necessary," Jay said drily. "I'd already read your flouncy text."

Mason winced, but Jay didn't seem too bothered, smiling as he poured the champagne. "Bottoms up." He winked. "As they say…"

By the time they reached Park Lane, Mason had downed two glasses of excellent champagne, and his mood was much improved. In fact, he was the perfect degree of buzzed as he stepped out of the car and onto the red carpet, relaxed enough to drape himself elegantly over Jay, pouting and preening for the cameras, without being so drunk that he made an arse of himself. Jay was up for the display as well, sliding one arm around Mason's waist and laughing as he pressed a quick kiss to Mason's lips for the benefit of the flashing cameras.

And if *that* didn't get them into the gossip mags, Mason didn't know what would.

They toned things down once they reached the bar, both intent on doing the rounds.

Jay made a face as he sipped the inferior champagne being offered around on trays by a fleet of uniformed servers. "I think," he said in a stagey, horrified whisper, "this may be *Prosecco*."

He was joking. Maybe.

Mason smiled along and stuck with him as they mingled. Everyone wanted to talk to Jay, and it was a fantastic way for Mason to get introductions to the industry people who mattered. Dutifully, he listened and laughed at their jokes, concentrating on looking his best and, as always, conscious of the eyes upon him.

People were always watching him, drawn in by his looks. Usually, it was the only thing about him they noticed.

At least there was no sign of Lewis Hunter and his entourage at the reception, although Mason kept his eyes peeled for Misty Watson-King. Eventually, about five minutes before they were due to take their seats, he spotted her strolling into the bar. Mason murmured his apologies to the couple he and Jay were talking to, and threaded his way through the crowd to where Misty stood talking to a younger woman. Mason was surprised to recognise her as Misty's latest intern—and personal dogsbody—Naomi.

"Mason!" Misty said, looking over as he approached. She was obviously pleased to see him, which was encouraging. Although perhaps she was just pleased to see a familiar face. "Look at you! Beautiful, as always."

"Thank you," he said. "You're looking beautiful yourself this evening."

Misty was a tall, slender woman, and tonight, she wore a floor-length, gold chiffon dress that Mason recognised as a last season Ralph Lauren, her ash-blonde hair cascading over one shoulder.

They bumped cheeks, air-kissing, and then Mason turned to Naomi. "You look lovely, too."

"Oh." Flustered, Naomi smoothed down her demure little black dress. "Thank you."

He noticed that she clutched a tablet in one hand and carried a large bag over her shoulder. She wasn't here to *work*, was she? That would be odd.

"I was looking forward to meeting your husband," Mason said to Misty. "Couldn't he make it?"

Misty made a face. "Stuck in Singapore in some arbitration thingy. Still, his loss is Naomi's gain, isn't it, Naomi?" She looked expectantly at her intern.

"Oh, yes," Naomi said brightly. "It was lovely of you to bring me."

Misty smiled complacently, then turned to Mason. "Your slot was very good this week."

Mason turned back to her, his stomach fizzing in sudden excitement. "You think so?" He managed to hide his eagerness behind a nonchalant smile. "I'm really enjoying it. More than I thought I would. Marc is great, of course."

"Marc's solid," Misty said airily. "But your little bit of off-piste flirting was enormous fun. I'd love to develop that in a more permanent way. Get a real buzz going around the show, you know? Although not with Marc, obviously. We'd need someone more, uh, in your league."

That sounded hopeful. Carefully, Mason said, "So there's a chance of something permanent on the show? That would be amazing."

"We're seeing some very positive feedback on our socials, Mason. *Very* positive. Obviously, you already have a substantial platform, which helps. You need a bit more experience in front of the camera. If we could just find something else for you to do with a wider appeal than male cosmetics..." She tilted her head to one side, considering him. "Let me think about it. I *like* you, Mason, and it's important to me to work with people I like. I mean, at the end of the day, that's what this show's all about."

Mason tried to play it cool, despite the flutter in his stomach. "Yeah?"

Misty continued, her expression earnest. "Wellness isn't a gimmick to me, Mason. It's a real passion. And part of personal wellbeing is recognising what matters to you and making mindful choices that give effect to that, right?"

She seemed to expect a response to that, so Mason nodded, saying slowly, "That makes sense."

"Right. And for *me*, that means I need to work with people who I like and respect and who like and respect me in return. Naomi will tell you that I don't tolerate negative energy in my people. Right, Naomi?"

Naomi, who had been frantically typing something on her phone looked up, startled. "Er, yes, right. Definitely not."

"I totally get that," Mason agreed, taking another sip of champagne.

Misty beamed. "I knew you would. I'm a *very* good judge of character." She gave him a self-satisfied smile. "Yes, I think we're going to get along famously, you and I…"

CHAPTER THREE

OWEN

"You didn't tell me the hotel was on Park Lane," Owen said to Lewis as their limo drew up outside the awards dinner venue.

"Didn't I?" Lewis sounded totally uninterested. He'd never been impressed by glitz and glamour.

Tag, who was sitting beside Owen, opposite Lewis and Aaron, chuckled. "The last time I was here, I was waiting tables. I wonder if I'll see anyone I know."

Tag had a boyish sort of handsomeness that verged on prettiness and a ridiculously cute smile, with teeth so white they had to have been bleached.

"You worked here?" Aaron asked, sounding tickled by the idea.

Tag grinned. "Yeah. Not full-time, though. I have a flexible temp gig—I pick up shifts for events like this quite often. They pay pretty good if you can be available on short notice —which I can be now *Bow Street*'s about to wrap for the season."

Lewis opened the limo door, and they all piled out onto the street, four men in more or less matching black tuxes.

"We look like we're going to a James Bond convention," Owen said once they were all standing on the pavement. He tugged uncomfortably on the cuffs of his rented tux.

Aaron laughed, and Lewis said drily, "I'm pretty sure James Bond's hair is tidier than yours."

Owen chuckled and ran a hand through his dark mop. "Sorry, I meant to get it cut, but I didn't have time."

"Right," Aaron said in a take-charge voice, rubbing his hands together. "We should get a move on. We missed the champagne reception, and they'll be serving dinner soon." He tugged Lewis towards the red carpet set out in front of the hotel entrance, leaving Owen and Tag to follow.

"I *like* your hair," Tag murmured, bumping Owen's shoulder with his own as they followed Lewis and Aaron inside. "It's sexy. Though it's definitely more *Game of Thrones* than *007*."

Cameras began to flash as they approached the front door of the hotel, manned by two men in red-and-gold livery. Lewis raised a hand at the line of photographers as he passed but didn't bother stopping, so Owen and Tag kept walking too, though Tag looked a little wistful as they entered the hotel.

They followed Lewis and Aaron towards a wide, winding flight of stairs on the other side of the foyer and began to climb. An avalanche of sound cascaded down: music, laughter, shouted conversations.

"Do you think dinner will be served soon?" Tag said. "I'm bloody starving."

"Well, it's supposed to be served at seven-thirty, and it's seven twenty-five now," Aaron said over his shoulder. "So hopefully, yes."

"The food'll be crap," Lewis warned. Which, from Lewis,

could mean anything from cordon bleu cuisine to rubber chicken.

"Who else is on our table?" Tag asked.

"RPP people mostly. Toni obviously." Aaron glanced back at Owen. "Have you met Toni?"

"Yeah, a couple of times. She's lovely."

"Everyone likes Toni," Lewis said. "She's bringing a date, but she was pretty cagey about who, so that'll be semi-interesting."

"Misty Watson-King and Henry Armitage will be there too," Aaron added. "They're from the Factual Programming department."

"Both boring as fuck," Lewis put in. "And their spouses are even worse. Misty's husband is a hedge fund manager or something. Some finance thing—don't ask him if you can help it. He could bray on about it for hours, and Misty's favourite conversation is herself. As for Dinah Armitage, she goes on about her fucking charity work so much you'll be ready to open a vein by the pudding course if you end up next to her."

"Sounds awesome," Owen said faintly.

"At least Jay and Mason will be there," Tag said. "Don't forget them."

No danger of that, Owen thought. He'd spent way too long thinking about Mason Nash in a tux—and *out* of a tux—over the last few days…

At the top of the stairs, black marble gave way to a swath of ugly hotel carpet which led through several sets of double doors and into a sea of tables in a vast, echoey ballroom. The lights were low, and the music was loud and tinny. Almost everyone was already at their tables.

Aaron checked the table plan. "Table twenty-four," he said and patted Lewis's shoulder. "Come on, let's get you your award."

"We're not going to win," Lewis said flatly.

"Yeah, yeah," Aaron said, giving him a little shove.

They began to weave their way through the tables. After a minute, Owen spotted Toni waving at them. She looked striking in a burgundy gown with a plunging neckline. A neckline of obvious interest to the mildly attractive middle-aged man sitting next to her who seemed to be having trouble keeping his eyes on her face as they talked.

There were two other couples at the table, Owen saw, as they got closer. The first was a complacent-looking pair who Owen reckoned were in their sixties. The woman's hair was cut in a pageboy style from another era. She wore a frumpy lilac evening dress with a pie-frill collar. Her companion rocked a receding hairline and gold-rimmed glasses. That had to be Henry Armitage and his wife.

The other pair were two women, one much younger than the other, so it seemed the hedge fund manager husband was not in attendance. They didn't look like friends, though. Their vibe was very much boss and underling. The older woman had long, blonde hair and wore a slinky, full-length gold dress. She was talking while the younger one typed industriously on an iPad. The younger woman was dressed more demurely in a black velvet dress with a single strand of pearls round her throat and a slim Alice band decorated with pearl beads holding back her black hair. Despite the velvet and pearls, the outfit looked curiously uniform-like.

There were six empty chairs at the table waiting to be claimed, and as Owen's party drew closer, he saw their last two table companions closing in from the opposite direction: Jay Warren and Mason Nash, glasses of champagne in hand—they must have made it to the pre-dinner drinks reception then.

Owen's mouth went dry, his heart pounding insanely. Why was he so bloody nervous?

Jay led the way to their table. Like nearly every other man in the room, he wore a classic black tux. Of course, his tux was probably custom-made. It certainly seemed to be perfectly tailored to his tall, well-made frame. Not like Owen's, which, despite the salesman's assurances, didn't feel like it fitted quite as it should.

Mason followed in Jay's wake, his body moving in that confident, loose-limbed way models used as they stalked down the catwalk. And fuck if he didn't make every other man in the room look stuffy and overdressed. He hadn't bothered with a tux or even a tie. His velvet suit was a rich, deep blue, and he wore the jacket open to display a slim-fitting shirt that was a riot of tulips and dog roses. His pale hair was swept back from his flawless features, his spectacular eyes framed by lush lashes. Owen couldn't see from this distance, but he knew those eyes were a vivid summer green, the colour of life and growing things.

He was a vibrant splash of colour in an ocean of monochrome. And sexy as hell.

Lewis, who was a couple of paces ahead, turned to raise a brow at Owen and his expression—God damn him—was amused. He winked, and Owen glared back at him.

Moments later, they reached the table. Lewis and Jay shook hands in a familiar way, laughing like friends. Then Lewis leaned in to Mason, saying something Owen couldn't hear that made Mason smile politely, if not particularly warmly.

Owen hung back, letting Aaron and Tag move forward next to greet Jay and Mason, only stepping closer when they were done.

"You remember my brother, Owen?" Lewis said, clapping Owen on the shoulder.

"Of course," Jay said warmly, offering his hand.

Owen took it. "Actually, we haven't met," he clarified with a smile. "I think Lewis was talking to Mason."

Jay flushed with embarrassment. "Oh, sorry," he said. "I meet a lot of people. It's difficult to keep track sometimes."

Tag gave a little bark of humourless laughter at that, and Jay shot him a sharp look.

"It's fine, honestly," Owen said, unoffended.

"Well," Jay said. "You're very lucky to have Lewis as a brother. He's a good friend and an incredible writer." He laughed before adding, "I mean, obviously, I'm a beneficiary of his amazingness, so I would say that."

"Yes," Owen agreed, smiling back. "He certainly got the talent in our family."

Mason sighed loudly at that and rolled his eyes. "And you've still got a modesty fetish, I see."

Christ, he was a brat! Owen felt his lips twitching but suppressed the smile, raising a single eyebrow instead.

When Jay glanced between them questioningly, Mason said, "Owen's an amazing landscape gardener. He did Terry Prescott's place—do you know Terry? The photographer?"

"Yeah?" Jay said, scrambling on an expression of polite interest.

"Yeah, God forbid he blow his own trumpet, though," Mason went on before Owen could respond. "He's not a fan of shameless self-promotion, are you, Owen?"

Owen blinked, surprised and a little confused by that comment, but then his attention was stolen by Tag tugging at his sleeve and saying, "I think we need to take our seats."

Murmuring an *'excuse me'*, Owen turned dutifully back to the table. Lewis was already taking the seat next to Toni, Aaron settling into the empty one beside him. Tag bent to examine the place cards.

"Looks like we're here," he said, taking the seat beside Aaron and patting the one on his left for Owen. As Owen began to lower himself into the chair, he glimpsed the place card in front of the seat next to his own: *Mason Nash*.

Well, hell.

If he was a superstitious man, he might think it was fate, but he wasn't superstitious. Nope, definitely not. Besides,

29

Mason was here with Jay—a famous, successful actor—and he barely knew Owen existed.

"He's an amazing landscape gardener. He did Terry Prescott's place…"

Okay, fine, he remembered that much about Owen. But still his expression hadn't exactly been friendly…

Just then, Mason and Jay took their seats, preventing Owen from chewing over the matter any longer.

For the next few minutes, everyone was busy putting their napkins on their knees, selecting bread rolls from the basket one of the waiting staff brought round, and deciding whether to have red or white wine. But eventually, all of that was done, and they settled in to chat to their neighbours. Since Tag was laughing with Aaron about something, and Jay was listening politely to the blonde woman, Owen turned to Mason.

He offered a wary smile. "You're looking well, Mason."

"Uh—thanks," Mason said, eyebrows lifting in surprise. After a moment, he added, "So are you."

It didn't sound sincere exactly, and Owen chuckled.

"Tuxes aren't really my style," he said ruefully. "But I suppose they're mandatory at this sort of shindig."

"*I'm* not wearing a tux," Mason pointed out.

"True," Owen agreed, "but your outfit probably cost more than all our tuxes put together."

Mason glanced round the table. "Not Jay's," he said at last, "but yes, that's probably true for the rest of you." He smiled slightly, a wry, attractive expression, and Owen felt a tiny surge of excitement in his belly, just at having those clear green eyes meeting his own.

He opened his mouth to tease Mason back, but before he could get a word out, Jay's neighbour, the blonde woman in the slinky gold dress, leaned over the table and said to him, "I don't think we've met? I'm Misty Watson-King."

"Nice to meet you," Owen replied. "Owen Hunter. Lewis's brother."

Misty looked like she was going to respond, but right then, Lewis stood up and addressed the whole table. "Hey everyone, can I interrupt for a second?" Everyone quietened, turning their attention to him.

"I just want to introduce my brother, Owen." He pointed at Owen and grinned. Then he indicated Tag and added, "And for those of you who haven't met him, this is Tag O'Rourke—he's one of the cast in Aaron and Toni's new project, *Bow Street*. You know, the one Toni's been banging on about at all our monthly meetings?" A couple of people laughed, and Toni stuck her tongue out at him. Lewis grinned at her before turning his attention back to Owen. "Owen, you already know Toni, my boss. And this is Poor—er, Geoff Hall. He's...?" His eyebrows rose in what was clearly a silent question for Toni.

Smoothly, she said, "Geoff's considering investing in RPP, so I thought it would be a great idea for him to see some of our amazing people being recognised by the industry tonight."

For a moment, Lewis looked like he was about to say something more—probably something tactless by the look in his eye—but apparently, he thought better of it. And that had to be Aaron's influence, no doubt about it. Lewis pointed at the smug couple next. "Henry and Dinah Armitage—Henry's head of Factual Programming at RPP." Dinah gave a tiny wave with just the tips of her fingers, while Henry lifted his champagne glass by way of greeting. Owen nodded back.

"And this is Misty Watson-King and Naomi Lee," Lewis said, gesturing at the blonde woman and her black-velvet-and-pearls companion. "Misty's a producer in Henry's department. *Weekend Wellness* is hers. It's up for an award tonight. And Naomi is—"

"Best daytime programme," Misty interrupted chirpily,

cutting Lewis off. "Our team is like a family so we're all pretty excited, aren't we, Naomi?"

Naomi looked startled to be asked a question. "Oh, um, *yes*. Super-excited." She smiled nervously, eyeing Misty.

"Okay," Lewis said, clapping his hands together, "introductions done. Now we can all get pissed."

CHAPTER FOUR

OWEN

For some reason, Misty seemed to find Owen fascinating. She kept staring at him, so much so that he shifted in his seat, uncomfortably conscious of her gaze skewering him across the table. She'd been studying him for a while now, eyeing him in a way that made him feel like he was something she was considering buying. He didn't think it was sexual interest, but it was *some* sort of interest. Something acquisitive that made his skin crawl, just a little.

She was quite attractive in her way, though not his type. Early-to-mid-forties, he guessed, and sort of *long* all over. Long blonde hair, obscuring one eye, a long, elegant nose, and a long, slim body that looked toned and well-maintained. She reminded him of a well-groomed Afghan hound.

"So, Owen," she said. "What is it that you do?"

"Oh, I'm just a gardener," he replied with an easy smile.

"Bollocks," Lewis interjected from the other side of the table. He was spreading his bread roll with a thick layer of butter. "Don't listen to him. He's not just a gardener; he's a

33

successful businessman. He has a thriving garden design and landscaping business with a waiting list as long as your arm."

Owen forced a smile, but that little comment—*He's not just a gardener; he's a successful businessman*—got to him. Sometimes he couldn't help but wonder whether Lewis thought that being a mere gardener wasn't good enough. He always seemed to want Owen to be doing *more*. He'd offered to invest in the business several times so Owen could expand and bring in more work. More money. He never seemed to get that Owen didn't *want* that, no matter how many times Owen told him.

"Gardening?" Misty said. She tilted her head, examining him even more closely. "Yes, I can see that. With those shoulders…"

Christ, she was making him feel like a side of beef.

He was grateful when her attention was interrupted by the arrival of a man at her shoulder.

"*Hello*, old thing!" the man said.

Misty looked up, surprised, then beamed when she saw who it was. "Austin! Bloody hell, I might've known I'd see *you* here!"

He laughed, bending down for a quick *mwah mwah* on each cheek, and they began to talk in low voices.

Owen eyed the man, wondering if he was famous. He was pretty nondescript. Average height, average build. Average beard. Dark hair and little shoe-button eyes behind squarish, heavy-rimmed glasses. *Austin*. The name didn't ring any bells, and he didn't look familiar, but then, Owen wasn't really into TV. As he looked away, he caught a glimpse of Jay and was surprised by the tight expression on his handsome face and the way he angled his body away from the new arrival.

Beside him, Tag said, "Shall I top you up?"

Owen turned to find Tag holding a wine bottle aloft.

"Um, I'm fine," he said. He'd barely touched his wine yet, which had only just been poured.

"Mason isn't," Tag said, leaning past him. "More wine, Mason?" Sure enough, Mason's glass was empty.

"Yeah, why not," Mason said, though he sounded more weary than enthused. "I'm going to need a lot of booze to get me through this. Awards dinners are so fucking *long*."

Tag topped up his glass. "Well, you've probably been to a ton of them," he said. "I'm a newbie, so I'm excited."

Mason looked briefly chagrined. "Ignore me. It's just—it's been a week, you know? I'm kind of—" He stopped.

"Peopled out?" Tag suggested, his tone part sympathy, part humour.

Mason smiled. "Something like that."

The man—Austin—moved away, and Misty turned back to them.

"Imagine seeing Austin here!" she said, flipping her hair back in a preening gesture. "I can't believe it."

Owen turned his head to Tag and murmured, "Who's Austin?"

"Journalist," Tag whispered back. "He writes a column for one of the big papers. Does quite a lot of reviews. TV and films mostly."

Was it *that* surprising to run into a TV critic at a TV awards ceremony? Owen wondered, eyeing Misty.

She turned to Jay. "You were very quiet. I thought you and Austin knew each other?"

Jay's expression was closed. He shrugged. "We went to the same school." His tone did not invite further conversation on the point, and after a moment of silence, Misty took the hint. She turned to Naomi.

"I told Austin we *have* to get him on the show," she said. "Pop a reminder in my diary to give him a call on Monday, and get us a table somewhere half-decent for lunch mid-week."

Naomi, who had been trying to eat her bread roll, hurriedly dropped it back onto her plate and bent down to fetch her iPad. Jesus, did she ever get a break?

That train of thought was interrupted by Tag saying waspishly, "I suppose he's beneath your notice now that you're so famous?"

Owen glanced at Tag, surprised by the uncharacteristic venom in his voice, but Tag didn't even notice his look. His own gaze—glare, really—was trained on Jay.

Jay stiffened with offence. "We're not friends. Do you keep up with everyone *you* went to school with?"

"No, but I'd say fucking hello to them if they were standing right next to me," Tag shot back.

Owen leaned back in his chair and glanced at Mason. "Do they always bicker like this?" he asked under his breath as Jay and Tag continued sniping at one another.

Mason gave a huff of unamused laughter. "Yeah. I don't think they even notice the rest of us are here." As though to illustrate the point, he swiped Jay's still mostly full glass of champagne from the table and necked it in one go. His own champagne glass was empty, his wine glass newly topped-up by Tag. His bread roll hadn't been touched. Owen glanced at him, noting the slight flush over his cheekbones.

Reaching for the water jug, Owen poured out two glasses, sliding one casually in front of Mason.

"Excuse me," Jay bit out suddenly, drawing Owen's attention back to the other guests. "I'm going to go and say hello to my agent." He stood up and stalked away from the table, shoulders tense.

Owen turned to Tag to ask what had provoked that reaction, but Tag seemed to be deep in conversation with Aaron, so he turned back to Mason, only to discover that Misty had moved into Jay's seat and was leaning over Mason to get closer to Owen. "Tell me, Owen," she said. "How long have you had your gardening business?"

Owen smiled. "Well, I've been gardening for quite a long time, but I've only been in business myself for ten years. At the start, it was just me and my best friend, Mac, but now I employ a whole crew."

"And how many is a whole crew?"

"Six people full time, plus one apprentice." He smiled. "Being able to take people on has been one of the best things about owning my own business, but it's kind of the scariest part too."

"Being the boss, you mean?" Misty said. "Oh yeah, do I get that!"

"It's not so much being the boss," Owen said. "It's more that… well, it's pretty amazing to get to be the person who gives someone a job, you know? One of my guys is someone I took a chance on when he wasn't in a great place, and watching his confidence grow has been incredible. And now I'm taking on kids out of school and helping them build a career from scratch. That's really satisfying, but also the responsibility is pretty huge. I need to make sure the work keeps coming in, and I need to help people keep developing their skills so the job stays interesting for them."

Mason huffed, not quite a laugh. "Very noble," he said in a tone that implied that, if he wasn't exactly rolling his eyes, he was thinking about it.

Brat, Owen thought again, reluctantly amused. Mason really didn't like being ignored, did he?

"Oh, *absolutely*," Misty chimed in, apparently missing Mason's sarcasm. "Helping your team develop is *so* rewarding."

Owen's gaze flickered to Naomi, who was on her phone now, one hand over her other ear as she listened, frowning. Probably still trying to get a table at a fancy restaurant for Misty's lunch next week.

"Am I right in thinking you and Lewis grew up on a council estate?" Misty asked then.

Owen dragged his gaze back to her, frowning at the question. "Um, yes, we did."

"That's amazing," she cooed. "How on earth did you get from such a difficult start in life to having your own successful business?"

Owen wasn't wild about the patronising note in her tone, but he forced himself to be polite. "It took a while," he said mildly. "I left school at sixteen and worked in a supermarket for a while, before getting a job as a labourer in construction —I wanted to get a trade, you see, but it was hard back then unless you had some kind of 'in'. I wanted to do joinery or plumbing, but I was getting nowhere. Then I met this guy who did landscaping on a job I was labouring on. He liked me and offered to give me a start, and I discovered I loved plants and gardens. It went from there. Took me a while to get where I am now, but I'm a slogger."

"Wow! I knew Lewis was from a deprived background, but—"

"I wouldn't call it *deprived*," Owen interrupted. Okay, they'd grown up on a rough estate, and they'd had some tough years, but he'd done his best by Lewis.

Misty looked taken aback by his admittedly quite defensive reaction.

There was a brief awkward silence. It was broken, surprisingly, by Mason, who said to Misty, "You probably know Owen looked after Lewis when their mum passed away, right?" She nodded, and he went on. "According to Lewis, Owen was an absolute saint about it. Lewis certainly wasn't deprived." He laughed lightly, then added, "He probably got more attention from Owen than I got from both my parents combined when I was a teenager."

Owen felt a stab of gratitude. That was Mason's second sort-of intervention on his behalf this evening, he realised with faint surprise.

"Oh, yes," Misty said to Mason, her gaze narrowing. "You and Lewis used to be together, didn't you?"

Mason's smile tightened just a fraction. "We had a brief casual thing for a while." He shrugged one shoulder as though to emphasise the *casual* point.

Misty opened her mouth to respond, and for some reason he couldn't quite put his finger on, Owen found he really didn't want that line of conversation to continue. Without thinking about it, he found himself blurting, "So, you work in factual programming, Misty? That sounds exciting?"

Her gaze flicked back to him, her expression instantly brightening. "Yes, it is! I'm very lucky to work in a field I'm so passionate about. I produce *Weekend Wellness,* which is our flagship lifestyle show. Do you watch it?"

"Um…" Owen scratched the back of his neck. "Not usually, but I did actually see the part when Mason was on last weekend."

Mason arched a brow. "I thought you had better things to do than watch TV?"

"I watch *Leeches*," Owen protested. Then he shrugged. "But yeah, I don't have time for much else. But, like I said, I did watch your bit on Misty's show, and I thought you were great. You were really…" He waved a hand as he struggled to find the right word. "Animated."

"Oh, Mason's a natural," Misty said, tossing a long sweep of golden hair over one shoulder. "People *loved* all the spontaneous flirting with Marc."

Her expression changed then, her head tilting to the side as she seemed to consider something. "You know, Owen, I've wanted to add a gardening segment to the show for ages, and I think you'd be very telegenic."

"*Me?*" Owen said, astonished. "Oh, no. I'm not the television type."

"No, really," Misty insisted, setting her elbows on the table and leaning closer. She gazed at him intently. "I've got a great eye for this, and you've got a fantastic face."

"Who's got a fantastic face?" That was Tag.

"We're talking about Owen," Misty told him. "I think he'd be very telegenic. What do you think?"

Tag studied Owen closely for a few moments, and Owen shifted uncomfortably. "I agree," he said at last. "After all, Lewis photographs well, and you're very alike."

"No, we're not," Owen protested. "Lewis is handsome."

"For God's sake," Mason put in, and this time he really did roll his eyes.

Owen scowled at him. "Lewis is *way* more handsome than me."

"Rubbish, and you know it," Mason said dismissively. "You've got a whole other thing going on." He waved his hand in a lazy circle. "Hot gardener vibe. It's wholesome as fuck."

"Yes!" Misty said. "That's it. He's got that sort of honest-farmer look. I could totally see him in"—she leaned back, narrowing her eyes as if envisaging some other version of him— "tattersall shirts, tweed gilets, green wellies. Yeah?"

"Um, I usually just wear t-shirts, shorts and work boots."

Misty pursed her lips, considering. "Work boots? *Hmm.* We could probably work with that."

Owen shook his head, feeling hunted now. "I'm really not —that is, being on TV is not something I've ever wanted to do."

Misty opened her mouth to argue, but luckily, she was interrupted by the arrival of a fleet of waiting staff who moved through the room depositing starters on tables with military precision, directed by supervisors wearing radio earpieces and barking orders.

Some kind of cheesy quiche type thing appeared on a plate in front of Owen. It was a tiny little tartlet, dribbled with a couple of swirls of a dark sauce. Pretty fancy but absolutely miniscule. Out of old habit, Owen glanced over at Lewis to see him prodding his food suspiciously with a fork.

Owen leaned towards his brother. "You could just have the bread rolls," he suggested. He pointed at his own. "Want another?"

"Don't encourage him," Aaron said repressively. "There's nothing remotely exotic on the plate. Just bloody try it, Lewis. You might like it."

Lewis sighed, adopted a martyred expression and took a bite.

"Sorry," Owen said to Aaron under his breath. He blamed himself for Lewis's poor eating habits, but even before their mum had died, Lewis had been fussy. And afterwards... Well, Owen had been seventeen and spending every hour God sent grafting for the money to keep a roof over their heads. Back then, chicken nuggets and chips had felt like pushing the boat out.

Aaron's mouth quirked up in a grin. "At least he's trying it," he said softly. "Look."

Owen did, and had to stifle a laugh at the disgusted expression on Lewis's face.

The dish was actually quite nice. Owen wasn't sure why Lewis disliked it so much. He glanced at Mason to see what his reaction was—he was cutting careful slices and chewing thoughtfully.

Perhaps sensing Owen's eyes on him, Mason glanced up.

Owen said, "This is pretty good." He sounded heartier than he'd intended. "What do you think?"

Mason shrugged, reaching for his wine. "It's not bad, for a mass catered event. I like the hint of smokiness. That'll be the Scamorza, I suppose."

"Yeah, probably," Owen said, wondering what Scamorza was. He ate the second half of his tartlet in one bite, and this time, yes, he noticed the smokiness, which seemed to come from the cheese. Was Scamorza a cheese? "I expect you go to a lot of these things," he tried. "Award dos and stuff?"

"Obviously. It's part of my job." Mason didn't sound exactly happy about it, though. In fact, he sounded pretty defensive, and Owen decided to change the subject.

"You were very good on *Weekend Wellness*," he said. "Do you see yourself working in TV in the future? Is that your goal?"

"Er..." Mason blinked a couple of times, as if trying to work out whether Owen had asked a trick question. "A regular TV role would be good for me career-wise." He gave a shrug. "I mean, it's easy money. Definitely better than modelling pays."

"Really?" Owen teased. "I thought you models didn't get out of bed for less than ten grand."

Mason huffed, not quite a laugh. "Yeah, well, we're not all Kendall Jenner. And male models—even the top ones—get paid a lot less than female models. I earn a decent amount from sponsorships, though. I've got pretty good numbers on Insta, and if I got more TV work, that would help me build my following up even more. So yeah, like they say, all publicity's good publicity." He took another hefty swig of wine.

"Do you enjoy it?" Owen asked.

"Enjoy what?"

Owen smiled at Mason's confusion. "Your work—modelling and... the other stuff. Is it fun?"

"Fun? Well, no, not really." This time Mason really did roll his eyes. "Modelling *is* actually hard work, you know? We don't just laze around all day admiring ourselves in the mirror. I mean, there are worse jobs, but it's not exactly fun. Whose job *is* fun, though?"

Owen wasn't sure how to answer. He loved his work, although maybe 'fun' wasn't the right word. Rewarding described it better. Even when it was physically demanding and the weather was crap, he loved being outdoors in people's gardens, nurturing things, watching them grow and thrive. It gave him real satisfaction, real pleasure. "I could definitely do without the paperwork," he admitted, which was true.

Mason looked surprised. "Don't tell me there's something in Saint Owen's life that isn't perfect."

Saint Owen?

"Trust me," Owen said. "There's plenty in my life that isn't perfect."

In that moment, their gazes met and held, and it felt weirdly intimate, as if they were connecting in a new way. Misty and Naomi had their heads together, while Tag was deep in conversation with Aaron. It almost felt like he and Mason had come here together, as partners.

And then Misty whipped back towards them, bursting into their little bubble with an excited exclamation.

"Oh my God, Mason! I've just had the most brilliant idea!"

Mason turned away and the moment was over. "It must be good to get you this excited," he said to Misty, half-laughing. "What is it?"

She wagged her finger between Mason and Owen. "You two, together. *Gardening*."

Owen stared at her, at a loss. "I'm sorry, I don't... What?"

"On the show!" She pressed her hands over her chest. "It's perfect. Gardening is so big at the moment—and it's really great for mental wellbeing—I mean, look at you, Owen. Gardening saved your life!"

Saved his life? Owen frowned and opened his mouth to contradict her, but she was already moving on.

"I've been desperate to get it into the show in a way that's relatable to our audience, you know? No more old, posh, straight, white men going on about their bloody herbaceous borders—instead we have young, hot guys bonding over growing produce together. This could be so perfect. Owen, you're a *real* gardener. I love the authenticity of that. And Mason is just like our audience—completely clueless."

"Sorry," Owen said, holding up his hand. "What are we talking about here?"

"A regular gardening slot on *Weekend Wellness*—you sharing basic gardening techniques with Mason that can help everyone get outside and get in touch with nature, and Mason doing what he does so well—looking insanely pretty."

Bemused, Owen shook his head. "No way, I'm… I couldn't be on telly."

"Why not?" Misty whined. "You're perfect. I'm not looking for glamour, Owen—Mason can bring that—I'm looking for something you can't fake. Something real. Real knowledge. That's what our viewers want. They want to see ordinary people, *diverse* people. Gardening's often seen as a middle class, middle-aged thing, right? But you're neither of those, and of course you two are—well, it's perfect."

"I'm sorry," Owen said. "But you've got the wrong brother. Lewis is the TV guy. And anyway, I really wouldn't have time. My business is—"

"We're only talking about a ten-minute slot a week," Misty interrupted. "It's no more than a couple of hours' commitment, max. And obviously, we'd pay you. *Obviously.* I don't ask talent to work for exposure. Not on my shows."

"Yeah, but I'm really not—"

Misty ignored him. "Lewis," she called across the table, interrupting Lewis's conversation with Toni and Geoff. "Tell your brother he needs to agree to be on my show."

Lewis looked up. "To do what?"

"A weekly gardening-for-wellbeing spot with Mason," Misty said with relish. "Don't you think that's an awesome idea?"

"With *Mason*?" Lewis grinned at Owen. "That *is* an awesome idea. You'd fucking love that."

Owen glared at him.

"The gardening, I mean," Lewis said, his grin widening. "Fuck, yes. Do it. You could be the next Monty Don. Only gayer."

"Bugger off," Owen muttered, feeling his cheeks heat.

"Sorry," Lewis said, laughing. "But honestly, it *is* a good idea. Just think what it would do for the profile of the business."

"The business is fine. We're really busy."

"It's not just about being busy, though, is it?" Misty put in. "It's about getting the highest-quality jobs out there. The interesting ones that help your staff develop their skills and keep learning. The ones that enable you to give your apprentice the best and most diverse training you can."

Owen felt a pang of guilt. He hadn't considered that. He'd been focused on thinking about how busy he was and his own lack of interest in being on TV, but yes, something like this might well have benefits for the business and the rest of the guys.

And then it suddenly occurred to him that there was someone else whose views had not been considered.

Turning to Mason, he said, "What do *you* think?"

Mason blinked, seeming surprised that Owen had asked. Eventually, he said, "Well, I'*d* certainly be up for it, although I don't know anything about gardening…"

"Which is *perfect*," Misty interrupted. "It's *real*, you know? It's not a setup. You'd genuinely be learning alongside our viewers, and Owen would genuinely be teaching you." She turned to Owen. "Looks like it's down to you then, Owen. What do you say?"

Owen looked around the table. At some point, everyone else had started listening in, and all he could see were expectant faces. Lewis in particular looked pleased and excited in a way he rarely did, and somehow, that complicated the whole thing even more. He didn't want to disappoint his brother.

Owen cleared his throat. "To be honest, this is pretty far

out of my comfort zone," he said. "But... well, it does sound interesting."

"Fantastic!" Misty crowed. "Naomi can start—"

Owen held up a hand. "Sorry, wait, that's not a definite yes. I need to think about this properly, but I *will* think about it and get back to you."

Misty frowned at that, but after a moment, her expression smoothed out, and she nodded. "I'll need an answer quickly, though. Tomorrow, really."

"That's fine. I'll get back to you."

"Naomi will give you my contact details," Misty said. Naomi dutifully began rifling through her bag, from which she produced a business card. Rather than just pass it down the table, she got out of her seat and brought it round to Owen.

"Uh, thanks," he said, tucking it away as she scurried back to her seat.

After that, everyone drifted into smaller conversations. When Owen turned to look at Tag, Tag was grinning.

"Bet you didn't expect that opportunity to fall into your lap tonight," he said.

"No, I did not," Owen said truthfully.

Tag lifted a hand and vigorously rubbed Owen's arm.

"What are you doing?" Owen said, puzzled.

Tag raised a brow. "Hoping some of your luck rubs off on me."

CHAPTER FIVE

Mason

"...and the winner of Best Teleplay in a Drama Series goes to..."

Dramatic pause.

Everyone on the RPP table held their breath, staring at the host. All except Mason, who found himself surreptitiously watching Owen from under his lashes. Like everyone else, Owen's gaze was riveted on the stage, one hand gripping the table hard.

"...Lewis Hunter for 'Over the Rainbow', *Leeches*."

The crowd roared, Owen shot to his feet, whooping in delight, and Lewis, laughing, grabbed Aaron and kissed him thoroughly on the lips. Grinning from ear to ear, Owen darted around Tag and Aaron as Lewis rose, pulling his brother into a bear hug, speaking earnestly, his words lost beneath the clapping and cheering. Lewis nodded, gruff as ever, and hugged Owen back, holding him hard for a long moment before letting go and making his way to the stage.

Owen got his phone out, then, taking pictures, his pride in his brother obvious. Watching him, Mason felt... odd. Out of sorts. The whole display was completely OTT, he decided, but there was a strange, tight feeling in his chest as he watched Owen, and he couldn't help wondering what it would be like to have someone like that, strong and dependable, in your corner. Lewis hadn't talked much about his background when they were together, but the one topic he was forthcoming on was his perfect older brother, who had fought so hard to take care of Lewis after their mother's death.

Watching Owen now, Mason wondered what it had cost him. The weight of responsibility must have been crushing, and perhaps it was a weight Owen still carried. Responsibility, once assumed, was almost impossible to put down.

As Mason well knew.

"I can see why you're staring," Misty said, leaning across Jay's empty seat—he'd been poached by one of the RPP bigwigs at the neighbouring table a while ago. "He's a hunk, isn't he? The housewives will *love* him."

Mason blinked at her. He probably shouldn't have had so much wine. His gums were starting to feel numb. "Owen?"

"Yes, Owen," Misty laughed. "*Obviously.* I can see you're into him."

"I'm not into him," Mason protested, horrified. Had he really been *staring*?

"No? Not even a little?" She paused, then gave a little shrug. "That's a shame. It would be good if you were."

Mason glanced at her sharply. Her gaze was calculating, just as it had been when she'd said that stuff to Owen about doing the show for the sake of his employees. Mason couldn't believe he'd fallen for such an obvious line, but he had. Mason had seen it in his eyes.

"What would be good about it?" Mason prompted.

"You have chemistry. That's important between co-presenters."

"Chemistry," Mason repeated, slowly.

"He can't keep his eyes off you, Mason." She smiled, her

gaze amused. "And you've been watching him too. Don't deny it."

Mason's face heated.

"The thing is," Misty went on when Mason stayed silent, "a bit of flirtation between you and Owen would play really well in any slot you two do together on *Weekend Wellness*. Viewers absolutely love that sort of thing. And with you having so many followers on Insta, I'll bet you could create a decent buzz around it. We'd certainly love to improve our numbers in the 18-35 bracket." She raised a brow at him. A question.

Flirting? With *Owen*? Mason wasn't sure whether it was fear or excitement making his heart suddenly race. Either way, even if Owen agreed to do the show—and Mason seriously doubted he would—he surely wouldn't agree to something like this.

He can't keep his eyes off you, Mason.

Would he?

Misty was staring at him expectantly, waiting.

"Well," he said slowly, "I *am* good at flirting."

She smiled at that, pleased. "You really are," she agreed. "You had Marc eating out of your hand the other day. He said—" She broke off when the audience quietened, turning to look over her shoulder, and when Mason shifted his own gaze to the stage, it was to see that Lewis was standing at the podium, award in hand. He leaned toward the mic.

"This episode was inspired by, and written with, my partner, Aaron Page"—Lewis lifted the award up to shoulder height—"so I'll be giving this to him." And with that, he nodded and began to walk away. He hadn't gone two steps before he stopped abruptly, leaning back towards the mic to add quickly. "Also, the team that works on *Leeches* is the best fucking crew in the world. You're all amazing. And my brother, Owen, is the best fucking brother. I couldn't do this without you all, so thanks." And with one last curt nod, he stalked off-stage.

Mason couldn't help but laugh. It was such a typical Lewis speech.

Jay slid into his seat just in time for the cameras to descend for Lewis's triumphant return to their table, his megawatt smile firmly in place as he smoothly rose to greet Lewis as though he'd been sitting there the whole time. Pulling Lewis into a bro-hug, he deftly manoeuvred him into place for the obligatory photo call that Lewis would have brushed off given the chance, beckoning Aaron over to join them. Jay really did have star quality, Mason had to admit as he watched him work, and not just in terms of looks. He had that elusive charisma too, that certain something that drew the eye.

Mason looked away, feeling suddenly flat.

The awards continued, and as they did, the wine continued to flow.

Misty didn't win her category, much to her obvious and jaw-clenching dismay, and after that, she lost all interest. After a while, Jay went off to speak to someone he went to drama school with, and Misty took the opportunity to move into his seat again. She started regaling Mason with stories about her children, Oscar and Mabel, which he listened to politely while he worked his way steadily through the remains of the last bottle of too-warm Sauvignon Blanc on the table. Tag had disappeared too, not very long ago, and Owen had moved into his seat to chat to Aaron, leaving an empty chair beside Mason—which made Mason scowl at his wine glass. Stupid to feel abandoned, but he did.

"...Mabel's always been a voracious reader," Misty droned on. "So, I bought her *The Iliad* last Christmas, and now she's *insisting* we spend half term in the Greek Islands instead of skiing." She laughed. "Apparently, she'll 'just die' if she doesn't visit Knossos."

"Right," Mason said, topping up his glass again.

Misty needed no further encouragement. She carried on without drawing breath, allowing Mason's increasingly drunken thoughts to amble back towards Owen. Like most of the men here, he wore a classic tuxedo. *Unlike* most of the men, he looked amazing in it, the clean lines flattering his solid, masculine body, even as his thatch of tousled brown hair and rugged features undermined the suit's formality. Even here, dressed up to the nines in the ballroom of a luxury Mayfair hotel, Owen Hunter looked somehow windswept and outdoorsy.

Yum, Mason thought, then caught himself and scowled. That was the wine talking. He was *not* into Owen Hunter.

Perhaps conscious of being studied, Owen glanced over, and their eyes met briefly before he looked away again.

He can't keep his eyes off you…

Probably, Owen wanted to fuck him, Mason thought—and his gut clenched with sudden, unexpected want.

Christ. *Was* he into Owen?

Mason's mind started racing. Maybe this was a good thing? If Misty thought a bit of flirtation would be a selling point for this possible new opportunity… Well, it would be a lot easier if there was a genuine mutual attraction there, wouldn't it?

Shit. He really needed to not get his hopes up about this.

He went to reach for the wine bottle to refill his glass, only to realise, with dismay, that it was empty.

And Misty was still wittering on about her bloody kids.

"…and so *obviously* her birthday party had to be Ancient-Greek-themed," she was saying. "Well, if you've ever tried to find Odysseus party favours for thirty eleven-year-olds—"

Mason couldn't sit through this without a drink. He lurched to his feet. "Can you excuse me for a sec?" he said. "I just need to pop to the bathroom."

Standing up that fast set the world spinning, but he

managed to steady himself as he moved away and began weaving a path between the tables. He headed for the set of double doors that led to the bar area, where the pre-dinner drinks reception had been held. As soon as he walked in, though, the first thing he saw was Tag and Jay.

They were standing at the bar itself, and it was obvious they were arguing. Jay's brows were drawn together, and Tag was gesticulating wildly as he made some point.

Mason moved towards them, conscious of his own unsteady gait.

Neither of them even noticed his approach. Bloody typical, he thought. Weren't these two meant to be competing to be seen out with him? If so, how come they never even seemed to notice he was there?

When he reached them, he said loudly, "I wondered where you two had got to."

They both startled, almost comically, and turned to look at him.

"Mason," Jay said. "God, sorry, I—" He broke off, his face colouring.

Tag was staring at Mason too, his expression dismayed. "We, uh, lost track of time, I guess. We were so busy arguing—"

Mason scoffed. "*Arguing*. Right."

"We were!" Jay said. "I was having a quiet drink in here when Tag spotted me and came over to tell me off for abandoning you with Misty." He made a face. "He was right. I'm sorry. She's just really hard work, you know?"

"*Now* you admit I was right?" Tag exclaimed, throwing up his hands.

"I never said you weren't *right*," Jay retorted angrily. "It was the way you said it, like I was being—"

"Jesus Christ!" Mason interrupted. "What *is* it with you two?"

They both stared at him in guilty silence. And no wonder

—this competitive fake-dating was supposed to have been fun. And okay, Mason had got what he wanted out of it: lots of great 'casual dating' content for his socials that enhanced his profile as a popular, young, famous gay guy. But there was something downright humiliating about the fact that, for Tag and Jay, the whole thing was obviously about something completely different. They were so focused on each other, *beating* each other, that they didn't even notice whether Mason was in the room.

"You know what?" he snapped. "I don't even care. Whatever. Let's just...end this farce, okay? No more dates. With either of you."

"What?" Tag exclaimed in dismay. "No. Mason, I—"

He held up a hand to shut Tag up, but the gesture somehow knocked him off balance and made him stumble sideways. "Come off it," he said, catching himself against a bar stool. "Who do you think you're kidding with this bullshit anyway? Why don't you just go fuck each other's brains out already, instead of pretending this weird competition has anything to do with me—"

They both stared at him with matching horrified expressions; then Tag turned to Jay and hissed, "See what you've done?"

"What *I've* done?"

"Yeah. You left him alone all night!"

"*You* could have talked to him. But here you are, haranguing me, instead!"

Mason covered his face with his hands and started laughing. He couldn't help himself. It was either laugh or cry. Or maybe throw up. Perhaps he'd do all three because fuck, he really was *very* drunk, and suddenly, everything was just so stupid and sad, and he felt so pathetically alone—

"I don't think we need any photographs," a new voice said.

It took Mason a moment to realise that the new voice

belonged to Owen Hunter. Owen, who was somehow now standing right beside him, placing himself squarely between Mason and another random bloke standing a few feet away. Mason blinked. No, not a random bloke—that was Austin Coburn, the journalist who'd been speaking to Misty earlier.

Austin stiffened. "I *beg* your pardon?" he said, in a haughty *Do you know who I am?* tone of voice.

Owen was unmoved. "I saw you taking pictures on your phone, and I don't think anyone here wants that right now." He glanced over to where Tag and Jay were staring at him like a pair of stunned mullets, his gaze skipping past them to land on Mason. "Right?"

Mason nodded, and then Jay, thin-lipped with anger, said, "Yes, that's right. Do run along, Austin, old chap."

Austin fixed a venomous glare on Jay, then turned the expression on Owen. "And you are, what? The hired muscle?"

Chuckling, Owen shook his head. "Just being a friend," he said. "I'm sure there's plenty of other people here who'd like to have their pictures in your mag."

"My…" Austin spluttered in outrage. "My… *mag*?"

Mason couldn't suppress his snort of amusement. Among other things, Austin Coburn had a regular column in the arts section of one of the broadsheets and was used to being feted, even feared, by those aspiring to be taken seriously in the creative industries. The fact that Owen clearly had no idea who he was obviously pissed him right off.

As if to hammer his complete indifference home, Owen gave an apologetic shrug and said, "I'm afraid I don't know who you work for."

Austin's lip curled into a sneer. "Clearly. How embarrassing for you." And with that, he stalked away.

Owen turned back to face the rest of them. "Sorry about that, but I saw him sneaking photos of you, and you all looked like you were, er, preoccupied…" He trailed off, his gaze landing on Mason with a slight frown of concern. "I hope I haven't put my foot in it or anything?"

"Not at all," said Jay, recovering his usual savoir-faire. "Quite the opposite in fact. Austin Coburn is a pompous prick who's hated me since prep school. I'm grateful you spotted what he was up to."

Tag rolled his eyes. "*Prep* school."

Jay shot him an irritated look, then turned back to Owen. "Watching you put him in his place is the most fun I've had in what's been a very long and tedious evening."

He probably hadn't meant that comment as a slight to Mason, but Mason was drunk and dejected and in a sensitive frame of mind—and he had come to this fucking dinner with Jay after all. Blowing out an irritable breath, he folded his arms, well aware it looked like a flounce. "Thanks a bunch."

Jay's eyes widened. "Oh, Mason, I didn't mean anything by it—"

"No you never *mean* to be insulting, do you?" Tag muttered. "But somehow, you always are."

"*Insulting*?" Jay rounded on Tag again. "You're the one…"

All at once, Mason had had enough—of them, of the night, of everything. He turned away sharply, which proved to be a big mistake because the room took a sudden and sickening spin. "Shit," he muttered, swaying queasily. "Fuck."

"Whoa." A strong arm closed around his waist, holding him upright. "Easy there."

Owen. Confusingly, Mason felt a rush of relief. *It was Owen.*

For a blissful moment, he relished the way Owen pulled him in close like that, confidently pressing him against Owen's strong body. Unfortunately, though, his head was spinning, and now his guts were getting in on the act and starting to pitch and roll like the deck of a ship.

Was he sweating? He felt hot; his face felt damp.

Owen steadied him, looking even more concerned than before. "Are you okay? You've gone really pale."

"Fine," Mason said through gritted teeth. It was a lie. "Ah, fuck, I'm really drunk, actually."

"Yeah. You want to sit down? Let's sit down."

Too late. With a rush, like a milk pan boiling over, nausea surged. Mason staggered, pressing a hand over his mouth. "Going to be sick."

"Okay," Owen said, calm and no-nonsense. "Bathroom for you." With one hand on Mason's back and the other at his elbow, he guided him quickly through the maze of couples and tables to the toilets.

Thank God, they were empty.

"How do you feel?" Owen asked once they were inside. "Are you really going to be sick?"

Mason squinted in the bright light, catching a glimpse of his ghastly pallor in the floor to ceiling mirrors. He looked like shit. "No... maybe." Abruptly, that changed—"*Yes*"—and he dived for one of the cubicles as an acid rush of bile heaved up his throat.

And then he was kneeling on the hard tile floor, retching and coughing into the toilet. He felt like death. This was so fucking mortifying. And he could do nothing but crouch there, clinging to the toilet like a life raft, as his stomach heaved and heaved.

Outside the cubicle, he was aware of Owen pacing. Then he heard the outside door open, laughing voices, and Owen speaking to someone, telling them to find a different set of toilets. Thank fuck. He did *not* need any witnesses. One was bad enough.

A few moments later, he felt a presence at his side. From the corner of his eye, through a veil of damp hair, he saw Owen's polished shoes appear. Helplessly, Mason heaved again, all but sobbing in misery and humiliation, but then a warm hand came to rest on his back, another sweeping the hair off his sweaty forehead.

"You're okay, petal," Owen murmured. "You'll feel better in a minute. Then we'll get you some water."

Bloody hell, had an angel descended from on high? Mason almost laughed at his own absurdly grateful reaction.

"Wanna go home," he whimpered, before heaving again.

"Yeah, I know," Owen said soothingly. "I'll take you home." A pause, then, "Unless you'd rather Jay—"

"No. Christ, no. Not after that fucking fiasco in the bar." He groaned and looked pleadingly at Owen. "I can't face them right now. Would you take me… Please?"

"All right," Owen said simply, rubbing comforting circles on Mason's back. After a couple more minutes of on-off retching, his stomach was finally empty.

The relief was enormous.

"Here," Owen said then, handing him a wad of paper towels to wipe his mouth and stepping back as Mason climbed shakily to his feet, flushing the toilet before turning around. He felt dismal but, if not quite sober, at least less wretched than before.

"Fuck," he whispered, closing his eyes. "I'm so sorry."

"No need to be sorry," Owen said gently. Was he always so fucking gentle? "Come on. Wash your hands and face."

Glancing down at himself, Mason was grateful that he'd at least managed to avoid getting vomit on his clothes. He sloshed water on his face, rinsed his mouth, and washed his hands. When he looked up, dabbing his face dry with a paper towel, he stared at his pallid reflection. The *Masculin* mascara and eyeliner he'd put on had smudged and smeared into dark circles around his eyes. "I look like crap," he said, pushing a hand through his wrecked and sweaty hair.

"You look fine," Owen assured him. "Pretty hot, actually, for someone who just puked his guts up in the toilets of a Mayfair hotel."

Mason almost smiled.

Owen said, "Do you want to go back to the table before we leave?"

"Do you think I should?"

Owen's expression softened. "Not if you don't want to, no. I can fetch your jacket and take care of everything while you wait in reception."

Thank God. He really couldn't face anyone looking like this; what would they think? What would *Misty* think? It was bad enough that Owen Hunter had witnessed his humiliation without wrecking his nascent TV career into the bargain. "That would be amazing, if you don't mind."

"I don't mind at all." Owen put a hand on Mason's back again, large and warm and comforting, guiding him towards the door. "Come on, let's get you home..."

CHAPTER SIX

MASON

Sooner than Mason would have thought possible, he found himself slumped in the back of a black cab, eyes closed, trying to quiet his unhappy stomach as they inched through south London's busy Saturday night traffic.

And trying to ignore the warm presence of Owen by his side.

Not that they were touching or anything. Owen had carefully fastened Mason's seatbelt after he'd flailed around trying to find the bloody thing in the dark and then retreated to his side of the cab and fastened his own seatbelt. Even so, his presence filled the silence between them.

Christ, he must think Mason was such a fucking loser.

What kind of idiot got himself so plastered that he puked at an awards dinner where he was meant to be schmoozing his way into a job?

Mason Nash, ladies and gentlemen.

His internal groan of dismay must have escaped because Owen said, "You okay? Do you need us to stop?"

"No."

"Because it's better to say something if you're going to puke again."

"I'm fine. I'm not going to puke."

From the front of the cab, the driver made a disgruntled noise.

"So, tell me," Owen said quickly, in a hearty 'I'm distracting him from puking' tone of voice, "what's your take on this TV gardening thing Misty was on about? Is it…?" He sounded doubtful. "Is it really something you're interested in doing? No offence, but you don't strike me as the gardening type."

Mason rolled his head sideways on the headrest and peeled open one eye to look at Owen, grateful that at least the horrible spinning had abated. In the orange glare of the passing streetlights, he studied Owen's face. There was something of Lewis there—you could tell they were related —but they really were quite different. Owen's hair was a warm, nut-brown rather than Lewis's severe sable, and he was bulkier than his brother in an honest, wholesome sort of way. He looked like a man who used and enjoyed his body rather than a man who honed it at the gym, and Mason liked that. Owen's nose had a slight bump in it too, as if he'd broken it at some point. Lewis's face had no such imperfections.

The biggest difference was the eyes, though. Not so much the shape or the colour, though Owen's were a lighter blue. No, it was the expression. Owen's gaze was kind. Gentle even…

Mason blinked. What the hell was he thinking?

Jesus. Get a grip.

Forcing himself to sit up straighter, he said, "You're right. I'm *not* the gardening type." And then he added, bluntly, honestly, "But I'd do pretty much anything for a regular slot on that show. Or any show. I've been trying to get into TV for ages."

Great, now he sounded desperate. Drunk and desperate. What an alluring combination.

And why the fuck would Owen ever agree to do the show with him now, after seeing Mason at his worst, throwing up in a hotel toilet?

Just then, the car braked sharply, and his stomach lurched up into his throat. He clamped his mouth shut and covered it with his hands.

"It's okay. We're nearly there," Owen soothed as Mason breathed determinedly through the wave of nausea. "Just another couple more minutes according to Google Maps." He smiled reassuringly, little lines crinkling around his eyes.

God, he really did have ever such nice eyes.

Ugh, of all the people to see Mason like this, why did it have to be Owen? And why tonight, when long-awaited opportunity had finally come knocking?

Mason closed his eyes and let his body move with the car's motion.

He must have drifted off a bit because when Owen touched his knee lightly, he jack-knifed up, blinking confusedly for a moment.

"We're here," Owen said softly.

Sure enough, the cab was turning into the small parking area in front of Mason's building on Clapham Common North Side. The common itself opened up into a dark expanse of night on the other side of the road, his own building half obscured by a line of trees.

"Anywhere is fine," Mason told the cabby, struggling to undo his seatbelt. At least he was feeling slightly less pissed now, although with returning lucidity came deepening mortification.

To Owen he said, "I'm sorry I fucked up your evening. Maybe if you head straight back, you and Tag can still—"

"Tag's fine. He wasn't my date," Owen said, undoing his own seatbelt. "Besides, I don't fancy spending what remains of the evening watching him and Jay squabbling—or whatever it is they think they're doing." He glanced at the cabby, at the still-running meter, and lowered his voice. "If it's all right with you, I'd like to come in and make sure you're okay before I head home."

The cabby snorted, somewhere between a cough and a laugh.

Owen ignored him, although he ran a self-conscious hand through his mop of hair. "You're still white as a sheet, and I don't want to leave you alone until I know you're okay."

"You don't have to..." Mason began, but then he trailed off. Why not? Why not just let this nice, capable guy take care of him for a little bit? God knew it was what he wanted—hell, what he *needed*. That thought brought a sharp sting to his eyes, though he quickly blinked it away.

Owen pulled out a battered leather wallet and said to the cabby, "What's the damage?"

Belatedly, Mason reached for his phone and fumbled open the payment app. "No, I'll get this—"

Too late. The contactless reader pinged, and Owen got out of the cab with a friendly, "Cheers, mate!" for the driver.

Shit. Mason was still putting his phone away when Owen opened his door. "All right?" he said, offering a hand to help him out.

Fuck, was he for real?

Mason felt a little silly taking his hand, but again, he thought, *Why not?* And when Owen's large hand closed over his own, his heart skipped at the sensation. Besides, the world did rather lurch when he stepped out of the cab and the cold night air slapped him in the face.

"Careful," Owen murmured, setting his other hand on the small of Mason's back to steady him. His touch was warm through the fine cotton of Mason's shirt, provoking a little involuntary shiver. "You should put your jacket on," Owen said as the cab pulled away. "It's freezing." Then he peered up at the terrace of substantial period houses, each one converted into flats. "Which one's yours?"

Mason rummaged in his pocket for his keys. "It's this one," he said, heading for the second building to the left. His was the garden flat, with its own entrance accessed down a steep flight of stairs to the side of the front path.

Being in the basement meant the flat could be somewhat dark at times, but he'd taken it purely because he'd fallen in love with the glorious kitchen. Or, more accurately, with the potential of the glorious kitchen.

The distinctly unrealised potential.

"Let me go first," Owen said, keeping hold of Mason's hand as he went down the steep steps, steadying Mason as he followed. Christ, he was chivalrous. Any moment now he'd be laying his cloak over a puddle, and it was doing silly things to Mason's insides.

The motion-activated security light flicked on as they reached the bottom step, revealing the tiny empty courtyard in front of Mason's bedroom window. Mason wove towards the door, and maybe he *was* still quite drunk because the lock seemed to be bobbing about, dodging his key as he tried to slot it in. He swore under his breath.

From behind him, Owen said, "You could do some pot down here."

"What?" Mason glanced over his shoulder, surprised. "Uh, no thanks, I don't really do pot or—"

Owen looked confused and then laughed, a broad and friendly sound. "No, I said you could do with *some pots* down here." He gestured around the barren space. "It's shady, but you could have some nice ferns, lily of the valley, even cyclamen. Brighten the place right up."

"Oh." Feeling like an idiot, Mason gave an embarrassed laugh. "Like I said, gardening's really not my thing."

Owen chuckled again but didn't say any more, and Mason

turned back to the door, trying to get his key into the shifting lock. "Shit, this fucking thing keeps moving."

"Let me see," Owen said, and Mason felt a sudden warmth against his back as Owen reached around him to take the key and easily slid it into the lock. "There you go."

Slightly breathless, Mason turned the key and opened the door, feeling for the light switch as he led Owen down the short hallway, past his bedroom and into the kitchen with its warm wooden floors and gleaming stone surfaces. Wobbling a little, he balanced himself with one hand on the wall as he walked.

"Come on," Owen said when they reached the kitchen, taking Mason gently by the elbow and guiding him to sit at the small table. "You should eat something."

He shook his head. "I'm not hungry."

"Still queasy?" Owen said, crouching down next to the chair to study him. "You're very pale."

"No, I'm just..." Again, his eyes stung, and he blinked rapidly, embarrassed, then dropped his head into his hands. "Shit, I'm sorry. I never do this."

Jesus, what was wrong with him? A guy showed him a little kindness and, what, he was ready to bawl?

Owen touched his shoulder gently as he stood. "I'll get you some water."

Mason listened to him opening a couple of cupboards, running the tap and filling a glass. Listened to Owen's footsteps as he drew closer again and to the gentle thud of a glass on the table. "Start sipping that," Owen said, "and I'll make you some toast. Where's the bread?"

Mason looked up, squinting in the bright kitchen light. Owen was standing next to his chair, a frown creasing his brow as he gazed down at Mason.

"I try not to eat bread."

Owen looked as incredulous as if Mason had just

announced, 'I try not to breathe air'. Then his expression cleared. "Oh, are you allergic?"

Mason laughed grimly. "Only to the carbs. Honestly, I fucking love bread, but I have to be strict when I've got a shoot coming up."

A lot of guys Mason had gone out with would have said something sarcastic or judgmental about that, but Owen just looked thoughtful, then said, "Have you got something else that might soak up the booze? I guarantee you'll feel better tomorrow if you eat something." He glanced around the kitchen, as if for inspiration. The surfaces were all spotless, everything in its place, and barren of food. That had less to do with Mason's tidiness and more to do with the fact that he didn't have much reason to cook very often.

After a pause, he admitted, "There's a loaf in the freezer. I keep it for emergencies."

"I think this counts as an emergency," Owen said, heading to the freezer and pulling out Mason's guilty pleasure: a loaf of cheap, white, plasticky bread. He pried free a couple of slices, then stood in the kitchen, looking around.

"Don't you have a toaster?"

"It's too much temptation," Mason admitted. Truth was, he dearly loved a cup of tea and a slice of toast. It reminded him of coming home from school, him and Frieda sitting down at the galley table, eating hot buttered white toast and drinking tea together while he told her about his day. That had been before the twins came along, of course. And before Kurt left.

Owen said, "You must have a grill?" He sounded somewhere between bemused and indulgent.

"Yeah," Mason admitted. "It's above the main oven." He pointed out the controls, then watched as Owen got the grill going and began toasting the bread.

"Butter?" Owen asked.

"In the fridge." Mason closed his eyes and let his head

sink back into his hands. He reckoned he was still pretty drunk because this weirdly domestic scene with a not-quite-stranger was churning up all sorts of unwanted, inappropriate emotions.

Shit, he was never drinking again.

"Here you go," Owen said a little later, his voice, and the delicious aroma of buttered toast, reaching Mason at the same time. He looked up to find Owen sitting opposite him at the table, a plate of toast and two mugs of tea between them.

"Go on," Owen said, nudging the plate towards him. "You'll feel better."

And fuck it, why not? Reaching out, Mason picked up a piece of toast and took a massive bite, almost groaning at the sweetish flavour of the toasted bread and the salty, melted butter.

Across the table, Owen smiled. "Good?"

"So good." Mason pushed the plate back towards Owen. "Have some."

Owen grinned and grabbed a slice while Mason took another big bite of his own toast. Already, he was feeling better, his body eagerly responding to the gloriously unhealthy fix of refined carbs, fat, and salt.

They ate in silence for a while, quickly munching through the whole plate. It was surprisingly comfortable, and Mason felt the distress of the evening begin to ease as his stomach settled. When the toast was gone, he reached for his tea. It had milk in. He usually made himself drink it black, but he preferred it with milk, and when he took his first sip, he sighed in pure unadulterated contentment. God, there really was nothing more comforting than a cuppa, made just the way you liked it.

Maybe that was why he found the courage to ask, "So do you think you'll do the *Weekend Wellness* thing?"

Owen glanced at him. "I don't know… TV isn't something I've ever thought about doing, and I've got a couple of really busy months coming up." He tipped his head, looking Mason in the eye and frowned. "But you could still do it, right? They'd easily find another gardener. Someone way better than me, I'm sure. I'd be useless on telly."

Mason tried not to let his disappointment show. "Honestly, I think Misty only suggested it because of you. So if you're not up for it…" He trailed off meaningfully.

But Owen didn't take the bait. "Because of *me*?" he said, frowning. "I doubt that."

Mason stared at Owen, wondering how to respond. Part of him—a big part—wanted to work on Owen, use everything he had to persuade him to do the show. But another part of him was fiercely rejecting that idea, and he honestly wasn't sure why.

"Misty thought we had…" He paused. "Look, it doesn't matter. She'll probably move onto something new tomorrow anyway. That's how this industry works." He was going to stop there; he really was. But somehow he found himself adding, "You have to seize your chance in the moment, before it slips away."

Owen's frown deepened. "So you'd be missing out on that chance if I said no?"

Mason stared at him, unsure what to say. He suspected that if he agreed with that assessment, Owen would do it, even if he didn't want to. It was a heady realisation, and he wasn't quite sure what to do with it.

"I don't want to fuck things up for you," Owen added quietly, earnestly.

For a split second, Mason hesitated. He just had to say the word, but somehow he couldn't bring himself to do it. Instead, he gave a shrug and said lightly, "It wouldn't be the end of the world."

Owen said nothing, but his gaze stayed on Mason, warm and heavy.

Mason looked away, swallowed the last mouthful of

his tea.

"Listen," he said, setting down his mug, "if you don't want to do the show, don't do it. Misty's bullshitting about it only being half a day's work. That's probably how long it'll take to shoot, but there'll be a ton of prep and meetings, and we'd need to talk about it and probably rehearse since you've not done this before and I'm pretty new to it too. It's a bigger commitment than you realise."

Owen frowned. "What would rehearsing involve?"

Mason tried not to stare at Owen's fingers wrapped around the mug of tea, tried not to remember how comforting they'd felt stroking the hair back from his forehead. "It'd be pretty informal, probably." He cleared his throat because his voice was coming out a little husky. "Just you and me getting together a few times to go over ideas for the show, talking about how we'd want to present stuff. That kind of thing."

"Hmm," Owen said. "That could be—"

"—time-consuming. I know."

One corner of Owen's mouth tugged up in a sexy half smile. "I was going to say doable."

"You were?"

"Yeah, I mean it *would* be extra work, and I have just taken on another big project—so the timing isn't the best—but on the other hand, it would be publicity for the business. And sometimes you have to grab your chances when they crop up, right? That's how I started my business, by taking a punt. And I could set some limits, I suppose. Maybe just sign up for a few weeks to start with, to see how it goes."

Mason's heart kicked in excitement. If this worked out, if the segment was successful, it could change everything for him. "So…are you saying you're interested? In doing the show?"

"Yeah, I'm interested," Owen said slowly. "If you are?"

"Definitely," Mason said. "A regular slot is exactly what I'm looking for, but… You're honestly okay with this?"

Owen smiled. "I am, yeah."

"Wow, *thank you*." He was grinning now; he couldn't help it. "I would totally owe you, big time."

"No." Owen set down his mug and looked Mason straight in the eye. "If I agree to do the show, it's because I want to do it, not because you've talked me into it. Not because I'm doing you a favour. You don't owe me a thing. We're both grown-ups here. Got that?"

Mason nodded, a little taken aback by Owen's stern tone. A little…turned on by it too, if he was honest. He swallowed. "Got it." Then, with half a smile, he added, "So who's going to give Misty the good news?"

Owen laughed, grimacing. "I'll do it tomorrow. Naomi gave me her card."

"Okay," Mason said, trying to dampen his obvious excitement. "Could you text me after to let me know how it goes? I'll send you my number just now. What's yours?" He pulled out his phone and swiped to messages, plugging in the number Owen told him and sending a quick, *Hi, it's Mason* text.

Owen's phone pinged in his pocket, and they smiled at each other, their eyes meeting across the table. Owen's lips moved, as if he were about to say more, before he looked away and stood up to gather the empty plate and their mugs.

"You're looking better now," he said, carrying everything to the sink and running water over them. He stayed there for a moment before turning around to lean against the counter. "I should get out of your hair. Let you sleep it off."

Mason studied him, considering the broad expanse of his shoulders, the stretch of his dress shirt over his chest, shirt-sleeves rolled up to expose strong, tanned forearms. Owen was an incredibly attractive man. Mason was attracted to him. Physically for sure, but also—tonight—to his kindness, his gentleness, his warmth.

Suddenly, powerfully, he didn't want Owen to leave. He didn't want to be alone.

Pushing to his feet, relieved to find the world holding steady, he padded across the kitchen to where Owen stood by the sink. "Do you have to go?" he asked, smiling at the flush rising in Owen's cheeks. "Stay for a while."

Owen wasn't classically handsome like Lewis, but it struck Mason in that moment that, for Mason's money, Owen had the nicer face. It was an approachable face, trustworthy and friendly. The face of someone Mason would like to get to know better.

But it seemed that Owen didn't feel the same way, because he cleared his throat and stepped sideways, putting space between them. "I really should get going," he said. "It's quite a trek to Beckenham from here."

"That's where you live?"

"Yep."

"I've never been to Beckenham."

Owen laughed. "Well, it's not really a place people go to visit, but I like it. There's plenty of green space, you know?"

"There's green space here," Mason said, stepping closer again. "Clapham Common is great. We could go for a walk."

Owen's eyebrows drew together in confusion. "Now?"

"Why not?"

"Uh, because it's cold and dark outside, and, to be honest, I think you're still a bit pissed. In fact, why don't you get ready for bed while I dig out some painkillers for you?"

Mason scowled, annoyed by Owen's recalcitrance. "I don't need painkillers."

Owen smiled, and it was an indulgent sort of smile, like he thought Mason was cute or something. "Trust me," he insisted in a tone that was somehow gentle yet brooked no argument. Bossy, but in a way that made Mason feel cared for, even as it triggered a little thrum of excitement in the pit of Mason's belly. "You'll be glad you took them in the morning."

Still, Mason hesitated, but there was something about Owen's gentle bossiness that was difficult to defy. Reluctantly, he made his way along the hall to his bedroom at the front of the flat. It was a large room, painted white like the rest of the place, with a bay window overlooking the tiny, empty courtyard at the bottom of the steps. In the dark, lights from the cars passing on the busy road outside flashed through the window, sending weird shadows dancing across the walls.

Mason sat down on the side of his bed and switched on his bedside lamp. He felt cold, suddenly. And alone. He wanted desperately for Owen to stay. Partly that was because he was horny, but it wasn't just that. He wanted more of that cosseting and care.

Fuck. He rubbed his face. He must still be pissed—he usually ran a mile from any sign of emotional neediness, either in himself or his lovers.

Sitting up straighter, he mentally shook himself, shoving the emotional bullshit to one side and focusing on the other part of Owen's appeal. The fun part that would involve them getting naked in bed together. And okay, that was probably a bad idea too, but Mason really did feel horny, and actually, it would probably help on the *Weekend Wellness* front. After all, Misty had made it clear that Mason's chemistry with Owen was key to her whole gardening idea—and what was this if not chemistry?

He'd be an idiot not to use it to his advantage.

He was still sitting on the bed when Owen appeared in the doorway, holding Mason's water glass and a packet of ibuprofen. His expression was a little curious, a little cautious as his gaze flicked around the bedroom.

Mason rose. "Thanks," he said, moving to take the glass and pills from Owen and carrying them over to his bedside table. "You're very kind, you know? To do all this for someone you hardly know."

"Well," Owen said with a self-deprecating laugh, "Lewis always says I love playing the knight in shining armour."

"Yeah? What does that make me then? The damsel in distress?" From across the room, he gazed into Owen's warm, expressive eyes and noted the spark there. The interest. It wouldn't take much to fan that spark into a flame, if he wanted.

And to hell with it—he *wanted*.

Tossing his hair back, he walked towards Owen with a hint of catwalk strut. Owen's eyes widened, his gaze darting down over Mason's body and back up to his face as Mason stopped in front of him, biting lightly at his lower lip and looking up through his lashes.

He could practically hear a camera click and whirr.

"Could you help me?" he said softly, making a half-hearted attempt at undoing the buttons on one cuff. "These are so fiddly."

It was blatant, but it always worked.

After a moment, Owen released a controlled breath and said, "Okay. Let me see."

Mason lifted his arm, presenting Owen with his wrist, watching as his big, surprisingly nimble fingers undid the tiny buttons, one by one. "There," Owen said huskily, as the cuff fell open. "Other one?"

Mason silently complied, lifting his other cuff for Owen to unbutton. Then Mason pouted and gestured to the rest of the buttons on his shirt, raising his eyes to Owen's in a mute plea for assistance.

Owen pressed his lips together, a hint of amusement in his expression now. "All right," he said, and Mason loved the note of soft indulgence in his tone.

Carefully, he started to unbutton the shirt. This close, Mason could smell notes of cardamom, sandalwood, and vetiver on Owen's skin, warm and masculine and a little intoxicating. "Tom Ford, Oud Wood?"

Owen glanced up. "What?"

"Are you wearing Oud Wood cologne?"

"Uh, maybe?" He smiled self-consciously. "It's something Lewis got me last Christmas. I can't remember what it's called."

Mason smiled. "It suits you," he said, leaning in so that his bare chest brushed Owen's fingers where they were working on his buttons. He inhaled deeply. "Very manly and outdoorsy."

"Uh, these are dog roses," Owen blurted, staring down at the fabric of Mason's shirt. "And lilies. On your shirt, I mean."

Mason looked down. "Are they?"

"Tulips, too. It's a nice pattern."

"Yes, it's Simon Carter." They were standing very close now, Mason's body humming in anticipation. It wasn't just the booze, either; he could feel a warm rush of desire in his blood, making his heart bound and his fingers tingle. Reaching up, he stroked Owen's jaw, enjoying the soft scratch of stubble beneath his fingertips. Not quite a beard, but sensual to touch.

Owen froze, his bright gaze lifting to Mason's eyes. Mason smiled encouragingly. Owen was about his height, but a lot broader, giving Mason a delicious sensation of being engulfed. Leaning in, he let his lips part, wetting them with the tip of his tongue.

Owen visibly swallowed, Adam's apple bobbing.

Smiling, Mason allowed gravity to draw him in, to pull him into Owen's orbit, so close his lips brushed Owen's mouth and—

A firm, gentle hand on his chest stopped him, eased him back. "I don't think this is a good idea." Owen sounded regretful.

Mason froze. "Why not?" Then he drew back, offended. "Never mind. Forget it."

"It's not that I don't—"

"I said forget it!" Mason turned away, face burning in humiliation. No one ever turned him down for a fuck. The fact that it was Saint bloody Owen, sounding gruff and pitying… Christ, it was unbearable. "Fuck, I'm still half-pissed," he said. "I should just sleep."

"I think that's a good idea," Owen said gravely. Then, "Take a couple of pills first, yeah? And try to drink all that water."

Mason, whose throat had closed in a suffocating knot of mortification and frustration, could only nod. Fuck, of course Owen wouldn't want him. What had he been thinking? Owen had never thought Mason was good enough for Lewis, so why would he want him for himself? Especially now, after he'd just watched Mason puking on a toilet floor and been forced to leave his brother's awards dinner to pour Mason into a cab. Jesus. Mason hadn't even brushed his teeth yet.

Worse than all that, though, he'd probably just killed off any chemistry between them. And with that went Misty's interest in the whole gardening slot.

Fuck. Fucking *fuck*.

And still Owen was being obnoxiously patient and gentle because that was the sort of Mr. Bloody Perfect he was. The sort of man who'd want nothing to do with a self-promoting piece of arm candy like Mason Nash.

"Are you going to be okay?" Owen said. He sounded closer, as if he'd taken another step into the bedroom.

Mason just nodded.

"Okay, well…" Owen cleared his throat, shuffled his feet. "I'll just turn out the lights in the kitchen and head home. You get into bed and sleep it off. You'll feel better in the morning."

Another nod, and then he managed a scratchy, "Yeah, thanks. Thanks for…" His voice gave out, and he couldn't finish the sentence, screwing his eyes shut against another swell of regret.

Why had he done it? Why?

"Any time," Owen said, then gave an awkward laugh. It was the first time all evening he'd sounded less than genuine. "Not that I think you should make a habit of this."

"I won't. I *don't*," Mason assured him, arms wrapped around himself now in a desperate attempt to hold together what was left of his dignity until Owen had left.

Perhaps sensing that, Owen said, "Right, well, goodnight then."

With that, his footsteps disappeared down the hallway. Mason heard the kitchen lights switch off, then the hall light as Owen walked back past his bedroom to the front door. Finally, he heard the sound of the front door opening and closing.

Through his window, Mason watched Owen trot up the steps back to pavement level. He paused at the top for a long, long moment before eventually shoving his hands in his jacket pockets and walking quickly away.

That, Mason guessed, was probably that. Tomorrow, a text would arrive from Owen saying he'd given it some thought and he couldn't do the show after all. Too much on. Too busy.

And Mason had no one to blame but himself.

CHAPTER SEVEN

OWEN

The morning after the awards dinner, Owen woke at six, hard as a rock, with the image of Mason, standing in his bedroom, vivid in his mind. Mason's eyes gleaming with seductive promise, his open shirt revealing the pale, beautiful architecture of his body. The delicate wings of his collarbones, the lean musculature of his chest, his taut, flat belly and sharp hipbones.

Posed like a cover model, all artful allure.

For a moment, Owen thought it was the lingering ghost of a dream. Then he remembered—it had really happened. Mason had lured Owen into his bedroom. Mason had tried to *kiss* him.

And Owen had pushed him away.

He threw one arm over his face and groaned.

Fuck his life.

It was for the best—no doubt about that. He was under no illusions as to why Mason had come onto him last night. Mason was drunk and feeling horny, and Owen was... well, he was there, and he had a pulse. For some guys, that was all you really needed.

But yeah. No.

There was a part of him, though—okay, it was his dick—that was pissed off at last-night-Owen for doing the right thing and turning down a night of meaningless sex. Because, physically, at least, Mason was so very much Owen's type, it wasn't even funny. And yeah, maybe it wasn't *just* the physical stuff. That moment when he'd pouted and pointed at his shirt buttons, practically demanding that Owen undress him? Owen let out an embarrassed laugh at the memory. Christ, he was a sucker for a spoiled brat…

Owen's dick throbbed with need. Groaning, he wrapped his fingers around his shaft under the bedcovers and stroked, allowing himself the luxury of wallowing in the memory of Mason leaning in towards him…

The soft pout of his sulky mouth.

Owen's hand moved faster as he let himself imagine a different ending to the evening. One where he pushed Mason down to his knees, ripped open the fly of his tux trousers and shoved his cock down that lovely throat.

Within moments, Owen's hand was stripping his cock desperately, his breath coming hot and fast. When he came, it was sudden and violent, too soon and so hard that he curled in on himself, groaning as the hot semen splashed his belly, his chest.

He lay there for long moments afterwards, stunned by the intensity of his reaction. How quickly he'd come, how strongly the image of Mason on his knees had affected him.

Christ, was he really that superficial? Apparently so.

If the world was fair, that would have been enough to deal with his preoccupation with Mason for one day. But the world wasn't fair. Thoughts of Mason intruded all through his morning run, and all through the long, hot shower he took afterwards. Even as he made, then ate, his breakfast.

And for some reason, it was the moments when he'd seen Mason at his most vulnerable that kept coming back to him.

The hurt expression on his face when they'd been in the bar and Jay had said that the most fun he'd had all evening was when Owen had got rid of that journalist.

His gratitude when Owen had taken care of him when he was being sick.

His angry mortification when he'd tried to kiss Owen, and Owen had pushed him away.

Hell.

Perhaps his impulsive decision to do *Weekend Wellness* wasn't as rational as it had felt last night. He really *didn't* have the time for another project, and in the cold light of day, the "good for business" angle felt really quite thin.

No, he had to own it: he'd been swayed by Mason. By his beauty, and by that knowing, sexy pout that seemed calculated to go straight to Owen's cock.

It certainly hadn't been Owen's *head* making the decision. Well, it was too late now to pull out. He'd told Mason he would do it, and he'd stand by that decision. He'd just have to make sure he set some clear boundaries with Misty Watson-King about his availability. Oh, and pretend that pass last night had never happened.

After breakfast, and before he headed off to his first job, Owen bit the bullet and called Misty. He half-expected her to say she'd thought better of the idea overnight and it had just been the wine talking, but no, she was just as enthusiastic as she'd been at the awards dinner. And when Owen told her he'd decided to do it, she was positively triumphant. After commending him on recognising that her offer was not an opportunity to be missed, she said Naomi would send him and Mason information on next steps over the weekend.

Once he'd hung up on Misty, he texted Mason.

Called Misty about WW—she's over the moon. You'll be getting an email in a day or two :-)

He stared at the screen of his phone for a few minutes after sending, but there was no response, and eventually, he tucked it away and headed out to work.

Hunter Gardens occupied a fairly basic unit at an industrial park a few miles from Owen's house. It wasn't exactly glamorous, but it had a decent-sized office, ample secure storage for his gear, and parking for the vans.

As usual, Owen was the first to arrive, though Mac wasn't far behind him.

Mac, Owen's best friend from his school days, was a tall Amazon of a woman who wore her long, curly hair scraped back in a ponytail and not so much as a scrap of make-up. Prior to working for Owen, she'd spent most of her days stoned with one loser boyfriend after another. But after agreeing to help Owen out temporarily when he was trying to get the business off the ground, she'd decided—to Owen's eternal astonishment—that she actually preferred hard physical labour and early mornings.

"Wotcher," she said—her traditional greeting—when she entered the office.

"Morning," Owen replied, swigging his instant coffee. "Kettle's just boiled."

Mac grunted and shuffled over to the tiny kitchen area to make herself a cuppa.

Owen finished pulling together the week's timesheets, then emailed them over to the guy who did their payroll. Next, he pulled up the rotas for the next two weeks, and he and Mac discussed the alterations they'd need to make for the new job they'd taken on.

"It's kinda tight," Mac said at last, "but it should be fine. They'll all be up for some weekend overtime, I reckon."

By then the crew had begun arriving. Owen helped Steve and Ally load up the vans for the day ahead while Mac got everyone organised. She headed off with two of the guys for a day of maintenance contract work in the north and west of the city, while Owen took the others with him to the Chelsea job for what he knew would be a tough day, clearing out a mature hornbeam hedge and digging up a bunch of concrete paths to prepare the ground.

He didn't get a chance to check his phone for a couple of hours, and when he did, he found a string of texts from Mason waiting for him, the last sent just a few minutes earlier.

OMG that's awesome!

Thanks, BTW. I thought you might have changed your mind after last night.

Also, sorry about that. Hope I didn't make you feel uncomfortable.

I mean, obviously I did. Sorry again.

If it makes you feel any better, I have a bloody awful hangover today.

Owen stared at the messages, reading them over and over. Then he typed a quick reply.

Honestly, no need to apologise. It was no big deal. Consider it forgotten.

He followed that up with,

Sorry you've got a hangover :-(

A minute later he got back,

Thanks <3 <3 <3

He stared at the last message—at the stupid little row of hearts—for too long before he put his phone away and got back to work.

Mason had been absolutely right about the time involved in working on *Weekend Wellness*. Over the next few weeks, it took up way more than the couple of hours Misty predicted. RPP ended up suggesting eight ten-minute slots for the show to be filmed in three sessions. It didn't seem like that big of a commitment, and Owen agreed without thinking too much about it. However, within a few days of confirming, his inbox was brimming with invitations to production calls and meetings.

It turned out there would be a four-week lead-in to the airing of their first segment. During that time, they needed to secure a piece of ground to work on and get ready for filming —Misty apparently had somewhere in mind that had *'allot-ment energy'*—while Owen planned what plants to put in, and the basic gardening content for each slot. Misty wanted details in advance so that her team could work on a *'loose script'* and get hold of the plants and equipment they needed.

"I thought you said you wanted us to talk naturally," Mason said when she mentioned the script again. It was a chilly spring morning. Misty had asked them to come and see the plot, which turned out to be an area of semi-abandoned land next to the RPP studio.

"And you will," Misty reassured Mason. "We definitely want to make the most of your spontaneous style. This is just about giving you guys some structure to help shape the conversation and make sure we're hitting our key messages each week."

Owen wondered what their 'key messages' might be, but decided not to ask. The presenting stuff was Mason's department. He wanted to concentrate on checking out the space that was to be their garden.

Clearly, at some point in the past, this had actually been a garden. According to Misty, it was currently used by some staff for smoking breaks. There were a couple of disreputable-looking plastic chairs and a pile of cigarette butts on the concrete slab patio area to prove it. A few scraggly bulbs were poking up through the weeds, most of them coming up blind. An overgrown buddleia, probably self-seeded, dominated one corner of the rectangular plot. It was, at least, south-facing, and the brick side of the studio would be sheltered and warm. He could imagine a jasmine or honeysuckle climbing up the brickwork, perhaps trained over a small wooden arbour with a bench where you could sit and soak up the beautiful fragrance with the evening sunshine…

"…is that okay with you, Owen?"

He blinked and found Mason's eyes on him, head slightly cocked as he waited for an answer. Over the last couple of weeks, they'd got to know each other a little better, and Mason had definitely softened towards Owen, dialling back the sarcasm and joking around in a more friendly way. By silent agreement, they'd put that night in Mason's flat, when Mason had made a pass at Owen, firmly behind them. Which didn't stop Owen noticing how gorgeous Mason looked every time they met. Today, he wore jeans and Converse, an over-sized baby blue sweatshirt, and a slouchy beanie hat. The early sunshine gleamed in the wisps of pale blonde hair that framed his face, and his cheeks and nose were pinked by the chilly air.

Mason's sculpted eyebrows arched questioningly, and Owen realised that he still hadn't replied.

"Uh, sorry," he said, scrubbing a hand through his hair. "I was just thinking about planting options. What did you say?"

Mason nodded towards Misty, who was, amusingly, dressed in green wellies and a Barbour jacket. "Misty was just saying that we'll have a rough script to work from, with talking points and so on, to keep us on track rather than us trying to ad lib the whole thing."

"Sounds good to me." Owen was honestly relieved that they'd be getting some guidance on the presenting side. He had no idea what to say in front of a camera and had visions of freezing as soon as a lens was pointed in his direction.

Maybe Misty recognised his unease because she grabbed his arm and added, "Don't worry, Mason will take the lead on the conversation. He'll keep the discussion moving along while you"—was she squeezing his bicep?—"concentrate on covering the gardening content."

"And you're sure that's going to work?"

"Of course," she said, frowning a little. "Obviously, we need to do a screen test first, but I'm never wrong about these things."

Owen blinked at her. "A…what?" He had an atavistic dread of the word 'test'.

"Nothing to worry about," she said with the breezy confidence of a straight-A student. "A formality, before we sign the final contracts. We'll just get you and Mason walking around the garden, chatting. It's to make sure the chemistry is there on-screen." She gave a stagey wink. "Which it *obviously* is. I just know our viewers are going to love the two of you together. Oh, and we'll probably test some costumes at the same time."

"Costumes?" Owen echoed.

"Not *costumes*," she backpedalled. "But, well, *clothes*. I'm thinking of a gilet for you, Owen, maybe with one of those sexy utility belts with tools hanging off it."

Owen felt his eyebrows hit his hairline. "Tools? Like what? A trowel?"

With surprising diplomacy, Mason said, "Maybe Owen should just wear whatever he usually wears when he's working? You know, for authenticity."

"Which is pretty much this," Owen said, gesturing at his olive-green sweatshirt with its discreet company logo, cargo shorts, and muddy work boots. He was on his way to a job, which was why this meeting was so early in the day.

"Well," Misty said, giving Owen a swift, unimpressed once over. "There's authenticity and then there's *authenticity*."

Whatever that meant.

She waved a hand. "Look, don't worry about it. We'll try some options out at the screen test and you can see what you think." Gazing around the scrubby plot of land, she added, "Given the current state of this, I suggest we do the screen test in a proper garden. I was going to scout somewhere, but then *everyone* said I should volunteer my own garden. Although heaven knows why. I'm not really a gardener. I just dabble, you know?" She laughed, then added, "But who am I to argue with my team? So, my place it is. Naomi will be in touch with times and such, but the sooner we can do this, the better. We need to get those contracts signed, boys!"

Which was how, two days later, Owen found himself pulling up outside a substantial house in Primrose Hill. It was three in the afternoon, and he'd been working nonstop since eight, finishing a large job in Hampstead. Mac was dealing with the final sign-off. Even though she and the rest of the crew thought it was brilliant, and hilarious, that Owen was going to be on telly, Owen still felt guilty leaving the job early. Ordinarily, it was a matter of pride to him that he personally saw every job finished to the customer's satisfaction, and he didn't like leaving that to someone else, even Mac.

Not for the first time, he wondered whether he'd made a mistake in agreeing to this whole *Weekend Wellness* thing. What on earth had he been thinking?

The probable answer to that question arrived as he was studying himself in the van's wing mirror, trying to tame his hair—he *really* needed to get to the barber. A car pulled up in front of his van, and a familiar, slim figure climbed out of the back seat.

Mason.

Owen sighed at himself, even as his stomach did a strange flip-flop. Mason glanced over at Owen's van, probably recognising the logo, and lifted a hand to wave.

Feeling awkward, as if he'd been caught staring—well, he *had* been caught staring—Owen grabbed his phone and wallet and scrambled out of the van.

Mason smiled, waiting for him. "Are you ready for this?"

"To be honest, I've been so busy with work I haven't even had time to think about it. I hope I don't muck it up for you."

"Of course you won't," Mason said, patting his arm. "Just be yourself."

Owen grimaced. "Easy for you to say."

Mason looked puzzled, head tilted in query.

"I mean, look at you. You always look perfect, like you've spent hours at a spa."

A complex expression crossed Mason's face.

"Well," he said lightly, after a moment, "we shameless self-promoters have to make sure we look good at all times, you know."

"Oh God, not this again," Owen groaned. Apparently, this was a reference to some joke Lewis had made at Mason's expense when Owen had first met him. Now Mason lobbed it into conversation whenever he wanted to make a dig at Owen.

Mason smiled placidly. "Come on," he said, turning towards Misty's house, a large Victorian villa with a nice wisteria growing around the front porch. "Let's get this screen test over with."

The house was pretty much exactly what Owen had expected; he'd worked on a hundred places just like it in North London. Reclaimed hardwood floors and muted Farrow and Ball paint dominated the original front part of the house, while the back of the house was all hard-edged gleaming surfaces and glass.

Misty's assistant, Naomi, today dressed in a neat white shirt and cropped black trousers, led them through a huge, open-plan kitchen-living space, and out into an immaculate but curiously soulless garden.

Like her house, the garden had been designed to tick all the right boxes: home gym with glass wall at the garden's far end, two-storey timber treehouse for the kids, green slate patio with luxury furniture, and, of course, a wood-burning pizza oven. A golf-course-perfect lawn and uniform rows of depressingly manicured plants were the only concessions to nature. It could have been out of a magazine. All very aspirational but, in Owen's opinion, the antithesis of what a garden should be. Like someone had tried to bring the indoors outside.

Misty was standing in the middle of the lawn having a heated discussion with a grim-faced man holding a long pole with something huge and furry on the end.

"It's a dead cat," Mason said quietly.

"*What*?"

Mason chuckled, eyes sparkling. In the afternoon sunlight, they were a gorgeous mossy green. "The fuzzy cover on the boom mic is called a 'dead cat'. The fur stops the wind hitting the microphone and screwing up the sound."

"...don't care if it's her birthday. We need it tomorrow, so you'll just have to get it finished tonight." Misty turned away from the guy holding the microphone, who glared at her back. Her expression shifted into a bright smile when she caught sight of Mason and Owen. "Ah, here they are!" She hurried over and gave Mason a stagey kiss on each cheek, which he reciprocated politely.

"You look gorgeous!" she exclaimed. "As always. *Loved* your post on Insta this morning. That's exactly the content we're looking for—wholesome but a little naughty."

"Yeah, it got some traction." Mason threw a quick look at Owen. Was he expecting Owen to have seen it? He hadn't. He didn't waste time on social media. Owen had Facebook and Instagram pages for the business, and he rarely even looked at those.

"Owen." Misty turned to him, leaning in for the same *mwah-mwah*.

"Misty," he said, aware he sounded, and probably looked, stiff. This, all of it, was really not his scene. Lewis or Aaron, or even Tag—maybe especially Tag—would be far more comfortable here.

"Don't you look handsome?" she said happily. "Very rugged."

When she looked down at her phone, scrolling with her thumb, Owen glanced over at Mason to roll his eyes. Mason gave a funny little half-smile and looked away.

"Now, let's get you changed," Misty said, looking up again. She turned her head and yelled, "Naomi, bring the outfits over!" before turning back to Owen. "I'd love a gilet, ideally with one of those tattersall shirts—you know, the checked shirts countryside people wear? With your colouring, I'm thinking blues and browns…"

"I really don't think—"

But there was no arguing with her, and a few moments later, Naomi appeared looking flustered and carrying an armful of clothes.

"Welcome to my life," Mason murmured, grinning as, without a hint of self-consciousness, he started unbuttoning his own shirt.

Owen flashed back to Mason's bedroom that night, his face heating, watching helplessly as Mason stripped the shirt off and took the t-shirt Naomi held out to him. Owen caught his breath. He couldn't help it because Mason's body was… Well, he was gorgeous. Of course he was gorgeous. Lean, lightly muscled with pale skin, his chest was smooth—waxed, a dizzy part of his brain suggested—with dark pink nipples that pebbled in the cool spring air.

Mouth dry, heart pounding, Owen tore his eyes away, his cock thickening in instinctive, powerful desire. Shit, had anyone noticed him staring? He swallowed, but his throat felt dry as a bone, and he cleared it, trying to be quiet.

"…no, no. The blue one," Misty snapped. "I said *blue*. Are you colourblind?"

"Sorry," Naomi said, rummaging through her armful of clothes. "Here, try this."

Owen, still hyper-aware of Mason pulling on clothes in his peripheral vision, yanked off his own sweatshirt. He had never been shy about his body, but now, he felt weirdly self-conscious, perhaps because it was only him and Mason getting undressed while everyone else just watched them.

Or perhaps it was because *Mason* was watching, and Mason—as a model—would be used to seeing beautiful, perfect bodies all day long…

Fuck.

Owen determinedly shoved that thought aside and quickly shrugged into the shirt Naomi handed him, trying to appear unconcerned as he fastened the buttons.

"Mmm," Misty hummed, tipping her head from side to side as she studied him. "Sleeves rolled up, I think. Show off those glorious forearms."

Naomi moved hesitantly forward, reaching for Owen's cuff.

"It's okay," he said quickly. He undid the buttons and turned up the sleeves to expose his forearms.

"Yes, good. *Very* nice," Misty purred. She glanced at Mason, who was now wearing a tight-fitting violet t-shirt with a prancing cartoon unicorn on the front and a V-neck that exposed the hollow at the base of his throat.

Owen had a sudden, powerful vision of himself licking into that little hollow. Of kissing Mason there. He could almost taste the salt on Mason's warm, smooth skin…

"Okay, you'll do," Misty decided. "We'll lose the light if we don't start now." She clapped her hands. "All right everyone, let's begin."

Owen felt a sudden panic as the guy with the microphone, and another man hefting a huge camera on his shoulder, approached.

Shit, this was really happening.

"Take a breath," Mason said, stepping closer.

He squeezed Owen's arm, fingers cool on Owen's bare skin, driving an unhelpful spike of desire through Owen's already pounding heart.

"You know about gardening, right?" Mason was looking at him seriously, his hand still lingering on Owen's arm. "So just tell me about stuff. I know nothing, so there's plenty to say."

Owen nodded. "Okay." His voice sounded tight and rough.

"You'll be fine," Mason said and threw him a wink. An actual bloody wink. Cute, and sexy as all hell. Christ.

Misty told them where to stand and said *'action'*. Just like in the movies. Owen felt a sudden urge to laugh hysterically.

"So here we are in this *gorgeous* garden…" Mason began, and suddenly he was *on*. Performing. He was still himself, just a bit more so. It was a subtle difference, but obvious to Owen, and he knew that he couldn't do the same, that he'd feel and look ridiculous if he even tried.

Shit.

Panic flapped in his chest, and he was about to tell them all to stop, that he couldn't do it, when Mason said, "So, Owen, would you call this a modern, contemporary garden?"

"Uh," Owen said, glancing at the camera, then away because Misty had told him to never look at the camera. "Sort of?"

"Yeah? What does that mean, then? What makes a garden contemporary? Or should I say, what makes a contemporary garden?" He shrugged, frowning in a cute, puzzled way that made Owen chuckle despite his nerves.

"Well," he said. "As you can see, there's a lot of sleek, elegant features in this garden. Those concrete planters on the patio, for example. There's a fantastic contrast between the clean, simple lines of the containers and the plants inside. I love that feathery fern in the tall planter and the spiky rosemary too. Rosemary is such a great all-year-round plant. It's evergreen, it grows like crazy, and it smells amazing. Plus, it's a magnet for pollinators."

"Also, you can cook with it," Mason said. "It's awesome in a hearty stew. And I make an *amazing* rosemary focaccia—I'll give you the recipe; it's totally *orgasmic*. But what if you only have a very limited space? What can viewers like me do to create something beautiful in a small area and hopefully attract some pollinators?"

Owen was grinning now, enjoying Mason's cute, flirty style and the easy way he'd fed him that cue. "There's tons of options," he said, thinking back to the patch of barren courtyard outside Mason's flat. "You can actually do loads even with a very small space. You need to think about growing vertically, using walls or fences, even balconies. Pots are great too, because you can move them around to maximise sunlight or shade, and there's a bunch of different plants you can choose to attract bees and butterflies…"

And they were off, Mason asking the questions and Owen answering. At one point, Owen squatted down and pulled out a few weeds, showing Mason the difference between geraniums and creeping buttercup. It felt good, grounding, to get his hands in the earth, and even better when Mason's fingers brushed his own as they compared the geranium leaves with the buttercup leaves. Mason seemed genuinely interested. Owen wasn't sure whether that was real or just a performance, but it looked real. The smile in Mason's eyes looked real. His enthusiasm looked real as he guided them around the garden and got Owen to demonstrate some of the basic gardening tools Misty had left out, making a few funny remarks and provoking a laugh or two from the crew, and from Owen.

This was a new side to Mason—engaged, enthusiastic, happy—that Owen hadn't guessed at until he'd started getting to know him properly. Over the last few weeks,

Owen had begun to see him in a new light. Had realised that there was more to Mason than the spoiled and rather vacuous model Owen had assumed him to be when they'd first met. It turned out that Mason was smart, quick-witted, curious, and a natural presenter, with an ability to talk easily on just about any topic, and today, all those qualities were on show.

If Owen hadn't been having so much fun, he might have started to worry that he was in way over his head.

As it was, when Misty called 'cut' and the screen test came to an end, he felt almost disappointed that it was over so soon. And as they trooped into the kitchen to watch the footage back on Misty's laptop, he realised he was nervous. What if he'd been rubbish? Suddenly, he really *really* wanted to do this again. With Mason.

It turned out, though, that he had no need to worry. Misty loved it.

"I was right!" she crowed, her expression pure self-satisfaction. "I knew you two would work on-screen. Let's think about punching up that flirting a bit, yeah? A little bit of *will-they-won't-they* will go down a storm." She gave them a wink and turned her attention back to the screen.

What the fuck?

Perturbed, Owen glanced at Mason, but he didn't seem remotely bothered. In fact, he was grinning too, as though what Misty had just said made perfect sense.

Well, maybe it did? Maybe Owen was being silly. After all, Mason had flirted with that silver fox presenter during his first slot on *Weekend Wellness*, and that hadn't meant anything. And what did Owen even know about TV?

"My garden looks *amazing*," Misty said as she played the footage again. "It would make a fantastic location. Maybe we could get you to do a couple of extra slots from here? I *was* thinking of putting in some cold frames. Maybe a project like that would work…"

Mason made a soft harrumphing sound at that, but Misty didn't seem to notice, too caught up in her own thoughts.

Later, though, when they'd left Misty's house and Owen was giving Mason a ride to the tube, he fumed about it. "And what was all that about Misty trying to get you to install some cold frames in her garden for free? She's such a fucking freeloader!"

Owen laughed. "She certainly takes after her namesake."

Mason frowned. "Namesake?"

"Did you know her name is short for Mistletoe?"

"*What?*" Mason laughed.

Owen grinned back. "Lewis told me. Apparently, she was a Christmas baby."

"Oh my God, that's hilarious, but what's it got to do with being a freeloader?"

"Mistletoe's a parasitic plant," Owen explained. "It gets all its food and water from its host."

Mason snorted. "Is it enormously impressed with itself, too?"

"Now that I don't know," Owen said, chuckling—Mason could be surprisingly wry. "But it *is* poisonous, so watch out…."

For a few moments they were both silent. Then Mason said, "Despite all that, I had a lot of fun today. Did you?"

Owen glanced over, catching Mason's eyes for a moment. "I did, actually. I was quite nervous at first—"

"I could tell, but you were great. Really natural."

"Yeah? *You* were amazing. Feeding me all those lines. You made it so easy."

Mason's cheeks flushed. "I think this'll be good," he said as Owen pulled up on a double yellow line outside the station. "It'll be *great*. I'm going to start posting about it." Someone hooted, and Mason quickly undid his seatbelt. "Once the contracts are signed, is it okay if I put something on Insta? A pic of us from today?"

"Uh, yeah, okay. Of course."

"Not too self-promoting for you?" Mason said, raising one brow, lips ticking up in a cheeky smile.

"No," Owen said, smiling back. "I think I can live with that."

"Great," Mason said, opening the van door and climbing out. At the last minute he turned back, sticking his head inside the van. "You should follow me on Insta. I'm @mason-isamodel. We should get a little banter going. For publicity, you know? Misty will love it."

"All right," Owen said, smiling too. "I will." God only knew when he was last on Instagram. It had been so long that he'd have to ask Naaz to show him how to log on.

"Great. And thanks for the lift." He closed the door and strode off.

Despite the irritable hoots of cars trying to get around him, Owen didn't move, watching until Mason had crossed in front of the van and headed into the station, naturally grace-ful, long legs striding out and blonde hair gleaming in the golden evening light.

"Jesus Christ, Hunter," he said to himself as he pulled out into traffic, giving a wave of apology to the grumpy cab driver glaring at him. "Stop fucking staring at the guy."

He was smiling as he said it, though. He was smiling all the way home.

CHAPTER EIGHT

Mason

The Sunday after the screen test, Mason was slumped down in a seat at the back of the carriage on a train from Clapham Junction. The spring sunshine streamed harsh and bright through the window, which was good because it meant Mason could keep his sunglasses on without looking like a wanker.

Not that Mason got recognised constantly, but it did happen, and always at the worst time.

This was a worst time.

Visiting his mum always put him in a mood, one that wouldn't lift until he was on the train heading back to London and his own life. Not that he didn't love his mum. He did. Of course he did, but sometimes—okay, often—she felt like an enormous weight sitting on his shoulders.

What would I do without you? she'd say when he sorted out another problem for her. *My beautiful boy.*

You'd be fine without me. That was what he wanted to say. *You're a grown woman.*

But he didn't say it because saying it would have been

impossible. Even hinting at it would have strayed too close to the things they didn't talk about.

Didn't dare talk about.

Like the way Frieda had broken down after Kurt walked out and left her alone with Mason and his twin sisters. And the way that Mason, at thirteen, had been the only one there to pick up the pieces.

Somehow, he was still picking them up. Or, rather, taking care that his patched-up mum didn't fall apart again, doing whatever was necessary to help her through life. Back then, it had been cooking and shopping, taking the girls to the park, or to nursery. Comforting Frieda when she cried over Kurt, taking care of her when she had one of her nervous stomachs or three-day migraines.

Things were easier now, but mostly, that was because Mason had money.

Funny how people said money couldn't solve your problems. The truth was, everything was easier when you had money—*everything*. Anyone who said otherwise was talking out of their arse.

True, it didn't solve every problem, but it was a big fucking cushion, and Mason would rather have it than not.

Now, with Mason's financial support, Frieda and his sisters lived in a leafy London suburb, in a flat close to the river. Somewhere Frieda could take Pilates classes with nice ladies-who-lunched, dabble in her art, and not have to deal with anything as traumatic as a job. She led as stress-free a life as Mason could buy, which meant she could just about cope with parenting his sixteen-year-old sisters, while *he* was more or less free to live his life in London.

Mason's gut began to twist as the train drew closer to his destination, a sign of his rising anxiety. He did a good job of compartmentalising most of the time, locking his family responsibilities into a box he could ignore—but reality always intruded sooner or later. Like when he had to deal with Frieda's money issues or intercede with Kurt. Or like now, sitting on the train, contemplating the possibility that he'd turn up to find Frieda in one of her fragile moods.

To distract himself from his anxiety, he scrolled through his phone. He'd posted a picture of him and Owen at the screen test the previous evening—#WatchThisSpace #GardeningHottie #WeekendWellness—and it had got decent traction, plenty of heart eyes and a few eggplant emojis.

Better still, Owen had replied with 'That was fun' and a thumbs up. They'd need to work on his social media skills, but even so, it had made Mason grin. It was a great picture too, Owen laughing and Mason mugging for the camera in that ridiculous unicorn t-shirt.

Misty had WhatsApped him too, early this morning, but he was only now checking his messages.

Saw your post on Insta last night! You guys look GREAT together!! LOVED your chemistry on-screen. Let's go hard on the flirting in your segment. Viewers pant over 'Are they/Aren't they?' stuff, really positive for ratings. Would be awesome to see you teasing it on your socials too. Dinners out, pap pics in the park holding hands etc? See how far you can push it, sweetie. <3

He read her message a couple of times, considering.

Misty wasn't wrong. He knew that. He and Owen *did* have chemistry, but who wouldn't have chemistry with someone as easy-going and friendly as Owen Hunter? Sexy as fuck too with that touchable mop of dark hair, those big shoulders and arms, and that quietly spoken self-assurance that gave Mason goosebumps.

Among other things.

Yeah, the chemistry was real despite the debacle at his flat the night of the awards dinner.

The question was, would Owen be up for embracing it? Playing it up for the cameras a bit more?

Mason wasn't sure he would. Owen was such a *what-you-see-is-what-you-get* sort of guy. He might be okay with gentle on-screen flirting, but Mason had the feeling that he wouldn't like the idea of pretending there was more going on between them.

Not if that wasn't true.

He sent a quick message to Misty.

Not sure O would be keen to push it—he doesn't really do social media. Might not get it.

He saw that Misty was writing an immediate response, but then she stopped, and a moment later, his phone rang.

Uh-oh.

"Mason, sweetie," she said as soon he picked up, "you're the pro, here. You do realise that, don't you? You're the media professional, and Owen needs to take his lead from you."

Mason glanced around the carriage, but it was mostly empty. Even so, he sank lower into his seat and kept his voice quiet. "Yeah, I know, I'm just saying that kind of thing won't come naturally to Owen. He's a very straightforward guy."

Misty made a dismissive sound. "Of course he is. That's what our audience is going to love about him, but I have to be honest with you, sweetie—" Her voice raised about ten decibels. "Oscar Watson-King! *What* do you think you're doing with that violin?"

Mason pulled the phone away from his ear, grimacing.

When he tentatively put it back, she was saying, "...not going to be geraniums that excites our audience, is it? It's going to be the sizzle between you and Owen. And, frankly, if Owen isn't prepared to go there—"

"I didn't say that," Mason jumped in hastily. "Just that he probably won't get why we need to stage a bunch of fake stuff for Insta, you know?"

"Well," Misty said crisply, "who says it has to be fake?" When Mason didn't respond, she added, "You're both attractive young gay men, aren't you?"

Mason laughed, almost speechless. He couldn't tell

whether she was joking. "Are you...? Are you suggesting I *fuck him* for ratings?"

After a pointed pause, Misty said, "All I'm doing, sweetie, is giving you a heads-up on what you need to do if you want this to be a success. You do want that, right? *I* do—I want it to be a *huge* success for you. I *like* you, Mason, and I'm thrilled to be giving you this fantastic opportunity. Obviously, it's up to you how far you run with it...."

She rambled on for another few minutes before abruptly hanging up—something about her son and orchestra practice. Mason wasn't really paying attention. His thoughts had already returned to that night in his flat.

The thing was, as crass as Misty's suggestion was, Mason *was* tempted. He remembered the transparent desire he'd seen in Owen's eyes that night.

Drunk or sober, Mason knew when a man wanted him. And Owen *had* wanted him.

Still wanted him, in fact, because Mason saw that same interest every time he and Owen met. Owen was reserved and respectful, yes, but Mason wasn't blind—he saw the way Owen looked at him. He saw the obvious attraction that was simmering beneath the surface.

Saw it and returned it.

So, what would be the harm in turning up the heat a little?

Obviously, he wouldn't tell Owen that Misty was encouraging them to mess around—Owen wouldn't like that any more than Mason did—but that didn't matter. The fact was, Mason *was* genuinely attracted to Owen. Who wouldn't be? He was a lovely guy, and Mason had been fantasising about getting him into bed for weeks now. If Owen felt the same—and hadn't been put off by Mason's last clumsy come-on—why shouldn't they have some fun? And Mason was pretty sure Owen *did* feel the same. Now that he knew Owen better, he could see that he was the sort of man who liked to get to know the people he slept with before he jumped into bed with them. The sort of man who'd probably be more easily seduced with a home-cooked meal and a cosy night in than the sort of blatant pass Mason had attempted before…

Well, Mason could certainly provide a home-cooked meal. It would be fun, in fact, a rare opportunity to cook something fabulous.

Then… well, they could just see how things went, but a friendly fling while they filmed and then promoted the show would be pretty sweet. It would definitely help Owen get on board with creating the sort of social content Misty wanted. Not that Owen would really understand that—or even be interested in what it could do for his own profile—but that was fine. Mason could take care of that side of things for both of them. Because Misty *was* right: if viewers got invested in their relationship, it would be *awesome* for the show, for Mason's long-term career, and—whether Owen realised it or not—for his business too.

It was a win-win proposition all round

"The next stop is Surbiton," the train's automated announcement told him. *"This is the Hampton Court service calling at Surbiton, Thames Ditton, and Hampton Court only."*

Sighing, Mason pocketed his phone and pushed to his feet, making his way to the doors as the train pulled into the station. When it stopped, the doors beeped and opened, and Mason stepped out onto the mostly empty platform. At this time on a Sunday, there weren't many people around.

It was a ten-minute walk, fifteen if you took your time, from the station to the three-bedroom flat he helped his mum rent on a tree-lined street one road back from the Thames. A lot of the buildings were older, Victorian maybe, but his mum's block was modern, and although she didn't have a garden, she had a small balcony with room for a table and chairs. It was way nicer than the flat they'd been in when Mason had lived at home, back before he started modelling.

As always, he felt a familiar anxiety dragging at him as he

rang the bell and then pulled open the building's door when the buzzer sounded. Avoiding the lift, he climbed the stairs up to the second floor, taking them slowly to delay the inevitable as long as possible.

It didn't take long though, and a couple of minutes later, he was walking down the short hallway to their flat at the end. The front door stood ajar, and his stomach flip-flopped uneasily. "Hello?" he called, pushing it open. "Frieda?"

It had been years since she'd had one of her black moods, and yet every time he saw her, he still felt that childlike fear of what he'd find. But when he walked in, he found her in the kitchen fiddling around making a salad, frizzy blonde hair loose about her shoulders— greying now, like tarnished gold —in a baggy sweatshirt and leggings. And when she turned around, she was smiling.

Immediately, Mason relaxed, his stomach unwinding.

"Angel!" Frieda beamed. "There you are. It's so good to see you!"

He winced inwardly. Angel was his given name. Mason was his own invention, a name he'd picked out after his agent had walked up to him in the street and handed him his card. His real name, along with his pretty face and unconventional parents with their canal boat home, had given the other kids at school way too much ammunition to mock him with, and he'd been desperate to be rid of it.

"It's good to see you, too," he said and tried to mean it, slipping off his jacket and hanging it on an overcrowded coat hook in the hall. "Are the girls in?"

Frieda looked shifty. "You know what they're like. There's always something going on with their friends. Anyway, I thought it would be nice for us to spend some quality time together. Just you and me." She crossed the room, holding her arms open for a hug. He obliged. "It's been too long since I've seen my beautiful boy!"

"It's been six weeks," he said around a mouthful of her frizzy hair as he hugged her. "I *have* phoned."

"I know," she said, patting his face. "But it's not the same. And I want to hear all about *Weekend Wellness*!"

Of course she did.

"I've made us a nice tuna salad," Frieda went on, bustling back into the kitchen. "I know you have a shoot next week, so there's no pudding. And it's probably for the best that I couldn't spring for a bottle of wine!"

She laughed, and Mason sighed, taking his cue. "As it happens, I've got a nice Pinot Grigio in my bag."

Just like he always did when he came to lunch.

Frieda beamed. "Angel, you do spoil me."

They ate at the kitchen table, shoving aside Frieda's art supplies. She fancied herself something of an artist and sold a handful of things—handmade greetings cards, mostly—on Etsy. It didn't make any money, but Frieda found her art relaxing, and so Mason had always encouraged it.

"You were so good on *Weekend Wellness*," Frieda rattled on. "So handsome! I had my girlfriends over, and we watched it three times on catch-up, with a few glasses of pink fizz. Shelly said you were a natural, much better than that other bloke—the old one. And her daughter works in the theatre, you know, so she knows about that sort of thing."

Mason gave a noncommittal hum and forked up another mouthful of claggy tuna salad.

"So..." Frieda sent him a sidelong glance. "What's next? Has Frankie got you anything else? They have social media stars on *Strictly* these days, you know."

"Frieda..."

"This could be your break, Angel. The big time!"

He shrugged, weirdly reluctant to tell her about the gardening slot with Owen. Why, he wasn't sure, but for some reason he found he wanted to keep it to himself, as if sharing the news with Frieda would sully it in some way. Which was stupid; it was only a job, like any other gig he'd taken over the last six years. Shoving his discomfort aside, he ploughed ahead. "You'll be happy to know that I've just signed to do a series of slots on the show."

"Oh my gosh!" Frieda squealed. "That's brilliant! I *knew* that would happen. I told Shelly it would! Those cosmetic companies must have been wetting themselves, having someone as gorgeous as you promoting their stuff."

"It's nothing to do with cosmetics actually," he said. "It's a gardening feature."

"Gardening?" Frieda looked baffled. "What do you know about gardening?"

"Nothing. I won't be *doing* the gardening, obviously. I'll be learning about it. They've got another guy—he's called Owen. He's…" He bit back a sudden smile, looking down at his plate and pushing a lump of mayo-clogged tuna around. "He's very cool. The idea is that viewers learn along with me."

Frieda shrugged, tapping her wine glass against his in salute. "As long as they're paying you, that's what counts. And it's all good exposure." Then she sighed, and Mason braced himself. "Such a shame *we* don't have a garden. Then I could have learned too. Gardening can be so mindful."

"You have a good size balcony," Mason said, unable to suppress his reflexive instinct to fix her every problem. "Owen knows a lot about gardening in small spaces, including balconies, and we're definitely going to be talking about that."

"Hmm," Frieda said. "That's just pots and things, though, isn't it? Not really connecting with the earth. When we lived on the boat, we had so much green space around us. It was like we were part of nature. I do miss that."

Alarm fluttered in his chest, the way it always did when his mum expressed any displeasure.

"You're a two-minute walk from the river," he pointed out. "And there's that lovely walk all along the towpath…"

"Oh, I'm not complaining," she said, which was what she always said when she complained. "You're very good to us, Angel." She covered his hand with her own, squeezing. "I don't know what I'd do without you."

And there it was, the concrete slab of responsibility he had no choice but to shoulder, the chain he couldn't break. Her hand tightened on his, and her lips began to wobble. He knew what was coming next.

Freeing his hand from her grasp, he picked up his fork and stabbed at a piece of tomato. "So, Kurt's late with this month's payment again?"

"Yes…" Frieda said, fiddling with her hair, tucking it behind her ears. "And, well, things are a bit—" She trailed off feebly.

"Tight?" Mason supplied.

Kurt did make most of the payments eventually, but he was almost always late, and despite Frieda's complaints to Mason, she was useless at confronting Kurt about it. Which was why Mason always ended up having to get involved, both to push Kurt to pay up and to sub Frieda so she could pay the bills till the money arrived. And since Frieda wasn't great at managing money, and overspent most months, the subs just disappeared into the bottomless pit of her bank account.

"The thing is," Frieda went on, "the girls have their GCSE French trip this term. They have to go. It's part of the curriculum, but it's four hundred pounds each…"

It was tempting to just say *how much do you need?* He could transfer the money on the spot and fuck off home. But that's not how they did things; he had a role to play first.

"Don't worry," he said, smiling for her. "I can cover that."

"Oh, Mason, I didn't mean—"

JOANNA CHAMBERS & SALLY MALCOLM

"No, I'd like to. They *are* my sisters, remember? It's the least I can do."

"Well, it's very good of you," she said. "If Kurt could just pay up on time, but his new girlfriend…"

She trailed off, and Mason felt another pinch of anxiety when he saw her downturned mouth. "Regan?" he said with a deliberate laugh. "She won't last. She's awful."

Frieda gave a watery smile.

Regan *was* genuinely awful—grasping and boring as hell. Not that the details mattered. Mason's job had always been to tell Frieda exactly how terrible Kurt's latest girlfriend was and all the ways in which Frieda was superior. After Kurt had walked out, it was Mason's exaggerated description of the woman he'd shacked up with that had first brought a smile back to Frieda's face. He'd been doing it ever since.

Luckily, this time, he was saved by the bell. Or, rather, by the doorbell.

"Oh, those girls!" Frieda exclaimed, getting up from the table and going to the entry phone. "They never remember their keys."

A few moments later, Harmony and Melody burst into the flat in a riot of colour and noise, phones in hand and Mel talking a mile a minute.

"Mum, we're going to Brooke's house. Her dad's going to —Mase!" she squealed, and he just managed to get up from the table before she barrelled into him, her frizzy red hair soft beneath his chin.

"I didn't know you were coming," she said, squeezing him tight around the waist. "Mum, why didn't you say?"

After hugging his sister, Mason pulled back and nodded to Harmony. Taller and quieter than her sister, Harmony—Min, for short—was always less effusive than Mel, just giving him a lift of her chin from the kitchen door.

"Hey Min," he said fondly. "How's it going?"

"Terrible."

He smiled. "Great."

A slight smile curled one corner of her lips, and she went back to her phone.

"Girls," Frieda said happily, "your brother's going to pay for your French trip. So, you don't need to worry now. You can definitely go."

"Really?" Mel said, beaming at him. "Ohmygod, thank you *so* much."

"No thanks needed. We've got to get you *parlez-vous*-ing with the best of them, right?"

Mel snorted, but Harmony looked up at him from beneath a fall of sleek blonde hair so like his own. "Why can't Dad pay?" she said. "It's, like, literally his job?"

Frieda frowned, flustered, and threw a helpless look at Mason. "Now, Min, don't be—"

"I offered to pay," Mason cut in quickly. "I want to. You know how I love making you guys do *even more* schoolwork. So come on," he sat back down at the table and patted the chair next to him, "tell me about your trip. Where are you going? And don't say 'France'..."

CHAPTER NINE

Over the next few weeks, it seemed like Owen had endless calls and meetings with the RPP team.

The three days of filming were going to be roughly three weeks apart. RPP was arranging for the hard landscaping to be done before they started—clearing the ground, creating raised beds and putting up a small greenhouse in the corner. On the first day, they'd film Owen and Mason preparing the soil and doing some sowing and planting. Owen had planned out a mix of vegetables, herbs and flowers, since Misty was keen to get some produce back to the studio to use in the cooking section of the show. The second day of filming would capture progress and cover tending and maintenance work, and the third would show off the results of their efforts and hopefully include some harvesting of produce.

At this early stage, it wasn't entirely clear how the content would be sliced up into the weekly slots. Misty said it would depend on what the footage looked like—what worked, what didn't and how it dovetailed with the other content they were scheduling. The format of the show meant that they were making content decisions right up to the day before broadcast.

As well as the pre-recorded slots, Misty wanted Owen and Mason to come into the studio for at least one live appearance.

"Maybe we'll do more if you go down well with the viewers," she'd said with a smirk. Owen found it difficult to believe the audience could get *that* excited by gardening basics, even if Mason did flirt with him, but what did he know?

When Owen had asked if the live appearances would count as one of the eight slots he had agreed to, Misty pointed out that the contract—which he'd blithely signed without the benefit of any legal advice, something Lewis had chewed his ear off about later—obliged him to do whatever additional promotional appearances RPP might 'reasonably request'.

Lesson learned, if a little too late.

During those initial planning weeks, it wasn't easy to meet all his commitments. Even with RPP being flexible about scheduling calls and meetings, his working day was extended by a couple of hours most days, and, between the *Weekend Wellness* stuff and catching up on paperwork for the business, he was now working most of his weekends too.

There was one positive coming out of it, though: getting to know Mason. Even, amazingly, becoming *friends* with Mason. Because Mason wasn't actually the shallow 'shameless self-promoter' that Owen had had him pegged as. Yes, he spent a lot of time working on his social media profile and thinking about what his thousands of followers thought of his every move, but that wasn't—as Owen had so uncharitably assumed—because Mason was a self-obsessed narcissist. It was just… part of his job, a part he took seriously. And one on one? Away from other people, Mason was softer, sweeter, surprisingly thoughtful. As the weeks passed, it began to feel to Owen that their initial camaraderie was deepening into something that felt like a real, lasting friendship.

When Owen had, early on and a little diffidently, asked Mason if he wanted to help with planning what they'd actually plant, Mason's enthusiastic response had taken him aback. They'd spent several evenings poring over Owen's gardening books to reach their final list, and when Mason had emailed him a whole set of detailed notes afterwards, setting out how different herbs and vegetables could be incorporated into other slots on cooking, pickling and preserving, Owen had been stunned by how much work Mason had put into it.

"This is amazing," he'd said as he scrolled through the notes on his phone over a quick coffee they'd grabbed one lunchtime. "How do you know so much about this stuff?"

Mason shrugged carelessly, but Owen had seen the quick, shy smile he'd hidden. "I used to cook a lot. I don't get much chance to do it these days."

"Yeah? You cook?"

Mason laughed. "Don't look so surprised. My skills aren't limited to pouting and wearing clothes, you know. I'll even prove it, if you like."

"Prove it?"

"Yeah. I'll cook for you." He smiled a smile Owen wasn't quite sure how to interpret. "Why don't you come to mine tomorrow evening? We'll get these notes finished and sent off to Misty, and I'll make us some supper."

Which was how Owen found himself standing in his bedroom on Thursday evening after getting home from work, wondering what the hell to wear.

This is not a date, he reminded himself for the hundredth time as he towelled his hair dry and examined the contents of his wardrobe. *He's just cooking supper. We're having supper as friends.*

Over the next half hour, Owen tried on a bunch of different shirts and trousers, but everything he put on made him look like he was going on a date. Or at least like he *thought* he was going on a date. Which he definitely wasn't.

In the end, hot and flustered from all the pulling on and off of different outfits, he settled for some nice but very old jeans and a navy-and-green checked shirt in soft, brushed flannel with a plain, white t-shirt underneath.

Casual, he thought. *Relaxed and casual.*

He spent a few minutes trying to calm his messy hair, cursing himself for still not having gone to the barber's again this week and resolving to definitely go this weekend. Having tamed his mop into submission with hair product, he impulsively reached for the Tom Ford aftershave Mason had commented on before. He liberally sprayed himself, only to breathe in and realise just how much he'd used. Hell. Now he *reeked* of Oud Wood—and when he looked in the mirror, he groaned at the sight of his weirdly, uncharacteristically neat hair.

"Shit."

Running his hands through his hair, he messed it back up, then scrubbed himself with a damp washcloth to get rid of the aftershave scent as best he could.

"Calm the fuck down," he scolded his reflection in the bathroom mirror. "This is *not a date.*"

And if he didn't get a shift on, he was going to be late.

He was locking his front door when one of his neighbours, Susie, walked past on her way home from work.

"Hey, Owen," she said cheerily, slowing her pace. "You look nice. Hot date tonight?"

"What, me?" he said, giving a strained laugh. "No. No date tonight."

She looked puzzled by his vehemence but said lightly, "Okay. Well, have a good night, whatever you get up to."

"Yeah, thanks," he said. "You too."

Damn. He should probably change, but he really didn't have time now. Instead, he jumped in the van and spent the drive over to Mason's place worrying that, despite his determined attempts to appear casual, he still looked like he thought he was on a date. After all, why had Susie jumped to that conclusion? Was he usually *so* dressed down that just putting on a clean shirt looked like a major effort on his part?

"This is not a date," he muttered as he pulled the van into a parking spot round the corner from Mason's flat. "It is absolutely *not* a date."

He grabbed the bottle of wine he'd bought to take over—was that another mistake?—and forced himself to get out.

He paused when he reached Mason's front door, but before he could even press the bell, it opened... and there was Mason in a pair of loose, tatty, grey shorts and a tight navy t-shirt with a floury handprint on it. His narrow feet were bare, and his lean, lightly tanned legs were smooth and hairless.

Owen realised he was staring at Mason's legs and dragged his gaze back up.

"Hey," Mason said, his smile warm. "I saw you coming down the steps."

"Hi," Owen replied. His voice was husky, and he cleared his throat self-consciously. "Um, I brought some wine."

Mason reached out to take the offered bottle, and Owen stared at the twisted leather bracelet on his wrist, the dark brown leather contrasting with his pale gold skin.

"Thanks. Oooh, a Riesling, that's perfect. Come on in." Turning around, Mason headed back into the flat, and Owen followed, closing the door behind him.

"Wow, it smells amazing in here," he said, sniffing appreciatively as he entered the kitchen.

Mason grinned at him. "Grab a seat. I'll open this."

He picked up a corkscrew and efficiently uncorked the wine. There were glasses on the table already.

"Um, I drove over actually," Owen said. "I probably shouldn't drink."

"Your choice, but you could have one glass," Mason

replied. "I can make you some coffee to have with pudding to sober you up after."

"You made pudding?" Owen said, surprised.

"Of course! I invited you over to show off my skills, didn't I?"

"What are we having?"

"Halibut with beurre blanc and sauté potatoes followed by tarte au citron."

Owen's eyes widened. "That sounds… wow. I was kind of expecting some pasta or something. Maybe some garlic bread if I was lucky. In that case, okay, I'll have some wine. Seems a shame not to."

Mason grinned and poured the Riesling.

"I better get the halibut started," he said. "Everything else is pretty much ready to go."

"Do you need me to do anything?" Owen said, half-rising from his chair. Mason set a hand on his shoulder and pressed him back down.

"All you need to do is sit there and look pretty," he said, chuckling.

Owen's face flooded with sudden heat. "Um, that's really more your thing, isn't it? Maybe we should swap places."

Mason's full lips quirked up in an amused smile. "Unless you can make a beurre blanc, tonight it's your thing, big boy."

Big boy?

Owen shifted uncomfortably in his seat, but as he watched Mason cook—slicing butter into a cast-iron pan, setting the fish inside, seasoning and basting and turning it—his awkwardness began to melt away. Mason's movements were practised and assured, his confidence evident. After a few minutes, he took the pan off the burner and slid the whole thing into the oven. An orgasmically good garlicky scent escaped when he opened the oven door, and Owen's stomach grumbled loudly.

"Hungry?" Mason said, his green eyes dancing with mischief.

Owen's breath caught. Mason's face was pink from the heat of the hob, his hair was flopping messily over his forehead, and he looked… happy.

It was a good look on him.

"Yeah," Owen said, after a pause. "Starving actually."

Mason winked. "Just the beurre blanc to go." He lit one of the burners under another pan that was already sitting on the hob and headed off to the fridge. By the time he returned, with a bowl full of cubes of butter, the pan was giving off an aromatic winey fragrance.

"That's a hell of a lot of butter," Owen said.

Mason smiled. "Well, it *is* a butter sauce. Don't worry. You'll like it." He tossed a handful of butter cubes into the pan and began whisking.

"I'm sure I will," Owen said, practically drooling. "I love butter. You'll have to stop me eating it. I'll be licking my plate."

Mason's smile widened, pleased with that response. "Lick away," he said, waggling his eyebrows at Owen. "You work hard, and you cycle tons—you can afford to splurge on a few calories."

"So can you," Owen pointed out.

Mason gave a strangely charming half-grin. "I sort of can actually, for once. I don't have another shoot for ten days. I'll be doing double workouts till then, though." He took a glug of wine, tossing another handful of butter cubes into the pan, his whisk moving constantly.

For a few minutes, Owen just watched him contentedly, sipping his wine. "You really look like you know what you're doing," he said after a while.

Mason shrugged. "Well, I did used to be a chef."

Owen blinked. "*Did* you?"

Mason looked amused by his reaction. "Yup. I was

working as a chef de partie in a Michelin two-starred restaurant when I got spotted by my agent. It actually took him a while to convince me to give modelling a go." He opened the oven and extracted the halibut. "This needs to rest for a few minutes."

"What made you agree in the end?" Owen asked, genuinely curious. Mason seemed so comfortable cooking. It was the most relaxed Owen had ever seen him.

Mason sighed. "Long story."

"You don't have to tell me," Owen said, sensing reluctance.

"It's fine. But maybe once we're sat down." He added more butter to the sauce pan—by now the sauce contained an eye-watering amount—and kept whisking. "I'll be ready to serve in five minutes. Could you get out some cutlery?" He gestured at a drawer to his left.

Owen rose and went to the drawer, plucking out knives and forks. Then he topped up Mason's wine and put the bottle in the fridge.

When he turned back, Mason was plating the food with all the concentrated precision of a professional chef.

"Wow," Owen said as Mason set the plates down on the table and they slid into their chairs. "This looks incredible."

Mason's smile was somehow shy and confident at the same time. "Try it," he urged.

Owen did, forking up a piece of halibut, liberally coated in beurre blanc. Christ, it was good. Fishy and sweet and succulent and buttery. He tried the little cubes of potatoes next and groaned with pleasure. They were garlicky and crispy and melting inside. And the asparagus, drenched in beurre blanc. And the green beans, soft but still bright green and full of flavour.

"This is amazing," he got out at last. "It's so good."

Mason pressed his lips together, but Owen saw the smile he tried to suppress, and it made his heart skip a beat. He reached for his wine and took a mouthful, and that was amazing too, fresh and fragrant, cutting through the richness of the buttery sauce.

All too soon, he had finished his plate. He stared down at the remains of the sauce pooled there, wondering if it would be crass to ask for a spoon. Mason seemed to understand his dilemma. He got up and came back with a few slices of rustic-looking bread on a plate.

"I'm afraid I didn't make this myself," he said. "It's sourdough from a Swedish bakery near here. It's really good, though."

Owen took a slice—and then another—using the delicious bread to mop up every bit of the sauce.

Mason ate more slowly than Owen, only eating his final bite of fish at the same time that Owen popped the last scrap of buttery bread into his mouth. Mason left the remainder of his sauce on the plate, eschewing the bread altogether. He did eat everything else, though, with obvious relish, as well as polishing off two large glasses of wine.

When he was done, he leaned back in his chair with a happy sigh. "That was good."

"It was," Owen said, and he didn't only mean the food. It had been good to watch Mason cook and eat with such obvious pleasure. Good to see him so relaxed and happy.

"I'll sort out pudding in a minute," Mason said.

"No hurry." After a moment, Owen added, "You seem to really love cooking. And judging by your expression when you put that fish in your mouth, you really love food too."

Mason laughed softly. "Yeah. I do. I wanted to be a chef from being really young."

"So why did you give up the kitchen for the catwalk?"

Mason made a face. "It's actually a pretty boring story."

"Tell me anyway," Owen urged.

Mason sighed and leaned back in his chair. After a few moments, he said, "Getting a position at a top-end restaurant isn't easy. The pay is terrible for junior chefs, and the hours are really long, so getting a second job is impossible. And of course, living in London is ridiculously expensive." He shrugged. "But I really wanted to do it. In fact, it was the only thing I had ever wanted to do, and I figured it would be okay, despite the challenges, because at least I could keep living at home, which cut down on my expenses."

"Was it just you and your parents at home, or…?" Owen trailed off, inviting an answer.

"My mum and two sisters," Mason confirmed. "My dad lives with his girlfriend." He gave a crooked smile. "When I was a kid, before my dad left, my parents were kind of hippyish—we lived on a canal boat when I was little." He smiled at the memory, his green gaze softening.

"A canal boat? That sounds like fun for a kid."

"It was," Mason said. "For a long time, it was just the three of us, and yeah, it was great. Frieda—that's my mum—didn't work, and she was tons of fun to be with back then. Kurt works for a charity."

"Kurt's your dad?" Owen said uncertainly.

Mason nodded. "Yeah, it's confusing, I know, but I've always called them by their first names. My sisters call them 'mum' and 'dad', but they're much younger. Ten years younger actually."

"Ten?" Owen exclaimed, his eyebrows shooting up.

Mason shrugged. "They were a surprise, apparently."

"A big one, I imagine, being twins," Owen replied. After a pause, he added, "So why did you call your parents by their names?"

Mason gave a half-hitched smile. "Back then, Kurt thought that titles like 'mum' and 'dad' were authoritarian emblems of the patriarchal society we live in."

"Oh."

Mason laughed at whatever expression he saw on Owen's face. "Anyway, yeah, we didn't have tons of money, but it was fine. Frieda had inherited some from a relative, which they used to buy the canal boat. Kurt didn't earn a huge salary, but it was enough. But then, when I was ten, Frieda got pregnant with the twins, and everything changed. The boat was too small for us all. Plus, my sisters were premature when they were born and needed extra care, so we ended up moving to a poky flat in Newham." Mason gave a little laugh. "Sorry, I'm really dragging this out. Long story short: after that, money was tight, and family life was busy and hard and a lot more stressful. By the time the twins turned three, Kurt had had enough. He left to move in with a twenty-one-year-old he met at work."

Owen made a face. "Shit."

Mason gave another little laugh. "Yeah. Pretty much. Money had been tight before, but after, it was *really* tight, and Kurt... well, he isn't exactly reliable. Not that that changed anything from my perspective—not right away anyway. My goal was to be a chef, and I knew that meant I'd have to put up with low pay and punishing hours for a while. And I knew I'd have to live at home and give most of my wages to Frieda to help with the rent."

Owen had worked out what was coming by now. "But then you got spotted?"

Mason smiled. "Yup. And not just spotted—spotted for a specific campaign. Which meant money straight in the bank. A lot of money, or so it seemed to me at the time. Certainly more than we'd ever had before." He sipped his wine. "It was...impossible to turn down. I had this idea that I'd take advantage for a couple of years, stash some cash, then go back to working in kitchens, but—well, sometimes things don't work out how you plan, you know?"

Owen smiled wryly, thinking of his own convoluted career path. "Yeah," he said. "I do."

"I didn't realise that more money *in* also meant more money *out*. It didn't take long to start amassing a bunch of

116

extra expenses. Frieda and the girls got a better flat, which I subsidised. And then I moved out. Initially, I shared with a couple of other models from the agency, but later on, I got my own place. And once I had a taste of independence, I really couldn't imagine living at home again. Plus, suddenly I had all these other expenses too: a gym membership, grooming stuff, clothes—though I do admittedly get quite a lot of good stuff for free." He sighed. "And then there's Kurt."

"Does he ask you for money ?"

"No, but like I said, he's not reliable—he spends most of his time and money on Regan, his latest girlfriend. He's supposed to give Frieda money every month, but he's late all the time, and he sometimes misses a payment altogether. Frieda isn't very—" He shrugged, then smiled, clearly changing his mind about saying more. "Well, she still has a soft spot for him, despite everything. She always lets him get away with it."

"So… you help out when your dad doesn't pay on time?"

"Yeah. And honestly, even if he was on time every month, he doesn't really earn enough to cover everything Frieda and the girls need. Like I said, I sub their rent anyway, but every couple of months, I end up giving Frieda extra money on top, and it's got so that—" He broke off, his mouth twisting ruefully as he rubbed at the back of his neck.

"What?" Owen prompted gently.

Mason met his gaze, and suddenly, Owen realised that all the happiness of earlier had leached away, and he looked sad and a little defeated. "It's just that they rely on me, you know? Which means I can't really afford to stop modelling. Not until I get something else in place that pays similar money."

To Owen, it sounded like Mason's parents took him and his money for granted. Not that he had any right to judge how their family operated, but it was clear that Mason was struggling under the weight of all that responsibility. And

Owen knew how that felt, even if his own situation with Lewis had been very different.

Curiously, he said, "Don't you like modelling?"

Mason shrugged. "It's okay. I actually quite liked it at the start, but that wore off, and now"—he made a face—"well, I'm pretty sick of having to be so strict about my diet and exercise. And it doesn't really challenge me. The influencer and TV stuff is better, but they don't pay enough yet. I've got some brand work, but Frankie—he's my agent—says I need to hit a 100,000 followers on Insta to start making bigger money on that." He met Owen's eyes, his expression rueful. "That's why I want to get on TV. I feel like I've achieved my limit in terms of organic growth. I need something high profile to bump me up."

"And you think our *Weekend Wellness* slot will make the difference?"

Mason's smile was wide. "You have no idea. TV exposure will help *so* much."

Owen leaned forward and set his hand on Mason's. "Well, in that case, I'm really glad I decided to do it." He smiled, and their gazes caught. For a couple of long moments, they just stared at each other. Then Mason swallowed, a visible shift of his throat, and suddenly, Owen realised that he was smoothing his thumb over the back of Mason's hand.

"Sorry," he muttered and began to pull his hand back, except Mason turned his own hand over, sliding his fingers into the spaces between Owen's, preventing him from pulling away.

"Don't be sorry," Mason murmured. "Not for that."

Owen's pulse began to race.

Mason bit his lip—God, he was gorgeous. It wasn't fair; it really wasn't. "I'm not drunk this time," he said quietly. "So, if you reject me again, I'm going to have to take it personally."

"Me?" Owen breathed, incredulous. "Reject *you*?"

"You did before."

Owen's heart felt like it was being squeezed in a hard fist. "I didn't want to," he admitted. "But you *were* pretty drunk, and I couldn't take advantage of that. Not knowing you might regret it in the morning." He swallowed. "Besides, I'm not really a one-night-stand type."

"Yeah," Mason said, with a small smile. "I figured that." He took a deep breath. "Look, I like you, and maybe I'm wrong, but I think you might like me too? And not in a just-friends way."

"You're not wrong," Owen said hoarsely. "I do like you. A lot."

"Okay." Mason smiled tentatively. "Well, I can't see into the future, but if it helps... I don't see you as a one-night stand."

"No?" Owen whispered.

Mason shook his head. "So what do you think?"

"I think," Owen said, "that pudding can wait."

CHAPTER TEN

Mason led him into the bedroom. When he turned to face Owen, his green eyes were sultry, his body language open and inviting, but he made no move towards him. After last time, he probably wanted Owen to make the first move. Well, that suited Owen just fine. Now that he knew Mason was interested in more than a one-time hook-up, he was more than comfortable taking the lead.

Stepping closer, he raised one hand to trace the sharp line of Mason's jaw with his fingertips. He liked that Mason was almost as tall as him, that they were looking each other in the eye. Liked too that he was bigger than Mason in every other way.

"Can I kiss you?" he murmured, curving his hand around the back of Mason's neck, fingertips threading into the short hair at his nape.

Mason's breath hitched in a way that made Owen's already-stiff cock throb in his jeans. "Yeah," he whispered.

Owen touched his lips gently to Mason's, just a light graze of his mouth. When he drew back, Mason whimpered and leaned forward slightly, trying to maintain contact. Owen laughed softly and kissed him again, another soft, grazing touch. When Mason shuddered with pleasure, Owen rewarded him with another kiss, a little harder this time, followed by a sweep of his tongue over Mason's full lower lip, then another kiss, and another, each succeeding one deeper and more thorough.

His other arm snaked round Mason's waist, yanking him closer, and he ground their hips together, his clothed, aching cock throbbing painfully at the delicious friction.

"Oh God," Mason breathed between kisses. "*Owen.*"

His hands had been resting against Owen's chest, but now, he slid them up and over Owen's shoulders, winding them round the back of his neck as he pressed closer. Their kisses had grown hot and wet and deep, their tongues sliding together, exploring. Christ, you couldn't get a breath between them now, and Owen loved it. Loved having Mason's body plastered against his own.

Eventually, he tore his mouth free. "I want to suck you," he growled.

"Same," Mason said breathlessly. "Sixty-nine?"

"Fuck, yeah," Owen replied with a grin. He reached for the hem of Mason's t-shirt and yanked it up over his head, tossing it aside, admiring the lean, muscled planes of his smooth chest and shoulders. His hands went to the waistband of Mason's tatty shorts next, pushing them down, groaning when he discovered there was nothing underneath.

"No underwear?" he murmured as Mason kicked the shorts aside, standing naked in front of him. "Careful, I might think you were planning a seduction…"

"Me?" Mason looked up through his lashes, playing innocent.

Owen grinned. "You're a very bad boy, do you know that?"

Mason gave a soft, almost desperate laugh. "Maybe you can spank me later."

"Jesus Christ," Owen muttered curving his hands over the smooth mounds of Mason's arse even as he leaned back so he could eye his long, slender dick. "I would fucking love that."

Mason's eyes went wide. "You would?"

Owen looked up. "Fuck, yeah. If you would. I'm not *always* Mr. Nice Guy, you know."

Mason gave a shaky laugh. "Um—wow. Okay, yeah." He swallowed hard, his eyes a little glazed.

"First things first, though," Owen said, muscling him over to the bed. "I need to taste you. Get on the bed, petal."

While Mason lay down, Owen quickly stripped his own clothes off, enjoying the obvious desire he saw in Mason's eyes as his body was revealed. He might not have model-worthy chiselled abs, but he was a fit guy with an attractive body and a more-than-decent-sized cock. And yeah, Mason obviously liked the look of him. There was no faking the expression he wore now, eyes hazy with lust, full lips parted.

Owen got on the end of the bed and knee-walked towards Mason, settling himself between Mason's spread thighs, his eyes eating up every delicious inch of smooth skin laid out before him.

Leaning over, he lapped the very tip of Mason's cock, collecting the fat bead of sticky fluid gathered there, making Mason gasp. Then slowly—very slowly—he circled his tongue over the plump head, before beginning a languorous, downward circling that had Mason arching up in an effort to force Owen to swallow his dick.

Owen chuckled, pinning Mason's hips down before beginning his slow teasing again, adding a little more suction, a little more pressure, as he gradually took more and more of that delicious cock.

"Fuck, *Owen*."

And then Owen took him deep, right to the root, making

him cry out with the pleasure of being thoroughly blown, of having his dick enthusiastically worshipped.

"Fucking hell," Mason stuttered out at last. "If you don't let me suck you soon, this is all going to be over before I even get my mouth on you."

Owen pulled off his dick with a rude slurp. "Can't have that," he said. He moved up over Mason, shifting his knees to straddle Mason's lean chest. Then he paused, just gazing down at him for a moment, admiring his beauty in an uncomplicated way.

"Come on," Mason pleaded. "I need your dick."

Jesus.

Owen took his rock-hard shaft in his hand and brushed it over Mason's plump lips. "Kiss it then," he said hoarsely.

Mason gave a stifled moan of pleasure, pressing his lips to the glans, then swiping his tongue over it, his hands sliding up to grip Owen's muscular thighs

"Fuck," Owen breathed. He shifted his position again, bracing himself against the headboard so his cock was angled at Mason's open mouth. "Now suck me."

Mason made a guttural sound of approval, opening his mouth wide, and Owen pressed inside, pushing his hips forward, careful not to cut off Mason's air. Not that Mason seemed to care about that as he greedily swallowed Owen down, his tongue stroking the underside of Owen's dick with maddening skill.

Fuck, it felt amazing, and Mason was obviously loving it, his fingers digging into Owen's thighs as he worked his shaft.

After a few minutes, he pulled off, gasping, "Sixty-nine?"

"Yeah," Owen agreed. "I need your dick in my throat. Shift down a bit and get on your side."

Mason began to wriggle down the mattress. "You know, you're pushier than I'd have imagined."

Owen lifted a brow. "Do you want me to stop?"

123

Mason grinned. "No, I fucking love it," he said, and Owen grinned back.

They moved onto their sides and, after some frantic shifting around, Owen got his mouth back on Mason's lovely cock, relishing the faint burst of salt from the precum gathered on the tip. Moments later, Mason took Owen into his mouth too, and they fell into the mad mind-fuckery of sixty-nining. One minute, Mason's mouth would be greedily working Owen's cock, and the next, it would be going slack and inattentive as the pleasure of Owen blowing him made his brain melt. And God, it was just as bad—or good—for Owen, the synapses of his brain firing in twenty different directions as pleasure built and overloaded, built and overloaded.

After a while, Owen tore his mouth off Mason's cock and shifted further down to lap at his tender balls, gently at first, then a little more firmly as Mason responded with noisy appreciation, shifting his thighs to give Owen more room to work. Owen went lower still, lapping at his perineum with the flat of his tongue, loving the hoarse cry that ripped from Mason's throat.

"I want to rim you," Owen growled. "That okay?"

"Oh, fuck," Mason almost sobbed. "Yeah, do that. Rim me while you shove your cock down my throat."

Owen shifted onto his back. "Come on then," he said. "Get on top and wrap your lips round my dick."

Mason's face was flushed, his eyes glittering with lust as he followed Owen's orders, turning around to face Owen's feet, then settling his lean frame in place, a knee on either side of Owen's torso. Owen smoothed his palms over the perfect mounds of Mason's absurdly gorgeous arse, gasping as Mason's lips glided down the length of his dick, enveloping his throbbing shaft in hot, wet heat.

For a minute or two, he allowed himself the selfish luxury of just letting Mason expertly blow him. But eventually, he tugged at Mason's hips, drawing him closer. Close enough to lick a slow, wet stripe from his balls all the way to his tight hole.

Mason tensed, crying out with each stroke of Owen's tongue, and then again, more loudly, when Owen began to tease at the delicate edges of his hole with his tongue. Tease and then probe and then, gradually, open him up.

Christ, but he was perfect. He was fucking perfect, and *damn,* but now his mouth was back on Owen's dick, and that was about as amazing as anything got. Somehow, it was easier to keep rimming Mason while Mason blew him than it had been to keep sucking Mason's dick. Maybe because Mason was rocking back onto Owen's face, practically demanding his tongue. Yeah, that might be it.

Mason's dick was grinding against his pecs now, the driving movements getting more frantic as Owen relentlessly worked at his hole. When Owen pressed his tongue inside, Mason howled around his cock and began to buck wildly. It was messy and chaotic and incredibly hot. Moments later, Mason's whole body tensed up, and he began to shoot, his warm spunk striping Owen's chest.

"Oh, fuck," Mason gasped, finally stilling. "Fucking *hell.*"

Owen gave a helpless laugh at the sheer astonishment in Mason's voice. "Good?" he asked.

Mason turned his head to look over his shoulder. He was smiling dopily, his hair flopping in his eyes. "Insanely good." He sighed happily, then added, "Let me take care of you now. Lie back."

So Owen did. He let his head fall to the mattress with a soft thud, his eyelids closing as Mason's mouth engulfed his cock again. It didn't even take a minute. He came in a rolling, exuberant burst of pleasure, back arching, so much come flooding Mason's mouth that Mason spluttered, then laughed, then coughed.

"Sorry," he gasped when he'd recovered, manoeuvring

himself around till they were lying side by side. "That was very un-smooth."

Owen stretched out a hand and tenderly brushed the long strands of Mason's floppy fringe out of his eyes. "Was it?" he asked, smiling. "I don't mind. I quite liked you choking on my spunk."

Mason's eyes widened, and he laughed again, an abrupt, shocked sound. "You are... *very* surprising, do you know that?"

"Am I?" Owen replied, tugging Mason closer so that his head rested on Owen's shoulder.

"Yeah," Mason said, lifting his chin to meet Owen's eyes. "You're so sweet in everyday life that I was kind of expecting you to be all—I don't know—romantic in bed."

Owen lifted a brow. "Did you think that because I'm not into one-night stands, I'd want to scatter the mattress with rose petals and make sweet, beautiful love to you?"

Mason snorted. "To be honest, that *is* closer to what I was expecting."

Owen kissed his forehead. "I can be romantic," he said. "I can do rose petals if you want."

"Yeah, no. Not really my thing," Mason said, nuzzling into his shoulder. "I think I'll take the rimming and the spanking if it's all the same to you. We can save the romantic stuff for when we're cuddling on the couch. Or on a date in publ—" He stopped abruptly, as though he'd just realised what he was saying. Quickly, he added, "Sorry, I shouldn't assume that..."

"Hey," Owen said softly, urging his chin up again. Mason let him do it, but his gaze was wary.

"I *want* to go on a date with you," Owen said. "And I *really* want to cuddle on the couch."

"Okay," Mason said with a wobbly smile. "In which case there's no time like the present."

CHAPTER ELEVEN

MASON

As so often happened after mind-blowing sex, Mason felt a little … tender, a little at sea as he padded back into the kitchen. He'd cleaned up and dressed, leaving Owen to use the bathroom while Mason went to serve pudding, but the sight of their empty plates still sitting on the kitchen table felt oddly jarring, as if he was waking from a particularly delicious dream.

Only that had been no dream; his body was still alive with pleasure, humming with it, his limbs honeyed and relaxed.

Christ, Owen was…not what he'd been expecting.

And, he guessed, why not? Why couldn't you be an all-round nice guy, kind and easy-going, and also scorching in bed? Just because Mason had never met that particular unicorn before didn't mean they didn't exist…

Misty will be pleased.

The thought intruded unpleasantly. It was true, though. She'd be over the moon if she knew how far he'd managed to 'push it' with Owen. This was exactly what she'd wanted to happen. Or, at least, exactly what she wanted *viewers* to want to happen. And no doubt tonight would make Owen's response to Mason's flirting all the more authentic—Misty's favourite word—whether that was on-screen, out in public, or online.

He chewed on his bottom lip as he set the coffee maker going and started plating up their dessert: slices of tarte au citron, creme anglaise, and a few mixed berries.

When he'd told Owen that he didn't consider this to be a one-night stand, he'd been telling the truth. A one-night stand wasn't what he wanted. So how come he felt kind of... dishonest?

Careful, I might think you were planning a seduction...

Well, yeah. Nothing wrong with planning a seduction, was there? Not if they both wanted it. It wasn't as if Mason faked anything. He hadn't needed to because he really *was* into Owen, and the sex had been... Christ, it had been off the charts good. For both of them.

Still, he should probably talk to Owen about the public aspect of their relationship. Owen wouldn't have a clue about what Misty would expect of them. Mason should at least give him a heads up, help him leverage the attention to promote his business. Yet he felt curiously reluctant to mention it, as if doing so would puncture the intimacy of the evening.

Hearing Owen heading into the living room, Mason shook off his unease and concentrated on the task at hand, dusting each dish carefully with icing sugar, before setting everything on a tray and carrying it through.

Pausing in the living room doorway for a moment, he drank in the sight of Owen relaxed on the sofa, long legs stretched out across the cushions, hair still delightfully sex-rumpled, bare feet crossed at the ankles. He looked unbelievably sexy in those butter-soft jeans that hugged every line of his muscular legs and that flannel shirt that Mason longed to rub his cheek against. Hell, the thought of curling up next to Owen and snuggling into his chest was nearly irresistible.

"Hey," Owen said, smiling warmly and shifting his legs to make room for Mason on the sofa. "Okay?"

"I think you fucked my brains out," Mason said, laughing. "I could barely remember how to make coffee."

Owen grinned as Mason set the tray down on the low coffee table and came to sit next to him, hip to hip, their eyes meeting in one of those intensely intimate moments they'd been sharing since that night at the awards dinner. It occurred to Mason that Owen's eyes were the exact same faded blue as his jeans.

"That was really great," Owen said seriously. "You were amazing."

Face heating, Mason felt himself grinning. "You were pretty amazing, too."

"Yeah?"

Mason leaned in and kissed him, a gentle kiss this time, all soft lips and smiles. "Yeah." Sitting back, he picked up one of the dishes on the coffee table and handed it to Owen. "Now try this."

Owen's gaze lingered on Mason for a moment, then turned to the plate in his hand. "Wow." He looked impressed. "This is so pretty. It feels wrong to eat it."

"You'd better eat it," Mason said, nudging him. "And you'd better take the leftovers home, too. I can't afford that amount of temptation in my fridge."

Owen groaned around his first spoonful, a low, sexy sound that had Mason's cock twitching again.

Christ, what was it about Owen Hunter that made him so fucking horny all the time? He'd gone out with men who were probably more conventionally handsome, but, somehow, he couldn't think of anyone who had even a quarter of Owen's appeal. There was just something about Owen that drew Mason in, a compelling mixture of intense sexual attraction coupled with a desire to just... snuggle into him.

"Bloody hell, that's good," Owen said, between mouthfuls. He polished off the whole dish in less than a minute and quickly agreed when Mason offered him seconds.

"Have your own first, though."

"It's okay," Mason laughed, getting up. "I haven't even started yet."

He brought Owen a larger slice the second time, watching him demolish it as Mason slowly made his way through his own serving, relishing every mouthful. He didn't eat sweet things very often and rarely something as good as this, even if he did say so himself.

Once they were done, he fetched the coffee. He knew by now that Owen liked it strong and black, and when Owen sipped the rich, dark brew, his tiny sigh of contentment made Mason smile.

Owen leaned into the corner of the sofa, stretching one arm along the back and lifting an eyebrow in invitation. After a moment's hesitation, Mason scooted closer and snuggled up against Owen's side.

"Perfect," Owen said, sighing happily.

Mason agreed, feeling ridiculously sated and cosy.

They stayed there together for a while, quietly sipping their coffee, and Mason's thoughts began to drift. Their empty plates sat together on the coffee table, forks askew, and he realised with a beat of frustration that he hadn't taken a pic of their desert for Insta. Shit. Unless…

Actually, this might work better.

Pulling out of Owen's hold, he grabbed his phone from the coffee table, then settled back and snapped a quick pic of their two plates, just a sliver of his leg looped over Owen's in the foreground. He showed Owen. "What do you think?"

Owen appeared nonplussed. "Uh…about what?"

"I'm going to post it on Insta. Something like 'This evening's going well…'" He turned to look at Owen, who was frowning slightly. "Is that okay?"

"Uh, sure," Owen said. Doubtfully, he added, "Is that the

sort of thing your followers like? I'd have thought they'd rather see a picture of you."

Mason smiled, nudging his knee. "Well, they see a *lot* of pictures of me. This is like…a glimpse into my life. A tease of…you know, us."

"Right," Owen said slowly. "Well, I'm sure you know more about it than I do."

That was clearly true, and Mason felt another beat of unease. "I'll tag you," he said as he posted the pic—#GardeningHottie #WeekendWellness #WatchThisSpace. "Then you can reply. You'll get the hang of it."

"Yeah, maybe." Owen set down his empty mug, tugging Mason close again. "Now come back here."

Mason did, leaving his phone and mug on the table, resting his cheek on that soft flannel shirt and slipping an arm around Owen's middle. God, he felt good to cuddle.

Owen gave a happy sigh and began toying idly with Mason's hair. It felt amazing, that touch, intoxicating. Closing his eyes, Mason smiled as he pressed his head into Owen's hand, content as a cat.

After a while Owen said, "So what next?"

"Next?"

There was a long pause. Then Owen said softly, "I'd like to do this again. All of it, I mean. Not just the sex. Although definitely the sex."

"Yeah?" Mason looked up at him, close enough that his nose nudged Owen's jaw and he breathed in the faded scent of Tom Ford aftershave and the subtle hint of sex that lingered on Owen's skin. It set off a squirmy, sexy feeling in his stomach. "Is this your way of asking me to cook for you again?"

"What? No." Owen's cheeks pinkened. "I mean—*yes*, obviously you can cook for me any time you like; you're a bloody genius in the kitchen—but there's lots of other stuff I'd like to do with you too."

"Same here," Mason said. He hesitated, then added, "I suppose the question is, how open do you want to be about it?"

"What do you mean?"

"Well, you know Misty wants us to flirt on-screen, right? Tease the audience with some will-they-won't-they stuff?"

Owen waggled his eyebrows. "Will-they-won't-they? I'd say they already did. With bells on."

Laughing, Mason said, "Yeah, well, that's the thing. Like, do we tell Misty at this point, or...?"

Owen was quiet. Then he said, "Do you think she'd care? It's not really any of her business."

"Oh, she'd care. She'd fucking *love* it. But she wouldn't want the audience to know yet."

"That's kind of weird, but okay," Owen said. "Maybe we keep it on the down-low then? I mean, you can still flirt when we're doing the filming, right? That's what Misty really cares about, and it won't affect that. Might even make it better."

"Sure," Mason agreed lightly. Then, to be clear, he added, "But she does expect us to flirt on social media, too."

"Flirt?"

"You know, it gets the audience going. It's part of it."

"Okay," Owen said slowly. "But that's just to promote the show, isn't it? It's not part of *this*." Owen tightened his arm around Mason's shoulders. "This is private, right? This is the real us."

"Yeah." Mason lifted his head again to look at him, their eyes meeting, holding. "This is just us, doing what feels good."

And if it happened to play well with the audience—and Misty—then that was just an added bonus.

Owen's eyes twinkled. "Talking of feeling good..." He leaned forward, lips brushing against Mason's, their noses bumping, stubble catching.

"We should eat out next time," Mason said, a little breathlessly. His head was starting to spin, in the best possible way. "There's a pop-up Peruvian-Japanese restaurant I've been dying to try, if you fancy it?"

"Mmm, sounds interesting." Owen nuzzled Mason's jaw and throat, then returned to his mouth for more kisses, his plush lips moving against Mason's, teeth nipping, tongue sliding, slow and sensuous and patient. "I'd like that, yeah."

Smiling, Mason leaned back against the sofa cushions, drawing Owen with him. "How about next Saturday?" he said, unfolding his legs as Owen moved forward, covering Mason's body with his larger frame and sliding one strong arm underneath his shoulders to pull him closer. It felt *fantastic*.

"Sounds like a date," Owen murmured, dipping his mouth into the hollow at the base of Mason's throat, licking him there, sucking gently. Teasing.

"Fuck, *yes*," Mason gasped, arching up as Owen's hand slid beneath the waistband of his shorts and closed around his aching cock with a gentle, commanding pressure. "It does, doesn't it?"

CHAPTER TWELVE

For the rest of the week, Owen ended up being crazily busy and barely saw Mason.

The new job, the complete redesign of a huge garden surrounding a detached house in Greenwich, was sucking up most of his time. Not that it wasn't interesting work, and lucrative, but the client was demanding, and on top of Owen's regular contract work, and two smaller design projects already underway, it was putting pressure on his resources. He'd been forced to split his crew between all three jobs and put in a bunch of extra hours himself. He managed to make time for lunch with Mason one day, but otherwise, they only spoke on the phone. Well, that and flirted on Instagram, which seemed to be Mason's favourite method of communication.

Owen was... still getting his head around Instagram. He'd set up an account for the business a few years ago but hadn't really had the time—or the inclination—to get to grips with it. After a couple of weeks, he'd just sort of forgotten about it.

Mason seemed genuinely shocked by Owen's paltry

134

twenty-nine followers—which was hardly surprising given that Mason had over 80,000 of them—but then Mason was a professional influencer who made actual money off the platform. He clearly understood the ins and outs of how to make it work in way more depth than Owen ever would.

Mason had tried to explain it to Owen. How to create a brand, how to use hashtags, how to build a following. A whole bunch of stuff that Owen would never use. Even so, it was interesting to see how much time and work went into creating the profile of someone who, on the face of it, appeared to be living a pretty carefree life.

By contrast, Owen felt like a total amateur. Hell, he couldn't even manage to take a half-decent selfie—which was what he found himself messaging Mason about from his living room sofa, the night before their first day of filming.

Mason was trying to get him to post a pic of himself on Instagram, arguing that Owen couldn't just keep commenting on Mason's posts without having posted anything recent himself.

"What about when people click to see who you are?" he asked, clearly expecting Owen to immediately see his point.

"Why would they do that?"

"Because we're posting flirty comments at each other on my posts that make it obvious we're spending time together," Mason had pointed out patiently. "And some of my followers are getting curious about you. But when they click on your account, all they see is a handful of photos of gardens that you worked on three years ago. You have literally no pictures of yourself on the account."

"It's a business account."

"So what? You think people don't want to see who owns a business? Hell, most people expect that these days. And don't you want to connect with new customers? Why would you *not* use everything you've got to sell your services?"

"It's not the same for me as for you," Owen had said. "You get hired based on the way you look—I don't."

Mason had frowned, eyes dipping briefly to the table before saying, "Look, forget the business angle. Just put a photo up for me, will you?" Then he'd batted his lashes shamelessly. "It will help with Operation 100K."

And, of course, Owen had agreed.

Mason had even given him the text and hashtags for the post. It was to say *"Big day tomorrow with @masonisamodel"* and the hashtags were #bigday, #nervousandexcited, #instapic, and #followme. Apparently, this was "keeping it simple". When Owen had asked how that could be simple when the hashtags took up more characters than the message, Mason had just shaken his head in despair.

Well, Owen had said he'd do it. So… now it was selfie time.

He stretched out on his couch, leaned back and angled his phone, squinting at the screen. He was wearing a faded black t-shirt and PJ bottoms—both Mason-approved—and his hair was messy, which, weirdly, Mason seemed to like. He forced himself to smile and took a bunch of pictures, then scrolled through them, frowning. Why could he never seem to get a photo that didn't make him look like a moose? Picking out the best of a bad bunch, he sent it off to Mason with a quick message. *How about this one?*

You look constipated, Mason messaged back half a minute later, complete with laughing-crying emojis.

Cheeky sod, Owen thought, chuckling.

He sent another.

Nope.

Another.

Jesus. No.

A thought occurred to him then, and he grinned, shoving down his loose PJ bottoms and taking his cock in hand, stroking it a few times till it was fully hard before snapping a quick pic.

This any better?

Bubbles appeared, then, *Yum*. Then more bubbles. *But no dick pics on Insta. Sorry.*

Owen laughed again. *Aw, come on!*

Nope.

I don't have any more!

Fine, use this instead.

A picture appeared a second later. Mason must have taken it at the coffee shop where they'd met for that quick lunch date while Owen was zooming between jobs.

Owen studied the picture. He had to admit he looked good in it, his smile wide and natural, eyes bright with happiness, the coffee shop bustle in the background. He couldn't even remember Mason taking it.

I don't look 'nervous and excited', he messaged.

You look fucking hot, though. Use it.

Owen stared at the screen and those words: *You look fucking hot…* He still wasn't quite used to the idea that Mason actually liked him in that way. It wasn't that he didn't believe Mason, but somehow, it was easier to accept when they were together. When he actually saw the lust and appreciation in Mason's green eyes for himself.

When they were apart, he would sometimes think about Lewis saying it was his fame that had been the main attraction for Mason, or that, not so long ago, Mason had been dating Jay Warren. And then he'd think, *Why is he interested in a nobody like me?*

That wasn't fair, though. The Mason he'd got to know over these last weeks wasn't the shallow celebrity wannabe Lewis had accused him of being. He was obsessed with Instagram, that was true, but in fairness, it was an important career tool for him.

Pulling up the app, Owen dutifully added the photo and pasted in the text and hashtags Mason had provided. Then he waited.

Mason quickly commented on the post, as though he'd just seen it—*"OMG, me too! Can't wait!"*—followed by an excited stream of emojis: a grinning face, a sunflower, some kind of vegetable, and a bunch of rainbow hearts. And then Mason must have posted something of his own that drove more people to Owen's post because as Owen watched, with vaguely horrified amazement, his post began garnering likes, a lot of them, and he began acquiring new followers too. Fans of Mason? They must be, from some of the comments that began appearing on his post.

Are you the guy who's going to be on TV with Mason?

Is this M's new BF?? OMG I'M SCREAMING

U R so hot! You and Mason must be beautiful together! Pls post lots of pics! #loveislove

And finally:

Okay, who are you and what have you done with my boyfriend's brother?

Owen blinked in confusion at that last comment before he realised it had been posted by none other than @aaron_scriptdoctor. Grinning, he replied to that one with the comment, *"Been getting some Insta lessons from an expert,"* and quickly got back, *"So I see!"* from Aaron.

After a few more minutes of checking and liking comments, his eyelids began to droop. It had been a long day. He'd started not long after dawn, missed lunch, been run ragged all day, and now it was almost midnight. And he was due at the RPP studio at seven a.m. tomorrow for their first bit of filming. Which he really *was* nervous and excited about.

With a jaw-cracking yawn, he shoved his phone in his pocket and headed upstairs to bed.

The first day's filming didn't wrap up till four-thirty, more than nine hours after they started.

Owen really shouldn't have been surprised by how long it took—he'd realised ages ago that everything related to *Weekend Wellness* took way longer than he'd have ever imagined—but even so, as he and Mason walked back to his van afterwards, he grumbled about it.

"So much for '*a couple of hours.*'"

Mason snorted. "I told you."

Owen sighed. "I know."

In truth, though, he was having to fake being disgruntled. Despite the stupid script notes Naomi, Misty's intern, had pressed on them, and all the hanging around—seriously, they'd spent more time waiting to be filmed than actually *being* filmed—and despite it being as cold as a witch's tit all day and there being nowhere near enough coffee, it had been a pretty good day. A great day, actually. And yeah, that was mostly because he'd spent it with Mason.

He honestly couldn't remember the last time he'd enjoyed another person's company so much, and it wasn't just because he fancied the pants off of Mason and wanted to fuck him six ways till Sunday. He liked Mason. Mason made him laugh, and he could be surprisingly thoughtful. During the filming, he was unflaggingly cheerful, despite having to brave near-hypothermia, and endearingly friendly to the whole crew, from the director right down to Eddie, the junior runner who spent the whole, long day doing constant errands.

"It was actually a pretty normal day for me," Mason said as they neared Owen's van. "There's loads of waiting around on shoots as well. At least today I didn't have to contort myself into uncomfortable positions for hours on end. Following you around and chatting while you worked was a lot more entertaining than posing for pics."

Owen flashed him a grin. "I don't think Naomi was very happy with our chatting, though, do you?"

Mason laughed. "Oh my God, no! But what did she expect giving us all those script notes when we were just about to start? There were, like, twenty pages of them!"

"She obviously thought we should be mugging up on them whenever we weren't being filmed," Owen said, pulling out his keys. He unlocked the doors, and they both got in.

"To be fair, they were Misty's notes, not hers." Misty hadn't been able to make the filming, thankfully.

"Yeah," Owen said. "I can see why Naomi wouldn't want to have to report back that we'd ignored them. Misty'll probably give her an earful about it."

"We didn't ignore them," Mason pointed out once they were inside, turning in his seat. "We did *sort of* read them. And we did that first cringey intro bit they put in. But it's not like we were going to be able to learn all of it in between takes. We're not bloody actors!"

"Christ, no," Owen agreed. "It was all I could do to hold a vague conversation with you, never mind remember all that gubbins. I can't even remember most of what I did say."

"You were awesome," Mason said firmly. "And I thought we got some really good banter going. Lucy seemed to like it, anyway."

Lucy, the director, had been great. She'd been easy going and positive about the sections they had filmed, waving off Naomi's anxious comments about them not using Misty's script notes.

"This is working fine. They've got a good back and forth going, so let's not mess with it."

That back and forth had all been thanks to Mason, starting with his opener of *"just think of me as a puppy following you round the garden"* followed by his quick-fire questions about what breed of puppy he would be—Owen had finally decided on a cockapoo—while Lucy captured footage of them doing basic soil preparation tasks.

And then there had been that ridiculous debate about what flowers Owen would bring Mason if they ever went on a date, with Mason arguing for two dozen red roses and Owen arguing for either no flowers at all—"*Who brings someone flowers on a date?*"—or maybe just a few handfuls of sweet peas plucked straight from the garden because they smelled so amazing.

That had naturally led into them talking about the sweet peas they'd be planting in the *Weekend Wellness* garden, training the plants up over a tripod of branches and canes Owen planned to build in the sunny south-west corner. And *that* conversation had gone so well that Lucy had sent Eddie off to get the materials they needed so Owen and Mason could build the tripod there and then. Which they did, while Mason spouted endless *double entendres* about the length and girth of the canes they were using.

So yeah, they really *hadn't* needed the script notes, and when they'd wrapped for the day, Lucy had grinned and said she had tons of good material, and the only problem was going to be choosing which bits to use.

"I felt like I was okay," Owen admitted now, smiling at Mason. "But you were amazing—you kept the conversation moving so easily. And God, I laughed so much! Sometimes I forgot the cameras were there." He chuckled, remembering. "You know, you're a really funny person. I never realised that about you when you were going out with Lewis. You always seemed a bit—" He broke off, realising he might be straying into dangerous territory. But when he glanced at Mason, Mason didn't look offended, just sort of curious.

"Go on," he prompted. "How did I seem to you back then?"

"I don't know," Owen said uncertainly. "I just don't remember you laughing much those times I met you." Which was strange, really, given how much time Owen spent laughing with his brother. But yeah, as funny as Lewis could be, he was also… intense.

Mason smiled crookedly, a little ruefully. "That's fair. Lewis and I were never really on the same wavelength, if you know what I mean? Whereas with you…" He trailed off, blushing.

"What?" Owen said softly.

Staring down at his hands, Mason said, "I don't know. It's easier to be myself around you. You're good at making people feel comfortable." Glancing up again, he added quietly, "I don't think I could have done all that stuff today if it was anyone *but* you."

Owen's chest pinched. Beneath the polished exterior, there was something soft and vulnerable about Mason. Something that appealed deeply to Owen. Tapped into his Knight in Shining Armour complex, perhaps. He wanted to look after Mason, protect him and care for him… and at the same time get naked and fuck like minks. Helpless against the impulse, and even though they were in full view of the studio and anyone passing, Owen reached for him, leaning across the gear stick to kiss him, an urgent, sensual kiss, overflowing with all those confusing feelings.

Mason's answering kiss was hot and hungry and everything Owen needed.

When Owen finally drew back to catch his breath, Mason gave a soft huff of discontent that went straight to Owen's dick. Fuck, Mason could switch from sweetly vulnerable to poutingly hot in a heartbeat, and it drove Owen wild.

Biting at his full lower lip, looking up through his lashes, Mason said, "So, do you have plans this evening…?"

Tragically, Owen did: the metric ton of paperwork that had been piling up thanks to all the time he'd spent on *Weekend Wellness*. He groaned, "I've really got to catch up on…"

"Oh?" Mason looked disappointed, even a little disgruntled. "Got a better offer?"

"Are you joking?" He reached out to squeeze Mason's leg. "I'm not making an excuse. Trust me, there's nothing I'd like more than to take you home tonight and jump your gorgeous bones." He waggled his eyebrows and was rewarded by a softening of Mason's tight expression. Christ, did he really think Owen would voluntarily turn him down? "But we've got our date tomorrow, right? Peruvian-Japanese food, wasn't it?"

Mason softened further. "You're still up for that?"

"Yeah, course I am. If you are?"

"Definitely." He added, "I've booked a table for eight, if that's okay?"

"Perfect." With reluctance, Owen let go of Mason, turning away to fasten his seatbelt before he could change his mind about tonight. His resolve was weak, and he really did need to get through that paperwork this evening. "Send me the details and I'll meet you there."

"How about we meet first for a drink?" Mason said, reaching for his own seatbelt. "There's a fabulous cocktail bar not too far from there. Say, seven?"

Owen smiled and started the engine. "Even better."

"And, uh…" From the corner of his eye, Owen could see Mason squirm a little. "Maybe we could go back to my place after?"

Owen's grin broadened. "Should I pack a toothbrush?"

"Yeah, you should." This time, there was a smile in Mason's voice. "If you're good, I might even cook you breakfast in the morning."

Owen's heart swooped alarmingly. It was scary, how much he already liked Mason. He'd always been an all-in, no-half-measures kind of a guy. But even for him, it felt like this was happening pretty damn quickly. Maybe too quickly.

He didn't show his disquiet to Mason, though, instead

adopting a teasing, growly voice and saying, "And what if I'm *bad*?"

Mason gave an adorably breathy little laugh. "Then I'm *definitely* cooking you breakfast. With all the trimmings. And a cherry on top."

CHAPTER THIRTEEN

MASON

The object of going to Cosmos for drinks was to be *seen*. Mason had been there with Jay a couple of times, and they'd always got a lot of attention. Good for both of their profiles, but especially for Mason's. Once, after Jay's character, Skye, came out in *Leeches*, Mason had gained over 2000 followers when a pic of him and Jay made it into a clickbait piece about gay actors playing gay characters.

Tonight, though, Mason would have to do the heavy lifting, and so he needed to look suitably eye-catching. Not that he wouldn't want to look good for Owen, but unlike the men Mason usually dated, Owen was completely unimpressed by designer fashion or statement pieces. He'd told Mason he looked 'amazing' in the ancient blue sweatshirt and cropped jeans he'd worn to set yesterday. Which was adorable—he smiled at the memory of the genuine admiration in Owen's eyes—but didn't help him with his current dilemma.

He had three possible outfits laid out on his bed. One was pretty high fashion, relaxed Brunello Cucinelli dog-tooth trousers paired with a red shirt and cotton blazer, which he'd been given following a shoot he'd done in the States before Christmas. The others were more restrained—a deconstructed baby pink linen suit that he knew showed off his long legs, or his favourite pair of jeans and a flamboyant Claudio Lugli shirt. Spying an opportunity, he snapped a picture of himself puzzling over the clothes, cropped and filtered it, and popped it up on Insta.

Choices, choices. Hot date tonight but what to wear…? #fashiongram #fashioninsta #love #me

The replies flooded in quickly, with a satisfying number asking whether the date was with *@OwenHunterGardens*. Mason replied with suitable 'my lips are sealed' emojis.

Misty responded with *Don't forget your wellies!* and a pride flag.

Owen didn't reply at all. Probably because he hadn't seen it or was working. Or both. Unlike the rest of the world, Owen didn't have his phone riveted to his hand. On a couple of occasions when they'd met up for meetings or rehearsals, he'd even left it in his van.

Inconceivable. Mason got the jitters if he misplaced his phone for more than thirty seconds.

Anyway, the general consensus on Insta was that Mason should wear the Brunello Cucinelli, but in the end, he decided to dress down in his jeans but spice it up with his commando-soled Chelsea boots and a Tom Ford quilted velvet bomber jacket. A photographer had once told him that the soft teal made his eyes pop.

He didn't want Owen to feel uncomfortable by over-dressing, and besides, people would draw their own conclusions if he and Owen dressed more alike. In fact, it would be great if he could get a pic of himself casually wearing something of Owen's—the olive-green sweatshirt with his company logo on it would be perfect...

He made a mental note to try and get hold of one.

After deciding what to wear, Mason went for a long run on the common to burn off some of his nervous tension and then indulged in a hot and very thorough shower. He wasn't sure exactly what the evening would bring, but he wanted to be prepared for anything. To that end, aside from personal grooming, he changed the sheets on the bed and made sure there were condoms and lube to hand in the bedroom. And the living room.

Then he took a few pics of himself in the full-length mirror, giving it a little catwalk pout, until he had one that he liked. He posted it—*Feeling flirty!* :)—and headed for the tube.

By the time he got out at Battersea, he was feeling more nervous than flirty. Which was stupid, because it wasn't like this was an ordinary date with some random guy desperate to get him into bed. This was Owen, who had somehow, over the last few weeks, become his friend.

His *friend*.

Mason considered that as he headed for the bar. He'd never been good at friendships, not since he'd turned twelve, hit puberty, realised he was gay, and changed schools all in one year. Not that he hadn't been noticed—for as long as he could remember, people had noticed him.

He's going to be a heartbreaker, random strangers used to tell Frieda when he was a kid, smiling as they'd passed him in the street.

Yes, Mason had always had plenty of attention, and these days, that attention was paying his bills, but attention wasn't friendship. Sometimes attention meant being coveted—Jay and Tag weren't the first guys who'd competed to be seen out with him. Other times, attention was driven by envy, which usually turned into sly comments about his vanity or intellect. Whatever form it took, though, it meant being different. Being other. It had made Mason wary of people, and it was difficult to make friends with people whose motives you didn't quite trust.

Mason had a lot of acquaintances. People he saw at parties and took selfies with. People whose posts he always liked and added a gushing comment to. He *looked* like he had a lot of friends, but the truth was, that was all just so much surface. Whereas these last few weeks, with Owen…

His musings were cut short by the sight of Owen standing on the pavement outside Cosmos. There was something…odd about Owen tonight, and it took a moment for Mason to realise that he looked uncomfortable. Nervous. His expression relaxed when he saw Mason, and he lifted a hand to wave, but he still looked uneasy as Mason drew closer.

"Hi," Owen said. Then, "Wow, you look great."

Mason smiled. "Thanks, so do you." He did, too, in jeans and a soft-looking dark sweater that Mason wanted to snuggle into and strip off him all at once.

"Yeah?" Owen looked doubtful and glanced over his shoulder towards the bar. "I had a look inside… You didn't tell me it was so posh. I'm a bit underdressed."

"It's not posh," Mason objected. The place was a favourite with celebrities and the media crowd, which was exactly why Mason had chosen it, but it wasn't posh. Although he supposed the clientele might look rather glitzy to Owen's eyes. Mason was used to the place, but perhaps he should have prepared Owen. Was that what a friend would have done?

"Look, if you don't fancy it, we can go somewhere else, but there's no dress code or anything. And you look scrumptious." He stepped closer and ran a hand over Owen's chest, his sweater as soft and cosy as he'd imagined and perfectly outlining Owen's firm pecs. "Mmm," he said, teasing, "Insta-ready."

Owen smiled. God, he had a lovely smile. It started in his

eyes and then nudged his lips up on one side of his mouth, then the other. "Well," Owen said, "I trust you. If you think I look okay, let's head inside."

"You look more than okay," Mason assured him, sliding his fingers down Owen's arm to take his hand. "Come on, let's get a drink. They make *amazing* cocktails."

Owen's fingers threaded with his, squeezing. "Do they do beer?"

"Oh, I expect so, but you have to try a cocktail first." Mason led him inside, pausing for a moment at the entrance, both to scan the bar and to ensure he'd been noticed. He recognised a couple of faces, people Jay had introduced him to, and saw several pairs of eyes turn in his direction. Good. As a reasonably successful model, Mason just about scraped into the minor celebrity category these days. People often recognised him but usually weren't sure why.

Since it was relatively early in the evening, one of the tables in the window was still open, and Mason led Owen over. There was a loveseat on one side, a deep armchair on the other. He toyed with the idea of snuggling up next to Owen in the loveseat, but wasn't sure how comfortable Owen would be with that kind of public exhibition. Besides, he was meant to be teasing their relationship, not confirming it, so he dropped—elegantly—into the armchair instead. Owen, glancing around with interest, took the loveseat.

"This is nice," he said. "Not my usual sort of place, but nice."

"What's your usual sort of place?"

"Well." Owen laughed, picking up the cocktail menu and starting to read. "Just a normal pub, really." His eyebrows shot up. "Bloody hell."

Mason felt his face heat. The prices *were* steep, even by London standards, and he should have considered that Owen's budget might be different to his own. "My round," he said breezily. "I recommend the Aviation. That's what I'm having. Gin, Maraschino, Creme de Violette and lemon. Fragrant, aromatic, a little sour."

"Sounds good," Owen said, closing the menu with a slight frown. "But I'll get them."

"Owen—"

"My treat. You did all the organising for tonight."

And there was something about the mulish set of his mouth, a harder expression than Mason was used to seeing on his face, that warned him to accept the offer graciously. Perhaps money was a sensitive subject for Owen. Mason could see how it might be; Lewis was loaded, and, as Mason well knew, that kind of wealth disparity within a family could cause all sorts of stresses and strains. So instead of arguing, he simply smiled and said, "Thank you."

It was the right call because Owen visibly relaxed, setting the menu back on the table, and gesturing for a waitress who glided over from the bar to take their order. As Mason watched her, he glimpsed a couple of women sitting at the bar eyeing him and Owen. He didn't recognise them, but he did recognise their giggling interest and the way one of them was subtly holding her phone like a camera. It was exactly the situation Misty had told him to create and why he'd chosen Cosmos in the first place, so he made a little show of shucking off his jacket to reveal the slim-fitting Claudio Lugli shirt—an outrageous print of pink and blue feathers—and leaned across the table to take Owen's hand.

"So," he said, smiling into Owen's eyes, "all set for next week's production meeting?"

Owen threaded their fingers together, looking pleased and a little flushed. "Yes—if by 'all set', you mean I saw that Misty sent some kind of feedback email that I haven't opened yet..."

Mason laughed, exaggerating it for their audience, not letting go of Owen's hand. "Yeah, I read it. Basically, you won't be surprised to know that she loved all the flirting we did and wants us to ramp it up even more next time. She thinks you should bring me some sweet peas from your garden, by the way. Like, as a gift?"

"Next time we film?"

"Yeah. You know, because you said you'd give them to someone on a date…"

Owen shook his head, looking both bemused and amused. "Okay, first off, I said *nobody* gives people flowers on dates. And second, I won't have any sweet peas in my garden by then. And *third*—"

"There's a third?"

"Yeah, there's a third. *Third*, I thought this was meant to be a slot about gardening, not flirting."

Mason patted his cheek, grinning. "Sweetie, it's about both, of course. Viewers love shipping people."

"*Shipping* people…? Please don't say in crates."

Mason laughed, shaking his head. "Oh my God," he said, lifting Owen's hand to his lips, pressing a swift kiss to his knuckles. "You're unbelievable."

And Owen laughed too, although his eyes widened deliciously, darkening as his fingers tightened around Mason's hand. "Yeah, yeah, I know what shipping means. Aaron's always banging on about people 'shipping' the characters in *Leeches*." His smile faded. "But that's different from us. They're fictional characters. It's just a story. This is real."

Mason shrugged, throwing a casual glance at the two women at the bar, who both looked away quickly. "The thing is," he said, turning back to Owen, "when you're on TV, or in the public eye in any way, you sort of become a fictional character, you know?"

"That's not true."

"Okay, but there's a persona," Mason explained, dropping Owen's hand as the waitress came over with their drinks. She set down two thick cocktail napkins, then, with infinite care, the brimming coupe glasses. The spirit was milky and bluish, and a plump black cherry nestled in the tiny indentation at the bottom of each glass, spiked by a miniature silver sword. Like a heart, Mason thought. He smiled and thanked her, and as she moved away, he turned back to Owen. "You have to create a persona, or it's just too intrusive."

"Is that what you do?" Owen asked. Before Mason could respond, he added, "It is, isn't it? I actually saw you do it when we were filming—you were a sort of exaggerated version of the real you. A bit louder, a bit friendlier, a bit more outspoken." A strange look came over his face, and he added, "It's how you were when Lewis first introduced us."

That observation left Mason feeling oddly exposed, but he tried to cover up his reaction with an airy wave of his hand. "Yes, well, it's not like having a completely different personality. You just… turn it up a bit."

"I don't think I could do that, though. I'm a what-you-see-is-what-you-get kind of guy."

That was true; Owen was always himself. It was one of the things Mason really liked about him. There were no sides to Owen Hunter, no angles. "That's okay," Mason said. "Viewers will respond to your authenticity."

Owen cocked an eyebrow. "Is that what Misty told you?"

Laughing, Mason said, "Yeah. Sorry, but she's right. People do respond to authenticity, probably because it's so rare."

Owen considered that as he picked up his glass and took a sip, his large hand making it look dainty. Mason found himself holding his breath, watching Owen's expression as he tasted his drink—thoughtful, surprised, then pleased. "Wow, that's delicious."

"It is, isn't it?" Satisfied, Mason took a sip of his own drink, savouring the burst of flavour. "It's my favourite." Then he set it down and reached into his pocket for his phone. "Selfie time. Do you mind?"

"Er, I suppose not."

Scooting over, Mason wiggled into the space next to Owen on the loveseat.

"Oh, you mean with me?" Owen said, surprised.

"Of course with you. I've been teasing this on Insta all day. Okay, so pick up your drink." Mason picked up his own glass, holding his phone in the other hand. "Lean in and try to get your drink in the frame... Yeah, that's it. Oh my God, try to look less terrified."

"Bloody hell," Owen muttered, but he was laughing, and that was perfect. Mason held his finger on the button, and his phone rattled through a bunch of pictures as they pressed their faces together and posed for the camera. Well, Mason posed. He didn't bother going back to the other seat when he was done, just set his drink down and scrolled through the pictures looking for the best ones.

"How about that?" he asked eventually, showing Owen. In the pic they were both smiling, Mason's face slightly hidden by the rim of his glass, but he liked the way the light had caught his hair and Owen's eyes.

"Okay," Owen said with a shrug, settling back against the cushions and sipping his drink. After a while, he added, "Do you have to do all that now?"

Mason nodded, fiddling with the filters and cropping the image just enough that some of the glittery background lights of the bar were still visible. He posted it, tagging Owen and Misty, and Cosmos, and wrote—*Looks delicious, yes? (What? I mean the drink!)* #cocktailporn #WeekendWellness #justgood-friends #instagay #love

The likes and comments started rolling in, and he smiled at all the rainbow hearts and *squeee*! Given that their first slot hadn't even aired yet, the reaction was fantastic. Misty would be stoked. And he was excited to see how it developed, too; if the TV audience got behind the ship, it could be huge. Look at what happened to that YouTuber on *Strictly*.

Owen said, "It's amazing how much time you have to spend doing all that stuff."

"How much time do you spend gardening?" Mason said, pocketing his phone. "It's part of the job."

"Fair point," Owen admitted, although he was studying Mason with a curious look. After a moment, he added, "And…this is part of your persona? The social media stuff you post?"

Mason nodded. "Yeah. It's a curated version of my life, I suppose. It's not like I post pics of my dirty laundry. It's only the things I want people to see."

Thoughtfully, Owen nodded and sipped his drink. They were sitting close now, the knee of Mason's crossed leg resting against Owen's thigh. Comfortable. After a while, Owen said, "So are we, like, officially seeing each other on Instagram now?"

"No," Mason said. "We're just teasing it. If people ask, I'm saying we're just good friends."

"I don't mind people knowing." Owen smiled. "I mean, I sort of still can't believe it's real."

Mason stared at him. "What do you mean?"

"Well… Let's face it. You normally date glamorous celebrities." He winked and added, "You're way out of my league."

"That's bollocks," Mason scoffed. "For fuck's sake, practically the first time we met, you ended up holding my hair while I puked in the loos. Then you poured me into a cab and had to fend off the world's most cringeworthy seduction." He gave an exaggerated shudder. "I probably still had vom in my hair. Trust me, Owen, you are so *not* out of my league."

That made Owen laugh, his eyes twinkling in that way that made Mason's insides tingle. He *really* liked making Owen laugh. It was weirdly addictive. Leaning forward, close enough to murmur into Owen's ear, he added, "And you fuck like a randy porn star."

At which point Owen choked on his cocktail and Mason

ended up thumping him on the back, both of them laughing so hard half the bar must have noticed. Which was an *excellent* result.

After that, the evening went swimmingly. Nicely buzzed on cocktails, they made their way to Callao, the pop-up restaurant Mason had picked, which was way less pretentious than Cosmos. Owen's relief was palpable, his smile broadening into a grin as they ordered from the amazing menu and then tasted all of each other's food while they talked and flirted, bumping knees under the table and tangling their fingers on top.

The restaurant was small enough to be intimate, but buzzing with life. Just regular people, Londoners in all their infinite variety. Laughing conversations in a dozen different languages reached Mason's ears, and yet the only person he had eyes for was Owen.

And the only person Owen had eyes for was him.

"Are you ready to go?" Owen said at last, when the waiter had cleared their plates and they were playing with each other's fingers on the table top.

Mason smiled, nodding. "Very ready."

They got a cab back to Mason's flat, sitting close together in the back seat, legs touching from hip to knee, hands clasped. Owen's thumb kept stroking over Mason's knuckles, back and forth, a gentle soothing gesture.

Owen was a big, strong guy, but he had a soft streak a mile wide. Mason knew he had to be wary of that soft streak, wary of entangling Owen, maybe even hurting him. That would be awful. Mason never wanted to hurt anyone the way Kurt had hurt Frieda, and he knew he was very like his father; everyone said so. A real chip off the old block.

Which meant he had to take care that Owen didn't get too invested. That neither of them did. Not that they were there yet; this would only be their second night together.

He just had to make sure to keep things fun. Light.

They'd split the bill at dinner, so Mason picked up the cab fare when they pulled up in front of his building. Owen didn't object, although that may have had more to do with the desire dancing in his eyes as Mason led him down to his flat. This time, it wasn't booze but anticipation that had his hand shaking as he worked the key into the lock.

In the bright hall light, things were suddenly real, and Mason felt an inexplicable spike of nerves. He wasn't drunk, but he wasn't stone-cold sober either. Neither was Owen.

"Do you, uh, want a nightcap?" Mason said, slipping off his jacket.

"Not really." Owen was taking off his boots, and Mason did the same. He felt lightheaded when he stood up and laughed, a giddy sort of giggle, steadying himself on the wall.

Owen smiled, that thoughtful look back in his eyes as he reached out and took Mason's hand. "Don't be nervous."

Mason laughed again, a breathy sound. "I'm not."

"No?" Owen drew him closer, their socked toes brushing. "You certainly don't need to be. I'm going to take good care of you tonight, petal."

Oh Jesus, could he read Mason's fucking mind? "Yeah?"

"If that's what you want?"

"It is." He swallowed, pulse racing. "It is, yeah."

Owen nodded then leaned in to kiss him, one hand sliding into Mason's hair, holding his head lightly.

Just like in the van yesterday evening, Mason went up like a firework. Heat and desire surged through him as he opened his lips and felt Owen take charge, arms wrapping around him, holding him, kissing him deeply, thoroughly, before pulling back to bite lightly at Mason's bottom lip, then nuzzling at his jaw, kissing him just beneath his ear.

The only sounds were their rasping breaths and the soft, involuntary cries Mason made that he knew sounded needy and desperate but which only seemed to fuel Owen's fire.

"Fuck, I've been dying to do this all night," Owen panted, backing Mason up against the wall.

"Same," Mason gasped and gasped again when Owen rolled his hips against him, the rigid length of his cock mashing against Mason's through their jeans. "*Fuck.*"

"I want to fuck you," Owen said, pulling back far enough that his forehead rested against Mason's, their breath mixing steamily between them. "Would you like that? Do you like that?"

"Yeah," Mason said, heart rabbiting, banging around inside his chest. "I fucking love it."

Owen's eyes were bright with lust, but still smiling. Still warm and playful. "Now, let me see," he said, sliding a hand down Mason's back, dipping his fingers beneath the waist of his jeans. Mason sucked in a breath, eyes fluttering closed, head knocking back against the wall as Owen slid his hand lower, cupping his bare arse.

"No underwear *again*," Owen said, his voice teasing. "You *are* a bad boy."

"So bad," Mason whispered, thrusting his hips forward with a little whimper. Jesus, was this really happening?

Owen laughed softly at his desperate state. It did something wild to Mason, that laugh, and he wasn't sure why. The laughter was kind, not mocking, but it was a recognition of Mason's desperation—and Owen's control. And yeah… he kind of loved that. Feeling out of control. Feeling mastered, but mastered by someone who *liked* him. Who enjoyed his little display of needy desperation and was willing to indulge him.

"You know?" Owen growled. "I think I should smack that gorgeous arse of yours."

Mason thought he might pass out, so much blood headed south. Although his face felt as flushed as his dick. Swallowing, he said, "Yeah, maybe you should."

Owen pulled back once more, looking him straight in the

eyes. Something passed between them. "Yeah?" Owen said, softly. "Just for fun, nothing…extreme."

Mason bit his lip, heart beating wildly. "Yeah. Just for fun."

Owen studied him, as if confirming he meant it; then his expression melted into something almost helpless, dazzled. "Christ," he said, and leaned in to kiss Mason again, deep and powerful, both arms going around him, holding him so hard he could hardly move. Not that he wanted to move, he simply…relaxed, ceded control, let his body turn to honey in Owen's arms.

And then Owen was manoeuvring them both into the bedroom, still kissing, still touching, undressing each other as they went. "On to the bed," he said, when Mason was down to nothing but his jeans. Mason moved to slide them off, but Owen stopped him. "No. Keep them on for now. Hands and knees. Let me look at you." His voice was gentle, but firm, like he knew exactly what he wanted, exactly how this was going to play out.

Swallowing, Mason did as he was told, and it felt…terrifyingly vulnerable and astonishingly safe at the same time, because even though he wasn't sure where this was going, he trusted Owen to make it good.

When he looked over his shoulder, he saw Owen watching him. He wore nothing but a very nice pair of black boxer briefs, his sizeable cock straining the fabric. Catching Mason's eye, he smiled and gave himself a deliberate stroke through the cotton, biting lightly at his bottom lip. Fuck, he was sexy.

Owen said, "You look so bloody hot like that."

And *Christ*, the way Owen was looking at him with that compelling mix of heat and fondness —it just *did* something for Mason. Let him give up control, maybe, without worrying the other guy would lose respect for him.

He gave his arse a suggestive wiggle and said breathlessly, "Are you just going to look, then?"

Owen's grin was approving. "Such an impatient boy," he said and came closer. His warm hands landed lightly on Mason's hips, fingers ghosting up his sides, running over his ribs, leaving a trail of goosebumps across his skin before moving down over his back, thumbs either side of his spine, fingers spread, and finally settling on his hips again. Then, with a firm tug, Owen pulled Mason to the edge of the bed, close enough that Owen's cock could nudge against Mason's denim-covered arse.

Mason rocked back into him with a helpless, needy whine, and for a while, they just moved like that, Owen thrusting lazily against him while Mason whimpered, his iron-hard cock trapped in his jeans. He needed to touch himself, but he couldn't, so he clenched his hands into the duvet instead.

Finally, with a hitching breath, Owen pulled back. "You're going to make me come before I can even get inside you," he murmured. "Such a bad boy."

His hand landed in a light swat across Mason's backside.

It didn't hurt, but the sound and the feel of it, the *thought* of it, ran through Mason like an electric bolt. He cried out in shocked pleasure, cock pulsing and straining inside his jeans.

Owen did it again, a little harder, and Mason gave another of those helpless, needy cries.

"Fuck." Owen swatted him again. "You have no idea —Jesus."

Mason laughed, and it sounded shaky and desperate. "Take them off. Take my jeans off."

"Hey." Owen smacked him again. "Who's the boss here?" But his hands were already undoing Mason's flies. Pulling his jeans down slowly, with obvious relish, Owen gave another of those husky hitched breaths. "Fuck, Mason, look at you."

The cool air on his arse and the reverence in Owen's voice made Mason shiver. And then another of those light smacks landed, this one skin to skin, bringing a stinging tingle. Mason gasped, elbows giving way, face landing in the duvet.

"So fucking hot, I can't get enough," Owen was saying. "I'll never get enough." Another swat landed, and it ran like fire though Mason's blood, liquifying him. And then a different sensation, firm hands spreading him, hot breath against his skin, the soft scratch of stubble, and a sudden silken pressure as Owen's tongue slid across him, lapping and probing at his hole.

Mason had to fumble for his stiff cock and grasp it in a firm fist to keep from coming right then. "Jesus," he hissed as Owen licked and kissed, teasing fingers sliding between Mason's legs to caress his balls, tongue flicking and exploring. All coherent thought fled, leaving Mason suspended in a glorious, timeless space of sensation and touch, of kissing and caressing, of light tingling swats. Being petted and chastened and spoiled.

Then Owen husked, "Lube, condoms?"

"Bedside table." Mason pressed his face back into the duvet and just…let it happen. He floated in that perfect place of sensation while Owen toyed with him, kissed him, played with him until he was a hot mess of want, and finally—*finally* —he felt the blunt head of Owen's cock at the entrance to his body.

"Okay?" Owen said, voice hoarse with restraint.

Mason pushed up on his elbows, giving himself more leverage so that he could push back against that pressure. "Give it to me," he growled. "Fucking *give* it to me."

"So impatient…" Another swat on his arse, and then—oh Christ—then Owen was pressing in, slow and steady, unrelenting. Filling him. And Mason held nothing back because Owen loved all his whimpering, needy noises. They were like firecrackers thrown onto a bonfire, each one triggering a grunt from Owen as he began to move. A careful rhythm at first, his hands hot on Mason's hips, strong and firm, and then—like a burst of starlight—another sharp smack on his arse that made them both cry out.

Fuck, it was good. So good.

And then Owen began to really pick up the pace, one hand on Mason's shoulder to keep him in place, the other on his hip as he fucked him, hard, and Mason was just taking it. *Loving* it. Shouting with every shuddering thrust, his body tightening, his stomach and legs clenching, drawing up, muscles contracting.

Inevitable, unstoppable, his orgasm began to rise. And somehow Owen must have known because he pulled out, lifting and turning Mason in his powerful arms till he was on his back, staring up at Owen.

For a moment, Mason lay there, gasping, Owen above him flushed, his cock swaying heavy and hard between them, his eyes gleaming. And then Owen was kissing him, devouring his mouth, grabbing Mason's wrists and pressing them into the mattress above his head with one large hand as he smoothly entered him again in one powerful thrust.

Mason cried out with the pure abandoned joy of it, wrapping his legs around Owen's waist, lifting his hips off the bed as Owen angled into him just fucking *right*. Right *there*.

He was so close now, so fucking *close*. But he couldn't quite get there, not on his own. "Need to… Fuck." He whined and whimpered, thrashing desperately. Mastered, and loving it. Too pleasure-soaked to be coherent. "Fuck, I can't… I need to…"

"Say please," Owen said softly, a smile teasing the corner of his mouth. There was just a hint of a taunt in his voice, but his eyes shone with real affection.

"Fuck."

"Say it…"

"Fuck. Please. Fucking *please*!"

Owen's smile widened. Sweetened. "Good boy," he husked, brushing his mouth over Mason's before finally—

fucking *finally*—taking Mason's cock in his strong hand. "Now do it," Owen growled, hand moving perfectly. "Come on, angel, I want to see you come."

The shock of hearing his real name on Owen's lips, of that firm, commanding grip, and the deep pressure of Owen's cock pounding into him, twisted off the cap. Mason came like a detonation, shooting into Owen's hand as he cried out and arced up off the bed.

Owen groaned, thrusting hard—once, twice, three times—and went rigid, fingers biting into Mason's hips, gasping his release.

"Jesus," Owen panted, collapsing over him, the words a hot caress against his throat. "Jesus, Mason. Fucking *hell*…"

After a few stunned moments, Owen shifted unsteadily, still breathing hard, and carefully withdrew from Mason's body before he stood up to deal with the condom.

Mason rolled over, pressed his hot face into the duvet, aware of his jeans still tangled around one foot, dangling off the edge of the bed. He felt abruptly unmoored, vulnerable, and a little uncertain.

Angel.

Did Owen *know*? How could he? Or was it just a pet name?

But then Owen was back, gently tugging Mason's jeans the rest of the way off his foot. The bed dipped beneath his weight as he sat down, one hand stroking Mason's back.

"Hey, still with me, petal?"

All teasing had disappeared from his voice, nothing left but that familiar, gentle warmth. Mason moved, his leaden body responding sluggishly, lifting his face from the duvet, the wreck of his hair flopping over his face.

Owen watched him with smiling blue eyes, looking flushed and happy. "Okay?" he asked, pushing Mason's hair out of his eyes. "Was that good for you?"

Mason nodded, and Owen smiled, then gave a little tug on his arm. "Come here, then. Let's have a cuddle."

And it was exactly what Mason needed, snuggling under the duvet together, his flash of vulnerability melting in the steady warmth of Owen's arms.

After a while, Owen gave a low chuckle, the sound a deep reverberation against Mason's ear. "That was… Christ, that was hot."

Mason laughed too, burying the sound against Owen's shoulder. "It really fucking was." And maybe it was the drowsy warmth beneath the covers, or the feel of Owen's strong body keeping him close, or simply the surge of contentment swelling inside him like a balloon, but Mason heard himself saying, "Why did you call me Angel?"

"Why not? You're beautiful enough." Owen threaded a hand into Mason's damp hair, pushing it away from his face to look at him better. "Christ, you're *so* beautiful."

You're so beautiful.

Mason stiffened at those familiar words. He didn't say anything, though. He never did because it sounded silly and ungrateful, but this time, he didn't have to say anything because Owen noticed his reaction.

"No?" he said, frowning. "That bothers you?"

Shaking his head, Mason had no intention of explaining himself. Yet somehow, under Owen's steady gaze, it felt okay to say, "It's just… I can't help how I look, you know? It's not like I can take any credit for my face, but sometimes it feels like it's all people care about." He winced, hoping he hadn't offended Owen. "Sorry, I know it's stupid, and I didn't mean to—"

"It's not stupid," Owen said. "I've seen the way people ogle you. It must feel … objectivising. I don't want to make you feel like that."

"You don't."

"You *are* beautiful, though. There's no getting away from

163

it." Owen stroked his thumb over Mason's cheek again. "You're also funny and fun to be around, smart and sweet, a little shy, interesting to talk to…"

Mason started to smile, then laughed as the list went on.

"… engaging, professional, generous to your family, warm-hearted…"

"Okay, stop."

"…and not to mention a talented cook—"

"Hey! *Chef.*"

Owen grinned. "Chef," he corrected, waggling his eyebrows. "And you look dead sexy holding a whisk…"

Mason snorted.

"I'm serious!" He looked very serious as he leaned in, lips brushing Mason's. "There's nothing sexier than a man who knows what he's doing."

"Mmm, well, I won't argue with that, Mr. Sexy Gardener."

Owen gave a soft laugh, and he looked so perfect right then, so exactly what Mason wanted, that he added hoarsely, "Angel's actually my real name."

Owen blinked. After a stunned moment, he said, "You're kidding?"

"Nope. I changed it to Mason when I started modelling."

"Ah… So 'Mason Nash' is part of your public persona, then?"

"I suppose." He'd never really thought about it like that. He'd just wanted to get away from all the stupid jokes, from the boy he'd been at school.

Studying him again, Owen lifted a hand and traced a fingertip over Mason's face, following the lines of his cheek-bone, his eyebrows, his jaw. "Angel," he mused softly. "Angel Nash. I like it."

"Yeah?"

"Yeah." Owen's eyes twinkled, teasing. "I mean, it's not every guy who can say he's shagging an angel."

Mason groaned, burying his face in Owen's shoulder. "And *that's* why I changed it."

"Oh, come on. That was funny." Owen grinned. "Maybe you should tweet *that* on Instagram."

"You don't tweet on—" Mason began, then broke off, laughing. "Yeah, okay, maybe I will," he said fondly, reaching up and stealing another kiss. "Maybe I will tweet that on fucking Instagram."

CHAPTER FOURTEEN

OWEN

April

Their debut *Weekend Wellness* slot was airing on the first Saturday in April, and Aaron was set on throwing a brunch party to celebrate the occasion. Owen had already firmly rejected the offer, partly because he didn't want a big fuss made over what was, in the end, a ten-minute TV slot, and partly because he and Mason had plans for a small celebration of their own. But when he met up with Aaron and Lewis at Owen's local, the Bat and Belfry, a few days before the airing, Aaron determinedly made one last-ditch attempt.

"Oh, come on," he wheedled. "Why not?"

Before Owen could answer, Lewis arrived back at their table with another round of pints and some crisps and peanuts.

To Aaron he said firmly, "Leave him alone." Then he sat down and turned to look at Owen. "I don't know what's got into him with this cooking and entertaining obsession. It's weird."

"First," Aaron said as he reached for his pint, "cooking *one* meal, then suggesting *one* brunch almost two months later, is hardly an *obsession*, and second, I want to do something nice for your brother for his big TV break. What's wrong with that?"

Lewis eyed Aaron silently for a moment, then glanced back at Owen and mouthed, *Obsessed.*

Owen laughed, and laughed again when Aaron elbowed Lewis and Lewis gave a short *hmph.*

"It's not a big deal," Owen said, grabbing a pack of Scampi Fries and ripping it open. "It's just a short bit—blink and you'll miss it. Besides, between that and the business, I've been working like crazy all month. Saturday morning will be the first chance I've had in ages to veg out in my PJs."

"Hear that?" Lewis said, giving Aaron a significant look. "He doesn't want to trek all the way over to ours to eat fucking smoked salmon bagels. He wants a lie-in."

Aaron sighed. "Well, what time is it on? We can at least make sure we watch it."

"Misty said it'd be about eleven-fifteen," Owen said.

Aaron opened his mouth again, but Lewis forestalled him with another look. "We'll be watching," he assured Owen. "And you can come to ours for dinner on Sunday to celebrate instead. Deal?"

Owen grinned. "Deal."

Aaron looked mollified by that compromise, at least.

"Speaking of Misty, how are you getting on with her?" Lewis asked.

Owen took a drink of his Fullers. "Okay. She's a real sergeant-major, though, isn't she? Poor Naomi, her assistant, looks like she's on the verge of nervous breakdown most days."

"Misty would be so pissed off if she heard you say that," Lewis said, looking highly amused. "She told me the other day that if I shared more of my inner self with my team and

167

encouraged them to bring their whole selves to work, like she does with her team, I'd get more out of them."

Owen rolled his eyes. "That's rich. From what I've seen, her whole team's terrified of her. Luckily, she likes Mason, and I get a free pass by riding on his coattails."

Lewis raised a brow at that, a question in his eyes that Owen wasn't too keen on answering. He pretended fascination with his Scampi Fries, poking around inside the bag.

"From what I overheard the other day, I think you've earned your own free pass," Aaron said. When Owen looked up, interested, he added, "Misty and Naomi were ahead of me in the canteen queue, and they were blabbing about you—well, Misty was. Naomi was just listening. It was pretty obvious Misty knows you're not that bothered about being on TV. I think she realises she needs to keep you sweet."

That surprised Owen. It certainly hadn't seemed to him like Misty was trying to keep him sweet. But then, it wasn't like he asked her for anything. He mostly tried to avoid her, letting Mason do all the heavy lifting on that front. Mason seemed to know how to keep Misty on-side.

"What else did she say?" he asked, curious.

Aaron looked amused. "Well, she was talking about all the flirting Mason's been doing with you on social media."

Owen felt his cheeks warm. "Yeah?"

"Yes, she's *very* happy about it—thinks it's going to play out well with the viewers."

"What's all that about anyway?" Lewis said then. "You've never been one for social media before."

Owen opened his mouth to speak, but Aaron got in first. "Oh, you know Mason and his Instagram. He's got to have a new celebrity boyfriend to show off every month. It's all a bit —" And then he broke off, shooting a slightly mortified glance at Owen, as though just remembering he was there.

"All a bit what?" Owen said, amazed that his voice came

out sounding so easy and normal when he felt suddenly and weirdly uptight.

"Oh, you know," Aaron said, shrugging. "It's all a bit... well, *fake*."

"Fake?" Owen echoed. "Fake how?"

Lewis said quietly, "Aaron—" but Aaron didn't seem to notice.

"Look, I *like* Mason," he said, "but have you looked at his Instagram? More than the recent posts, I mean? If you actually believed what he posts there, you'd think he has this amazing, wonderful life, and he's blissfully happy. It's all... it's all very *airbrushed*, you know?"

"Well, sure, it's 'curated'," Owen replied, trying not to sound too defensive. "But the photos he's posted of the two of us together—we weren't *pretending* to smile and laugh in them. We were having a good time." He paused, then added self-consciously, "And I *do* like him. He's a great guy."

There was an awkward silence for several long moments. Then Aaron said, too brightly, "You know what? You're right. He probably *is* just that happy. I mean, why wouldn't he be? He's a gorgeous model who goes to flashy celebrity hangouts and gets given expensive stuff for free all the time. Hell, if I was him, I'd probably be sticking all that on Instagram too."

Lewis snorted. "Sweetheart, you're flailing."

Aaron groaned. "I know." He met Owen's gaze. "I feel like I've read this all wrong. I kind of assumed from what Misty said that you and Mason were just pretending—"

"For the record, *I* didn't think that," Lewis interrupted.

Aaron ignored him. "Did I assume wrong? Have you and Mason got something real going on? Not just for the show, I mean?"

Owen rubbed the back of his neck uncomfortably. He felt stupidly panicked by Aaron's assumption and wasn't sure whether he wanted to talk about this or not, but equally, he didn't want to lie. Didn't want to deny Mason.

"Yeah," he muttered at last. "It's very new, but... yeah, it's a real thing." He glanced at Lewis. "Are you okay with that?"

Lewis rolled his eyes. "Haven't we already had that conversation? I have *Aaron* for fuck's sake. Besides, I was only with Mason for about eleven minutes. But if you need me to say it, yes, it's fine. *Jesus.*"

"It was a *bit* more than eleven minutes," Aaron said drily.

"You know what I mean," Lewis said with a wave of his hand. He turned back to Owen. "So, tell us how it's going. You just said you really like him..." He raised an eyebrow in question, inviting Owen to expand. "More than just a little fun?"

Owen screwed up his face. "Honestly, it feels weird talking about this with you. I mean, when you were going out with him, you used to moan about him to me."

"Yeah, well, you know me. It's nothing personal, I just don't really... do people."

Owen gave a fondly rueful laugh. "Yeah, I know."

"The fact is," Aaron interjected, pointing at Lewis, "you and Mason were never suited. It was pretty obvious actually."

"That's true," Owen agreed. "For one thing, you're both kind of highly strung, so that was never going to work."

"Highly strung?" Lewis echoed. "I'm not fucking *highly strung*. I mean, okay, I can be a little intense I suppose, but, you know, that's because I'm the impulsive, artistic type."

Aaron snorted amusement. "I think you mean you're the hot-tempered, obsessive-workaholic-with-no-time-for-other-people type."

"Unfair!" Lewis protested.

Aaron bumped him with his shoulder. "I don't mean me or Owen," he said soothingly. "I mean other people."

"Oh," Lewis said. "You mean people-people." He thought about that for a moment, then shrugged. "Yeah, fair enough."

"Anyway, the point is," Aaron went on, "Owen's obviously a better fit with Mason."

"I am here, you know," Owen grumbled.

Lewis grinned at him. "He's right, though."

"I am, aren't I?" Aaron said, warming to his subject. "I mean, Owen, you're so different from Lewis. You're kind and patient and thoughtful. And you have that competent caretaker thing going on that—"

"Hey!" Lewis protested. "I'm not so bad."

Aaron batted his eyelashes at Lewis. "You know I love you and only you."

Lewis grunted and subsided. "Yeah, well. Just remember that."

"Joking aside, you do have a point," Owen admitted. "Mason is"—he searched for the right words—"I think he *needs* a bit of kindness and nurturing. When I first met him, I thought he was pretty shallow, but now that I've got to know him, I see he's not like that at all. He's actually a lot more down to earth, and even a little bit shy." His cheeks felt suddenly warm, and he reached for his pint to hide behind, throwing back the last of his beer.

When he set his empty glass back down, it was to discover Lewis watching him with a faintly troubled expression.

"What's that look for?" he said warily.

"Listen," Lewis said carefully, "I don't really disagree with anything you just said. And I do think you two could be a good fit. But Mason is—" He gnawed at his lower lip for a moment. "He really is quite *into* the whole celeb thing. You probably remember me moaning about him nagging me to go to more industry events and take him along, and always wanting to post stuff about us? And I'm not slagging him off for that. That's fair enough. It's what he does with his whole branding thing. I get it. But I think you should... be aware of that. Maybe be a little bit cautious, you know?"

Owen's face felt red hot now. "Jesus, Lewis," he muttered. "I'm not getting too—" But then he broke off without finishing the sentence and looked away. Because he was, and he knew it.

"Okay," Lewis said reasonably. "Just bear it in mind, that's all I'm saying. I know that, right now, working on the show is throwing you two together a lot, and obviously, Mason's capitalising on the publicity, but it's not going to be like that forever. You said you don't see yourself trying to carve a TV career out of this, so maybe have a think about what things will be like with Mason once the show's done. Will your lives still mesh then?" He shrugged. "Like Aaron said earlier, Mason has a lot invested in his Instagram life. Don't underestimate that."

Owen sighed. "Okay, I'll think about it."

Lewis clapped his shoulder, squeezing once before dropping his hand. A rare show of affection that made Owen's chest tighten.

Another pint. That was what he needed. He stood. "My round I think. Same again?"

Owen and Mason's private celebration for their first TV appearance together was taking place at Owen's house. Mason was doing a beach shoot all day Friday and wouldn't get back to London till late, so he was going to come straight to Owen's place—his first visit there—to spend the night. Then they'd have a celebratory breakfast the next morning while watching the show.

Owen felt a strange mixture of excitement and apprehension at the thought of Mason coming over. He loved his house and had the vague, unsettling sense that once Mason had been here, once he'd lounged on the sofa and pottered in the kitchen, and lain in Owen's bed, those memories might be difficult to shift. But it was too late now to change his plans. He'd invited Mason, and Mason had said yes—he could hardly uninvite him. So instead, he focused his efforts on making plans for their fancy breakfast, which he was determined should be celebration-worthy.

When he got home from work on Friday evening, he had a bite to eat, gave the place another quick tidy, and changed the bedding to the new absurdly-high-thread-count set he'd bought earlier in the week. Finally, on an impulse, he went out into the garden and picked some of the early blooming tulips, scarlet red ones and creamy white ones. He didn't have a proper vase since he generally preferred his flowers to stay in the ground, but he found a plain glass jug and stuck them in there with lots of water, and they looked very pretty, if somewhat haphazard.

At ten he got a message from Mason.

On my way back. Hoping to get to yours around midnight.

Owen sent back, *Looking forward to it. Fancy some Champagne when you get in?*

Bubbles appeared in the message window, then went away again. Then reappeared and went away twice more. Finally—

Honestly, I'd prefer a cup of tea. I'm freezing, knackered, and have sand in unspeakable places. Sleeping-face emoji.

Owen laughed softly. He felt weirdly pleased by the message—more pleased than he would have been by enthusiastic agreement to popping the fizz open, to be honest, because it made him feel trusted. Like Mason felt okay showing Owen his vulnerable side.

Happy to help you wash off the sand. Let me know when you're five minutes away and I'll have a cuppa waiting.

He was rewarded with a quick *Can't wait* and three hearts in response.

He killed the next couple of hours in front of the TV, sipping his way through a couple of beers while a series of panel shows flickered on the screen, each one merging into the last. Finally, his phone buzzed again.

Be there in ten.

His smile in response to that simple message was big —too big.

Christ, he really was in trouble.

He switched off the TV, then decided it was too quiet and set up some music in its place, fiddling with the volume obsessively till he was satisfied it was just right. Then he popped the kettle on and began pacing the kitchen, excited and nervous in equal measure.

No sooner had he poured the hot water in the teapot than the doorbell went, and his heart began pounding. Rubbing his hands down the front of his thighs, he forced himself to take two deep breaths, then strode to the front door.

"Hey," Mason said when he opened it, giving a crooked smile. He looked tired but ridiculously gorgeous in threadbare joggers, an old denim jacket and a striped beanie.

"Hey," Owen echoed, smiling wide and fighting the urge to grab him and just *enfold* him in a huge hug.

Play it cool, he schooled himself silently.

He stood back to let Mason enter, smiling even wider when Mason paused to kiss his cheek, then followed him into the house.

"Straight down the corridor to the door at the end," he directed.

Mason paused when he entered the living area, turning in a slow circle as he took in the big squashy sofa, the sturdy, mostly oak, furniture and the myriad pot plants that filled every nook and cranny, from the spiky yucca plant in the corner to the big, leafy japonica beside the glass doors that let out onto the garden.

"Wow, this is beautiful," Mason said, his eyes shining with real pleasure. "And I love your kitchen." He headed towards it, and Owen followed slowly, watching his reactions.

Mason ran a finger over the hob of his range cooker and

raised an eyebrow at Owen. "This looks very clean," he said, quirking a smile. "Almost as if it's not been used much."

Owen chuckled. "That's fair, but I will be using it tomorrow."

"Really?"

Owen waggled his eyebrows. "I have plans for breakfast."

"Intriguing," Mason said, his wide smile transforming suddenly and comically into a huge, jaw-cracking yawn.

"You really are tired," Owen said, moving forward and settling his hands gently on Mason's hips, tugging him forward, loving the little moan Mason gave as their chests bumped.

"I'm totally wiped," Mason admitted. "Been up since four and on the go the whole day."

"Yeah?" Owen said. "Poor baby."

Mason gave a funny, little laugh that was a bit embarrassed and a bit pleased. Encouraged, Owen kissed his nose, then drew back. "Bloody hell, your nose is like ice!"

"I'm like that all over," Mason said. "That beach was fucking freezing."

"Were you modelling swimwear?" It hadn't been warm today—in fact it had been grey and overcast. Definitely not nice enough to be mostly naked outside.

Mason shook his head. "Nope, high-end tailoring, would you believe? But the photographer had us barefoot in the water for ages, splashing in the shallows, then sitting around on wet rocks looking wistfully out to sea. The water was fucking freezing, and it was pretty windy at times." He shrugged. "He was pleased with the results, though, so that's good."

Owen let go of Mason's hips and reached for his hands, twining his warm fingers with Mason's icy ones. "Let's get you warmed up," he said. "Do you want to take a hot shower while I make you that tea I promised?"

Mason shook his head. "Maybe later. Could we just…" He

trailed off, his cheeks pinkening. He wanted to ask for something but couldn't seem to find the words, and for some reason, Owen found that incredibly cute.

"You want to go to bed?" he guessed. Mason nodded, but Owen could see from his hopeful expression that there was something else too that he wanted.

"Okay," Owen said agreeably. "Let's go to bed and I'll take care of you."

Mason sighed happily and let Owen tug him towards the bedroom.

Once they got there, he seemed to be too tired to do anything but just stand while Owen undressed him, shepherded him into bed, and then gave him a long, slow, thorough blowjob, edging him a couple of times before finally letting him come in big, greedy, exuberant pulses.

"Tha' was so good," Mason mumbled as Owen settled in behind him spoon-style, tugging Mason closer, one arm anchored round his waist. "Wha' 'bout you, though?"

"I'm great," Owen said, smiling against his neck. "I can wait till tomorrow. Just go to sleep."

Mason probably didn't hear that—he was already gone.

Owen leaned up on one elbow and watched him for a few minutes. The lines of exhaustion were already smoothing out as he breathed, slow and deep. And as Owen's own iron-hard erection slowly subsided, a warm ache of helpless affection took its place. It was an odd feeling. A hazy, unknowable compass point located somewhere between joy and fear.

You're overthinking it, he told himself. *Just go to sleep.*

And at last, he did.

~

It was almost nine hours later that Owen finally woke, blinking in astonishment at the alarm clock. He never slept this long. His job required him to be up and about early most days, and it had become an ingrained habit to rise around six, even at weekends.

Well, not today apparently. It was nine-forty already, and *Weekend Wellness* would be starting in twenty minutes.

Owen slowly sat up, his gaze snagging on the man lying beside him. At some point in the night, he had let go of Mason, and Mason had moved away, curling in protectively on himself. Now, his face, turned into the pillow a little, was mostly hidden by his messy hair. He was still sleeping soundly.

Owen eased himself out of bed, careful not to wake him. He had Things To Do.

Padding through to the kitchen, he quickly set the coffee maker going, then pulled up the recipe on his phone that he'd decided to make—Eggs Benedict.

He started by getting out all the ingredients and equipment that he needed. Already he had a sneaking feeling that it might have been a better idea to buy the ready-made hollandaise sauce he'd spotted in the supermarket yesterday, rather than making it himself from scratch, but he was where he was. And it couldn't be that hard.

Before he started on the sauce, he split the muffins ready for toasting and put on a pan of boiling water for the poached eggs—those would only take a few minutes when the time came, so he just needed to be ready to go. What else? Oh yes, *bacon*. He set the grill as low as it would go and put the bacon on to cook slowly so it would get nicely crispy. The coffee machine beeped then, and he quickly poured himself a cup and took a huge swig. Okay, now he was ready to tackle the sauce.

He started by melting the butter in one pan and skimming the whitish milk solids off the top while, in the other pan, he whisked together egg yolks and tarragon vinegar in a bowl over a pan of water. His gaze darted anxiously between the two pans as the minutes ticked by. The yolk mix was supposed to thicken—that was the cue to start adding the butter—but it seemed as thin as ever. Was the difference subtler than he'd thought?

"*Fuck,*" he cursed under his breath. He stopped whisking, wiped his hands and grabbed his phone, swiping the recipe open again, then scrolling down to the video option near the bottom. Snatching up his coffee, he found the part where the chef was making the sauce and hit play. He was so absorbed that he forgot about his pans for a few crucial minutes. When he remembered, he lurched back around, yelping when he saw the egg yolks were beginning to look distinctly scrambled. "*Fucking fuck!*"

Abandoning his coffee cup on the worktop, he grabbed the whisk, and started furiously beating the eggs, but it only seemed to be making things worse, the egg mix turning into a thick, curdled mess. And *fuck*, he was sweating now. When had the kitchen got so hot?

That was when the smoke alarm started screeching—*fuck*, he'd forgotten about the bacon too!

"*Shit, shit, shit,*" he cursed, abandoning the eggs again, this time to yank out the grill pan and stare in dismay at the charred remains of what had once been top-quality bacon. And hell, the smoke alarm was still shrieking, and Mason had been sleeping so peacefully!

Owen tossed the ruined bacon, grill pan and all, into the sink and snatched up the tea towel from the worktop, intending to wave it under the smoke alarm till that horrible piercing noise finally stopped. But he must have set his coffee mug down on a corner of the tea towel because, as soon as he pulled, the mug toppled over dramatically, spilling coffee down the length of the worktop and all over the split muffins waiting patiently to be put in the toaster.

"Oh, fucking *hell!*" he yelled.

And then the doorbell rang.

Owen dropped his head into his hands and let out a

muffled scream. When he looked up again, Mason was standing in front of him, biting his lip against a smile and looking ridiculously, *adorably* sleep-rumpled... not to mention deliciously naked.

"Having trouble?" Mason asked, raising a brow.

"A bit," Owen admitted.

The doorbell rang again, a long, leaned-on ring this time.

"Get the door," Mason said. "I'll sort this out."

"Okay," Owen said, relieved.

He assumed it was going to be a delivery guy, but when he swung the door open, he blinked at the two men standing there.

"Surprise!" Aaron sang, holding up a bottle of champagne and another of freshly squeezed orange juice.

"What—?"

Lewis grinned at him evilly. "You didn't really think we were going to let your *television debut* pass unmarked, did you?" He stepped inside, moving past a blinking Owen. "Did you burn your toast?"

Just then, the smoke alarm abruptly stopped—Mason must have managed to switch it off.

Shit, *Mason*.

Owen turned his head, "Lewis, wait—"

But Lewis was already disappearing down the corridor, and now Aaron was pushing past him too. "Just as well we brought food then," Aaron said. "I have literally every breakfast pastry known to man—or Waitrose, anyway. Baggsy me one of the hazelnut chocolate croissants."

Shit.

Owen shut the door and hurried after them, but already he was too late. By the time he reached the living area, Lewis, Aaron and Mason were all standing staring at one another. Mason was holding the tea towel—now stained with the coffee he'd mopped up—over his crotch like an improvised fig leaf, and somehow, it made him look way more naked than if he hadn't bothered.

"Wow, Mason! Hi!" Aaron gushed, too cheerfully. "Sorry, we didn't realise you were here, but it's great to see you."

Mason smiled weakly. "Hey, Aaron. I, um, just got up. That is, I was asleep, and then the—" He nodded helplessly at the smoke alarm.

Lewis turned to Owen and raised a brow. "It looks like your kitchen had a nervous breakdown."

"I was trying to make Eggs Benedict."

"Enough said," Lewis replied, adding for Mason's benefit, "He's only a very slightly better cook than I am."

Mason gave a slightly strangled laugh at that, mumbled something about putting some clothes on, and fled for the bedroom.

Once the door had shut behind him, Aaron turned to Owen with a rueful expression. "Sorry about this. We just wanted to surprise you—we didn't know you'd have company." He paused, then added, "We probably should have thought. Do you want us to go?"

"Don't be daft," Lewis said. "If we do that, Mason will think we don't want to be around him." Owen and Aaron both turned to stare at him. "And that's not the case at all," Lewis added hurriedly. "Look. Why don't you go after him and check he's okay while we sort out breakfast, and then we can all watch the show together?"

"Good idea," Aaron agreed. "Lewis, you get the Bucks Fizz sorted, and I'll warm up the pastries." He headed for the kitchen, and Lewis followed him.

And since Owen didn't have a better idea, he did as they said.

CHAPTER FIFTEEN

MASON

Mason let out a long, mortified groan. Why, oh why did it have to be Lewis and Aaron, of all people, who would walk in on him naked? Not that either Aaron or Lewis had seemed very interested in his dangly bits, but even so. It was fucking *embarrassing*.

He didn't even know whether Owen had told Lewis they were seeing each other. Well, if he hadn't, Lewis knew now...

The door creaked open, and he swung round, alarmed, relaxing when he saw it was just Owen.

"Hey," Owen said softly, stepping inside and closing the door. "Listen, I'm sorry about this. I wasn't expecting them this morning."

Mason managed to dredge up a small smile. "Yeah, I figured. Do you"—he cleared his throat—"want me to go?"

"What? No! Jesus, no." Owen looked gratifyingly unhappy at that suggestion. He stepped forward, sliding his hands over Mason's shoulders and gently squeezing, a warm, affectionate gesture that made Mason's stupid stomach turn over. "Would you be okay with them staying? They've brought breakfast, which is just as well since I fucked up the Eggs Benedict big time."

Despite everything, Mason couldn't help but chuckle at that. "Yeah—I saw. I don't know what was in that pot, by the way, but it definitely wasn't a hollandaise sauce."

Owen's expression had been faintly worried, but at Mason's gentle teasing, the anxious stitch between his brows relaxed, and a gleam of humour came into his eyes. "I think I tried to run before I could walk," he admitted. "Though I'm not as bad a cook as Lewis would have you believe. I can actually make a decent spag bol, and I do a mean roast chicken dinner."

He urged Mason closer, and Mason found himself going willingly, pressing his naked frame against Owen's clothed one. Owen trailed his hands down Mason's sides before curving them over his arse and tugging him closer still, his grip firm. And fuck but Mason loved the way Owen *manhandled* him. Not carelessly, like he was a piece of meat. More like he was irresistibly tempting, and Owen just couldn't stop himself from reaching for him.

Owen leaned in to kiss him then, and Mason sighed happily, parting his lips for Owen's tongue. And then they were moaning and kissing and humping each other like teenagers, till Owen somehow managed to drag his mouth from Mason's and step back, breathing heavily.

"Fuck," he said, sounding breathless. "Fucking *hell*."

They stared at one another.

"If they weren't here," Mason said hoarsely, "I'd say fuck *Weekend Wellness*—put your cock inside me right now."

Owen gave a pained moan and adjusted himself. "But since they are here," he said, "we'd better go and join them. If that's okay with you?"

Part of Mason wanted to be petulant. To wheedle with Owen to get rid of Lewis and Aaron so he could have Owen all to himself. To avoid the inevitable awkwardness with

Lewis that he'd honestly rather avoid. But it was only a small part of him. And besides, when Owen looked at him like that, his expression hopeful and concerned at once… it made him want to be good for Owen.

And so it was that he ended up taking a quick shower, dressing in soft flannel PJ bottoms and a t-shirt bearing Owen's company name—fantastic Insta fodder—then joining the others in the living area.

Aaron immediately pressed a glass of Bucks Fizz and a plate of pastries on him, while Lewis shifted up on the big sectional sofa to make room for him next to Owen, making a few jokey cracks that neatly broke the ice. And Owen… Owen was unselfconsciously affectionate, putting his arm around Mason without seeming to even think about it, while stealing bits of almond croissant from Mason's plate and kissing his temple for no particular reason. All that dopey coupley stuff that Mason usually avoided like the plague.

In anyone else, Owen's behaviour would have sent up warning flares. Hell, it *was* sending up warning flares, but Mason was choosing to ignore them. If he wanted to keep things going with Owen—and he *did* want to; he needed to— then he'd have to roll with the coupley stuff.

Roll with it? Hell, who was he kidding? The truth was, Mason was fucking loving it. Maybe there was a tiny bit of Frieda in him after all, a clingy, desperate part of him that was revelling in Owen's affectionate attention even though he knew it was dangerous. Dangerous for Owen because Mason didn't do long term. Not with anyone.

And for Mason? Well, maybe not dangerous, but certainly distracting. Hell, *Weekend Wellness* was already burbling away in the background, and he hadn't posted a bloody thing all morning. He pulled his phone out of his pocket to quickly check his notifications, wondering if he could possibly persuade Lewis and Aaron to be in a pic with him and Owen —friend groups always played well on Insta—when he caught sight of the time and realised he was too late. Their bit would be starting any moment.

"Hey, it's time," he said. "Owen, it'll be starting soon!"

Lewis grabbed the remote and put the sound up, and they all leaned forward, shushing each other.

Marc was sitting on a sofa next to his co-presenter, Leah, a younger woman with long, dark hair and a strong Lancashire accent. They were finishing off a segment with a guest, a well-known sportswoman who'd just come back from some far-flung trip doing a charity gig of some description.

Once they were done with the sportswoman, Leah turned to Marc and said, "I think you're going to be *very* interested in our next segment."

"Oh yeah?" he replied. "And why's that?"

"Well," she said in an arch tone, smirking at him, "if you remember, you had *quite* the flirtation going with one of our guests a few weeks back—let's remind ourselves of just how that went down."

An edited version of Mason's debut slot on *Weekend Wellness* began to play. It had been made to look much more flirty than it actually had been on the day and culminated in Mason's 'boyfriend material' joke. When the camera cut back to Marc and Leah, Leah was laughing, and Marc was pretending to be mortified, though you could see he loved being the centre of attention.

"Oh, my word," Leah said, fanning herself with one hand. "You were *loving* Mason's chat!"

"What can I say?" Marc replied, shaking his head. "He's a cutie, for sure."

"Well, unfortunately for you, you've got a rival for Mason's affections."

Marc pointed at her. "Hey you, I'm a happily married man," he said, then winked and added, "but tell me who this rival is."

"He's a hot, buff gardening *hunk*," Leah said. "And he's on a mission to teach our lovely—but, let's face it, pretty flaky—Mason how to design and create a garden from scratch. Let's take a look at how their first day went."

Flaky?

Mason's mouth felt suddenly dry, his stomach twisting with nerves. And then there he was, on the TV screen. Doing that cringey intro part.

"Hi. I'm Mason Nash. I'm a model and influencer, but today I'm trading in my Dior high-tops"—he held up a pair of incredibly expensive trainers that were not actually his—"for these." On-screen Mason lifted his other hand, displaying a pair of muddy green wellies, and made an *Ew* face at the camera.

Lewis and Aaron both laughed, and Owen shot Mason a quick grin.

The shot cut to Owen then, who looked bloody delicious, rough and wind-rumpled in his open-necked tattersall shirt, hair delightfully messy, blue eyes all smiley and honest. "Hi, I'm Owen Hunter," he said. "I'm a gardener, and over the next eight weeks, I'm going to be teaching Mason how to design and create a small garden full of amazing plants, flowers and kitchen produce."

The film cut away then to a short montage of them doing stuff in the garden—Mason digging ineffectually while Owen laughed; Owen demonstrating correct digging technique; Owen lifting a heavy bag of soil, muscles straining, while Mason watched admiringly; Mason doing an impression of a puppy capering after Owen; Owen very obviously eyeing up Mason's arse as he bent down to pull up a weed.

"Oh my God," Lewis said, laughter in his voice.

Mason wasn't sure how he felt about it. Part of him was thrilled—this was exactly what he'd wanted, wasn't it?—but part of him was appalled, his stomach churning unpleasantly as he watched. Whatever he thought of it, though, there was no doubt it was cleverly edited. In less than thirty seconds,

JOANNA CHAMBERS & SALLY MALCOLM

the story Misty wanted to tell was clearly established: Mason was cute, clumsy and spoiled; Owen was hunky, competent and kind. And they fancied the pants off each other.

Mason glanced at Owen. His grin had faded. Now he was watching intently, a slight frown between his brows. What was he making of this?

Mason jerked his gaze back to the TV as the music faded out and the actual slot began.

That part was better: straightforward and actually pretty informative. The editor had crammed in an amazing amount of content, partly because the format moved much more quickly than a typical gardening programme. Even with all the content, though, there were still plenty of Mason-Owen moments: Mason asking funny, and sometimes silly, questions and both of them laughing a lot. Mason tripping over and Owen helping him up, his gaze fond.

Mason's chest ached, seeing Owen like that, on TV. So open. Wide open.

Vulnerable.

God, why was he being so weird about this? He'd been teasing his followers on Insta about Owen for weeks and weeks, but now that he was seeing their relationship actually play out on-screen, he felt oddly stripped, his feelings for Owen—and Owen's for him—too obvious for comfort.

He glanced at Owen again, and this time, Owen met his gaze. He smiled at Mason, but it seemed a little forced.

On-screen, Owen was summarising what they'd covered and outlining what they'd be doing "next time", and then it was over, and the show cut back to Marc and Leah in the studio.

"That was great," Leah gushed. "Don't you think, Marc?" She raised an eyebrow at him.

"Those drainage tips will certainly be useful," Marc said. "I've been having some bother with my raised beds, and now I can see where I've been going wrong."

Leah playfully swatted him. "I don't mean that. I mean Mason and Owen. Was it me, or were things starting to sizzle in that garden?"

Marc rolled his eyes. "Are you matchmaking again?"

"I can't help it!" Leah cried. "They're so *cute* together." A couple of the crew behind the cameras laughed—that was a gimmick they used a lot on the show, to make it seem more homey and friendly.

Leah turned to face the camera square-on, addressing the viewers at home. "Let us know what *you* think of our gardening hotties." She rattled off the show's Twitter handle and Insta details.

When she was done, Marc stood up and began walking off, a camera following him.

"Our last guest today wrote her first cookery book when she was just nineteen. Six years on…"

Lewis switched the TV off.

Mason turned warily to the others. Lewis was grinning from ear to ear. Aaron was his usual composed and friendly self. And Owen… Owen looked like Mason felt. Unsure, like he needed time to process.

"That was so good," Aaron said, with every appearance of sincerity. "You two work really well on-screen together, and Owen! My God, you were so *natural*." He gave a soft laugh, then added, "I have to admit to being a little surprised. I mean, you've never been in front of a camera before."

Owen cleared his throat. "That's down to Mason. He put me at ease so much I forgot the cameras were there."

"Who'd have thought?" Lewis said, grinning in obvious delight. "My big brother, a TV star."

Owen huffed, shaking his head. "Hardly that…"

"Why not? Aaron's right—you're a natural. I'm proud of you."

"Thanks," Owen said, but the stitch between his brows

187

deepened. "Mason did most of it, though." Nudging him with his shoulder, he said, "You were fantastic."

"You think?" Hiding his pleasure at the comment, Mason mock-pouted and said, "I didn't come across as too 'flaky'?"

He'd been aiming for a light-hearted tone, but Owen didn't smile. Instead, he said, frowning faintly, "They're certainly playing that up—among other things—but I suppose it's part of your public persona, right?"

Was it? Maybe it was now. It hadn't really been until he appeared on *Weekend Wellness*, but now he thought about it, it was certainly in line with the 'dumb model' dynamic Misty had been pushing from the first time he'd been on the show. Mason hadn't objected, not once. After all, Misty knew what she was doing; she knew how to engage an audience.

Realising that Owen was still waiting for an answer, Mason forced himself to smile. "I suppose," he said lightly. But he didn't feel light. His stomach felt sour and queasy.

A brief silence fell, into which Aaron carefully said, "Were you guys expecting them to focus so much on your relationship? I know Mason's been posting things on social media, but I didn't think it would be such a big part of the slot."

Owen scrubbed a hand through his hair, leaving it standing up in spikes that Mason felt a silly desire to smooth down. As if by doing so he might soothe the unease he sensed in Owen.

"To be honest, I am a bit surprised," Owen admitted, glancing at Mason. "They made us look so…" Colour rose in his face. "I didn't realise I was being so bloody *obvious*."

A pang of guilt speared Mason, but he said, "That *was* the idea, though. Misty said from the start that we should play it up for the camera, right?"

"Well, yeah," Owen said slowly. "I mean, she wanted us to flirt, but that was…" He trailed off, apparently at a loss. "I suppose I'm not as good at acting as you. It all looked way more real than I was expecting."

Mason felt an odd lurch in his stomach, as though he was standing on the deck of a storm-tossed ship. Owen was right: it *had* looked real. Owen's smiles had been fond and unguarded, his feelings blazing through the TV screen. Mason felt a prickling unease that the world had seen the tender shoots of something genuine between him and Owen. Something that was growing in ways he'd never imagined when this whole thing began. Something he shouldn't allow.

And to see it play out like that, cleverly edited to accentuate every flirtatious glance and teasing smile, made it even worse. He was starting to feel… slightly sick.

Over the last few years, Mason had put his whole life online, posting news of his lovers and break-ups with as little thought as he posted pictures of his breakfast or his latest clothing purchase. So, why should this be any different?

But it was.

Somehow, having *this* relationship out there for everyone to see, comment and speculate on, felt different. Far more uncomfortable than he'd expected. And he knew that this was only the start…

Weakly, and more to reassure Owen than because he believed it, he said, "Don't worry. Everyone will know it was just for the camera. It's entertainment, that's all."

Aaron gave a noncommittal hum in response to that assertion, his slightly raised eyebrows a little judgy, and Mason felt his hackles rise.

"The thing about stuff like this," Aaron said, "is that once it gets some traction, the lines between what's real and what's for the camera tend to blur. So… maybe be a little careful? Misty Watson-King is—" He trailed off, uncertainly.

"Fucking ruthless?" Lewis supplied. "I wouldn't trust her as far as I could throw her."

"I was going to say 'focused'," Aaron said, "but yeah. Misty won't hesitate to use your relationship to build her audience."

"Well, that *is* kind of the point?" Mason said shortly, his unease morphing into defensiveness. "We *are* actually trying to build an audience."

Lewis was a fucking dinosaur when it came to social media, and for all Mason knew, Aaron was just as bad. He didn't need their advice about how to build a platform, thank you very much, and opened his mouth to say as much, only to be distracted by an insistent buzzing from his phone.

Notification alerts, a lot of them.

He took a quick look as Owen murmured something to Aaron. Mason didn't catch his words, though, because he was watching, stunned, as his notifications blew up.

"Oh my God," he said, a tentative smile tugging at his lips. "Looks like the viewers *really* liked it." He held out his still-buzzing phone to Owen. "Look."

Peering at the screen, Owen barked out a laugh, although it sounded slightly alarmed. "Right, wow…"

Mason's heart began to race. "Okay," he said breathlessly. "We need to post something."

"*Now?*"

"Of course now! Come here." He snuggled back against Owen, glad that he was wearing one of Owen's company t-shirts and that his hair screamed bed-head. "Okay, look at the camera and smile…"

Owen sighed; Mason felt the heave of his chest against his back, and his stomach clenched unhappily. Even so, Owen managed a smile, though it was noticeably less easy than usual. Which was okay. It was *fine*.

Snapping a few pics, he found a good one, cropped it and fiddled with the filters, pleased with how a jug of tulips was visible on the counter behind them.

Brunch and #WeekendWellness with my gardening bestie @OwenHunterGardens! #love #me

The likes and replies came flooding in immediately, which was gratifying and cheering. Alongside them came several messages on WhatsApp: excited gushing from Frieda and his sisters, congratulations from Misty, and a message from Frankie asking whether Owen was looking for an agent.

Mason laughed as he sent a quick reply to Frieda. "Hey, Owen. Frankie, my agent, wants to know whether you're looking for representation."

"Er, what?"

"That's actually a good idea," Lewis said. "You should definitely get an agent."

Owen sat forward on the sofa, dislodging Mason, who'd still been sprawled against him. He glanced up as they shifted around, unsettled by Owen's frown and by the way he was running both hands anxiously through his hair. "I don't need an agent."

"If you'd had an agent look over your contract with Misty," Lewis said repressively, "it wouldn't have that ridiculous promo clause."

Owen shrugged. "Fine, okay, but it's not like I'm going to be doing any more of this stuff."

"Why not?" Lewis said, grabbing the last of the pastries—a limp pain aux raisins—and shoving half of it in his mouth at once.

"Er, because I have a business to run?"

"Yeah, but this is…" Lewis stopped as Aaron put a hand on his thigh.

"What?" Owen said with a mulishness Mason hadn't seen before. "*Better*?"

"No," Lewis said with exaggerated patience. "Better paid, though."

At first, Owen looked like he wanted to argue, but the next moment, the expression fled, leaving his face curiously blank. As if he'd slammed shut a fire door. Standing, he said, "Anyone want another tea or coffee? Anything else?"

"Actually," Aaron said, also rising, "we should be off,

leave you guys to chill out like you were planning before we gate-crashed."

"We don't have to—" Lewis began, then caught Aaron's eye and shut up, shoving the rest of his pastry into his mouth.

"Congratulations again," Aaron said, his gaze moving between them. "Your segment was brilliant."

He smiled, but there was something cool and assessing in his eyes when he looked at Mason that made Mason feel a bit... grubby.

Standing, Mason slipped his arm around Owen's waist, welcoming the steady warmth and strength of his body. "Nice to see you both. And thanks for breakfast."

Lewis nodded. "Think about the agent," he told his brother, even as Aaron grabbed his hand and led him firmly towards the front door.

Owen didn't respond to that, almost appearing not to hear.

"See you both soon!" Aaron called over his shoulder. "We'll see ourselves out."

A few moments later came the sound of the front door closing, then silence.

Mason looked at Owen, taking in his closed-off expression. "Hey," he said, drawing Owen's attention, "where did you go?"

Owen blinked. "Go?"

"It's like you checked out for a moment." He cocked his head, considering. "You didn't like what Lewis said?"

Owen sighed, visibly coming back to himself. "I know he's trying to be helpful," he said, "but... I've spent years building up my business and about six weeks on this TV stuff. And *this* is what he's proud of?"

"I'm sure he's proud of you for lots of things."

"Yeah, maybe. He's certainly more interested in *Weekend Wellness* than he's ever been in my gardening business, though." He gestured around him. "Or this house, or my garden. Both of which are things *I'm* really proud of having, even if they aren't as fancy as Lewis's."

Mason studied his face. The earnestness and hurt in Owen's pale blue eyes felt like a dart piercing his chest. A sudden, unexpected pain. That had to be Mason recognising something of his own experience in Owen's, though. Nothing more profound than the sense of connection you sometimes felt when you found a fellow traveller.

Carefully, Mason said, "I understand. The only interest Frieda and Kurt ever took in my chef training was when I got them freebies in restaurants, but as soon as Frankie offered me the chance to model..." He shrugged. "In their minds it was a no-brainer that I'd take up the offer, even though I loved—still love—to cook. Fame and fortune, I suppose."

"There's more to life than fame and bloody fortune." Owen's expression had softened, though, and he looked more like himself as he lifted a hand to stroke the back of his fingers against Mason's cheek.

Smiling, Mason took his hand, turned it over and pressed a kiss to Owen's knuckles. And, despite the swell of arousal that was never far from the surface when he was around Owen, Mason heard himself saying, "Will you show me around your garden?"

Owen huffed a soft laugh. "You don't need to—"

"I want to." He threaded their fingers together. "I want to know about the things that are important to you."

And so, he found himself outside in the chilly spring morning, letting Owen show him around his small but meticulously nurtured square of garden.

"It smells so green," Mason marvelled as Owen led him down the artfully designed stone path that wound through the planting beds, somehow making the garden feel far bigger than it could possibly be.

A brick wall ran along the back of the garden, the well-trained stems of a plant growing along a section of trellis.

"This is an Albertine rose," Owen explained. "It'll be beautiful in June, absolutely covered in soft pink flowers that smell amazing…"

He went on, describing the plants growing happily in their beds, explaining what he was going to plant as soon as he had time. "Tomatoes here," he said, gesturing to another spot on the wall. "Plenty of sun, there. And this is a raspberry bush."

"Ooh." Mason's interest was piqued. "What kind of tomatoes?"

"I've tried a few over the years, but my favourites are *Astro Ibrido*. They're a plum tomato, and really flavourful. Quite sweet." He laughed. "I usually end up dropping off bags of them with the neighbours, though. There's only so many cheese-and-tomato sandwiches a man can eat."

"Oh my God!" Mason faked outrage. "Do *not* give them away. Or at least give some to me. I'll make you the best chicken cacciatore you've ever eaten. Ooh, and pan con tomate for breakfast."

Owen seemed to like that idea, because he grinned widely. "Okay, you're on."

"Do you grow any other fruit and veg? I love cooking with fresh produce. Most of the stuff you buy in shops is so flavourless, and I never have time to go to proper markets anymore."

"Strawberries will be ripe in July." He nodded to where several hanging pots cascaded artfully down the tall fence, short leafy stems peeking over the tops. "Beans, courgettes. They're easy, though, but my secret project…" He laughed, clearly self-conscious. "It's just for fun, but I'm attempting to grow pineapples in here."

"Pineapples!" Mason exclaimed, astonished.

"Yes, come see."

Owen led Mason to a small greenhouse tucked into the back corner of the garden.

"It can take up to three years for the plants to develop fruit, and I only planted these last summer, so they definitely won't fruit this year. They're growing well, though, and looking pretty healthy. See? I propagated them using the topknots of pineapples I bought at the supermarket."

"No way! That's brilliant." Mason examined the plants that did indeed look like the tops of large pineapples in pots. He pulled out his phone. "Mind if I post a pic?"

"Of a pineapple plant?"

"Well, of a pineapple plant and *you*."

Owen ran a hand through his hair again. "I don't know…"

"Please?" He fluttered his lashes. "Pretty please with a cherry on top?"

Owen laughed, shaking his head. "All right," he said, sighing as he crouched down next to the pots, strong thighs stretching the fabric of his jeans.

"Very nice." Mason gave him a long, lascivious look. "Very nice *indeed*."

And it *was* nice because unlike in the previous pic, Owen's genuine smile was back, the April sunshine glinting in his hair and a mischievous sparkle in his eyes as he gazed up at the camera. At Mason.

A soft, warming sensation filled Mason's heart as he studied the photo.

Too good to post.

The odd idea came from nowhere—a silly, counterintuitive notion. As if there was such a thing as a photo being *too good* to post. If you didn't post it, what was the point of taking it in the first place? Jettisoning the thought, he opened Insta.

Guess what @OwenHunterGardens grows in his greenhouse? (Don't say eggplants!) #GrowYourOwn #HealthyLifestyles #love #me

He'd just posted it when a large hand closed over his phone, obscuring the screen.

Looking up, he smiled to find Owen watching him with a

decidedly wicked gleam in his eyes. "I think it's time you put that away," he said in a voice that had Mason's cock filling fast.

Breath catching, he whispered, "Are you going to make me?"

"Are you going to resist?"

Mason grinned. "Maybe."

"Mmm." Owen slid one arm around Mason's waist, tugging him flush against his body. "That would be very, *very* naughty."

Mason pouted dramatically. "Then you should probably do something about it."

"Oh yeah," Owen murmured, nuzzling his neck, just below his ear, close enough that the words caressed Mason's skin. "I plan to…"

CHAPTER SIXTEEN

Frankie Slade, Mason's agent, was ecstatic about *Weekend Wellness*.

"Almost 9000 new followers!" he crowed when they met for breakfast a few days later. "And that's after just one slot. You're knocking on the door of 100K, Mase! And when we hit that magic number, we trigger the additional fee in the *Masculin* contract. Plus, Maya says there's two new deals just out this week we can put you forward for."

Mason poked at his egg white omelette. He'd ordered it to save himself a lecture—Frankie would have him living on oxygen and protein smoothies if it was up to him. "Yeah," he said, pasting on a smile. "I'm pretty stoked."

He *was* pretty stoked, actually, but that "we" Frankie used grated on him. Frankie had done nothing to help him with his influencer work. In fact, he'd been downright dismissive of it until *Masculin* had told him they were interested in Mason. That—well, the money they'd waved under his nose—had got Frankie's attention.

Frankie was fundamentally old school. He'd been in the

business for years, and modelling was what he knew best—and he *did* get Mason great modelling work; Mason had no complaints about him on that front—but whenever Mason tried to talk to him about developing his career in another direction, away from modelling, Frankie didn't even bother to hide his lack of interest. Or, maybe, lack of knowledge. Mason had the uneasy feeling that his relationship with Frankie had reached its sell-by date, and he wasn't sure what to do about it.

After breakfast, he headed out to Finchley for a casting. He didn't have to go to a whole lot of castings these days, but this was for a big job: the Christmas shoot for a well-known fragrance line. There would only be a handful of models there, all hand-picked for the shortlist.

The casting went well. He was friendly with the casting director, Dev, and the clients seemed to like him. They certainly made sure they got plenty of shots and film of him.

"I saw you on TV the other day," Dev said, as he walked him out, his hand on Mason's shoulder. "That was a very cute little piece you did with that gardener hunk. Where did you find him?"

Mason laughed. "Owen? He's Lewis Hunter's brother."

"Lewis that you used to…?" Dev trailed off meaningfully, his eyebrows raised.

Mason flushed. "That was over ages ago. It was nothing. We were never serious."

"Yeah, course," Dev said casually, though Mason knew he probably remembered the conversation they'd had over cocktails last year when Mason had complained about Lewis dumping him. Which was embarrassing on a number of levels, not least the fact that he'd been more irate about having to find a last-minute replacement to go to the British Fashion Awards with him than the fact that their relationship was over.

What was more disturbing even than that memory,

though, was the fact that he found himself wanting to tell Dev that he was with Owen now. That Lewis's hunky gardener brother was *his*. Jesus, what was *wrong* with him?

After he and Dev said goodbye, promising to meet up for drinks soon, Mason remembered that the café Tag O'Rourke worked at was nearby. He hadn't seen Tag—or Jay for that matter—since the night of the awards dinner. He'd texted back and forth with both of them a couple of times after that night, and it had been pretty friendly, but still, the last time he'd seen Tag face to face, he'd been drunk and pissed off, and since he was at a loose end, it would be easy to pop by to break the ice.

And if Tag wasn't there? Well, he could do with a coffee anyway.

Zipping up his jacket, Mason crossed the road and headed in the direction of the café. When he got there, the place was pretty quiet, just a handful of occupied tables and no line. And yes, Tag was in, busily cleaning up some drinks equipment in the sinks behind the counter while another barista stocked up the bakery cabinet with fresh pastries.

"Hey, Tag," Mason said as he approached the counter. When Tag turned, his eyes widened in surprise. Then he smiled, a bright, happy smile that lit up his whole face and made Mason's own mouth curve in response. Tag was always bemoaning the state of his acting career, but Mason was convinced that one day he was going to make it big. He just had that elusive *something,* and it was most obvious in that smile. He'd make a great model actually, but when Mason had offered to introduce him to Frankie, Tag had declined. He wanted to be an actor—a *serious* actor—and he was worried about acquiring a "model-turned-actor" label. Which was fair enough. Mason knew all too well the judgments people made about models' intellectual abilities. So, instead, Tag kept working here, and for his dad's construction company, as he tried to build up his acting CV.

JOANNA CHAMBERS & SALLY MALCOLM

"Mason," Tag said warmly. "Good to see you, mate! It's been bloody ages. You here for lunch?"

"Just a coffee," Mason said. "Have you got time for a quick break?"

"Lou," Tag called over to the other barista. "I'm going to take my break just now. That okay with you?"

"Go ahead," she called back without looking up. "You want me to bring your coffees over?"

"Nah, I've got 'em." Tag glanced at Mason. "Black Americano?"

"Please."

"Grab a seat. I'll be over in a minute."

Mason wandered over to his favourite table. It was next to the window and had two big comfy armchairs. He settled into one of them, and a few minutes later, Tag arrived with two coffees and a massive chocolate brownie.

"Want some?" Tag asked, pointing at the brownie.

It looked gooey and awesome, but Mason shook his head regretfully. God, he was bored of watching his diet so carefully.

Tag had no such reservations. He took a huge bite and washed it down with a slurp of latte before leaning back in his chair and sighing contentedly. "You'd think I'd get fed up with these brownies, but I never do." He gave a rueful smile. "I'm glad you dropped by, Mason. I've been feeling really shitty about what happened at the awards dinner." His face reddened. "How Jay and I were acting, I mean. You were totally right."

Mason waved that off. "That whole thing of fake-dating you both at the same time wasn't the best idea from the start. I mean, don't get me wrong, I got some great content—"

"Especially from Jay, right?" Tag said, raising a brow.

"From both of you," Mason said firmly. "I mean, Jay's famous so obviously I got a lot of likes on any post he was in, but my followers adored you."

Tag grinned at that. "Okay, I'm assuming that's code for 'Tag's content was better and he's a lot cuter.'"

Mason laughed. "*Still* so competitive?"

Tag laughed too, then his expression grew more serious and he said, "Look, it wasn't all fake for me. I really did enjoy our dates. I had a lot of fun with you." He paused, then added, "So... can we still be friends who go out together sometimes, just to have fun?"

The sincerity in Tag's gaze made Mason feel unexpectedly emotional. Maybe because Tag's friendship was what he'd really wanted all along, but hadn't known how to get it. Dates were a dime a dozen in Mason's world, but friendship? That was rare. "Yeah," he managed to get out in a hoarse voice. "That would be good. I'd really like to be your friend, Tag."

Tag grinned at that, another of those bright million-dollar smiles that were going to make him famous one day, and Mason couldn't help but grin back.

After that, they chatted easily while they drank their coffee. Tag gave him the latest on his TV debut show, *Bow Street*—the first season had finished filming a few weeks ago, and everyone was hoping it would be well-received. If a second season was commissioned, Tag's role would be expanded. In the meantime, Tag had auditioned for a theatre role.

"Do you think you'll get it?" Mason asked.

Tag made a face. "The audition went well, and I think the director wants me, but the money guys want someone famous." He sighed. "They might offer me the understudy role, I suppose. It'd be better than nothing." Then he brightened. "Anyway, what about you and Owen on *Weekend Wellness*? That's awesome, man!"

Mason grinned, pleased. "I know, right? Landing it was pretty much a fluke."

"Fluke or not, you were amazing. You're a natural presenter." Tag raised his brows. "Any chance you might slip into Marc's role? I hear he's thinking about moving on."

"How did you hear that?"

"Friends on the inside," Tag said with a wink. "I met a couple of the *Weekend Wellness* crew at the RPP Hallowe'en party. We meet up for drinks sometimes."

"You are unbelievable," Mason said, laughing. "I swear, you *always* know someone."

"Hey, I'm a friendly guy!"

"Yeah, you are," Mason said fondly.

"Anyway," Tag continued. "If Marc does move on, you have to be in the running."

"Maybe as a rank outsider," Mason said drily. Funny, the thought of landing Marc's role just didn't seem as exciting right now as it had when Misty had first hinted at it. "I'm still very inexperienced."

"Don't be so modest," Tag said. "You were really good."

"Yeah, but that's partly down to Owen. I'm not sure I'd have been as comfortable if I hadn't been working with him. Talking to him just felt really natural, even though it was on camera. I didn't even have to think about it that much."

"He is a great listener," Tag said, "and an incredibly nice guy." He waggled his eyebrows. "Is there anything behind all the flirting you two were doing on-screen, or was that just for the cameras?"

Mason gave a secret sly smile. "There *might* be."

"Ooooh!" Tag responded, clearly intrigued. "Tell me all about it!"

"It's early days," Mason hedged. "Maybe I'll fill you in more when we meet up next."

Tag eyed him for a moment, then sighed. "Fine," he said, pointing at Mason, "but next time, you dish. I'll text you about meeting up next week." He stood up then and began collecting their dishes together. "It's back to the grindstone for me. The lunch rush will be starting soon."

"Yeah, I should get going too," Mason replied, standing and reaching for his jacket. He paused midway, turning to look at Tag again. "By the way—"

"Yeah?"

"Did you and Jay take my advice that night?"

"Your advice?" Tag said, frowning.

Mason's lips quirked, and he raised a brow. "The advice about fucking each other's brains out?"

This time when Tag flushed, his pale complexion turned beetroot. "Jesus, Mason!" he hissed, looking around furtively, though there was no one else anywhere near them to overhear.

Mason chuckled. "I'll take that as a *no*," he said. "But I still think you should consider it. All that tension between you *definitely* has a sexual edge."

He left Tag spluttering in the middle of the café.

Once he was outside, Mason checked his phone. There were loads of notifications, most of them comments cooing over his latest Owen-related post, and a bunch of new follows, bringing him up to over 94,000. His numbers were steadily increasing every day, and he was excited to see what would happen after the second *Weekend Wellness* slot aired on Saturday.

Would Owen want to repeat last week's sleepover and breakfast so they could watch their slot together? For a moment, he was tempted to shoot Owen a quick text suggesting just that. So tempting that he shut it down immediately. Spending cosy Saturday mornings together was the sort of coupley behaviour that might give Owen unrealistic expectations about the direction of their relationship—and hurting Owen was the last thing Mason wanted to do.

He was frowning over that thought when he realised he

had three voicemails waiting for him, two from Frieda and one from his sister, Melody. If that wasn't a message from the universe, he didn't know what was.

Stomach tensing anxiously, he listened to the first message.

"Angel, it's Mel. Listen, Dad's missed his payment again, and Mum's freaking out. We need to pay the balance of our school French trip by Monday, and she's saying we have to cancel because now she needs your money for the gas bill! Can you call me? *Please?*"

Mason's stomach twisted. *Fucking hell.* Another bloody family drama.

He really didn't want to listen to the two messages from Frieda after that, but he did anyway, and clearly, she was, as Mel had said, freaking out. Tearfully, in that feeble, tremulous voice he so dreaded, Frieda went on about how she didn't know what to do, and how Kurt's new girlfriend was turning him against his family, and how her nerves were making her stomach play up again, and then she started sobbing, and Mason's anxiety pinched so hard he felt sick.

He couldn't deal with this, not again. It wasn't fair. It wasn't fucking *fair*. He was sick of Frieda's feebleness, but he was even more sick of Kurt's fucking selfishness and the fact that things only ever got sorted out when Mason gave him shit about it.

He began striding towards the nearest tube station and texted Kurt. *Are you in?*

Kurt worked from home most days, home being a tiny flat in Tufnell Park that he shared with his bloody awful, whiny girlfriend, Regan. They worked for the same charity, Kurt in a senior policy role and Regan in the communications team. Regan was only a few years older than Mason and one of the worst people Mason had ever met, but she looked a bit like his mum twenty years ago, which seemed to be the main qualifying criterion for becoming one of Kurt's serial live-in girlfriends.

A minute later, he got a reply. *Yup. Bit busy tho.*

Just need 5 mins, Mason texted back. *Be there soon.*

He called Frieda then, who immediately started sniffling down the phone again. He let her talk for a while, but as he got closer to the tube station, he cut her off. "Listen. I'm on my way to Kurt's just now. I'll talk to him, okay?"

She let out a big, shaky breath, and he felt a complicated pang that mingled sympathy, anxiety, irritation and love. His mother's emotional dependency drove him round the bend sometimes, but he knew the years since Kurt had left hadn't been easy on her.

"What would I do without you, Angel?" she said, still sniffing. "Can you call me again after? I'm supposed to send the money for the girls' school trip tomorrow and—"

"I know," Mason said soothingly. "Mel told me. Just—look, don't worry about that. I already told you I'd cover it, didn't I?"

She made a pained noise, then mumbled, "You've already given me the money for that. I shouldn't have to ask you for more. I just want Kurt to pay what he owes me."

Mason wanted that too, but he knew chances were high he'd have to sub Frieda till Kurt's money came through. And it wasn't like he'd ask for the money back.

After the tube ride, it was a ten-minute walk to Kurt's flat. By the time he got there, he'd had half an hour to work himself up into a spectacularly bad mood over the whole debacle, so he leaned obnoxiously on the doorbell till Kurt let him in, then pounded up the three flights of stairs to Kurt's floor. He was ready to pound on the door too, but it was open for him to walk right in. Kurt was nowhere to be seen. Plainly, he already had the measure of Mason's mood.

Mason stepped inside and slammed the door closed behind him.

"I'm in the bedroom," Kurt called out in a tight voice.

Mason followed his voice, and when he poked his head round the door, it was to find his dad standing over two open, half-packed carry-on suitcases. Kurt didn't look up as Mason walked in, just continued with his task of folding up a shirt.

"I presume Frieda called you," Kurt said tightly.

"It was Mel who called first, actually," Mason said and had the satisfaction of seeing Kurt wince. He did look up then, his expression wary.

Mason was going to look a lot like Kurt when he was older. Mason had an inch or two on his dad, but other than that, they were very similar. They had the same lean, fit physique, the same fair hair—though Kurt's was mostly silver now—the same green eyes. The same blessedly symmetrical features.

It was probably why Kurt, despite being far from loaded, had managed to land a succession of young and beautiful women after walking out on Frieda. And the idea that he and Mason might be alike in that way too, that Mason might one day turn into his dad, sickened him.

"Why did Mel call?"

"Has she mentioned a French school trip to you?" Mason asked in a hard voice. "The girls are signed up, and the balance is due Monday."

Kurt groaned and dropped his head into his hands.

"Frieda told Mel this morning she can't pay it—because you've *fucking* failed to pay up *again*, and now Frieda's having a breakdown over it."

Kurt scrubbed his hands up and down his face, saying nothing.

"Jesus Christ, Kurt. You do *fuck all* for this family. The only thing, the *one* thing, you're asked to do is pay that monthly money to Frieda, and you can't even be relied on to do that." Mason slammed the heel of his hand against the door frame. "*Jesus.*"

"Hey, that's not fair!" Kurt exclaimed, dropping his hands. "I'm just a bit late sometimes."

"You're *regularly* late, and you missed January completely! Probably because you had to pay off your credit card after using that month's money to buy Christmas presents for Regan. You certainly didn't spend it on the girls!"

Kurt scowled at his suitcase. "I gave Frieda extra in February."

"An extra hundred quid? Didn't exactly make up the deficit, did it? And I should know because *I* had to make it up. Just like I do every time you're late. And that's on top of the extra rent money I already give her, not to mention paying for all the other stuff the girls need because, apparently, *you* can't afford another penny."

"I can't!" Kurt yelled. "Bloody hell, Angel, I'm barely scraping by as it is!"

"Yeah?" Mason yelled back, gesturing at the suitcases on the bed. "So, what's this? You and Regan off for another little mini-break, are you?"

Kurt flushed. "It's her birthday."

"Oh, how nice!" Mason said sarcastically. "Where are you going?"

Kurt squirmed. "Rome."

Mason laughed, a bitter, angry sound. "Rome, right. Of course. So, you need Frieda's child maintenance money to wine and dine Regan for her birthday. Have I got that right?"

Kurt's shoulders slumped. "I'm sorry," he muttered. Mason gave a snort of disbelief, and Kurt looked up. "I *am* sorry—but I only do it because I know you're there for them. If they didn't have a safety net, I wouldn't leave them in the lurch."

A familiar feeling of angry hurt churned in Mason's gut. "Safety net," he repeated flatly. "That's how you see me? The family safety net?"

Kurt gave a harsh laugh of his own then. "Well, let's face

it. You earn a damn sight more than I ever will. And don't forget that Frieda doesn't earn a—"

"Leave her out of it!" Mason snarled. "You left her to bring up twin toddlers and a thirteen-year-old on her own— you're in no fucking position to criticise!"

"I know. I know I screwed up with your mother. I know I made a big mistake, and I'm sorry. You've no idea how much I regret my actions. I just—" Kurt broke off, swallowing hard, his eyes glittering with what looked like real tears. "I think Regan's seeing someone else. I think she's going to—"

Mason held up a hand and stepped back. "Stop," he said. "I really don't want to hear this."

Kurt screwed up his eyes and pinched the bridge of his nose. "Please, Angel, I just need to talk to *someone*."

And now his dad was doing the *Poor Old Me* act. Christ, this was exhausting.

Mason ran an impatient hand through his hair. He wanted to hold on to his anger, but despite everything, it was difficult when his dad was standing there looking crushed. "Kurt, trust me on this one," he said firmly. "You *don't* want to have a conversation about Regan with me. I know you think the sun shines out of her arse, but I really don't feel the same way, and if you insist on talking about her, I'm not going to be able to hold back."

Kurt nodded. "Okay," he whispered. "Can we—can we maybe sit down and have this talk over a cuppa?"

"So long as talking about it results in you paying up," Mason said bluntly. "I've got to phone Frieda after this and tell her what you're going to do to sort it out."

"Yeah," Kurt said. "Yeah, I know. And you're right." He tossed the shirt, which he'd balled up between his hands, onto the bed. "Come on, I'll put the kettle on."

By the time Mason left the flat an hour later, they had an agreed plan. Kurt was going to pay half this month's payment now, and half in two weeks, once his salary came through. In the meantime, Mason would cover the girls' French trip and give Frieda what she needed to tide her over until the end of the month. Kurt had also promised that next month's payment would be made in full and on time—that seemed pretty unlikely to be honest, and Mason was already resigned to repeating this scene again in a few weeks.

As he was leaving the flat, Kurt caught his arm. "I forgot to ask how *you* are," he said, flushing a little. "Sorry. Whenever I see you, we always seem to talk about me and Frieda and our problems."

Mason paused in the doorway. He honestly couldn't be bothered with this, after parenting his own father for the last hour. "I'm fine," he said woodenly.

"I see you've been doing some television—that's great."

"Yeah. Thanks."

They stared at one another.

"It's good to see you making a success of things," Kurt persisted, adding a tentative smile. "You've achieved a lot."

"I don't know about that. I'm a model, not a brain surgeon."

"Don't put yourself down. You've made a good career out of this, and you're developing into TV now. It's impressive. I know it may not seem like it, sometimes, but I'm really proud of you."

And maybe that should have meant something to Mason, but the sad truth was, it didn't.

It was only later, as he was sitting on the train going back to his own flat—after phoning Frieda and reassuring her he'd sorted everything out—that he realised why that was. The sad fact was that what Kurt valued most about him, what his whole family valued most about him, was his earning power. His dad had made that very clear with his safety net comment.

And God, was Mason sick of being a safety net.

Being a safety net was exhausting and thankless, and

worst of all, it was fucking *unfair*. And he couldn't escape it. His dad was unreliable. His mum was fragile and dependent. The girls needed stuff, and why should they suffer when Mason could help them? He wanted them to go to university. He wanted them to have chances he'd missed out on. But at the same time, he wanted to shove the heavy yoke of responsibility off his own shoulders.

What would have happened if Mason had walked away that day Frankie stopped him in the street and handed Mason his card? What if he'd tossed it? What if he'd stayed at the restaurant, working his arse off for a pittance? His parents would have *had* to manage.

That thought made him feel weird. Almost dizzy, as he imagined a different life, one where he wasn't on TV, where he was pretty much broke but doing work he was passionate about.

What if.

He thought about it all the way home.

What if.

CHAPTER SEVENTEEN

Something prickled between Owen's shoulder blades.

Unfortunately, it had nothing to do with the rambling rose he was training along the trellis he and Mac had just fixed to the garden wall of the pretty Victorian terraced house they were working at.

"I reckon you've pulled," Mac said under her breath as she started shovelling wood chip mulch around the newly-planted rose.

Owen flushed, which was ridiculous, but it was just so… odd. "She's really not my type."

His type, apparently, being gorgeous twenty-something male models with pouty lips, grass-green eyes, and a penchant for being taken care of, which somehow managed to soften Owen's heart and harden his cock all at the same time.

Mason had him dizzy, that was for sure. Even now he smiled at the memory of waking up on Thursday morning with Mason snuggled up next to him after they'd shagged each other senseless the night before.

Mason had come over unexpectedly, all riled up about his

parents and prickly as a hedgehog, hadn't wanted to talk, hadn't wanted to eat, had just prowled around Owen's kitchen with a look of needy desperation in his eyes.

Owen had known exactly what he'd wanted. No, what he'd *needed*. Like any other rare and beautiful bloom, Mason needed specific care and attention. Luckily, Owen knew exactly how to give it to him.

And give it to him he had, right there against the kitchen wall with Mason's legs wrapped around his waist, begging to come as Owen pounded into him. And then they'd gone for a second round in the bedroom.

Mason had been out like a light afterwards, falling asleep with his head against Owen's shoulder, one arm draped over his waist, and Owen's heart had swelled until it felt too big for his body. He'd kissed Mason's hair, felt his eyes burn, and known with joyful dismay that he was falling helplessly in love.

That he'd already fallen.

"She's not even pretending now," Mac muttered. "She's just fucking staring at you."

"She" was their client's next-door neighbour. Owen and Mac had been working this job for a day and a half—a full redesign of a small, city garden. Usually, it was one of Owen's favourite types of job. Not big or ostentatious, but satisfying. The garden was west-facing, which was great for sun later in the day, with the challenge of some deep shade cast by the flats that had gone up one street over, and a nice square shape to elongate with the clever use of design. The client, Verity, was nice too. An easy-going single woman in her sixties, she had a clear idea of what she wanted from the space but was only too happy to leave the details of the design and planting choices to Owen.

So, yeah, he'd have been as happy as Larry if Verity's much younger neighbour hadn't spent the whole time watching him and Mac through her upstairs window as they worked.

A few minutes later, Mac said, "I'm going to get another bag of mulch from the van. Need anything else?"

"Nah, I'm going to put that forsythia in, then take a break." By which he meant escape the neighbour's weird attention and see if Mason had messaged him. Which he probably had, since he was wedded to his phone.

The garden was accessed by a back gate that led onto an alleyway that ran behind the terrace of houses, and Mac headed out that way to find the van. Parking was a nightmare, and even with the resident permit Verity had given them, they'd still had to park halfway down the road.

After Mac left, Owen tied up the last of the rose's little branches. Standing back, he took a moment to admire how it looked against the wall and to imagine what it would be like in a couple of years, twining up the trellis.

Behind him, he heard the kitchen door open.

"Oh, it's looking so lovely!" Verity said warmly.

Owen turned around. "Yeah," he said, then froze when he saw that Verity was not alone. Another woman had followed her out into the garden—the neighbour who'd been watching them.

Forcing a smile, Owen told himself that she was just another potential client, but there was something avid in her expression that made him want to back up a step.

"I hope you don't mind," Verity said apologetically, gesturing towards the woman, who Owen could now see was probably in her late twenties or early thirties. "But apparently, Jen here saw you on television"—she gestured at the woman and cleared her throat awkwardly—"and, um, she asked to meet you." Verity's eyes pleaded for understanding. "She's my neighbour."

Jen blurted, "I'd love a selfie."

Owen stared at her. "What?"

"I'm such a fan," she gushed.

"You're a fan of *Weekend Wellness*?" he asked doubtfully.

Jen frowned as though puzzled; then her expression cleared. "God, no," she laughed. "I'm a fan of *Mason Nash*. Been following him on Instagram forever. He's so funny and cute and—well, beautiful, obviously."

Owen stared at her, taken aback.

"You and Mason are *adorable*," she added quickly, as though worried she'd offended him. "I *totally* ship you. Like, massively."

"Oh." Owen felt his ears burning, remembering that shot of him ogling Mason's arse. "Right. Um, thanks."

Jen lifted her phone and shook it. "So… selfie time?"

Owen made a pained expression. "I—"

But Jen was already moving towards him, swiping at the screen as she went. "You don't mind, do you?" she said, her tone clearly indicating that she neither expected nor required an answer.

And then she was right beside him, one arm sliding around his waist, her head canting onto his shoulder in a too-intimate pose that made him feel trapped and uncomfortable.

Gaze fixed on her phone, she took several bursts of images —hell, there would be loads in there, some of them probably awful. Owen glanced at Verity, who sent back a look of help-less apology.

"You're *so* lucky working with Mason," Jen said wistfully as she pocketed her phone again. "Is he even more gorgeous in real life?"

"Er…" Owen felt himself redden further. How the hell was he supposed to answer that? Would she write about this on social media? Shit, Mason would know what to do, but Owen didn't have a clue.

"And is it *real*?" Jen said, her eyes gleaming fervently. "*Please* tell me it's real."

"Real?"

"You and him," she said. "All the flirting and the posts on Instagram? Are you and he…you know, *together*?"

Verity said awkwardly, "I think you might be getting rather personal, Jen."

Jen just laughed. "Oh, don't worry. This isn't personal. These guys *love* people shipping them. If they didn't, Mason wouldn't be posting cute pics of them together all over the internet, would he?" She turned back to Owen and smiled. "You don't mind me asking, do you? Mason's always so wonderfully open about his life. It's one of the things I love about him. That and his bum—ohmygod, so squeezable!" She giggled. "You can tell him that from me."

Owen honestly didn't know what to say to that. Mason *was* kind of open about his life—well, the curated version of it—but Owen wasn't, and this conversation was making him really uncomfortable. It was like she thought she *knew* him.

Finally, Verity seemed to cotton on to his discomfort. "Well," she said briskly. "Jen and I should let you get back to work."

Owen flashed her a grateful look. "We do have quite a lot to get through, if you don't mind."

Jen looked quite put out at that—in fact, she looked like she was about to protest—but just then the back gate swung open, and Mac appeared, lugging a heavy bag of mulch.

"Ah, there you are, April," Verity said, blithely using the Christian name that Mac absolutely hated. "Would you like a cup of tea? What about you, Owen?"

"I'd bloody love one," Mac said. "Milk and one sugar, please."

"Yeah," Owen agreed quickly. "That would be great. Just milk for me." He watched, relieved, as Verity began to steer Jen away. "Come on, Jen. I'll make you one too, before you go."

"I guess I'll just have to keep up to date with Mason's

posts to find out how things go," Jen grumbled, but she let herself be tugged away.

Owen grabbed his spade to get back to work.

Turning, he saw Mac busying herself opening the bag of mulch while failing to hide her grin. "She actually came down to meet you?"

Owen shut his eyes, leaning on the spade, feeling its edge sink into the well-tilled soil. "She wanted a selfie," he muttered.

Mac chuckled. "I hope you're not going to start getting all high and mighty now you're famous. We can't be having you slacking off to sign autographs."

Owen wished he could find it funny, but honestly, that little scene had... bothered him. The fact that a random stranger had seen so much of what felt intensely private between him and Mason *bothered* him. And he hated that she'd probably see even more of it when the next episode aired that weekend.

"Why the hell does she think it's any of her sodding business?" he muttered, stamping his foot on the spade and digging it into the earth. "For God's sake."

After a pause, Mac said, "Well, it *was* on telly. What did you think would happen?"

Owen looked up and met his friend's gaze. "I don't know," he confessed. "But I didn't expect this."

Neither had he expected his feelings for Mason to bloom so fast, nor to root so deep. That was the worst of it, having something so tender and new so ruthlessly exposed.

Yet this was what Mason did—it was all part of building his public profile. Owen had scrolled through quite a lot of his old Instagram posts now, and yes, Jay, Tag, and even Lewis were all featured in there, along with a bunch of other guys. In fact, it seemed like Mason had a new man to show off every few weeks. Which made Owen wonder glumly whether Mason would soon be looking for someone new in his life.

He was still mulling that over at the end of the day, when he and Mac got back to the small unit where he kept his fleet of three vans and all the equipment and materials he bought wholesale.

Mac reached for her ciggies as soon as she got out of the van, leaving one unlit in the corner of her mouth as they unloaded their gear and took it inside. Owen made a point of never leaving anything in the van overnight. Not that this was a dodgy area, but good tools were expensive and he didn't like taking risks.

As he shouldered his way into the store room, he saw Mac standing talking to Naaz. She was showing her phone to Mac, one hand over her mouth and her eyes wide. "...think I should say anything?" she was asking.

"About what?" Owen said.

Naaz jumped and almost dropped her phone. "Shit. I mean, sorry. Er…" Her cheeks darkened, and her eyes widened even further.

Owen looked at Mac for an explanation.

She sighed heavily, shook her head, and held out her hand for Naaz's phone.

"My friend sent it to me," Naaz said, handing over her phone. "I didn't know whether to say anything, but…"

Hanging up his spade on its hook, Owen braced himself. "Is this about the TV thing?" he said, stomping over to Mac.

"Some bollocks by the look of it," Mac said, showing him the phone.

He peered at the screen, not quite sure what he was seeing, and took it from Mac to look closer. It was two photos. One was Mason and him sitting opposite each other in a bar, holding hands across a low table and gazing into each other's eyes. Possibly the night they'd gone to that fancy cocktail bar?

He had no idea who'd taken the photo, but whoever they were, they certainly hadn't asked permission. The other picture was of Mason standing at a different bar, laughing with someone else. With Lewis, in fact. The headline ran, *Trading Up? Is Mason Nash swapping gardening hottie, Owen Hunter, for his gorgeous TV mogul brother? Fans react to shock photo.*

"This is…?" Owen frowned. "What *is* this?"

"It's on that gossip site, *Echo*?" Naaz said as if she was explaining it to her grandpa. "My friend saw it on Twitter."

"Bloody hell." Despite knowing better, Owen clicked the link. The 'article' consisted of little more than some comments about how Lewis and Mason had a 'stormy past' and a few tweets from random people saying things like 'Owen's so cute. I can't believe Mason would cheat on him' and 'No way would Mason cheat—they're clearly totally in love!!!!'

Shaking his head, Owen handed Naaz back her phone. "Do people really read this crap?"

"I suppose? I'm sure it's not true, though. Mason seems so nice and—"

Owen cut her off with an embarrassed gesture. "That photo with Lewis is about a year old." He didn't explain that the reason he knew that was because he'd googled Mason ages ago, and he remembered seeing the picture then. It had been taken at some kind of industry gala, and it had stuck in Owen's memory because he'd thought how different Mason looked when he was smiling naturally rather than wearing his pouty model expression.

Of course, now that Owen had seen that smile up close and personal, he realised it wasn't as natural as he'd first assumed. Now he noticed the faint tension around Mason's eyes and the stiff set of his shoulders. Now he saw that Mason was not, in fact, at ease in the picture, but was performing for the camera.

Owen tried to ignore the unworthy kick of satisfaction that knowledge gave him and focus on the fact that he didn't feel remotely threatened by the article or the photo, at least not in the way it had been presented in this weird, fabricated story. He didn't like it though, not one bit. Leaving aside the nasty insinuation behind the 'trading up' headline, the idea that people he knew—and people he didn't know—might read and even believe this crap, bothered him.

What would Mason think if he saw it? What would Lewis and Aaron think?

Shit, what would his clients think?

"See?" Mac was saying to Naaz. "Don't believe anything you read on the internet. It's all a load of bollocks."

Naaz nodded, clearly relieved. "I know. I just thought Owen should see it."

"Thanks, Naaz, I appreciate that." He gave her a smile, although it felt strained. "Are you off home? Don't miss your bus."

She checked her phone and grimaced. "Yeah, I'd better run. See you tomorrow, boss!"

When she was gone, the door closing behind her with a clang, Owen let out a heavy sigh. "Bloody hell, Mac."

She grimaced in sympathy. "On the plus side, it's got to be good for business."

"Has it?"

"All publicity is good publicity…?"

"So they say." Owen rubbed a hand through his hair. "I hope I haven't made a stupid mistake with this."

Mac cocked an eyebrow. They'd been best friends since they were kids—other than Lewis, there was no one who knew Owen better.

"You've been whistling like a budgerigar these last few weeks," she said. "And I don't mean just like a bloke who's getting some regular action for a change. I mean more like before things went south with you and Michelle."

Owen ran a hand over his face. "Am I that bloody transparent?"

"Well… Yeah, you are."

He laughed sourly. "Great."

"Nothing wrong with that," Mac said, reaching for her lighter. "You're an honest bloke, and people see that when they meet you. That's why they trust you with their business."

"Yeah." Owen nodded. "Yeah, thanks."

"So you're really into this Mason bloke, then?" She smiled, teasing but fond. "Get you, going out with a supermodel."

"He's not a supermodel," Owen protested, although he was smiling too. "But, yeah, we're…together. And it's good. It's *really* good. Mason's great. I just wish I didn't have to deal with all this internet crap."

"What does Mason have to say about it?"

"About what?"

Mac eyed him. "The internet crap."

Owen shrugged, because of course he hadn't said anything about it to Mason. What would be the point? Owen had known all along that they'd be playing up their flirtation on social media. Misty had been clear about that from the start. So had Mason.

"Hmm," Mac said, "let me guess—you haven't talked to him about it. You've just done the Stoic Owen routine."

"The what?"

"Oh, you know," she said, shoving his shoulder lightly. "Shields up, head down, and bulldoze through anything you don't like instead of actually communicating with people."

Offended, he said, "I don't do that."

Mac didn't argue, just gave him one of those long 'you know I'm right' looks and said, "Anyway, don't brood over that crap Naaz showed you. Today's news is tomorrow's chip paper, and all that." She flicked her lighter on and off, clearly eager to light up. "Talking of which, I'm heading home via the chippy. You coming?"

Regretfully, Owen shook his head and nodded towards

the office. "Need to catch up on some paperwork. I have to take another day out for filming next week."

"All right, I'll leave you to polish your Oscars then." Mac grinned. "But don't work too late. Early start tomorrow."

At the moment, it was *always* an early start.

After making himself a coffee, and trying not to think about fish and chips, Owen dropped into the chair behind his desk and cranked up his ageing computer. There was a stack of invoices waiting to be sent out, but instead of opening Excel, he found himself opening his browser.

After a pause, he cautiously typed: Owen Hunter Mason Nash.

A stream of results popped up on the screen, most of them links to posts on social media, some to the official *Weekend Wellness* website, others to RPP.

"Shit," he said, leaning back in his chair as if the words and images might jump off the screen to bite him. Then, with distaste, he looked closer and started scrolling, his stomach getting more and more tense as he went.

When his eyes landed on one particular image, though, he stopped, hand frozen on the mouse, horrified.

It showed a zoomed-in screen cap from last week's show —that bloody shot where Owen was blatantly staring at Mason's arse. Someone had photoshopped labels onto it. *Pitcher?* across Owen's chest. *Catcher?* across Mason's backside.

With one disgusted click, Owen shut down the browser.

He felt sick to his stomach. What the hell was wrong with people? How dare they look at him—at him and Mason—and think about *that*? How dare they speculate about their lives, about the most intimate parts of their lives? And how fucking dare they put it up on the internet to snigger at for fun? For their amusement?

In a fit of angry frustration, he slammed his fist on the table, sloshing his coffee onto his paperwork. "*Fuck!*"

And the worst thing was that Mason loved this crap. Lapped it up. It was his life, his career, his *future*—and for the first time, Owen wondered whether that was going to be a problem.

Because he hated it. He absolutely bloody *hated* it.

CHAPTER EIGHTEEN

Early evening sunlight filtered through the gauzy curtains of Mason's bedroom, casting golden shadows across the ceiling.

"You like that, baby?" Owen murmured, his voice husky and his cock buried deep, deep inside Mason's body.

Mason nodded, eyes half closing against the pleasure rippling through him. One of Owen's big hands had captured his wrists, pressing them lightly into the mattress above Mason's head; his other arm was snug around Mason's waist, lifting his hips at the perfect angle.

Their eyes met, Owen's smiling and warm, his face flushed, lips curled in pleasure. "God you're so... *perfect*." He dipped his head, kissing Mason's mouth, the thrusting of his hips slowing as he released Mason's wrists and cupped the back of his head instead.

Subtly, slowly their kisses changed. Softened, sweetened. Mason's heart pounded high in his chest, almost in his throat as Owen lifted his head to gaze into his face, before kissing him again. Moments later, he pulled out of Mason's body, and Mason couldn't stifle a whine of frustration at the loss.

"Shh," Owen soothed, nudging Mason onto his side and lying down behind him. "Let's try it like this."

Mason managed a gasped, "Yeah," as Owen eased back into his willing body, reaching around to take hold of Mason's cock. His grip was strong and warm, and he stroked in a delicious counterpoint to the steady thrust of his hips.

Mason arched back, turning his head enough that they could kiss again. Messy, hungry kisses. He grabbed a fistful of Owen's hair and pulled him closer, nipping at his lips, losing himself in abandon.

Owen's pace quickened, both hips and hand, and then with a grunt, he rolled Mason over onto his belly. Mason's cock rubbed against the sheets as Owen nudged his legs further apart and thrust harder, deeper, faster. Overwhelmed, physically and mentally, as Owen's body pressed him into the mattress, Mason could do nothing but feel.

And he *loved* it.

"Fuck." Owen growled the word against Mason's ear. "Fuck, Mason. *Yes.*"

Breath stuttering, Owen got both arms around Mason, holding him tight as he fucked into him. The world slipped away, nothing left but the pleasure thrumming deep inside Mason's body, the cresting rush of climax tightening his thighs, his balls, his belly.

With a cry, Owen came, deep and deeper, shuddering as he buried his face against Mason's shoulder.

Then, breathing hard, he rolled them both back onto their sides, his cock still deep inside Mason. Slipping one arm under Mason's ribs to wrap around his chest, Owen held him tight against his body as his other hand once more took hold of Mason's cock.

Fuck, Mason loved the way Owen manhandled him. Took control. There was a kindness and attentiveness to it that made him feel spoiled and cherished and brought a ridiculous sting to his eyes as his simmering climax reached a rolling boil.

Muscles tensed, brain blanked. Close, so fucking *close*.

"That's it. I've got you," Owen murmured, mouthing the words against Mason's ear. "Let go, angel. Just let go…"

With a shout, Mason let go.

His climax surged, boiling over, hot and sticky across his belly and Owen's hand, muscles tensing as his body clenched and jerked in release.

Owen held him close, spooning them together as he laid soft, soothing kisses against Mason's shoulder, his neck, the side of his face.

Awash with endorphins, and unexpectedly emotional, Mason twisted around in his embrace, hiding his face in the soft juncture of Owen's shoulder and neck. He didn't want to look at Owen. Was scared of what Owen might see on his face.

Gently, Owen shifted them both, getting comfortable, but he kept his arms around Mason. Just… holding him.

After a while, as the flood of happy hormones receded and Mason started feeling more in control of himself, Owen said, quietly, "Do you mind when I call you angel?"

Mason huffed amusement against Owen's shoulder and looked up. His eyelashes felt wet. He hoped Owen didn't notice. "What's wrong with 'Mason'?"

"Nothing. I like Mason. A lot. But…" His smile turned self-conscious. "I like that nobody else calls you angel."

Mason cocked an eyebrow. "My *parents* call me Angel."

"Not the way I do." Reaching up, he pushed his fingers through Mason's tangled hair. "My sweet, debauched angel."

"Oh my God," Mason laughed, burying his face into Owen's shoulder again.

They lay like that for a few minutes longer, until the beeping of the oven timer interrupted the peace. Mason sat up. "Dinner," he said, smiling down at Owen.

Relaxed, happy, and totally unselfconscious, Owen sprawled in Mason's bed like he belonged there.

Because he does, Mason's heart supplied. *He does belong there.*

It was an electrifying thought, and it jolted him out of bed faster than the fear of over-cooked coq au vin. "I'm just going to take dinner out of the oven," he said, "then jump into the shower. You go first, though."

Dragging on shorts and a sweatshirt, he quickly washed his hands and dashed into the kitchen.

Half an hour later, hair damp from the shower, loose-limbed and glowing, he sat across from Owen at the kitchen table, grinning like an idiot. The evening had darkened to twilight, and Mason had lit a candle between them. The effect was ridiculously romantic, and Mason might have thought it was too much if Owen's eyes, gleaming in the flickering light, hadn't looked so fond.

"My God, this smells amazing," he said when Mason spooned a generous helping of coq au vin onto his plate from the casserole on the table. He was serving it with crusty wholemeal bread that he'd made that morning—sod the carbs —and some simple sauteed green beans.

Owen ate like he did everything else, with all his straight-forward feelings on display. In this case, pure pleasure. His groan of delight as he took his first mouthful might have raised Mason's interest if he hadn't just been so thoroughly sated. It did give him a warm glow of satisfaction, though.

"Incredible," Owen said, eyes wide. "Blimey, Mason, this is fantastic. It's like restaurant food."

Mason felt his cheeks warm. "Thanks." Praise for his cooking meant a lot to Mason. It gave him a sense of accomplishment he simply didn't feel when people told him he was beautiful. Beauty was just a genetic roll of the dice. This, though? This was something he'd created with his own two hands using talent and training. This was something that gave another person pleasure, that fed and nourished them.

This was something worthy of pride.

Owen concentrated on his meal for a while, and Mason concentrated on Owen. He loved watching the enjoyment on his face, the way he dabbed up the last of the gravy with the bread Mason had baked that morning, the line of his throat as he tipped his head back to take another mouthful of Pinot Noir.

After Owen had finished eating, though, his expression changed. The pleasure and relaxation were chased away by something else, something that brought a frown to his brow.

Mason frowned, too. "Penny for them?" he said lightly, topping up Owen's glass and then his own.

"Hmm?" Owen looked up, blinking. He'd been miles away, which was not a good sign after a fantastic fuck and a fabulous meal. "Sorry, I was…"

And now he looked uncomfortable, and the expression triggered a queasy flutter in Mason's stomach. Mason pushed his own plate aside, unfinished. "What is it?"

Owen shook his head and sipped his wine. "Nothing. It's stupid."

"It can't be both of those things." Aware that he'd sounded sharp, Mason forced a smile. "It's okay if you don't want to tell me, though."

Owen appeared to consider that, then said, "I'll tell you, if you want." He reached across the table, taking Mason's hand and squeezing. "Come on. Bring the wine and let's get comfy on the sofa."

The warm grip of his hand and the smile in his denim-blue eyes eased Mason's spiking anxiety. As he followed Owen into the living room, Mason wondered whether Owen was one of those people blessed with a high emotional IQ, or whether he and Owen were just especially in tune with each other.

Alarmingly, the notion made his heart skip.

Taking his favourite spot in the corner of the sofa, Owen stretched out one arm along its back in invitation, and Mason sat beside him.

Fiddling with his wine glass, he took a sip, swallowed, and made himself say, "Okay, out with it. What's up?"

Owen sighed, his expression reluctant. "I've been thinking about today's segment."

Despite Mason's reservations about getting too coupley, he hadn't been able to refuse Owen's invitation to sleep over again, and they'd watched *Weekend Wellness* together that morning, cuddled up on this very sofa. Mason thought their bit was even better than the first episode, and he'd already had a shedload of comments on Insta, as well as compliments from Misty and Frankie, both excited by the buzz growing around his and Owen's on-screen flirtation. The expression in Owen's eyes made Mason wary, though.

"I thought you were great," he said encouragingly. "You came across well. Everyone says how natural you are."

Owen grunted, and then, to Mason's surprise, pulled out his phone. It was an old model, with a smaller screen than Mason was used to.

"I found this online the other night," Owen said. "There's loads of stuff like it. I'm sure you've seen similar things, but…"

Mason took the phone and peered at the image on the small screen. It was a 'pitcher-catcher' meme, a shot taken from the first show. He snorted a laugh, but Owen's silence cut it short. Twisting to look at him, Mason said, "Does it bother you? Sorry, stupid question. Obviously, it does, but it's just… the internet, you know?"

"Does it *not* bother you?" Owen asked, and he seemed genuinely perplexed. "Random people thinking about… about what we do in bed?"

Mason shrugged, shifting to sit cross-legged opposite Owen. "I guess not really? I suppose I've got used to it."

Owen's expression tightened. "You mean, because you're a model? Because people..." His face flooded with colour. "Because some people maybe...fantasise about you?"

"It's not something I actively think about," Mason said, although the high colour in Owen's face had him curious. "But I'd be pretty naive to think it doesn't happen. And anyway, there's loads of crap like this online. Once your image is public property, it's fair game."

"Doesn't feel fair," Owen said quietly. "And this..." He waved at the phone. "I mean, what they're talking about is more than just fantasy fodder, isn't it? That's *us*. That's our relationship."

Our relationship.

The words made Mason's gut clench. "Well, yeah," he said slowly. "But we are kind of milking it for *Weekend Wellness*. I mean, Misty would *love* this." He waggled his eyebrows at Owen. "You should totally send it to her."

But Owen didn't smile. His lashes shuttered over his eyes as he took back his phone. "That's sort of my point. Pretending to flirt for a TV show is one thing, but it's real now. It means something. At least, it does to me. And that makes it different."

Mason's skipping heart sped up. He didn't know what to say to that, but somehow, he found himself reaching out to touch Owen's knee. "It means something to me too."

Owen smiled, covering Mason's hand with his own. "Yeah?"

Breathlessly, Mason said, "Yeah." And he sort of hated that it was true. This wasn't what he'd imagined when he took Misty's advice all those weeks ago to 'push things' with Owen. And now, thinking about that, about his deliberate seduction of Owen, made him feel uneasy.

"So…?" Owen said carefully. "You wouldn't mind… pulling back a little?"

"Pulling back?"

"On the public flirting stuff."

"What do you mean?" The knot of anxiety returned, yanking tighter this time. "On the show?"

"Well, yeah. And on social media. I don't mean in real life."

"But that's… I mean, that's what the show's about."

Owen frowned. "I thought it was about teaching people how to garden."

"Yeah, but the ship—the 'are they/aren't they'—that's why people are watching."

"Is it? Christ, that's depressing."

"I don't see why, if people are enjoying it."

"Because…" Owen eyed him, still frowning. "Because it's pretty shallow, isn't it?"

Mason's hackles rose. How many times had he heard a variation on *that* theme over the past few years? "Shallow?"

"I thought we were trying to do something more important," Owen said. "Helping people get the benefits of working outside and connecting with nature and the environment. Not just…titillating them on social media."

Stung, Mason moved away, perching on the edge of the sofa as he set his glass on the coffee table. "Well, I'm sorry you think that, but to be blunt, that's what's driving up the ratings."

"And your followers."

"Right. Obviously."

Cautiously, Owen said, "And it doesn't bother you at all?"

"What? Being so shallow?" His voice dripped with sarcasm.

Owen sighed. "I didn't say *you* were shallow. I meant all the internet memes and stuff. That doesn't bother you?"

"What some rando on Twitter thinks about how we fuck?

No, why should it?" He shrugged, making it look careless. "It's not like they're wrong, anyway."

Owen bristled, his expression tightening. "I see." He shifted too, so that they were sitting side by side with a few feet of space between them on the sofa. As if they were in a waiting room. "One of my clients' neighbours thinks you have a 'squeezable' arse, by the way. Asked me to pass that on."

"For God's sake…"

"I'm not making it up."

"I didn't think you were." He let out a breath, tried to rein in his galloping sense of unease. "Look, I get that the attention is weird for you. You're not used to it, and it must be uncomfortable having people make comments like that, but for me, it's just how it is, you know? It sucks, but you do get used to it."

"I don't *want* to get used to it!" Owen objected. "I'm not— this is *not* my life, Mason. It's not going to become my life, either. I only agreed to do the show to—"

He bit off the sentence, but Mason didn't need to hear the rest. "To get into my pants?"

Owen looked at him in horror, but there was a betraying flush in his cheeks.

"You think I didn't know?" Mason said coolly. "You think I don't know when a man's panting after me?"

His words landed like a slap. Owen physically recoiled, and, instantly, Mason regretted them. "Sorry," he said. "That was—" Hypocritical, to say the least. "Fuck, I'm being a dick. I'm just—"

His mind shot back to Kurt, to Frieda, to Min and Mel. It was easy for Owen. He could stand on his principles because he wasn't anybody's safety net. Not now. Nobody leaned on him like they leaned on Mason.

"I just need this, okay? Until I start making enough money."

"Enough money for what?"

Owen's voice sounded flatter than Mason had ever heard it. His heart clenched. See? It was just so bloody easy to hurt people.

"You've got a fancy flat, nice things. Fame," Owen went on. "What more do you want?"

Mason rose, paced to the window and stared out at the scrubby patch of communal garden. "It's more complicated than you think. My family... I told you what they're like. They rely on me." He laughed, aware it sounded bitter. "I'm their 'safety net', apparently."

"What does that mean?"

He shrugged. "What do you think? It means Kurt can piss off to Rome for the weekend with his fucking awful girlfriend and leave me to pay for the girls' French trip. It means Frieda can overspend every single month and then freak out and expect me to cover the shortfall. It means they know I'll pick up the pieces when they drop the fucking ball, because I always fucking *do*."

After a pause, Owen said, "It's not your job to be their safety net."

"So what should I do? Let the girls miss out on their trip? Let Frieda default on her rent? Send the lawyers after Kurt for child maintenance?"

Behind him, he heard Owen get to his feet. "Maybe, yeah."

"Maybe?" Mason turned to face him. "You'd do that, would you, if Lewis needed you?"

Owen's mouth pinched. "What's the alternative? Keep slogging away at a career you don't really want instead of pursuing what you love?"

For a frightening moment, Mason thought Owen was talking about himself. "What I love?" he said, faintly.

"You're a fantastic chef," Owen said. "And watching you cook?" He shook his head. "I can see how much you love it, how much it means to you. When you're cooking, you're so focused, so relaxed and happy. I don't see that when you're hamming it up for the camera."

"Hamming it up?" That stung. "Thanks for the vote of fucking confidence."

"I didn't mean it like that," Owen said, taking a step forward. Mason took one backwards, arms folded. Hurt. They both stopped. "I just mean… Look, you're great at the TV stuff, honestly, but I don't think you love it."

"Yeah, well, so what? Plenty of people don't love their jobs. At least mine pays well. And once I hit 100,000 followers—"

"The magic number, I know." Owen sighed. "Then you can sell more stuff you don't care about to people you don't know. Great! Then what?"

Mason glared at him. "Then I'll have enough money to comfortably cover my family's bills whether or not Kurt pays up every month. Maybe enough to save up a deposit to buy my own place, rather than having to keep my money accessible for family emergencies." He rubbed the back of his neck, then added softly, "It would just be really nice to have enough money that I could make some plans of my own for once, you know?"

Owen frowned. "Paying your family's bills shouldn't be your sole responsibility. Besides, if you earn more, won't they just want more from you?"

That thought closed like a fist around Mason's lungs, squeezing.

"Maybe you should start pushing back," Owen went on. "They're your parents, for God's sake, not your children. They can sort out their own problems."

"It's not—" It wasn't that straightforward. When he'd got his first modelling contract, totally out of the blue, it had felt like winning the lottery. Frieda had still been fragile, and the constant grind of making ends meet had been hard on her.

Hard on them all. It had been obvious that Mason would share his windfall with his struggling family, and somehow that had just carried on. He couldn't stop now. Why couldn't Owen see that? Impatiently, he snapped, "I know you've got a saviour complex, Owen, but I don't need you to fix my life, okay?"

Owen looked hurt, but he drew closer anyway, setting a hand on Mason's shoulder. "I'm not trying to *fix* your life. I'm just saying that you deserve to choose the life you live. You're not your parents' safety net, and it's not fair of them to expect that of you."

His eyes were kind, pitying. And Mason couldn't stand it. He shoved Owen's arm aside and moved around him, back towards the kitchen. With effort, he tried to force some brightness into his voice, but it came out harsh and brittle. Like ice. "All this because you were offended by a fucking meme."

"I wasn't offended."

"What then?" Mason said, spinning around to face him. "You're ready to screw up my best shot at a TV career over it, so it must be bad."

"That's not what I'm saying." Owen lifted his hands in surrender. "Look, I don't want to screw anything up for you. Forget I said anything, okay?"

Mason jammed a hand through his hair, hating the slump in Owen's shoulders and the defeated look in his eyes. Hating that Owen's distress bothered him so much. "I just really need this exposure," he said, his voice pleading now. "It could change everything for me."

Owen didn't reply, his lips pressed tight in disagreement. Well, he was entitled to his opinion.

Silence descended, heavy and solid. A few outside sounds leaked in around it—the hum of passing traffic, the honk of a horn, someone talking too loud on their phone.

Owen sighed and said, "Maybe I should go."

Don't. Mason bit back his instinctive response, wrapping

his arms around his chest to keep from reaching out. Owen *should* go; clearly, they were getting too entangled. It would be best to cool things off. He gave an offhand shrug. "If that's what you want."

"I have to work tomorrow, anyway. I was going to tell you."

"On Sunday?"

"Because I'm taking Wednesday off for filming next week…"

Another reminder that Owen, unlike Mason, had a 'real' job. He set his jaw. "Right."

"Look, can we…?" Owen hesitated, then took a step forward. "I don't want to leave when you're pissed off at me."

The smart thing to do would be to give another insouciant shrug. To let Owen go and then keep him dangling for a day or two. Maintain a cool indifference, put some space between them. But… he didn't want that. He really didn't.

Dry-throated, staring down at his own bare feet, Mason croaked, "Then…don't go."

"Okay," Owen said immediately.

Mason peeked up through his lashes, saw the rueful tilt of Owen's lips, and felt his own anger and frustration start to melt away. A gap had opened between them, though, a chasm that Mason didn't know how—or whether—to cross.

Owen, however, didn't seem to share his uncertainty. He simply opened his arms and took another step closer, "Come here, angel," he said, and it was exactly that easy. Helplessly, Mason walked into his arms and let them close around him.

"I'm sorry," Owen murmured, nuzzling into his hair. "I don't want to argue with you. I just—"

"I don't either," Mason said quickly, squeezing him tight. "Let's just forget it."

Owen's sigh was almost silent, no more than a rise and fall of his chest. Mason felt it, but didn't comment. He didn't want to talk about this anymore, so instead, he said, "I was going to make dessert if you fancy it…?"

"Dessert?" Owen pulled back, eyebrows twitching in a comic display of interest.

"Moelleux au Chocolat." He smiled at Owen's blank expression. "It's a kind of gooey chocolate pudding, with a raspberry coulis. And ice cream. Won't take long to make."

Owen smiled back, a hint of relief in his eyes. "That sounds amazing."

"Okay then," Mason said, brisk now. "You put some music on. I'll be through in fifteen minutes. We can have dessert on the sofa."

Owen released him. "Fifteen minutes? To make a real French dessert?"

Mason chuckled as he headed for the kitchen. "Yup. It's super easy." He made a shooing motion at Owen. "Go on, music."

Once back in the kitchen, though, Mason stood for a moment with his hands braced on the counter and his head down, trying to centre himself. What the fuck was he doing? Was he actually getting involved in a *relationship* with Owen? Was that what this was?

He'd never wanted that, never wanted to hold the kind of power over anyone that Kurt had held—still held—over Frieda. And yet here he was, allowing Owen to comfort and forgive him, even though, five minutes earlier, Mason had been hurling angry, hurtful words at him.

Christ, he'd always run a mile from emotional crap like this. So why the hell wasn't he running now?

His heart whispered the answer, but Mason dared not listen.

Pushing himself away from the counter, he distracted himself from his churning thoughts by gathering up the ingredients he needed and setting them out ready to use. He knew the basic proportions, but decided to do a quick recipe check on his phone for the exact measurements. His hand went automatically to his pocket, but his phone wasn't there. It must still be in the bedroom, he thought, from when he'd got undressed earlier. He smiled to himself as he headed for the bedroom, both at the memory of how Owen had fucked him and at the surprising realisation that he'd gone so long without even thinking to check his phone.

He found it face down on the bedroom floor. It must have spilled out of the pocket of his jeans in his haste to strip. Picking it up, he idly thumbed it open, stilling when he saw the latest notification. A message from Misty. It was the last in a series of messages, and he quickly navigated to the full thread.

Great socials this week—loved the pineapple thing! Pineapple emoji.

Actually, let's pick that up Weds. We can do something with it. Thumbs up emoji.

Can't wait for you to see the plot, btw—you and O won't recognise it from last time!

Also, journalist friend of mine keen to do a piece on you two— will intro. Smiley emoji.

One little ask—can O do a bit more online? Works better if you're both engaging.

Smiley emoji.

Grimly, Mason closed his phone and shoved it in his pocket.

CHAPTER NINETEEN

By the time the next day of filming rolled around, Owen was knackered. He'd worked the whole weekend, then late on Monday and Tuesday so he could take the day off, and now his body ached from the hard labour and long hours of the last few days.

He was a natural early riser, but even so, when his alarm went off at five that morning, he groaned, pulling a pillow over his face. Christ, he could use another hour or two in bed. But he forced himself up and into the shower, turning it cold for the last two minutes to really wake himself up.

Chugging down a strong coffee, he drove out to the RPP studio on autopilot, parked and headed round to the garden plot at the back. There were a few people milling about already—Lucy, the director, a sound guy he hadn't seen before, and a make-up woman, rifling through her kit. He almost groaned aloud when he saw Misty Watson-King. She was wearing a pair of distressed denim dungarees over a red vest top, clumpy red gardening clogs and a red-and-white bandana tied in a jaunty knot. Her outfit was probably designed to look relaxed and casual, but she looked anything but as she barked instructions at a harassed-looking Naomi, who was trying to take notes on an iPad. Hopefully, Misty wouldn't be there all day. Owen wasn't sure he could take eight or nine hours of her without exploding.

Just then, he caught sight of Mason, standing off to the side, looking at his phone. For what felt like the first time in days, he cracked a smile. They'd put Mason in some sort of navy-blue fisherman's-smock-thing over denim cut-off shorts and dark blue deck shoes. It was a ridiculous outfit but, well, Mason could pretty much carry anything off, and he looked just as hot as ever.

Owen jogged over to him. "Are you gardening or sailing today?"

Mason looked up, and the immediate, instinctive smile that spread over his face at seeing Owen made Owen's heart feel like it was being squeezed by a giant fist. A moment later, the smile shifted into a mischievous grin.

"I know, right?" He shoved his phone in the front pouch of the smock. "I quite like this big pocket, though," he said. "There's tons of room in here. Enough for a packed lunch."

"You look like a very sexy French sailor," Owen rumbled, moving in closer for a kiss. But when Mason flicked a nervous glance at the crew, he stilled. "Something wrong?"

Mason's expression grew uncomfortable. "There's a couple of new people here today, so we should probably keep things on the down-low."

For a moment, Owen felt a stab of gratitude. Mason *had* listened to him then. Had heard what he'd said about wanting to keep their relationship more private. But then Mason added, "I think we should try to work the *are they/aren't they* angle as long as we can, you know? Shippers always say they want couples to get together, but the fact is it's the anticipation they like the best."

Disappointed, Owen just stared at him, saying nothing.

Eventually, Mason seemed to pick up on his mood. "What's wrong?" he said. Then his puzzled expression hardened into something that looked like guilty defiance. "Sorry, am I being too shallow for you again? Excuse me for having a career."

Owen sighed and turned away. "I think I'll grab a coffee."

"Owen—" Mason said behind him, but Owen kept walking, making his way over to where the crew was standing. It was only then, as he moved into the middle of the plot, that he noticed the changes. He came to a halt between two raised beds, gazing down at them in confusion.

"What the hell?"

"What do you think?" Misty said, grinning widely as she approached him. "Pretty amazing growth for three weeks, right?"

Owen glanced up, taking in her self-satisfied look. "You've replanted these beds," he said, in disbelief.

"The magic of television," Misty said smugly. "We need to show more progress than real life allows for, I'm afraid. Luckily, there's a plant nursery near me so we bought up a bunch of the plants you put in during the first filming session and swapped them out."

Owen frowned, pointing at a row of foxgloves, and said, "Those aren't delphiniums. We planted delphiniums—those are totally different!"

"Near enough," Misty said dismissively. "Trust me, Owen, I know television, and—"

"And I know bloody gardening," Owen interrupted. "We had a whole bit in last week's slot showing me planting delphiniums and talking about them and how long they'd take to grow, and you've planted something completely different in their place! People will think I'm an idiot!"

Misty's eyes narrowed in irritation. "Don't be so dramatic," she said, her voice hardening. "Nobody will remember what you said. Viewers aren't interested in the details. They're interested in the *story*. They're buying into the idea of a hot guy spending his Saturday morning gardening with his cute, twinky boyfriend before taking him indoors to bend him over and—"

"Don't talk about Mason like that!" Owen snapped, cutting her off. Just then, a hand touched his elbow, and he turned to see Mason standing beside him, his brows drawn together in concern.

"Calm down," Mason said, frowning. "You don't need to get angry on my account." He glanced at Misty. "Come on. You can see it from his point of view, right? Owen's a professional. His reputation is important to him. Even if most viewers don't notice, *he'll* notice."

Misty rolled her eyes. "Let's keep this in proportion. It doesn't need to be a big deal. We didn't replace *everything*, just the plants in these two beds—which were bloody tiny by the way—and I'm sure *most* of them are the same ones you two planted last time."

Owen opened his mouth to respond, but when Mason sent him a pleading look, he pressed his lips together.

"Okay, how about this," Misty said briskly. "We start by getting some footage with these new plants, and then for the rest of the day, we go back to your plan on what we're covering. Fair?"

It wasn't fair. Owen had spent hours—bloody *days* actually—planning this garden and how he could use the different elements to actually teach some useful lessons while creating a pleasing space. Mason had done loads of graft too, contributing his ideas on the produce side and typing up all those detailed notes that Misty had seemed so happy with at first. And now she was changing the goalposts at a whim. He opened his mouth to say as much, but when he clocked Mason's tense expression, he subsided.

"Fine," he said tightly. "But I decide which plants in these beds we talk about, and if I want to mention that you've transplanted older plants in, I will."

"That sounds fair," Mason said, looking at Misty hopefully.

Misty eyed him for a moment, then shrugged one shoulder. "All right," she said, casting an unfriendly look at Owen. "You're the gardening expert."

"I am," Owen got out through clenched teeth.

She gave a small, tight smile. "Just remember—I'm the TV expert."

The next two hours were wearing. With Misty watching, Owen struggled to get back into the easy back-and-forth vibe he and Mason had established last time. He was still pissed off, and he hated the way Misty rode roughshod over everyone else, constantly overruling Lucy's decisions and issuing orders.

Once they'd finished the section with the new plants, a wardrobe girl brought fresh outfits for them to change into—just another tattersall shirt for Owen, in green this time, but for Mason, skinny jeans and a rainbow hoodie in some sort of hemp-like fabric. Owen wouldn't be seen dead in it, but, as usual, it looked good on Mason.

"I don't understand why we need to change?" Owen grumbled as he buttoned up the fresh shirt. "We didn't last time."

"Well, you *should* have, last time," Misty said, shooting a glare in Lucy's direction. "We're getting footage for multiple episodes here. Viewers will notice if you're wearing the same thing all the time."

Owen frowned. "In that case, should we think about when the different parts we're filming today will go out? That bit we've just done should be one of the later slots, given how mature the plants are. So should we do the part that will go out earliest now?"

He glanced at Lucy, who nodded and said easily, "That makes sense." She pulled out her copy of Owen and Mason's notes, which she'd scribbled all over. "Perhaps if we start with the—"

"No, no, no," Misty said, cutting across them. "Let's not waste time on that. We can sort that stuff out in the editing suite." She consulted her smart watch. "It's almost ten, and I need to be out of here by twelve. I want to get as much of the footage in the can as possible by then."

"But surely it'll save time if we think about it now," Owen insisted. "That way we won't end up having to reshoot anything that—"

He broke off when Misty laughed.

"Oh my God," she said, in the tone of someone asking for the gift of patience. "Owen, this is not the sort of thing we do reshoots on, okay? We need to *move this on*. We'll edit the slots as close to your notes as we can, and if one or two little gardening inconsistencies creep through, the world is not going to end, okay? Trust me. Viewers. Won't. Notice."

Owen said flatly, "So they won't notice that, but they'll notice if I'm wearing a blue tattersall shirt instead of a green one?"

Misty's eyes narrowed. "Pretty much, yeah." Without waiting for a response, she turned and began to stride away, clapping her hands forcefully. "Fi, touch up Owen's makeup! We'll go again in ten. Mason—with me."

Mason blinked at her peremptory tone, seeming taken aback. But then he set off after her. Owen almost caught his arm to tell him he didn't need to jump just because Misty had said so, but then he'd be just as bad as Misty herself. So instead, he watched Mason follow her over to the tiny greenhouse at the back of the plot, resolving to gently raise the subject with him at some future point.

"I'm really sorry about this," Lucy said beside him. Her expression was grimly resigned.

"Not your fault," he said simply. "But last time *was* a lot easier."

"Yeah," she agreed. "I know. It's not fun for any of us when Misty decides to turn up for filming. Just try to ignore her, okay? She's only going to be here for two more hours, and then we've got the whole afternoon to get some decent footage." She offered him a half-smile. "Last time was super easy, with that flow you and Mason had going. It would be great to see that again."

Just then, Naomi appeared in front of them, balancing a tray of coffees she'd just fetched and a huge bag full of muffins and pastries. Once again, she was dressed entirely in black-and-white—stripes, this time, on a knee-length dress— with her long black hair pinned back in a bun.

Owen smiled and thanked her, extracting his black Americano from the tray and selecting a lemon-and-poppyseed muffin from the pastry bag while Lucy grabbed her own coffee.

"Thanks," he said, grinning at Naomi, who smiled nervously back. "Looks like you get all the best jobs."

She gave a soft huff of laughter, shooting a look towards Misty and Mason. "Well, you know," she said in her plummy accent, "it's par for the course as an intern."

"Yeah?" Owen said, sipping his coffee. "What are you interning in?"

Brightening, she said, "Television production."

"I bet that's competitive. You've done well to get the job."

She gave a little half-shrug and said, "I suppose. I mean, it's not exactly a job…"

"It's training," Owen corrected himself through a large bite of his muffin. Thinking of the apprenticeship schemes he was familiar with, he asked, "Are there modules or…?"

Naomi shook her head. "It's pretty informal. I just, you know, shadow Misty and…learn as I go."

Well, that sounded dull. Owen didn't say as much, lowering his voice and saying with a grin, "I hope you get hazard pay."

Naomi laughed, then cut herself off abruptly and threw a worried glance at Lucy, who just smiled and lifted her coffee in salute. To Owen, Naomi quietly admitted, "Actually, it's an unpaid internship."

He felt his eyes widen. "*Unpaid?*" Christ, Misty had Naomi working all hours. "How's that even legal?"

"Er…" She flushed, seeming embarrassed. "Well, actually it was my stepfather who arranged it—he went to school with one of the RPP board members. Apparently, if you're shadowing someone, rather than working, it's allowed."

Shadowing Misty his arse! Naomi was working her socks off for free and apparently getting bugger-all training in return. Not that it sounded like she needed the money, but even so, Misty was obviously exploiting her. Not to mention the fact that this intern arrangement neatly excluded any candidates who couldn't afford to work for free. "Well," he said, trying to sound positive, "I hope it leads somewhere for you. I'm sure it will."

Inwardly, Owen cringed. He wasn't sure he really meant those words—after all, given her family connections, it wasn't in much doubt that Naomi would get wherever she wanted to go. But still, she *was* being treated like crap, and for that, there was no excuse. It made him marvel again over how Lewis had single-mindedly bulldozed his way into this industry with nothing but grit and raw talent on his side.

"Perhaps." Naomi eyed Misty again, shifting the tray she was holding. "Working in TV isn't as much fun as I thought it would be, though."

Owen huffed softly. "Yeah," he said, "you've got that right."

With a rueful smile, Naomi moved towards where Mason and Misty were standing. Misty was talking intently in a low voice while Mason listened, a tiny frown between his brows. She glared at Naomi when she approached, waving her off with an irritable gesture like she was no more than a dog, even though Misty was the one who'd insisted Naomi had to make a coffee run. Mason called Naomi back, though, smiling sunnily and chatting for a few moments as he got his coffee, his expression regretful as he declined the contents of the treat bag.

Owen smiled, glad to see that Mason was not completely owned by Misty. But as soon as Naomi scurried off, Misty was back in his face again, back to delivering orders while Mason nodded unhappily along.

It wasn't until sometime later, after they'd done another stint of filming, that he got a chance to ask Mason what that had been about.

Mason glanced at him anxiously, then said, under his breath, "I don't think you're going to like this, but... look, will you give it a fair hearing? I honestly don't think it needs to be a big deal. It's just a bit of fun."

Owen frowned, already wary. "What's just a bit of fun?" He had visions of being asked to flirt harder, or worse, do something he really wouldn't feel comfortable with, like kiss Mason on camera.

"Misty really liked the pineapple photo I posted on Insta. She wants to do a section on it on the show."

Owen frowned, honestly bewildered. "A section on *pineapples*?"

"Yeah, she loves the idea of growing a pineapple just from the top bit that normally goes in the bin. She loves the sustainability angle." He shuffled his feet, his body language screaming discomfort, even as he kept his voice cheerful. "She thinks it would be really fun if we could take one of your pineapples into the studio when we go in for the live show in a couple of weeks' time. Explain to the viewers how you grew them."

"You mean one of my pineapple plants?"

"No, she wants an actual pineapple."

Owen chuckled even as he frowned. "I don't *have* any

actual pineapples. I told you they take years to fruit. How am I supposed to grow one in two weeks?"

"You're not." Mason looked uncomfortable, his gaze shifting away. "Apparently, Misty bought a few pineapple plants that are, you know, a bit further along than yours." He cleared his throat. "So, we just… pretend they're yours."

"Pretend they're—" Owen broke off, shaking his head. "Okay, wait, where are these plants?"

"In the greenhouse," Mason said miserably. Then, when Owen started walking away, he added in a panicky voice, "Owen, wait—"

But Owen kept moving, heading for the tiny greenhouse and yanking open its flimsy door to be confronted by three pineapple plants on the shelf, each of which had clearly been growing for several years and each of which already had a baby fruit.

When he turned back to speak to Mason, it was to find Misty standing in the doorway, with Mason and Lucy hovering behind her.

Misty gave Owen a wintry smile. "Are you in here because you're ready to do this bit?" she asked sweetly. She glanced at her watch and added, "If we get started now, we can get it in the can before I have to head off."

Owen crossed his arms and smiled back. "Nah," he said. "We won't be doing this bit at all. At least, not the way Mason described it to me."

She got that determined, steely look in her eye that was becoming familiar, her jaw tightening and her eyes going hard. "You're not being very flexible today, Owen."

"I'm sorry you feel that way," he replied, his smile still relaxed. "But I have a few boundaries that I need to maintain, and this is one of them." He jerked a thumb over his shoulder at the pineapple plants. "I didn't grow those, and I'm not going to say otherwise. If you want me to talk about how to look after a pineapple plant that you buy from a plant nursery

247

with the fruit already on it, fine. I'll do it. But I'm not going to pretend those came out of my garden."

Misty shook her mane of blond hair irritably. "I don't understand why you are making such a *huge deal* out of this! You *are* growing pineapples in your own garden at home, right?"

"Yup," Owen agreed.

"So what's the problem?" She spread her hands in a help-less gesture. "You're not lying about growing pineapples—you *are* growing pineapples. I'm just asking you to show the stages in the process. You know, there's a reason it's called tele*vision*? We do actually like to show *visual* content to viewers rather than just talk them through a set of instructions!"

"And that's fine," Owen said patiently. "Provided we're up-front about it."

Misty gave a huff of frustrated laughter. "Oh my God, Owen, you're not going to be happy until you have all my viewers switching off in complete boredom, are you? This is a *Saturday morning* lifestyle show. People tune in to be *enter-tained*." She sighed dramatically, making a show of calming herself down. "Look, how about this? We'll show some photos of your own plants for the first stage, then we'll have the little slot on these plants for the second stage, and then, when you come into the studio for your interview with Marc and Leah, we can have the final product there."

"The final product," Owen said. "You mean, what—a full-size pineapple?"

She nodded. "Yeah. A nice juicy pineapple that we can hand over to our guest chef to turn into a delicious dish. From garden to plate. What could be more inspiring for our viewers?"

He pointed at the pineapple plants again. "You do realise it's going to be months before any of those baby pineapples are full-size?"

Misty gave him a long, hard stare. Owen didn't shift or let his easy smile fade.

Eventually, Misty sighed. She held up her hands, palms out. "Okay, okay, I hear you. Let's just film this. Just say what you're comfortable saying, and we'll take a look in the editing suite and decide where to go from there. Maybe we'll do the section. Maybe we won't."

Owen raised his eyebrows, surprised that she was giving in. Surprised, but pleased.

"All right then," he said. "Thanks for understanding."

She shrugged. "You have to be tough to work in television," she said, "especially on a content-driven show like ours. But I like to think that, as tough as I can be, I *am* fair, and I *do* listen." She gestured around the set and added modestly, "And I'm pretty sure all of the crew here would back me up on that, right guys?" She glanced around, and after a moment, there was an unenthusiastic muttering of insincere agreement. Though it may as well have been a standing ovation, given how pleased with herself Misty looked.

Somehow Owen managed to keep a straight face.

"Right then," Lucy said briskly from behind Misty. "Let's get this bit filmed so we can move on, shall we?"

CHAPTER TWENTY

The pineapple segment was a disaster.

Mason tried his hardest to keep the tone light and their easy banter flowing, but Owen was mulish about explaining, in excruciating detail, how long pineapples took to grow, that these specific pineapple plants were years old and had come from a nursery, and that they were definitely not plants he'd grown from scratch at home.

As much as he hated to admit it, Misty was right. Viewers were going to be bored rigid. So, it was no surprise when, as she was leaving the set, Misty called him over again.

"Walk with me," she said as she strode across the car park towards her huge Audi estate car, blonde hair flying out behind her.

Mason sighed and followed.

The spring sunshine was bright and warm, and Misty had pulled on a massive pair of square-framed Prada sunglasses. Very on-trend. When she turned to face him, Mason had the bizarre impression that she was looking at him through a couple of TV screens and had to bite back a smile.

"That was *not* good." Her tone quashed his amusement and replaced it with a bolt of fear. "Oh, I don't mean you, sweetie," she said, clearly having noticed his dismay. "You did your best, but I don't know what Owen's deal is today. He does realise he's not David bloody Attenborough, doesn't he?"

Anxiety stifled Mason's instinctive defence of Owen. Misty might cancel the whole slot if he couldn't fix this, and it wouldn't help the situation to piss her off even more. Placatingly, he said, "Remember that he's not done any media work before. He doesn't really get that things on TV aren't always what they seem."

She huffed, tossing her head and setting her mane of hair swaying. "I should never have agreed to work with a total amateur," she said, as if the whole thing hadn't been her idea in the first place. "Which is why I'm going to need your help to get things back on track."

"Yeah?" He tried not to sound as relieved as he felt. "Okay, what do you need?"

She waved a hand towards the set, and Mason followed her gesture with his eyes. He could pick out Owen right away, talking to Lucy, the director, with his arms folded across his chest. He'd barely unwound all morning and looked bullish, unmoving as the crew bustled around him.

"I'm going to need some more footage in the greenhouse," Misty said. "What we got today was useless, and Owen obviously isn't going to give me anything better." She flashed a smile, dropping her voice into a whisper. "But you're a pro, Mason. So I'm going to get Naomi to squeeze in another hour's shooting tomorrow morning."

"Oh," Mason said, uncomfortably. "I don't think Owen will have time to do a second day. He's been really busy with—"

"We won't need Owen." Misty's smile turned sharp, rendered weirdly inhuman by her TV-shaped glasses. Mason could see his own uncertain expression reflected back to him in the twin black screens. "I'll just need to get some extra footage of you, a couple of different angles and so on. That's all." She gave a brittle laugh. "Something to give us a fighting chance in the editing suite."

Okay, that didn't sound too bad. Thank God she wasn't demanding Owen drag himself back to set tomorrow. He suspected, given Owen's loose contract, she may have been able to insist, and it would only have pissed him off even more. This was better. Mason could shoot the extra footage needed, and Owen could get back to the day job that he clearly enjoyed so much more than shallow TV work.

Ashamed of that disloyal thought, Mason forced a smile and said, "I can do that. Happy to help."

"You're a *star*," Misty gushed, chucking him under the chin as if he were a five-year-old. "I'll get Naomi to ping you the details." She glanced at her watch. "And now I *must* go. Oscar's got orchestra practice this afternoon, and the au pair's chosen this week to be off sick!"

The rest of the day's filming went much better. Owen was more relaxed when Misty wasn't around, and he wasn't the only one. The whole crew seemed to let out a held breath, and the set felt lighter, with more space for laughter when things went wrong instead of tense cursing. By the time they lost the light, they had everything in the can for the next three episodes.

"I hope they'll actually let the plants grow this time," Owen said, casting a regretful look over his shoulder as they headed off-set. "I don't want to come back and find a couple of coconut trees poking out of the greenhouse."

Mason smiled wanly. "It's a balance, I suppose, between being real and looking real. I get where Misty's coming from, and where you're coming from, too."

"Being real and looking real?" Owen echoed, glancing at

Mason with an odd expression. "That's an interesting way to put it."

Shrugging, Mason pulled his jacket closer around him. Though the sun had been warm earlier, it was gone now, and the air was springtime-chilly. "That's the magical world of TV," he said. "All media, really. It's a facsimile of reality. Like how, if you don't wear makeup on TV, you look really weird?"

"I guess," Owen said, although he sounded doubtful.

They paused at Owen's van. Mason considered inviting him over for the evening; then he remembered that he'd have to be back on set by six. Naomi had messaged him with the time of the crack-of-dawn shoot, and explaining that would be awkward. Even so, Mason found himself craving more time with Owen. Despite working together all day, he longed for the ease he felt when they were alone together.

Which was probably reason enough *not* to invite Owen over, and yet he still dithered.

Luckily, before he could test his resolve, Owen gave a heavy sigh and said, "I've got a really early start tomorrow. I'd say come over tonight, but I'm knackered. Probably just going to hit the sack as soon as I get in."

Which was for the best, Mason told himself, even as his spirits drooped. It would be easier that way. No need to explain anything about tomorrow. Shoving his hands in his jacket pockets, he nodded. "Yeah, me too to be honest."

"Friday?"

"Can I let you know? I've got a collection launch I have to attend, and it'll probably run late."

Owen looked gratifyingly disappointed, but nodded. "Okay. Well, let me know. I don't mind what time you show up." He gave a self-conscious smile and added, "I just like waking up with you in the morning."

"Yeah?" Mason's heart gave a helpless flutter, and he

couldn't resist leaning in to brush a kiss across Owen's lips. "I like that, too."

For a long few moments, they simply smiled at each other, and Mason was struck by the sudden conviction that this thing with Owen was developing a life of its own. One he couldn't control. And, perhaps, one he didn't want to control…

Then Owen took Mason's hand, tangling their fingers together, and fixed him with a look so serious it pierced Mason's soul. "We're okay, right? It got pretty tense today. Sorry if I made things awkward with Misty. It's just that she doesn't—"

Mason touched his fingers to Owen's lips. "Shh," he said thickly. "It's fine. We're good. Misty's hard work. Everyone was more relaxed after she'd gone."

"Yeah, I noticed that. She doesn't respond well to 'No', does she?"

Mason gave a shaky laugh and considered telling Owen about tomorrow's filming after all, but he knew Owen wouldn't understand, and Mason couldn't bear to argue. Not now that Owen was smiling at him with those gentle blue eyes of his. So he just said, "I don't think many people dare say no to her."

Including himself, he thought ruefully.

That was something he bitterly regretted at six o'clock the following morning as he stood, shivering, in that sodding greenhouse wearing the same stupid hemp hoodie he'd worn the day before, hands wrapped around the fading warmth of a mediocre coffee.

Lucy looked no more impressed, lips pursed as she and Misty approached from craft services, coffees in hand.

"…and there I was, minding my own business, just waiting for Oscar after orchestra practice, and Camilla started droning on about her bloody villa in Cavalaire-sur-Mer," Misty was saying. "As though *that* somehow compensates for the fact that Oscar plays first violin in the school symphonia while Aria only bangs a triangle in the percussion band!"

Mildly, Lucy said, "I didn't realise parenting was such a competitive sport."

Misty chose not to respond. "Mason, sweetie," she gushed, striding over. "There you are. Goodness, where's Make-up? You look dreadful."

"I've already been in Make-up—"

She spoke over him, barking orders and sending people scurrying for Make-up and Wardrobe. "Now," she said, turning back to him. "I've got a few notes on what we need." She handed him a single sheet of paper. "I reviewed what we got yesterday, and I was right, of course. The pineapple slot just isn't working. We can't have Owen standing there glowering the whole time! So, we're going to try a different approach."

As she spoke, Mason scanned the page of text. To his dismay, it read more like a script than notes.

MASON

[Whispering as he enters the greenhouse, looking into the camera over his shoulder]

Okay, shhh… Don't tell him, but I've snuck into Owen's greenhouse early because I just have to show you these. I'm so excited! Look, aren't they ADORABLE? Tiny, baby pineapples Owen's grown from planting pineapple tops! Later, we're going to show YOU how to grow your own pineapples, but first, let's take a look at what's been happening in the garden since last week…

MASON
[Planting the pineapple]

Okay, so here's a top Owen prepared earlier. He knows a lot about tops, actually. He's very experienced.
[Crew laughter]
What? I'm talking about pineapples!
[Laughs]
Anyway, so basically, you just get your lovely top and pop him in a pot like this, all cosy, cover him with soil…

MASON
[Eating pineapple]
It's fresh, it's healthy, and it's packed with vitamin C. Best of all, when you grow your own, you know it's organic and pesticide-free.
[Eats another chunk]
Mmmm, delicious! Not to mention, it doesn't cost a bean, so it's great for your budget too!

Mason kept his face as expressionless as any catwalk model's while he read the, frankly cringey, script. Tentatively, he ventured, "I'm not an actor. I'm not sure I'll be convincing working from a script…"

"Oh, that's fine," Misty said breezily. "Put it into your own words, if you like, but that's the message we need to hit in each section."

"But the thing is… It's not all quite *true*? And Owen—"

Misty's good-humoured expression winked out. She held up her hand like she was stopping traffic and snapped, "Lucy, give us a minute."

With a sympathetic look for Mason, Lucy ushered her crew away. They all but ran, and Mason didn't blame them. Misty's face was thunderous.

"Okay, Mason," she hissed, once they were alone, "let me

be very clear. If you want a future with RPP, then I need you on board with this. Nobody's interested in all that crap Owen keeps spouting about growing times and whatnot. This is a *fun* story about sticking the top of a pineapple in a fucking pot and posting it on Instagram, okay?"

"Yes, but—"

"It's a fucking *story*! You understand that, don't you? The whole show is about selling uplifting stories to miserable people—whether it's that they can grow their own bloody pineapples or find gay love in a greenhouse. And trust me when I say this, Mason—if you want to keep working on this show, you *need* people to buy your stories. You need them to invest and tune in every week and post the fuck out of them online, because RPP is not going to waste money on a segment that doesn't wash its own face. Do you understand what I'm saying?"

Mason swallowed. "I do, but honesty's important to Owen, and he wants—"

Misty laughed nastily, her lip curling. "You weren't so bothered about honesty when you decided to—how did you put it?—*fuck him for ratings.*"

Mason's jaw dropped. "I didn't—" he began, then broke off, staring at Misty in horror.

"Sweetie," she said, "we both know you did. And believe me, the *last* thing I want is for Owen to find out—Christ knows how he'd react if he gets this worked up over a bloody pineapple."

Was she *threatening* him? The thought of Owen learning that Misty had suggested Mason deliberately seduce him made his stomach knot painfully.

Perhaps seeing his horror, Misty made an obvious effort to soften her expression, which was about as reassuring as a shark trying to smile. "Look," she said, placatingly. "We don't need to get into any of this stuff with Owen, do we? I get that he's not familiar with the media. Fair enough. He's an

257

amateur. But you? Mason, sweetie… For *you*, this is just a stepping stone. Who knows where it might lead if you play your cards right? You know that Marc's probably leaving the show at the end of the year, and I'm looking for a fresh face. And do you realise I've literally had Austin bloody *Coburn* on the phone desperate to interview you? Do you know who he is? He has a column in *Weekend Life*, Mason. *Weekend Life*! That's fantastic exposure for us—for *you*." She shook her head. "There's a choice to be made here—don't fuck it up."

Mason stared sightlessly down at the script he still held in his hands, the lines blurring as he tried to absorb Misty's mind-fucking whirlwind of threats and bribes.

He found himself recalling Owen's words too, the night they'd argued in Mason's flat.

You deserve to choose the life you live.

Easy to say, but in the real world, what choices did he have? Christ, if Misty told Owen that Mason had 'fucked him for ratings'… Mason's stomach twisted at the thought. It wasn't true, not really—but it was close enough to the truth to ruin everything. Mason felt sure, with cold certainty, that Owen would never understand—or forgive—Mason if he suspected that was the reason Mason had slept with him.

Then there was the fact that Austin fucking Coburn was interested in interviewing him—Austin Coburn who had a big splashy column in a fancy Sunday broadsheet and who appeared on TV panel shows. It was a *massive* opportunity. Frankie would wet himself if he knew, and Mason would be a fool to turn it down.

But still he felt queasy. He gave it one more try.

"I think Owen just wants to be upfront about—"

"Oh my God, *nobody cares!*" Misty cried, throwing up her hands. "It's a pineapple, for God's sake. Are you really going to throw everything away over a fucking pineapple?"

And yeah, that was the question. Mason understood Owen's point, but Owen *was* coming at this from a very narrow perspective, and did it *really* matter if they fudged the growing time for a pineapple? It was just fluff, just filler. And if Mason presented it, it wouldn't even reflect on Owen. Not really.

Misty had her hands on her hips, studying him. The morning breeze caught her long swath of blonde hair, and in the cool light, he could see a narrow line of grey roots along the centre of her parting.

"Well?" she said impatiently. "What's it to be, Mason? Are you on board or not?"

CHAPTER TWENTY-ONE

Owen didn't see Mason in the week following the second filming session. Work was insanely busy, and Mason's diary was crammed too—away for a few days at a catalogue shoot, then out with his family for his mum's birthday on the Thursday he got back. Then, on Friday, he was due to catch up with Tag for drinks. He offered to rearrange, insisting Tag wouldn't mind, but Owen was so knackered by then, he decided to take the opportunity for an early night, especially given they had to be at the RPP studio for seven the next morning for their live studio appearance.

"You go out and have a good time with Tag," he told Mason. He was leaning against the fence of the garden he'd been working in, watching Naaz and Kyle tidy up their gear. His shoulders ached from lugging heavy bags of sharp sand, topsoil, and compost all day, but the late afternoon sun was mellow, and he was smiling as he spoke, imagining Mason lounging on his sofa in his favourite tatty shorts and nothing else.

"Are you sure?" Mason said uncertainly. "I've really missed you this week."

"Yeah?" A bolt of pleasure zinged through Owen at that confession. "I've missed you too. But we'll be done by lunchtime tomorrow, and then I've got the rest of the weekend off."

"No overtime this weekend?" Mason said, sounding suddenly brighter.

Owen grinned. "Nope." Encouraged, he took a breath and added, "I was thinking, if the weather holds up, we could maybe go to the seaside. What do you think? Maybe book a night somewhere nice?"

A considering pause came down the line, and for a heart-stopping moment, Owen was afraid he'd pushed things too far with that suggestion. But then, with a rueful sigh, Mason said, "I'd actually love that." He sounded happy, and Owen could just imagine how he'd look in that moment, his smile soft, green eyes dreamy. "Can we get an ice cream at the beach?"

"Yeah. We'll get ninety-nines with Mr. Whippy ice cream," Owen promised. "Double-size ones."

"With two Flakes and strawberry sauce," Mason added, with a soft laugh.

"Strawberry sauce!" Owen teased. "Sacrilege!"

Mason laughed too, then added softly, "Can't wait to see you."

"Same," Owen murmured. Distantly, he was aware he was smiling like a complete loon, but he didn't care. The words *I love you* tingled on the tip of his tongue, but no, he wasn't going to say them now. It was still so early, and he didn't want to scare Mason off. Besides, you didn't say stuff like that for the first time on the phone. So all he said was. "See you tomorrow, angel."

"Yeah," Mason breathed, and then he paused, and it felt

like he might say more, but in the end, he only murmured, "See you," and hung up.

Owen stared at his phone, still smiling, after the call ended. Then, realising he probably looked like a right nob, he shoved it in his pocket and went to help Naaz and Kyle put the gear back in the van.

∾

When Owen's alarm went off the next morning, he woke feeling well-rested. He'd been sorely tempted to call Mason the night before, to see if there was any chance of him coming over after his drinks with Tag, but now he was glad he'd resisted temptation. He felt refreshed and could look forward to a whole weekend of just him and Mason—well, after he'd faced the horrors of the TV cameras anyway.

That thought had his stomach knotting up with stress, and he scrubbed his hands over his face. Funny how easy it had been to agree to today's appearance when it had been weeks and weeks away. Now that it was here, today, it felt like an insane decision. Being filmed was bad enough when you knew someone was going to edit the footage to try to make you look semi-coherent. Today was completely different. Today, he was going to have to sit under hot lights, being questioned by those toothy, overly cheerful presenters. Live on air.

Groaning, he got out of bed and headed for the bathroom.

At least he'd managed to get to the barber's, although now that he was facing his stark reflection in the bathroom mirror, he wondered whether he'd gone too short. Fed up with his mop, he'd asked the barber to take off more than usual, and the guy had really gone for it. Owen felt almost naked as he turned his head, checking out the result. Well, it was done now, and at least he wouldn't look scruffy on TV.

Picking up his razor, he carefully shaved all the scruff off his face, thinking about the ordeal to come. As the minutes ticked by, the vague nervy jitter in his stomach that had begun when he first woke up gradually grew into something that felt more like a writhing pit of snakes. By the time he was showered and dressed, he was feeling genuinely nauseous, unable even to stomach the thought of breakfast. Somehow, he managed to force down half of a mug of camomile tea—which did nothing to calm him down—before he finally headed out to the van.

All too soon, he was pulling into the RPP studio car park again. He parked the van and switched off the engine, then closed his eyes and forced himself to take five deep breaths in and out, filling up his lungs, then letting the air out slowly.

It didn't help. He'd never felt as nervous about anything in his whole life. *Why had he agreed to this?*

Mason, a little voice in the back of his head supplied. *You agreed for Mason's sake.*

He was in the middle of another series of five deep breaths when his phone pinged a notification. He pulled it out to find a message from Lewis.

Good luck today, I know you'll be awesome.

All Owen could think at that moment was that Lewis was awake. He swiped the call button with his thumb and waited. It rang twice; then Lewis answered.

"Owen?"

"I can't do it. Shit, Lew. I can't go in there."

Silence for a beat, then, "Bollocks. Of course you can."

"Nope." His breath was coming in short, panicked gulps. "Nope, can't do it."

"Come on, this is nothing." Lewis yawned, sounding sleepy. Probably still in bed, the lucky sod. "You're the brave one, remember? Nothing freaks you out."

Not true. That had never been true, although Owen always took care not to let Lewis see his fears and struggles.

263

Growing up, he'd had to be the strong one, and that hadn't changed.

"Right," he said, pulling all the other words and feelings back behind his teeth. "Yeah, you're right."

"Honestly, you'll be fine," Lewis went on. "Just make heart eyes at Mason and the audience will lap it up—Ow! What?" A muffled sound. Lewis said, presumably to Aaron, "I *am* being nice!" Then, louder again, "Look, Owen, this is Saturday morning TV. Most people watching will either be hungover, still drunk, or shagging. Just smile, flirt with Mason, and take the money." A pause followed. "They *are* paying you, right?"

"I have to go," Owen said. He didn't want to get into *that* argument on top of everything else.

"What the fuck? I told you to get an agent to look at—"

Owen hung up, switched off his phone, and threw it onto the passenger seat. Then he spent another minute staring at the studio door, willing his pulse to stop racing and his feet to start moving.

Mason's in there, he told himself firmly. *He's relying on you. You have to go in. Now. You're five minutes late already.*

Finally, steeling himself, Owen got out of the van and strode up to the front door, passing through security first, then reception, where he was given a visitor's pass and had to wait for a bored-looking production assistant bearing a name-tag that read 'Adam' to come and collect him.

Adam tried to take him to Wardrobe, insisting that Naomi had organised an outfit for him that he was supposed to wear —probably another tattersall shirt, Owen thought sourly.

"I'm fine as I am, thanks," he decided. "No need to put Wardrobe to any trouble."

Adam's expression grew pained. "Could you wait here a minute?" he said tightly, walking a few yards and turning away from Owen as he made a call, speaking in a hushed but driven undertone to whoever answered.

After ending the call, he came back and said briskly, "I've to take you to Make-up instead. Apparently, your co-presenter's already up there."

"Mason, you mean?"

"Yup," Adam replied, popping the 'p' irritably and stalking away.

Owen made a face at his back as he followed him through a maze of corridors, up a couple of flights of stairs, and past a bunch of doors. Finally, Adam opened one of the doors—to room 3.09, according to the grubby plastic sign—and gestured for Owen to enter.

It was a surprisingly small, windowless room containing three swivel chairs in front of a bank of mirrors. A massive three-tier trolley, stuffed with cosmetic products, brushes, and other paraphernalia, took up half the remaining floor space, and a bank of shelves on the far wall was packed with more stuff in various labelled boxes and containers. Two of the room's three chairs were empty, but Mason sat in the middle one, a small, blue plastic cape around his shoulders.

"Hey!" he said, his smiling reflection in the mirror turning comically wide-eyed. "Oh my God, you cut your hair."

Behind Owen, the door closed, and he turned reflexively to discover that Adam had apparently decided to leave them to it.

When he turned back, Mason had swivelled his chair around so he was facing Owen. Someone had already applied a layer of foundation over his face. In the harsh overhead light, it looked plasticky, masking the subtly expressive lines of Mason's face and making him seem somehow unreal, like a mannequin.

Owen ran a hand self-consciously over his cropped hair. "Too short?"

"No," Mason said, smiling, head cocked. "No, I like it… It's different, though. Very GI Joe."

"I thought I should, you know…" His voice wobbled nervously, and he cleared his throat. "Look smarter."

Mason's smile faded. "Are you okay?"

Owen blinked. "What? Oh, yeah, of course. Sorry, just a bit nervous, you know? I had to give Lewis a call when I got here before I could make myself come in."

"You're nervous?" Mason said. He sounded surprised.

"God, yes. Aren't you?"

Mason seemed to think about that, his gaze going inward for a moment as though he was checking himself. Then he shrugged and met Owen's gaze again. "A little. Nothing too bad."

"Really?" Owen said. "I feel like throwing up."

Mason gave a short, surprised laugh. Then whatever he saw on Owen's face made his laughter tail off, and he said slowly, "You're serious."

Owen nodded.

Mason got out of his chair and went to Owen, taking hold of both his hands and guiding him into the chair to the left of his own.

"You don't have to do this," he said worriedly. "Maybe you shouldn't? We can say you've taken ill if you like. You're white as a ghost, so they'll believe you."

Owen gave a weak laugh. "I'll manage. I just—need a minute."

"The thing is," Mason said, still holding his hands, "there's something you should—"

Just then, the door opened, and a large woman in a yellow-and-blue kaftan with a matching yellow turban sailed in.

"I told you to stay in that chair!" she exclaimed, staring accusingly at Mason.

"I promise I haven't touched my face," he said hurriedly. "Or even moved it!" He gestured his hand at his own face in a circular motion and added, "I've been totally expressionless just like you said."

"*Hmmpf.*" She eyed him suspiciously for several long moments, then grudgingly turned to Owen, examining him with impersonal interest. "You're the other one," she said at last. She glanced at Mason and added, "You have good taste."

Mason pinkened, and Owen's heart gave a little thud.

"This is Carmen," Mason said. "Carmen—Owen Hunter."

"I know your brother," Carmen said, raising her eyebrows. Owen wasn't sure whether that was a pleasantry or an accusation, so he just smiled.

"Nice to meet you, Carmen."

Carmen nodded, then bent to get something out of the bottom tier of the enormous trolley. When she straightened again, she had another of those little plastic shoulder capes in her hand. A pink one this time.

"Okay," she said. "Let's get you ready for the cameras."

After the delights of Make-up, Owen and Mason were taken down to the green room, which, disappointingly, looked more like a GP's waiting room than anything else, with two dispiriting rows of not-particularly-comfortable seats facing each other. There were some drinks and snacks, but Owen still couldn't stomach the thought of food. He took a seat on the row opposite Mason so they were facing one another, knees brushing, and sipped at some water, his palms damp, his heart racing.

He tried to think of the questions the presenters would ask —Naomi had sent them through a rough list in advance, so they could prepare—and how he had planned to answer them, but right now, his mind couldn't seem to settle to anything. It was racing and curiously blank at the same time.

Mason had gone quiet too, his fingers picking nervously at

the hem of his t-shirt, a pink one sporting a sequinned rainbow, clearly Misty's choice. Owen was vaguely aware of Mason watching him worriedly. He offered what he suspected was an unconvincing attempt at a smile.

"Sorry about this. I didn't realise I'd react this way." He swallowed hard.

Mason's frown was concerned. "Honestly, maybe you shouldn't go on. I'm totally fine doing it myself. It might even be—" He cut himself off and gave a weak smile.

"Might even be *better*?" Owen finished for him, half offended and half amused.

"No. I mean, yes, but better for *you*. We could—that is, should we speak to Adam about it? Maybe he can…" He trailed off, then blurted, "I really think you should just let me do it, you know? I think that would be best."

Owen shook his head. "It'll be okay, just… maybe… can you jump in and rescue me if I freeze or fuck up?"

"Of course," Mason said, offering another nervy smile. "Whatever happens, I won't let you crash and burn."

Owen felt a slight easing of the tension in his stomach at that assurance. "Thanks," he said, and he really meant it. "That… actually helps."

Mason's smile faded, and he pulled out his phone, starting to scroll restlessly. Clearly, Mason was more nervous than he wanted to admit, and somehow that helped too. If Mason needed Owen to do this with him, Owen would be there. No question.

He glanced at the clock. Adam was coming to get them in a few minutes' time; then they'd wait on-set for their spot to start. He took a deep breath and let it out slowly, then another, then another. It helped a bit, but the jittery, nervy feeling wasn't going anywhere. He could only hope that it would ease up once they were actually doing the slot and talking to the presenters.

"Thank God they sent us the questions," he said. "I mean,

right now I'm struggling to remember the answers I prepared, but at least I have an idea of what they're going to say. If I didn't know, this would be so much worse. Fuck, I don't think I could have done it. I think I might actually have chickened out."

Mason looked up sharply from his phone, his expression arrested. "What?"

"The questions," Owen repeated. "I was just saying that if I didn't know what was coming, I don't think I could have gone on."

Mason looked stricken. "You know it's just a rough list, right?" he said. His gaze slid away as he added, "The presenters might not ask all those questions. Or they might…take things in a completely different direction — they're supposed to make it seem spontaneous. It's live TV. Anything could happen."

"I know," Owen said. "It's not like I've rehearsed it word for word or anything. It's just—well, knowing most of what they're going to ask helps, you know?"

Mason rubbed uncomfortably at the back of his neck, and Owen suddenly felt bad. It wasn't fair to lay all this on Mason. Owen wasn't the only one doing this today. Mason might have done live TV before, but only once or twice. He was clearly feeling anxious too.

"Hey, I'm sorry. I shouldn't be—"

Mason looked up, and this time his gaze was anguished. "No, don't," he interrupted. "Please don't apologise, Owen. Listen, whatever happens, just follow my lead, okay?"

The door to the green room opened then. It was Adam, clipboard in hand, earpiece on.

"Time to go to the set, gents," he said. "Follow me."

"Can we just have one minute?" Mason broke in anxiously. "I just want to—"

"Sorry, no can do," Adam said briskly. "We need you on

set and ready to go." He held the door open, gesturing brusquely at them. "Come on."

Owen got to his feet. "It's okay, Mason," he said, trying to sound calmer than he felt. "I'll be fine. Don't worry."

Mason looked like he wanted to argue, but in the end, he got up too, and they both followed Adam out into the corridor.

CHAPTER TWENTY-TWO

MASON

Mason's stomach pinched as Adam led them to the main part of the set where the guest interviews took place. It wasn't the fact that this was going out live that bothered him, although his body was alive with the familiar rush of adrenaline that accompanied every catwalk show. No, his churning anxiety was all about the extra pineapple footage that hung over him like the sword of Damocles.

On set, there were two sofas set up in an "L" shape, one for the presenters and one for the guests. Marc and Leah were already in place, both of them looking polished and whole-some as they perused their notes. As Mason and Owen got closer, Adam explained in an undertone that their latest gardening slot was currently on air, pausing to point out the screen hanging beneath the autocue, which showed what was being broadcast right now. On the screen, Owen and Mason were crouching beside one of the raised beds, Owen pointing to different parts of a plant as he talked. Mason was nodding, his gaze flicking between the plant and Owen. Mason's stomach twisted to see the expression on his own face each time his eyes returned to Owen. The softness there. The painfully obvious admiration.

"When the slot finishes, we'll come back to the studio," Adam added quietly, drawing Mason's attention to the here and now. "At that point, we'll go straight into your interview."

Mason nodded, then cast his gaze around. "Where's Misty?" he whispered when he could see no sign of her.

"Production control room," Adam said, pointing to a door behind the cameras

Well, that was something at least. Mason was glad he wouldn't be able to see her while they were on air.

When they reached the sofas, Marc and Leah stood up to greet them. Mason watched Leah do a double-take when she caught sight of Owen, and no wonder—gone was Owen's touchable mop of nut-brown hair, in its place that buzz cut that made him look oddly exposed. Vulnerable, even. Especially here, so out of his element.

Secretly, Mason mourned the loss of his hair. Not that he'd say as much to Owen, but he hoped it would grow back quickly.

They took their seats, and Owen appeared reasonably calm he shook hands with the presenters, though it was obvious to Mason from his uncharacteristic silence and lack of expression that he was very far from being himself.

"It's great to have you on," Leah gushed once they were all seated. "The audience is loving your segment—we're getting loads of positive feedback."

Marc's smile was more grudging. "Yes," he said. "It's proving to be quite popular."

Owen said nothing, and after a slightly too-long pause, Mason hastily put in, "Yeah, we're pretty stoked about it, aren't we, Owen?"

"Yes," Owen said. He gave a quick, tight smile.

Marc and Leah glanced at one another, sharing a look, and

Mason felt a stab of unease. He eyed Owen worriedly. He was very obviously not okay, and Mason was feeling increasingly certain things were about to get worse. He wasn't sure exactly what was going to happen during this interview, but Misty had said they'd be showing his re-filmed section with the pineapple plants.

Fuck, fuck, *fuck*. Why hadn't he warned Owen earlier? He had *intended* to tell Owen about it, but he'd wanted to do it face to face. Except they hadn't ended up seeing each other all week. And yeah, okay, maybe he'd been putting it off because he knew Owen wouldn't be happy, but he really had thought he'd be able to do the deed this morning before the show started. Only he hadn't anticipated Owen having a freak-out about going on live TV. Owen was usually so calm, taking everything in his stride. It was one of the things that had first drawn Mason to him, that sense that Owen was easy in his own skin. So, to see him like this was…unsettling.

There *had* been a brief window of opportunity in the green room, but Owen had seemed so anxious that Mason hadn't wanted to stress him out more. So, he'd sat there, paralysed with indecision, till Adam came and took the decision out of his hands. But God, now Mason desperately wished he'd taken the bull by the horns because, as nervous as Owen had seemed then, being ambushed on live TV was going to be ten times worse, wasn't it?

"Mason?"

He blinked and focused on Marc, who was looking at him expectantly.

"Sorry. I was miles away. What was that?"

Marc frowned his disapproval. "I was saying we've cut the first few questions. We've decided to show some gardening pictures our viewers have posted online instead and then move straight onto the attention your relationship's been getting on social media—that's what the viewers want to see."

Mason glanced at Owen, wondering if the social media stuff would bother him, but he didn't even seem to be hearing Marc. His jaw was clamped with tension, there was a faint sheen of sweat on his forehead, bared by his short haircut, and his eyes were distant. It was as if he'd gone somewhere else entirely.

Mason felt a pang of worry coupled with a helpless sense of dread.

"Forty-five seconds," someone said. Marc and Leah both adjusted themselves on the sofa, assuming toothy grins in readiness for the cue.

Mason leaned across the sofa and touched Owen's hand. "Are you all right?" he whispered urgently. A production assistant glared at him, but he ignored her.

Owen nodded, but he was pale, his dilated pupils making his blue eyes darker than normal, his chest moving with shallow breaths.

"Listen, just follow my lead. I'll—"

"Mason," someone said sharply—he didn't know who, but it was enough to snap him back into the moment, moving back into his own space on the sofa as someone else counted down the final seconds and Leah picked up the cue.

"I don't know about you, Marc, but Mason and Owen have really inspired me to get back out into the garden," she enthused.

"Same here," Marc said. "My local garden centre must be getting sick of the sight of me!" They both laughed at the unlikeliness of that.

Leah looked back to the autocue. "Lots of you have been getting in touch to tell us how inspired *you've* been—and sharing your own gardening pictures online. Let's take a look at some of them."

The screen below the autocue began to flash up a series of images from Instagram and Twitter, complete with emojis and hashtags. Ordinary, smiling people in their gardens: a woman pruning a bushy shrub, a little boy pretending to dig with a huge spade, a man with a plant pot on his head pulling a silly face. Eventually, the screen returned to Leah.

"Amazing pictures!" she gushed. "And we're absolutely delighted to have Mason Nash and Owen Hunter, our gardening hotties, with us on the couch today." She swept an arm in their direction. "Welcome to you both!" A few crew members duly cheered as the cameras switched to them.

Mason flashed his best million-dollar smile. "It's so great to be here—in the studio, where it's warm!"

They all duly laughed, but when Mason glanced at Owen, he seemed unable to manage more than a vague grimace.

There was a brief silence. Then Marc turned to Mason. "So, Mason. I know you're a big Instagram star—what do you think of our viewers' pictures?"

Mason grabbed the cue gratefully and began wittering on about the pictures, mentioning one or two of them and making a couple of gentle jokes that got a few chuckles from the crew.

When he was done, Leah turned to Owen. "It must be rewarding for you, Owen, as a gardener? Seeing our viewers so inspired by what you and Mason are doing?"

For a second, Mason wondered whether Owen was going to respond at all, but after a heart-stopping pause, he cleared his throat and said briefly, "Yes, it's great." He swallowed then, visibly struggling.

Mason's heart twisted for him. "Owen is *so* modest," he said, "but I've seen how dedicated he is to his work. And how much he believes that gardening is for everyone. Right, Owen?"

Mason shot him a hopeful look, willing him to pick up and run with the ball he'd lobbed at him.

And, with a jerky nod, Owen said, "Uh, yes. Everyone would benefit from gardening because—"

"But it's not just *gardening* pictures we're seeing online,"

Marc interjected in a teasing tone, cutting Owen off. Mason could have killed him. "You two have been getting quite a lot of attention yourselves—I gather you've even got your own hashtag." He looked at Leah, pretending bewilderment. "What was it you told me? *Hashtag OwSon?*"

Leah laughed. "Yes, there's a *lot* of buzz online about these two. Never mind budding flowers. It's budding *romance* that has everyone excited. So, tell us, Mason"—she turned back to him with a toothy grin—"are the rumours true? Are you two just good friends, or is something more blooming in the *Weekend Wellness* garden?"

Despite the gap between them on the sofa, Mason could sense Owen stiffening.

Mason tried to laugh lightly, but it sounded strained. "Let's put it like this," he said, "we're *very* good friends. I don't think I've ever clicked with anyone as quickly as I did with Owen."

He glanced at Owen, who met his gaze with confusion, even as he tried to smile. The little lines around his eyes that creased so adorably when his smile was wide and genuine were making him look strained. Oh God, was he annoyed that Mason wasn't admitting they were together? Was he annoyed that Mason was talking about them at all? Couldn't he understand that this was simply part of the story they'd been teasing for *weeks* now?

Leah turned to Owen. "And what about you, Owen? What did you think when you first met our Mason?"

Our Mason.

Owen looked… pained. No getting away from it, he was hating this.

"Er, when I first met him?" He blinked, seeming a little confused. "Well, he was dating my brother back then, so…"

"Oh my God, *Owen!*" Mason forced a ridiculously camp laugh that probably sounded more alarmed than amused. Of all the bloody things he could have said, why *that*?

Leah leaned in, her innate nose for gossip twitching. "That would be Lewis Hunter, creator of the vampire drama, *Leeches*?"

Visibly panicking, Owen stammered, "No. I mean, yes, but, uh— Mason... That is, I thought he was pretty great." Another of those strained smiles. "He's very attractive. Obviously."

Pretty great? Very attractive?

Even though Mason knew Owen wasn't *really* lukewarm about him, the tepid words still hurt, bringing an unexpected lump to Mason's throat.

"I can see you're a man of few words," Marc said, filling the silence left by Owen's awkward reply. "And, as Mason said, you don't like to blow your own trumpet either, do you? But we happen to know that you've got a *bit* of a secret project on the go." He raised a brow.

"And it just so happens," Leah said, taking up the cue, "that we have an inside track on that." She grinned at the camera. "Take a look at this."

Shit. Mason's heart leapt into his throat. It was happening. Now.

The screen below the autocue came on, with sound this time, and there he was: Mason, standing in front of the greenhouse in that fucking rainbow hoodie that he suddenly hated.

"Don't tell Owen," on-screen Mason whispered. *"But I'm going to sneak you into the greenhouse because I just* have *to show you this. It's amazing."* He opened the door and beckoned at the camera—which was actually just Misty's phone camera, since she'd decided she wanted this bit to look like a spontaneous film Mason had done himself.

Mason glanced at Owen anxiously—he was staring rigidly at the screen, face pale, lips parted in astonishment.

On-screen Mason stood aside, revealing the pineapple plants. *"Look! Aren't they adorable?"* He bent towards the plants and prodded one of the tiny pineapples with his forefinger, making it rock as he crooned, *"Little baby pineapples!"* Straightening, he added, *"This is pretty wild, but did you know you can actually* grow *these from the top of a pineapple you buy at the supermarket? And I happen to know that because it's exactly what Owen did a few weeks ago."*

He waited for the next part to begin—him saying that Owen's own pineapple plants were back in his greenhouse at home, and that maybe next time Owen would let Mason show those plants off—but it didn't appear. Instead, the VT cut to Mason leaving the greenhouse and closing the door behind him with exaggerated care before saying in a stagey whisper, *"To find out how you can grow pineapples like Owen's, check out the* Weekend Wellness *website. In the meantime, let's go back to the studio where we have some sweet treats lined up…"*

Misty had waved off Mason's question during filming about the *"sweet treats"* sign off, making a vague comment about the next part of the show being the cooking segment. But as the film ended, and the camera went back to Leah and Marc, Mason had a sudden horrible realisation about where this was going.

The next few seconds seemed to unfold in slow motion. He watched helplessly as Marc bent down to retrieve something from the shelf under the table between the two sofas while Leah said, "So, we have a little surprise for you, Owen!"

Mason glanced at Owen and saw the expression of betrayed confusion in his eyes as Marc straightened, holding something in his hands…

A pineapple.

A fucking pineapple.

"Mason sneaked in one of your amazing home-grown pineapples," Marc said to Owen. He laughed. "If I'd known they were so easy to grow, I'd have tried it myself!"

Owen opened his mouth to respond, and Mason's

stomach dropped. Shit, was Owen going to call bullshit on the whole thing live on air?

Holding his breath, Mason fixed his expression into camera-ready blankness and waited for the other shoe to drop.

And waited.

And waited.

But Owen said… nothing. No denial, no confirmation. Nothing at all. Mason risked a worried sideways glance and found Owen staring at him, colour high in his cheeks. With his brutal haircut and closed expression, he was suddenly unrecognisable. Hard as stone. Like granite, and utterly unreachable.

Mason felt like he'd been struck. The world shifted around him, reality suddenly too bright, too sharp. Panic twisted in his belly, making him feel sick with guilt, and he had to work hard not to reach out to grab Owen's hand. To reassure him. To apologise. To show him that—

Shit.

Mason's throat tightened. With abrupt and shocking clarity, he realised that, as much as he didn't want to lose the slot on *Weekend Wellness*, he was far, far more terrified of losing Owen. And suddenly, that seemed like a distinct possibility.

It felt like forever that they sat there, staring at each other, but it was probably only a second before Leah cut through the awkward silence. "Well, *I'm* definitely going to be trying to grow one of these at home, Marc, but once I've harvested my pineapple, what can I do with it? There's only so many pineapple smoothies a girl can drink!"

"Funny you should ask…" Laughing his cheesy laugh, Marc rose and began walking away from the sofas towards the kitchen set a few feet away, still carrying the fruit. One of the cameras swept along its dolly track after him. "Because we have someone with us today who is going to show us some amazing—and *surprising*—things you can do with your home-grown pineapple."

Mason blinked, struggling to grasp how quickly that had all played out. The interview was done. Already, the glaring studio lights were off them, and Leah was up and striding across the studio floor towards a middle-aged guy with an earpiece and a clipboard, leaving Mason and Owen stranded on the guest sofa.

Heart pounding, Mason said hoarsely, "Owen, I'm sorry, I —", but before he could say more, Adam was there.

"Let's get your mics off," he said briskly.

Mason just kept staring at Owen, his stomach in knots. He wasn't sure what he expected to see, but it wasn't the utter blankness he encountered when Owen looked his way. Owen's blue eyes looked hollow, and for a long, horrible moment, he stared at Mason with that cold, empty gaze. As though they were strangers. Then, with a violent jerk, he yanked off his mic and stood up.

"Hey," Adam said moving forward, "careful with that."

Owen ignored him, tearing the mic free, pulling the battery pack off his belt, and throwing it all down on the table. Then he stalked away without another word.

"Owen, wait—" Mason called after him, embarrassed by how his voice broke.

For a moment, he just sat there, paralysed; then he pulled off his own mic and hurried after Owen, ignoring Adam's demand for him to wait. Ignoring the frowning faces of the crew, he pushed past.

When Mason burst out of the set, Owen was already halfway down the windowless inner corridor, striding towards the exit.

"Owen!"

Shoulders hunching, Owen didn't respond. Didn't look back. Didn't stop.

Mason sprinted after him, dodging around an alarmed-looking woman carrying a cardboard holder loaded with hot drinks. "Sorry," he muttered, not stopping as he raced after Owen.

By then, Owen was in reception, slowing down as he approached the glass doors, and Mason finally caught him up.

"Fuck's sake," Mason said, breathless as he grabbed Owen's arm. "Will you just wait?"

Angrily, Owen shook him off. His face was flushed, his eyes flinty. "Let go," he growled, glancing past Mason.

Mason followed his gaze and saw the security bloke at the reception desk staring at them with interest. Lowering his voice, Mason said, "Look, I know you weren't expecting that. Neither was I, but—"

"Give me a break," Owen growled and pushed open the glass doors, walking out into the grey morning. He didn't wait for Mason, just stalked across the car park towards his van.

Mason pushed through the doors after him. "Will you just listen for a sec?"

No answer.

"For fuck's sake!" Panicking now, Mason charged after him. "Talk about overreacting."

Owen spun around, his face blank and unrecognisably cold. "Overreacting?"

"All right." Mason held up his hands. "Look, I'm sorry that I didn't warn you, but I *was* going to, this morning. Except, when you arrived, you were *so* stressed out that I started thinking that maybe I shouldn't say anything, in case I made it worse and then—"

"Warn me about what?" Owen interrupted angrily. "The fact that you'd decided to make me look like a fucking fraud on live TV?"

Taken aback, Mason said, "That's not what—"

"You could practically see the supermarket label on that

fucking pineapple! It's obvious it wasn't grown in a London greenhouse."

"Nobody's going to notice—"

"*I* noticed!"

Mason shook his head, fear tightening his chest. "Owen, come on. It was, like, thirty seconds of TV. Don't worry about—"

"You don't get it, do you?" Owen stared at him, and it was like being studied by a stranger, a cold and angry stranger. "You made me look like a fucking fake."

"I didn't." Mason's protest sounded weak, and his throat seized and clicked as he tried to swallow. "I didn't know they were going to—"

"Bollocks!" Owen laughed without a trace of humour. "Didn't you see yourself in the fucking greenhouse talking about 'Owen's pineapples'?"

"Okay, yes, but there was another part they didn't show, and I..." He glanced warily back at the studio. Hazy sunlight reflected off the glass doors, hiding whoever was inside. For all Mason knew, a dozen people had their phones out. Misty might be watching. "Look, can we go somewhere else to talk about this?"

"No."

The word was shocking in its curt finality.

"No?" The panic in his chest began to squeeze his lungs. "Come on, just let me explain—"

Owen backed up a step. "No. It's done. It's over."

"What? You don't mean..." Mason tailed off, horrified, because he'd never seen Owen look like that before. Blank, unmoved. Steely eyes watching him. "You're blowing this way out of proportion," he said, lifting a hand towards Owen, only to drop it in the face of his hostile expression. "Owen, come on. It's just a fucking pineapple!"

"You *lied*," Owen said flatly. "Do you understand that?

You trashed my professional reputation for the sake of… of boosting your own career."

Mason felt heat steal into his face, a crawling sensation. Like shame. And yes, it was true. He shouldn't have gone behind Owen's back to do the extra filming, but Misty hadn't given him a choice. Not that he could explain that to Owen. But, Christ, it was such a minor thing. A fucking pineapple. "Owen, *please*," he said desperately. "It's not that big of a deal."

If anything, Owen's expression only grew colder. "You *knew* I didn't want anything to do with that stupid pineapple crap. You knew I didn't want to lie to the audience about my work."

Scrubbing a hand through his hair, Mason said, "Look, I admit I should have told you about the extra filming, but I didn't know Misty was going to edit it the way—"

"Screw Misty," Owen spat. "You heard what I told her. You *knew* why I didn't want to fake it. Do you just not care that I have a business to run, a reputation to protect? Christ, Mason, I have a team who rely on me for their *jobs*."

"Owen—"

"Oh, I know that's nothing compared to ten billion fucking Instagram likes," Owen went on bitterly, "but to me, it's everything. My business, my reputation. Fuck, my business *is* my reputation. And you—you trashed it. You stomped all over it like it doesn't even matter."

"That's not fair!" Christ, he sounded petulant, but it *wasn't* fair. And it wasn't true. "They edited it to make it look like that. What I filmed was different—and I didn't even know about the bloody pineapple in the studio this morning."

Owen's lip curled. "Come off it. You knew what Misty wanted, and you gave it to her. You *lied* for them, Mason. Do you understand that? You lied, and you made me a part of their lie."

"It's not a *lie*," Mason shot back, angry now. "It's a *story*.

Why can't you get that? We're telling stories, Owen, not giving lectures—and people understand that. It only has to be an approximation of the truth."

"An *approximation* of the truth?" A horrible look of understanding spread across Owen's face. "Fuck, I'm not sure you even know what's true and what's not anymore. Or maybe you just don't care."

The heat in Mason's cheeks turned into a burn. "Of course I bloody do."

But Owen wasn't listening, shaking his head as he retreated a step. "Was… Was *any* of this real to you…?"

"*This*? You mean *us*?" Mason's eyes pricked, his throat thickening. "For God's sake, you know this is real."

"Do I?" Owen backed away further, although his gaze was still locked on Mason. "Maybe it's just a story you're telling on Instagram. Maybe it's all part of the show. Maybe it was Misty's fucking idea in the first place!"

Mason stiffened, felt the betraying rush of blood to his face.

"Jesus," Owen said, recoiling in horror. "Jesus, it was, wasn't it?"

Staring at Owen's pale, angry face, Mason knew there was no point in denial. Owen had seen the truth in his reaction, and denying it now would only make things worse. Voice cracking, he admitted, "Sort of."

"*Sort* of? What the fuck does that mean?"

Mason closed his eyes, blotting out the sight of Owen's outrage, and made himself say, "Misty…suggested our dynamic might be more authentic if you and I—"

"Fuck," Owen said, hands on his head, bunching into fists as if to tug at the hair he no longer had. His eyes were screwed tight shut. "Christ, I'm a fucking idiot."

"No! Owen—"

"Don't." Owen held up a hand to stop him, his face growing bleak. "Just… don't."

And then the bleakness seemed to drain away, leaving only that blank coldness in its wake. A mask of indifference as effective as any 'keep out' sign.

Mason knew him well enough by now to guess that, buried beneath the stony surface, there would be pain and confusion, but Owen wasn't letting him see those vulnerable parts of him any more. Owen was closing that door on him, and Mason's throat ached to be cut off like that.

It was then, in that moment, that he realised something: when it came to Owen, he'd failed in everything he'd tried to do. And he'd especially failed at keeping things between them casual. In that, he had failed *spectacularly* because it was suddenly, painfully, obvious to him that he'd fallen in love with Owen. That he'd betrayed and hurt the man he *loved*.

It turned out that he really was no better—no less selfish— than his father.

That realisation crashed over him with such force that it punched the breath from his lungs, leaving him airless. After a struggle, he managed to whisper, "I'm so sorry. I should have told you. I just—I didn't think you'd understand." When Owen said nothing, Mason added desperately, "But it *has* always been real between us. For me it has, anyway. And that's the honest truth, I *swear*."

As soon as the words were out, Mason knew they were too small, too ordinary, to give Owen any idea of how he really felt. And sure enough, Owen just gave a bleak laugh, shook his head, and walked away, shoulders hunched and hands shoved into his jacket pockets. It was like watching the tide turn, inevitable and inexorable.

Mason lurched after him anyway. "Owen, please!" He needed to say more. He needed to put himself out there. Even so, he balked for a moment, before he forced out the painful truth in a hoarse cry. "Owen, please, I *love* you!"

Owen's stride faltered, just for a moment, but in the end, he didn't stop, and he didn't turn around.

A hopeless, jagged pain stabbed into Mason's chest, driving his eyes shut. Into that aching darkness came the slam of Owen's van door and the roar of the engine starting, each sound driving the pain deeper. Turning back towards the studio, Mason began walking blindly, his vision blurring and his throat thick. He scrubbed at his eyes and sucked in a shuddering breath.

He'd lost Owen. He knew it with bleak certainty. As kind and caring and gentle as Owen was, there was an immovable, unyielding side to him. Mason instinctively knew that there were certain things he would not forgive, and this was one of them. Honesty mattered to him.

Mason had thrown away the best thing that had ever happened to him, and for what?

A shot at a career that would never make him happy.

A career that, when it came down to it, he didn't even really want.

CHAPTER TWENTY-THREE

Work. That was the key. Keeping busy so there was no time to think. No time to remember the video of Mason in the green-house or the nervous guilt in his eyes that had betrayed his complicity.

Or those words, flung so carelessly after Owen in the car park.

"Owen, please, I love you!"

No truer than the rest of it, those words. The next chapter in the story Mason was spinning, a desperate attempt to keep Owen on board with his latest social media campaign.

We're telling stories, Owen... It only has to be an approximation of the truth.

Well, screw that. He refused to be the supporting cast in Mason's story anymore—the current love interest. Stupid to have believed he'd ever been anything more than that. From the start, Mason had been clear about the career-boosting benefits of their 'relationship', and Owen had known how much Mason's career meant to him. Known it, but let himself be sucked in anyway, by the romance and the drama Mason had spun around them. By the *story*.

What a bloody fool he'd been.

He found himself remembering that fan of Mason's, the one who'd come into the garden he'd been working in to ask for a selfie. He thought of the way she'd looked at him, all starry-eyed and pleading. *"Is it real? Please tell me it's real."*

Turned out he was just as deluded as she was.

The only difference was he had no excuse. Lewis and Aaron had tried to caution him about Mason, but Owen had been blind. Wilfully blind. It was sobering to discover that he was no more immune to the allure of a beautiful face than any other lonely soul looking for love. So much for his pride in seeing beyond Mason's looks.

"Wotcher," Mac said, stopping in the doorway to his office. "Blimey, I thought *I* was in early, but you look like you've been here a while?"

Owen blinked up at her from behind his desk, glancing at the clock on the wall over the door. It was six-thirty on Monday morning. He'd been in since five. And all of Sunday too, not that he was about to confess that to her.

"Thought I'd get on top of the paperwork," he said, gesturing at his unusually tidy desk.

Mac nodded, looking unconvinced. After a pause, she came more fully into the office, shrugging off her jacket and hanging it on the coat stand. "Saw you on the telly on Saturday," she said, her tone deceptively mild.

Trying not to react, Owen made a noncommittal sound. More like a grunt, really.

Mac turned around. "Your face when they brought that bloody pineapple out," she said, smiling. "I thought you were going to murder someone."

He grimaced, shaking his head. "It was fucking ridiculous."

"Yeah, it was." Her smile faded. "Everything okay?"

The last thing he needed was a heart-to-heart with Mac. Or anyone, come to that. He preferred to nurse his misery in private. And okay, maybe that was more of the *Stoic Owen routine,* but he wasn't sure how else to act when he felt like this.

It was embarrassing enough that his infatuation with Mason had been broadcast on TV for all to see. He'd at least keep their break-up and his fucking *feelings* about it to himself.

"Everything's fine," he said, getting up from behind the desk. He was looking forward to doing some real work today, getting his fingers in the soil and his boots in the mud. Reconnecting with his actual job and escaping all the fakery of *Weekend Wellness.*

"I'm going to join Kyle and Dave on the Langley Road job today. They need an extra pair of hands on that driveway. I was going to send Tommy, but—"

On his desk, his phone buzzed, and he glanced down automatically. Like one of Pavlov's dogs, he couldn't help himself, and sure enough, it was another message from Mason.

Please call me.

They'd been coming in since yesterday afternoon, all saying the same thing.

Please call.

I need to talk to you.

Owen had ignored them all. It was probably juvenile, but he just couldn't face talking to Mason. He knew he'd have to at some point—they were grown-ups after all, and he was still contractually obliged to do another round of *Weekend Wellness* filming—but not yet. Not when he felt so raw and so… *used.*

A sharp stab of pain made him grunt out loud. It took him like that, sometimes, the shock of losing what he'd had with Mason. What he'd *thought* he had.

Christ, he was pathetic.

Shoving the phone into his pocket, he turned to head into the main part of the unit, ready to start loading up the van for today's jobs, but Mac stepped in front of him, forcing him to stop.

He glared at her. "What?"

"You don't *look* fine."

"Well, I am," he replied irritably.

"No," she said, shaking her head. "You're not. Did something happen with Mason?"

Owen sighed, a huff of air that was part impatience, part surrender. "We broke up."

"Damn. Why?"

Owen lifted his hands and scrubbed them over his face. When he dropped them, he said wearily, "Because I'm a fucking moron. I thought he liked me."

Mac's face fell. "Did he dump you?"

Could you even *be* dumped when the person you thought was your boyfriend had just been using you for likes and follows?

Owen shook his head. "I can't talk about this right now, Mac. You know how I am. I just... I need to get out of my head." And spending the morning breaking up a concrete drive with Kyle and Dave sounded like the perfect task for that: tough, distracting and physically exhausting.

Mac's worried expression didn't shift, but she nodded. "Okay. Well, I'm here if and when you change your mind."

"Yeah, I know." He tried to smile, but could tell from Mac's face that it was a poor effort.

"Right then," she said briskly. "How about a cuppa?"

"Is the sky blue?" he said, forcing something like jollity into his voice.

Neither of them was convinced by the performance, but Mac gave a nod and went to fill the kettle.

Owen headed into the main part of the unit to check out the van Kyle and Dave had used the day before. He'd need to load up some extra tools since he'd be joining them. Tommy could do maintenance today instead and take Naaz with him.

His phone rang, buzzing against his thigh, and Owen's heart missed a beat.

Mason?

He scrambled the phone out of his pocket, even though he knew he wouldn't—*couldn't*—answer it. But when he looked at the screen, it wasn't Mason; it was Aaron.

Shit.

He'd avoided a number of calls from Lewis over the weekend, unable to face talking about what had happened on *Weekend Wellness*. A wave of guilt washed over him, and he forced himself to answer the call, even as his heart still pounded against his ribs. Trying to sound normal, he opened with, "Hey, Aaron. Everything okay?"

Aaron said, *"We're* fine. I was phoning to see how you're holding up. Lewis was worried about you after—" He broke off, then sighed and added, "Well, after we saw the show on Saturday."

Owen swallowed painfully. "Yeah, it was pretty much a car crash. At least, that's how I remember it. I've not been able to watch it back."

"It wasn't that bad," Aaron said, though Owen intuited from his evasive tone that it *had* been that bad. "But Lewis could tell you were freaking out and—"

Owen gave a bark of laughter. "Yeah, I suspect that was obvious."

Aaron was quiet for a moment. Then he said in a rush, "He feels absolutely terrible, Owen. When you called and told him you couldn't do it, he just brushed you off, and then when he saw you on TV, there was nothing he could do to help. He's been beside himself all weekend, and—"

"Lewis doesn't need to feel bad," Owen interrupted wearily. "There was nothing he could have done. I don't even know why I called him."

When Aaron fell silent, he pulled out his keys and unlocked the roller door to the unit, watching it rattle up. Sunlight flooded into the space, and he squinted against it, rubbing at his eyes. He'd not really slept the last couple of nights, and it was starting to catch up with him.

"What's that noise?" Aaron asked.

"I'm at the unit, getting ready to go out on a job," Owen said. "Look, why don't you tell Lewis I'll call him tonight?"

"Yeah, okay," Aaron said. "Just make sure you do."

"I will," Owen said. "Right, I'd better—"

"Before you go..." Aaron paused, then added carefully, "Owen, how are you coping with the other stuff? The online stuff, I mean."

Online? Christ, he should have realised. Of course Mason would have posted something about them.

He sighed. "So Mason's announced our break-up, has he?"

"You and Mason *broke up*?"

"Uh, yeah..." Owen scratched his head. "Isn't that what we're talking about?"

"No. I'm talking about fucking *hashtag-pineapplegate*."

Owen stared out at the car park, mostly still empty at this time. "What the hell's that?"

"Shit," Aaron said. "You don't know? Owen, it's all over the socials."

"Yeah, well, I don't give a shit about 'the socials'."

A long sigh came down the line. "I'm afraid you're going to have to. This is big, Owen, and not in a good way. They're saying the pineapple thing was fake—"

"It *was* fake."

"Yeah, well, the *#pineapplegate* fiasco is threatening to bleed over into the whole *Weekend Wellness* brand. Misty's throwing a fit. So's her boss. They're trying to work out how to play it, but..." He sighed again, and Owen could imagine his kind, concerned expression. "Owen, it looks like you're getting the brunt of it on social media. You need to call Misty, make sure you're on board with however they're going to handle it. Mason, too."

Owen screwed his eyes shut. "I'm not doing that."

"You have to! You can't let them—"

"I really don't give a shit about that stuff, Aaron. Honestly. I'll leave that to Mason—" His voice broke like a wave over his name, and he cleared his throat. "That's his area, not mine."

There was a brief silence. Then Aaron said, more quietly, "And you broke up? What happened?"

Owen blew out a breath. "You saw what happened. He made me look like a fucking liar on TV. They wanted me to film some crap saying you can grow a pineapple in a few weeks, and I refused, so Mason filmed it behind my back. The first I knew about it was when I was live on air. I should have said something then and there, but—" He broke off, unable to say aloud why he hadn't spoken up. Because the truth was humiliating. Even as furious as he'd been, he hadn't wanted to expose Mason. Not when his TV career meant so much to him.

"Oh, Owen—"

"And I know you're not surprised," Owen went on, unable to bear the sympathy in Aaron's voice, "because you warned me about him from the start. You were right, by the way. It was all—" Again, his voice cracked, and this time he couldn't shake it off. Sucking in a breath, blinking into the sunlight, he said, "It was all just about telling a story for him. Just for attention."

Softly, Aaron said, "I'm sorry, Owen. I thought... Seeing you two together, I'd hoped I was wrong about that..."

Owen ran a thumb under his leaky eyes. "Yeah, well. I'd hoped so, too. Love really is blind, I guess." He grimaced and blew out a breath before Aaron could say more. "Listen, I have to get to work. Thanks for the heads-up about the online stuff, but I really couldn't give a shit. *Weekend Wellness* can drop me tomorrow for all I care. If I never see another TV camera again, I'll be happy."

"Yeah, okay." Aaron sounded unhappy. "Just...be prepared for some blowback over this. I'll tell Lewis you'll call him tonight."

"Yeah." He smiled, although it felt watery. Aaron was a good guy, perfect for Lewis. They were perfect together, and dwelling on that was pretty much the last thing his broken, aching heart needed right now.

What he needed was work, and lots of it.

Luckily, there was plenty to hand.

The crew started trickling in then, and Owen got busy rearranging the day's jobs. Then he headed over to Langley Road with Kyle and Dave. With the three of them working on the drive, they had the brunt of the hard work done by lunchtime. Owen left Kyle and Dave to finish up and set off to do a quick maintenance job for Mrs. Dickinson, one of his long-standing customers. Grass cutting, weeding, a little pruning. He had a raft of customers like Mrs. D who he'd been seeing for years, older people mostly, who couldn't manage their gardens. Mac told him that he undercharged— and he probably did—but he did the work himself so he didn't need to cover staff costs and could keep the price affordable. Besides, the last thing he wanted to do was cut loose some of the first people who'd taken a chance on him back when his business was as green as spring grass. He reckoned he owed them his loyalty in return for their faith.

After that, he headed down to the community garden in Beckenham to put in a couple of hours weeding the beds and picking up litter. Years ago, the council would have had park keepers to do this kind of thing, but those days were long gone. Now, it was left to volunteers, and Owen helped out as often as he could.

Which hadn't been very often over the last few months.

Standing in the park, which was busy with primary-school kids and their parents on this sunny Monday after school, he realised how much he'd missed it. He'd kidded himself that the gardening slot on *Weekend Wellness* would bring gardening to ordinary people, but that had just been another lie. It had never been about gardening at all, but this... this park, these flower beds planted with blue salvia and pansies and petunias, would give real people pleasure all summer. This was gardening for the people. This was real.

He'd lost sight of that for a while.

Feeling his balance somewhat restored, he headed back to the office through the rush hour traffic and pulled up outside the Hunter Gardens unit just after six-thirty. He was surprised to see Mac's bike still outside. She was allergic to paperwork so didn't usually hang around once she'd finished working for the day.

Heading inside, he was even more surprised to see her sitting at his desk with her gaze locked on the computer screen.

"Don't tell me you're logging invoices," he said as he stepped inside.

Mac jumped, and in anyone else he might have described her expression as guilty. It changed immediately, though, to a grim distress that dropped a rock into the pit of his stomach.

"What's happened?"

"Shit, Owen."

"What is it?" His heart was thundering stupidly. "Mac—"

"You need to see this," she said, turning the computer screen towards him.

He couldn't make sense of the screen at first, expecting to see some horrible news of a disaster, someone hurt—but all he saw was the familiar banner of one of the biggest trade review sites and his own company's logo. Then he saw that the star rating, which had always been a healthy five, had dropped to an average of three and a half.

"What the hell?" Relief that nothing life-altering had happened was swamped by confusion, anger, and a little fear. "How the hell could it drop so fast...?"

"Naaz told me this afternoon that you were getting abuse online over that fucking pineapple bollocks. Apparently, some people were posting our listing and... well, we've had a lot of new ratings this weekend," Mac said grimly. "All one star. You have to read the comments..."

Scrolling down, he felt his heart sink as fast as his company's reputation.

One star. Show me the pineapples!!!!!

One star. Owen Hunter is a bully and a fraud. He's not even gay.

One star. DO NOT HIRE THIS MAN! He's a liar! #pineapplegate

"For fuck's sake," he said, reeling back from the screen to stare at Mac over the empty expanse of his desk.

"Apparently it's all over social media," she said. "Naaz showed me some of it, and it was bloody nasty, Owen. They dug up some photo of you with Michelle. They're saying you're not really a gardener, that you're not really gay—"

"I'm bi," Owen croaked.

"I know," Mac said gently. Then she swallowed and added. "They're even saying that you bullied someone."

He stared, unbelieving. "*Bullied* someone? Who?" He felt sick, a churning nausea rising in his throat. "Not Mason. Did *he* say that?"

Shaking her head, Mac pulled the screen back around. "No, but it was some kind of official post... Let me find it." She scrolled for a minute. "Right, here we go, it's from someone called Misty Watson-King? She said—"

"Jesus." Owen pressed a hand to his eyes. Of course it would be Misty.

"She says..." Mac let out a breath and turned the screen

back to him. "Well, read it for yourself. Obviously, we know it's total bollocks."

He looked closer, heart sinking deeper and deeper. It was an Instagram post, and over the faint image of a pineapple, there was a block of text in a scrawly font.

I'm mortified that Owen Hunter misrepresented the truth on Weekend Wellness. *Authenticity is the bedrock of our show, and this incident has caused me physical pain. Following these upsetting revelations, a junior member of our close-knit team came forward to tell me that they had been bullied by Hunter. I was shocked that this could happen under my nose without me noticing. I hold myself responsible for failing to protect my* WW *family from Hunter's bullying and lies.*

Mea culpa. Mea maxima culpa. #pineapplegate

Owen went cold to the bone, a fusion of fury and terror turning him rigid. How could she do this? How could she just straight-out lie?

"You should sue her," Mac said. "Sue her for libel."

Owen's head spun. He didn't give a crap about Misty, or what she said about him, but his thoughts kept returning to those bloody one-star reviews on the trade website. That was his livelihood, the future of his business, Mac's job and Naaz's apprenticeship. Kyle and Dave and Tommy. For their sakes, should he counter Misty's lies somehow? Reply to her post? Or would that just make it worse? He had no idea what to do.

Mason would know, he thought with a gut-wrenching lurch. *Mason would know what to do.*

And, God, how Owen wanted Mason's arms around him then, wanted his smile and his warm, reassuring touch. Wanted *him*.

Hands shaking with shock and outrage, he pulled out his phone. There were dozens of missed messages, but he ignored them all, swiping through his contacts. He hesitated at the last moment and then dialled.

"Owen?" said the familiar voice immediately. "Thank fuck."

Owen closed his eyes, stupid tears bunching in his throat. "They're hanging me out to dry, Lewis. You have to help me. I don't know what to do."

"Get over to my place right now," his brother growled. "We're going to fucking war."

CHAPTER TWENTY-FOUR

Monday afternoon had turned grey and drizzly in South West London, and Mason sat hunched against the weather on a damp bench overlooking the Thames. On the other side of the river, joggers and cyclists made use of the towpath that ran along the water's tree-lined bank, while on his side a young mum and a little boy threw bread into the water for the hordes of swans and geese.

A shrubby embankment shielded Mason from the street behind him, but he could still hear the hum of traffic and the hiss of tyres on the wet road.

All of it, though, seemed to be happening elsewhere. At a distance. Ever since everything had fallen apart on Saturday, Mason had been living in a spiralling nightmare, disconnected from the real world.

He hadn't thought it could get any worse than Owen ending things between them, walking away without even hearing Mason's side of the story.

"Owen, please, I love you!"

His throat closed at the memory.

And then it had got worse.

It had started with the comments about Owen's behaviour on the show. Mostly from Mason's fans, disgruntled with Owen's failure to play the part of besotted lover on live television. That had been bad enough—seeing Owen being called *surly* and *cold* and *not fit to lick Mason's boots* had angered and shamed Mason in equal measure—but then someone had posted that photo again. The one Mason had taken of Owen in his own garden, with his own pineapple plants. And before he knew it, there were photo comparisons being posted, and links about how to grow pineapples, and accusations being thrown about Owen's credentials as a gardening expert. Within hours, *#pineapplegate* was in full swing.

When the story first erupted on Insta, Mason had prayed it would be contained there—or, at least, contained online so that Owen, social media luddite that he was, wouldn't have to know anything about it.

He'd prayed the story would burn out fast, blink and you'd miss it.

Neither prayer had been answered.

Instead, Misty had posted her vile lies about Owen—clearly, he'd been chosen as the sacrifice to appease the ravening mob—and Mason had spent the night watching his notifications blow up, while ignoring his agent's desperate urging to *Just like Misty's fucking post, will you?*

He hadn't liked it, and he hadn't posted any comment himself either. What's more, he had no intention of doing so until he figured out a way to actually make things better, rather than just pour more fuel on the fire.

Maybe that's why he'd come here, to the place where Frieda and the girls lived. A childish instinct to run home and seek comfort from his mum. Not that she'd be able to offer much more than a cup of tea. Frieda was part of the problem, after all. A big part.

He sighed and looked down at his phone, at the article

Frankie, his agent, had sent him that morning—"*Sex, Lies, and Tropical Fruit: What #pineapplegate tells us about gender, class, and privilege in the post-truth world.*"

Even if Owen had escaped #pineapplegate over the weekend, he'd bloody well know about it now. This shitty article had been published in the online edition of one of the national broadsheets and picked up by loads of online feeds. *Everyone* had seen it, and it had been shared and liked all over the place. Someone Owen knew was bound to have mentioned it to him.

The words of the article were warped by the spiderweb of cracks across Mason's screen, the result of flinging his phone across his bedroom when he'd first read it. The author was none other than Misty's journalist pal, Austin Coburn—because, of course—and Mason could hear his sneering, pompous tone in every word.

If you've been entranced by the delightfully quirky lifestyle show, Weekend Wellness *(10 a.m. Saturdays), you'll be familiar with "gardening hottie" Owen Hunter, the* erastes *to model-turned-presenter Mason Nash's post-ironic* eromenos.

Last Saturday saw trouble slither into W12's Garden of the Hesperides, although in this case, pineapples, not apples, were the forbidden fruit.

Eagle-eyed viewers cried foul when a clearly imported pineapple was paraded around the studio. Why? Because 'honest gardener' Owen Hunter wanted us to believe he'd grown it himself in his small South London garden. In a fortnight.

Step up trusty Twitter fact-checkers. Insisting the claim was impossible, they began to question Hunter's horticultural bona fides. Among other things.

Which was when the plot thickened…

It transpires that Owen Hunter is actually the brother of Lewis Hunter. Yes, the *Lewis Hunter, writer of* Leeches, *that saccharine vampire melodrama so beloved by your teens.* Leeches *is produced by Reclined Pigeon Productions, who, surprise surprise... also produce* Weekend Wellness.

If you're asking why this sordid tale of nepotism and TV fakery matters, read on because #pineapplegate tells us everything we need to know about gender, class, and privilege in the post-truth world.

It comes as no surprise, for example, that the show's fearless female producer, Misty Watson-King, is the only person to fall (or was she pushed?) onto her sword in a heartfelt apology for #pineapplegate. Not only that, but she bravely disclosed, and took responsibility for, allegations of bullying by Hunter that will come as no surprise to those familiar with the toxic culture of television…

It went on like that, outright lies and vitriol dressed up in flowery language. Mason's fury at the article was eclipsed only by the distress he felt at the thought of Owen reading it. And Mason couldn't even talk to him about it because Owen wasn't responding to any of his messages or answering his phone. At least, not Mason's calls.

Eyes stinging, Mason looked up, staring out across the brown river and blinking hard.

A chilly wind blew, ruffling his hair. He shivered, but made no move to leave. Already, he was second-guessing his decision to come here. How could Frieda help? She was probably already freaking out about the situation, envisaging the end of Mason's career. The unravelling of her safety net.

In his hands, his phone vibrated with an incoming message.

Owen?

As always, his heart hoped before his mind had time to register the name that popped up on the screen—then sank like a stone when he saw it was Misty. Well, fuck. He'd wondered when she'd get in touch.

He stared at the notification for a long time, his simmering anger coming back to the boil. What was she messaging him about? He didn't expect any apologies. Maybe a bunch of bullshit excuses for her lying Insta post? Or a contract termination notice for the gardening segment?

He stabbed the message open. Read it. Stared, and read it again.

Frankie has details for Saturday's show. Need you at the studio by 8. You'll be live at 11. Marc's doing the interview—a few tears would be great ;) Naomi will send you talking points & content for post-interview socials. Expecting a HUGE audience. #pineapplegate getting lots of engagement on all channels ;) Was trending in the UK last night! This is BIG!!!

What. The. Fuck?

Zero attempt to justify or even try to excuse what she'd done. Not even an acknowledgement that she'd thrown Owen under a bus to save her own skin—that she'd *lied* about him. Just carrying on like nothing had happened. No, it was worse than that—carrying on like this was a welcome development. And that fucking winky-smiley emoji? Like Mason had to be as delighted as she was about the numbers? As he stared, disbelieving, at the message he saw three little dots appear in the corner, and a moment later, another message appeared.

Btw, don't worry about the gardening slot being cancelled (formal email from Legal following). Already speaking to Frankie about getting you another role in the show. Maybe a food slot? Give him a call—he's got all the details ;)

Un-fucking-believable! If Misty—or Frankie—thought he was going to help spread lies about Owen live on her shitty TV show, then she had another thing coming. No way. No *fucking* way.

Furious, he switched his phone off and shoved it in his pocket.

Too wound-up to sit any longer, he got up and stalked along the river to the end of the gardens and back up to the street. Frieda's flat was one road back, just a few minutes' walk away. For a moment, Mason hesitated. The station was in the opposite direction, but he could be there in fifteen minutes, heading home to…

To what? To sit in his flat and feel miserable? To brood and avoid Frankie's calls?

No, he didn't want to go home. Not yet. And he might be in two minds about going to his mum's, but the truth was, he had nowhere else to go. Which was a depressing thought.

Besides, the rain was starting to pick up too, turning from drizzle into a definite shower.

With a sigh, Mason turned on his heel and began striding towards Frieda's flat, away from the station. Head down, he walked fast enough that he was slightly breathless by the time he got there. He paused for a moment, then pressed the buzzer on the door.

After a moment, Frieda's voice came over the crackly intercom. "What have I told you about remembering your key, Melody? You're lucky I'm in."

Mason felt an unexpected swell of emotion at the sound of her voice. For all the strain in their relationship, she was still his mum, and right now, he needed some comfort. A simple hug, maybe. "It's me," he said, his voice hitching. He cleared his throat. "Angel."

"Angel?" Immediately, she sounded concerned, and the door buzzed open. "What's happened? Are you all right?"

"I'm coming up," he said, by way of an answer, and pushed open the door.

Frieda was waiting in the doorway to her flat when Mason reached the second floor, looking worried and all but wringing her hands. When she saw him, though, her expression changed.

"Oh, Angel, look at you. You're soaking wet. What happened?"

He didn't answer, found he couldn't speak. Emotion closed his throat, a heavy knot of sadness and anger and loss.

Shaking his head, he wiped at his wet face. Not only rain on his cheeks.

"Oh, love," Frieda said, taking his hand and patting it. "Come on. Let's have a cuppa. I've got a packet of chocolate digestives to open. I dare say you're allowed one or two in an emergency."

He sniffed a soggy laugh and followed her inside, hanging up his jacket on one of the hooks behind the door and toeing off his wet shoes. Then he padded into the kitchen after her.

Although he'd never lived here, it still felt familiar—a lot of the things he remembered from his childhood home had survived the move. Including the old kettle which Frieda was filling at the sink.

"Fetch me a couple of mugs and a plate, will you?" she said over her shoulder. Mason obediently went to the cupboard, drawing out two mugs, comfortingly familiar with their blue-and-white stripes, one with a little chip in the rim. They'd had them on the canal boat, back before the twins came along.

With the kettle on, Frieda busied herself opening the biscuits. "Are you all right, love?" She darted a look his way, her nervousness evident in the way she fluttered about the kitchen. "You don't look like you've been sleeping properly."

He handed her a plate for the biscuits, watching as she set them out in a neat circle. A thread of guilt stirred in his gut at the knowledge that him turning up like this was going to worry her. But while he usually made it his mission never to give Frieda any cause for concern, he found he couldn't regret coming over—he was glad not to be alone right now. Finally, he said, "It's been a tough weekend."

She grimaced. "Mel showed me all those pineapple posts on Twitter. Is it true that Owen faked being a gardener?"

"*No!*"

Frieda blinked at his vehemence, and he lowered his voice, adding, "Owen's the only one who *didn't* lie."

305

"I'm sure *you* didn't lie."

He let out a huff of breath, not quite a laugh, and didn't answer. Which was, of course, an answer of sorts, though one Frieda would probably choose to ignore.

The kettle was starting to heat up, but beneath its wheezing hiss, he could hear the faint thump of music coming from Min's room. "Are the girls home?"

"Only Min—she's got a 'free study' afternoon, but you know what that means."

He smiled ruefully, remembering his own less-than-stellar academic record. Hard to comprehend that Mel and Min were that age now; it only felt like five minutes ago that he was sitting his GCSEs. While also trying to keep Frieda on her feet, less than two years after Kurt had walked out.

"Come on then," Frieda said, carrying the plate of biscuits over to the kitchen table. "Tell me all about it." She threw him another worried glance. "Have they…? Are you still on *Weekend Wellness*?"

Mason braced himself for her reaction, leaning against the counter while he waited for the kettle to boil. "No," he admitted, "they cancelled the gardening slot—"

"Oh no!" Frieda's alarm made his stomach pinch guiltily. "But that's not fair. You didn't know Owen hadn't grown those pineapples."

Mason sighed. "Yeah, actually, I did. So did Misty, by the way—it was her idea to pretend he had. Owen refused to go along with it, so Misty got me to film an extra segment without him." He grimaced around a knot of remorse, pressing his lips together for a moment. "So stupid. I should never have done it. And now everyone's blaming Owen."

"Oh. I see." Frieda fiddled with the biscuits, turning alternate ones chocolate-side down to make a pattern. "I suppose that's lucky?"

Lucky? Mason felt a stab of irritation. "Not for Owen."

Frieda met his gaze, her expression uncertain. "What does Frankie have to say about it?"

"I haven't spoken to Frankie." Turning to open the tea caddy, Mason dropped a tea bag into each mug. "But apparently, he and Misty have cooked something up. They want me to do another interview on *Weekend Wellness* this Saturday." Bitterly he added, "To help Misty piss all over Owen's reputation even more."

"Language," Frieda muttered.

"Sorry." He sighed again. "Obviously, I'm not going to do it."

"You're not?" Frieda's voice wavered, and when he glanced over his shoulder, he saw the unease in her eyes.

"Of course not! Owen didn't do anything wrong. They're *lying* about him. How can I go along with that?"

"But…" Her lips pinched. "If you don't, what will happen to you? I mean, if people think you're taking Owen's side, could that damage your career? Everything you've worked for?"

Could it damage my safety net? was what she meant.

"*Taking Owen's side?*" Mason echoed angrily. "Owen hasn't even said anything. He doesn't care about any of this media crap. Hell, the only reason he agreed to do *Weekend Wellness* in the first place was because *I* wanted to do it, and the only reason he didn't dump me in it live on air last week was because"—emotion made his voice give out—*because he was protecting me.*

And yes, there it was. Another truth he'd been hiding from.

The kettle started boiling then, and Mason gratefully turned away to pour water into the mugs, getting himself back under control as he fished out the tea bags and added milk and one sugar to Frieda's, leaving his own black. Christ, he was sick of black tea.

Frieda was wearing a familiar mulish look when he set her

mug down on the kitchen table in front of her. "You can't mean to destroy your career over this," she said. "Not when you're so close to a breakthrough—a major brand endorsement could launch you globally. That's what Frankie said, isn't it?"

Mason settled into the seat opposite her. "It is, yeah."

Years ago, they used to sit just like this on the narrow boat when Mason got home after school. He'd told Frieda everything then, unburdened all his boyish worries and listened to her advice. He stared at her now, her face showing the signs of the passing years. Lines around her eyes, her mouth, a peppering of grey in her frizzy hair. She picked up a biscuit and dunked it in her tea, letting the chocolate slightly melt before taking a bite.

Perhaps it was nostalgia, but as he wrapped his hands around his mug, he found himself saying, "The thing is... I love Owen. I'm—*in* love with him."

Frieda froze, biscuit halfway back to her mug for another dunk. "It wasn't just for the telly then, all that flirting?"

He shook his head. "Couldn't you tell?" he asked, genuinely curious.

"Well, it looked real, but you always were a performer," she said with a smile.

Mason swallowed. Yeah, he was, wasn't he?

Frieda's smile faded at whatever she saw on his face. After a moment, she added, "It's difficult, if that's how you feel."

"Yeah."

"Does he feel the same?"

"I don't know. I thought so, but now he won't even speak to me." Mason shrugged. "Actually, I think he despises me, and I don't blame him, so..."

Frieda dunked her biscuit again. "If he feels that way, he doesn't deserve you, love, and you need to put your own interests first."

"*My* interests?" He met her wary gaze across the table and

added, tentatively, "If I'm honest, recently, I've been wondering what *my* interests are."

"Well, your career, surely?" she said immediately. "Your *future*, Angel. You're going to be a star."

"What if I don't want to be a star at Owen's expense?"

"But none of this will stop him from being a gardener, will it? You said he isn't interested in the media business. He'll probably be happier going back to his normal life."

Back to his normal life. Before he hooked up with Mason.

Yeah, he probably would be happier with that.

Mason's eyes burned, and he looked away from Frieda, his gut churning. But even if that was true—that Owen was better off, *happier*, without Mason—that didn't make it okay to give in to Misty's demands. And it hurt that his mum would argue that it did.

"It sounds like you reckon I should go along with the lies about Owen to save my career. Is that really what you think?"

For a while, Frieda was silent, but at last, she said, "You've been blessed with a gift, Angel. Your looks, your talent... I don't understand why you'd throw away a career that millions of people would give their right arm for to keep a man you think despises you."

"Maybe because it's the right thing to do?"

"Right for who? Not for you." She was angry now, frightened and angry. He could hear it in her voice. "You'd have to give up your flat. No more fancy restaurants or foreign travel..."

He shrugged, watching her, even as she averted her gaze. "Maybe I'm tired of all that. Maybe I want to do something more satisfying with my life."

Frieda snorted. "You're tired of earning good money?"

"There's more to life than money, right?"

Frieda's mouth twisted. "The only people who say that are people who don't have to worry about paying the rent or keeping food on the table for their children."

Annoyed, he said, "But I don't have any children."

"Well, I do!" she exclaimed, her voice turning tremulous with that feeble waver he knew so well. "And if this is how you feel, I suppose I'll need to start looking at schools for the girls in a cheaper area because we won't be able to afford—" She broke off on a sob.

A familiar wave of dread broke over him. *Fuck*, he shouldn't have said anything. What had he been thinking? He couldn't cope with one of her crying fits right now—he just *couldn't*, not when he was already feeling like shit. He had to try to head this off at the pass.

"Look, I'm not saying I'm going to quit," he said as calmly as he could manage. "But I can't...I can't turn my back on Owen, okay? I can't *do* that to someone I love."

"But you *can* turn your back on me and the girls? On your family? Don't you love *us* anymore?"

"Frieda, come on. Of course I love you!"

Tears stood in her eyes now, and she dabbed at them with the back of her hand. "You've always been here for us, Angel, and I don't want you to think for a minute that I'm not grateful, because I am, and I honestly don't know how we'd manage without you. I only react like this because I'm afraid that if you don't—"

"For God's sake, Mum!" a new voice interrupted. "*Stop!* Just fucking stop this right now!"

Startled, Mason turned to find Min standing in the kitchen doorway. She still wore her school uniform, a pair of huge headphones around her neck, and she was glowering at them both.

Frieda's expression hardened. "This isn't a conversation for your ears, Harmony."

"Why not? Mason's my brother."

"Min—" Mason warned.

But she cut him off. "No, Mase. Someone has to tell her, and I know it won't be you because you're too bloody soft."

Mason blinked at her. "I'm too soft?"

Min rolled her eyes. "Mase, you let Mum walk all over you."

Frieda bristled. "Harmony, go to your room."

"No. I won't," she said, hands on hips. "Why do you always do this, Mum? You lay this whole guilt trip on him, and it's not fair! Mase doesn't want to be a bloody model anymore. He just told you he's tired of all that, so why are you trying to force him to keep doing it?"

Frieda looked stricken. "I'm not. You don't know what you're talking about—"

"Yes I do!" Min had hit her stride, and there was no holding her back. "And I don't see why Mase should have to keep bailing us out just because Dad can't be arsed to pay what he owes on time, and you won't stand up to him."

Tears glittered in Frieda's eyes, her voice going frail and wobbly—she was bringing out the big guns. "I don't think you're being fair..."

"*I'm* not being fair? Can't you see you're ruining Mason's life with your 'woe is me' act? Mel says it's emotional blackmail, and you know what? She's right."

Stunned, Mason's gaze shuttled between his sister and his mum. He noted the colour rising on his mother's face with concern. "Min," he said carefully, "come on. Let's not—"

She jabbed her finger at him. "Don't let her get away with it. You *know* it's true!"

He did know it. But he hadn't thought for a second that his sisters had even noticed. And now he couldn't think what to say in the face of Min's vehemence.

Into the sudden, ringing silence, Frieda said brokenly, "It's not true. It's *not* like that. Is it, Angel?"

Of course not.

The reassuring words were on the tip of his tongue, an easy instinctive lie to calm the troubled waters. To keep Frieda from breaking down, to keep them all safe from the chaos her meltdowns caused. But Min was standing strong, blazing with fiery indignation, and telling that lie again would have been a betrayal of her. He couldn't do it.

And he didn't want to.

Instead, shakily, he took Frieda's hand in both of his, squeezed, and made himself say the truth. "If I'm honest, I do feel trapped by the responsibility sometimes. Like I'm stuck on this one road with no exit."

Frieda's free hand flew to her mouth, her eyes filling. "Angel," she croaked, "I never meant to make you feel like that. I thought you *wanted* to help us…"

"I *do*." His stomach pinched guiltily. "Of course I do."

"It's just that with Kurt gone, it's so hard for me to—"

"Oh my God, *Mum*," Min said, with more exasperation than Mason would ever dare show. "You're doing it again." Striding into the room, she put her hands on Frieda's shoulders, a gesture both quelling and reassuring. "You're all right, Mum. You've got me and Mel too, haven't you? We'll *all* make sure you're okay. Nothing terrible's going to happen if you let Mason live his life the way he wants to. Just chill."

To Mason's surprise, Frieda met Min's gaze and slowly nodded, covering one of Min's hands with her own. And for the first time, Mason saw his sister, brimming with youthful certainty, not as a child, the dependent he'd always considered her, but as a young woman emerging into the world on her own terms. His equal, with her own, different relationship with their mum. A healthier relationship, probably.

Over Frieda's head, their eyes met, Min's bright and unflinching, and he felt the weight of responsibility ease a fraction from his shoulders for the first time since Kurt left.

It was a revelation.

Frieda would always be anxious and needy. Nothing would change that after fifty-four years of life, but he wasn't the only one Frieda could lean on—and Christ, that was a liberating feeling.

Min gave him a wry smile, as if she knew what he was thinking. And maybe she did. She obviously saw a lot more than he'd ever realised.

"So," she said, raising her brows at him. "What are you going to do, Mase? Screw up your career or screw over your boyfriend?"

CHAPTER TWENTY-FIVE

Owen

"I've got a call provisionally lined up with Kushal for tomorrow at four," Lewis said. "Will that be okay for you timing-wise?"

Kushal was Lewis's lawyer. He was a media specialist and, according to Lewis, already had a number of ideas about the steps Owen could take over Misty's social media posts.

They were sitting at Lewis's kitchen table—Owen and Lewis and Aaron. Lewis had a notepad in front of him, covered in his spiky handwriting. Aaron had his laptop open and was periodically tapping notes into it.

"I'm not sure," Owen said worriedly. "That's going to cost a fortune, isn't it? I don't have that kind of money."

Lewis looked pained. "Owen, come on. You don't need to worry about that. I can—"

"No." Owen glared at him. "I don't need you to pay for stuff for me."

Lewis gave an exasperated huff. "I thought you wanted my help."

Owen felt a pang of shame. He *did* want Lewis's help, to the extent that he'd actually asked for it for once. All their lives, Owen had been the big brother, the one who took care of things. And that was fine—that was who Owen was after all. But yeah, right now, *today*, it felt good to have his brother on his side and so intent on sorting out all his problems. Because the truth was, Owen hadn't felt so beaten down by anything in a long time. Maybe ever. There had been too many hard things at once. The public humiliation, the worry of what #pineapplegate was doing to his business... and having his heart ripped apart.

"I'm sorry," he muttered. "I do want your help. I'm just worried. I spent so long building up the business, and these last few days—" Mortifyingly, his voice gave out. He covered his face with his hands. "Fuck."

Lewis gripped his shoulder.

"Hey, it's okay."

The lump in his throat felt huge. It *ached*.

Lewis's hand was solid and warm, his thumb gently rubbing back and forth in a soothing gesture—and why did that make Owen want to cry? He didn't cry, though. Instead, he forced himself to take a big breath, then another one.

When he finally looked up again, it was to find Lewis and Aaron both watching him.

Aaron said quietly, practically, "Listen, one call with Kushal won't commit you to anything. *Are* you free at four tomorrow? Or do you need it to be later?"

Owen pulled out his phone, checking his calendar. "Four's okay," he confirmed. Then, awkwardly to Lewis, "Sorry for being a dick."

Lewis's mouth quirked up on one side. "'S'all right. It's quite nice to be the non-dick brother for a change."

Owen laughed ruefully.

Lewis had been more than a non-dick actually. He'd been

pretty amazing, both him and Aaron. They'd checked out all the online shit before Owen arrived so he didn't have to look at it again. Then they'd listened as he'd vomited out the whole sorry pineapple story. And then Lewis had explained a bunch of stuff he and Aaron were already lining up—because yeah, Kushal was only part of the plan.

Lewis had also arranged a meeting with the head of HR at RPP to kick off an internal procedure, while Aaron had pulled together all the relevant RPP policies and started drafting up a detailed point-by-point complaint for Owen to file. Even if the call with Kushal came to nothing, they had a solid plan to take action against Misty through RPP's internal channels.

"And there's one other avenue we're following up," Aaron said. "Or rather, Tag O'Rourke is."

"Tag?" Owen echoed, surprised.

"Yeah," Aaron said, smiling. "He was furious about what happened. He's arranged to go out for drinks with some of the *Weekend Wellness* crew he's friendly with, to see what dirt he can dish up on Misty from them—and if there's anyone who might want to make a complaint of their own. He seems to reckon there might be, from what he's heard them say in the pub."

Owen blinked, genuinely touched by that. He didn't even know Tag that well. Nevertheless, he said, frowning, "I don't want to get anyone into trouble."

Aaron shook his head. "If there's no dirt, fine. But if there is, we should do whatever we can to bring it to light. The reason people in this industry get away with so much toxic behaviour is because of the power they have over the cast and crew who need the work. It may not feel like it right now, with all the shit you've had written about you, but the fact that Misty doesn't have that power over you means that you can speak up about stuff others may not feel able to raise." He shrugged. "And once you've done that, it may be easier for others to come forward."

Owen hadn't thought about that angle before, but now he found himself remembering all those painfully awkward moments during the filming when Misty had treated people horribly. The pervasive sense he'd had that this was the norm on-set at *Weekend Wellness,* and no one felt able to challenge it. Misty certainly hadn't liked it when Owen had stood up to her.

He remembered her peremptory *"Mason—with me"* when they'd been filming. And Mason's haste to follow her—because Mason was convinced that he needed the *Weekend Wellness* slot if he was going to break out of modelling and still provide for his family.

And Misty had seen just how much he wanted it, hadn't she?

"Owen?"

He looked up to find Aaron watching him.

"You're right," he said. "And that was really nice of Tag. Especially given we don't really know each other that well."

Aaron gave a lopsided grin. "Well, he kind of owed you, given he got to be your plus-one at that awards dinner. Besides, he's a nice guy."

Weird to think of that dinner now—the night everything had started with Mason. It felt like a lifetime ago.

As though he'd just read Owen's mind, Lewis said gruffly, "So. How are things with Mason?"

Owen grimaced and said flatly, "Mason and I are done."

Ordinarily, that would have brought the conversation to an end, but not tonight apparently. Lewis glanced at Aaron, who gave him an encouraging nod. Then he said, hesitantly, "Do you... want to talk about it?"

Owen let out a short, sort-of-amused huff. "Do you want to *hear* it?" he countered, a note of disbelief in his voice that he couldn't quite rein in. Lewis hated talking about feelings.

Lewis's frown deepened. "Of course I do," he said gruffly. "I know I'm crap at the touchy-feely stuff—Grace says it's

317

part of my whole avoidance thing—but it doesn't mean I don't care. You know that, don't you?" His voice got a little croaky towards the end, as though just saying that much was hard.

"Who's Grace?" Owen asked, frowning.

Colour flooded Lewis's face. "My, um—my therapist. I've been seeing her for a couple of months now." He let out an embarrassed laugh. "God, that makes me sound like a self-indulgent twat."

"Hey, there's nothing self-indulgent about it," Aaron interjected firmly. "Going to Grace has been really good for you." He turned to Owen. "She was recommended by someone we met a while back. She's great. Really straightforward." He bumped Lewis's shoulder with his own. "She's not what you expected, is she?"

"No," Lewis admitted. "She's actually… pretty normal." Glancing at Owen, he added, almost tentatively, "I've been talking about"—he cleared his throat—"about Mum with her."

A flood of emotions welled up inside Owen at that admission, with guilt predominating. He knew he hadn't handled things very well with Lewis when their mum died. But the truth was, at seventeen, he hadn't really known what to do. Lewis had seemed to want to ignore what was happening as much as he could, and it had been easier to just go along with that. After all, Lewis had only been fourteen. He couldn't help Owen and their aunt deal with the medical staff in those awful final days, or make any of the funeral arrangements, or grapple with the bureaucracy that had followed afterwards, as Owen tried to keep them together. At the time, Owen had told himself it was better to let Lewis avoid it all. But now he wondered if that was the worst thing he could have done.

"I'm sorry, Lew," Owen whispered, staring at the table. "I know I wasn't there for you the way I should have been. I just buried myself in all the stuff that needed to be done to block it out and—"

"Hey, don't you dare," Lewis interrupted almost angrily. "You didn't do anything wrong. *I* was the one who opted out. Jesus Christ, I was the one who fucking *ran away* the night she —" He choked up, the words dying in his throat, but Owen knew what he was referring to.

The night she died.

Owen stared at his brother, shocked by the wrecked expression on his face.

Lewis tried again. "Grace says I need to forgive myself, but I wasn't there at the end to…" Again, he trailed off, as though the words were too painful.

Whenever Owen thought about that night, it wasn't about the part when Lewis had run off, just after the nurse came and told them they were to come and say goodbye to their mum. Mostly, it was about what had happened after Lewis stormed away, after their aunt had urged Owen to go with the nurse while she went to find Lewis. He vividly remembered the minutes that followed. The long, grey, antiseptic-smelling corridor the nurse had led him down, the dim, beeping room she had shown him into, where his mother lay dying.

For some reason, he'd assumed she'd be awake. That *she* was going to say goodbye to *him*. But no, she'd been unconscious. He'd sat down and taken her cool, unresponsive hand between his own. And a few minutes later, she was gone. Just like that.

Owen swallowed hard at the memory and met Lewis's agonised gaze.

"Lew, there's nothing to forgive yourself for. She didn't even know I was there."

His voice was hoarse with the remembered pain.

"What?" Lewis breathed.

"And she didn't know you *weren't* there," Owen went on. "She was already unconscious when I went in." There were tears at the corners of his eyes, and he dashed them away with the heels of his hands. "It didn't matter that you weren't there. She didn't know; you didn't miss anything."

Lewis let out a wet, shuddering breath. "*Fuck*. Fuck, I—" He turned to Aaron. "Did you hear that?"

Aaron nodded, his concerned gaze fixed on Lewis.

For a while, they just sat there, Aaron rubbing Lewis's back as he slowly calmed.

None of them said anything, but the silence felt okay.

Eventually, Aaron stood up.

"I'm going to make some tea," he said quietly. Moments later, he was busying himself with filling the kettle and getting out mugs.

At length, Lewis said, his voice husky with emotion, "We should talk about this more, but can we do it after my next appointment with Grace?"

Owen nodded. "We can talk about it whenever you want. I'm sorry if you ever thought otherwise."

"Don't say sorry," Lewis pleaded, shaking his head. "I'm the one who—" Then he stopped and took a deep breath. "Damn. I'm supposed to stop saying stuff like that about myself." He gave a short, rueful laugh. "This is why I need to talk to Grace before we do this."

"Take your time," Owen said gently. "I'll be here whenever the time's right."

Lewis nodded gratefully. After another short silence, he said, "God, what were we even talking about before I hijacked the conversation and made it all about me?" He shook his head as though to dislodge something from his brain, then blurted, "Oh, fuck. I'd just been asking you about breaking up with Mason, hadn't I?" He groaned. "I'm such a self-absorbed arsehole."

Aaron appeared then with three large mugs of tea. He set them down and dropped a kiss on top of Lewis's head. "True, but you're *my* self-absorbed arsehole," he said fondly before wandering back to the kitchen.

"Do you *want* to talk about Mason?" Lewis asked then. "I promise to listen properly. You know, like an actual functioning grown-up."

And strangely, Owen found that he *did*. He began hesitantly, but soon found he couldn't stop. He was still talking when Aaron re-joined them with a plate of toasted, buttered crumpets. He talked all the way through two more mugs of tea and told them pretty much all of it, right up to that last terrible argument at the RPP studio.

He even told them about Mason saying he loved him.

"You really don't think he meant it?" Aaron asked carefully, when he was done. "For what it's worth, I thought he seemed genuinely into you, that time we came over to yours to watch *Weekend Wellness*."

Owen shrugged. "Yeah, well, I thought that too, but—" He broke off, unable to say the next part aloud. That he wasn't sure whether *any* of it had been real for Mason, not in the way it had been for him.

He'd been thinking about that a lot since their awful argument in the RPP car park. And the truth was, he just… didn't know. From the start Mason had made it clear that he was only too happy to go along with Misty's suggestion of teasing a romance between them as a hook for the show. And yeah, he'd wanted to post pictures of them constantly, seeming delighted with all the likes and comments he got in response. But despite all that, there had been times when Owen would have sworn that Mason really did *like* him.

Maybe even more than that.

When he thought about the time they'd spent together, how soft and vulnerable Mason had been with him, how right it had felt between them, it was impossible to believe that none of it had been real. But didn't that just make Mason's betrayal worse? Because even if some of it had been real, even if Mason hadn't deliberately set out to fake a relationship with him, he certainly wasn't above sharing all the details of that relationship on Instagram. The brutal truth was that, for Mason, the main value of their relationship had always been as… well, content fodder. A story to share, to tease at. A stream of pretty pictures, carefully filtered and curated. So, it wasn't really a surprise that, in the end, Mason had prioritised content over honesty. He'd prioritised content over *everything*. Because for Mason, all of that—the likes, the reactions, the comments—were more important than anything else. More *real* than anything else.

More real than anything he had—or could have had—with Owen.

Maybe that was why he hadn't thought it was a big deal to go behind Owen's back and film that extra footage, despite knowing how strongly Owen felt about it? Because ultimately, it was the story that mattered most to him. Not the messy stuff that went on behind the scenes. The boring real-life stuff.

"The thing I can't get my head around," Lewis said, interrupting Owen's depressing train of thought, "is Mason saying all that stuff about growing pineapples in a week *after* what you'd told him. I mean, he can be a pain in the arse, but I wouldn't have thought he'd be deliberately dishonest."

Owen shrugged, even now trying to hide just how painful he found talking about this. "He claimed they edited it to look like that."

"Oh? How did they edit it?" Aaron asked, his brow creased in curiosity.

Owen flushed. "I don't know. I didn't hang around to find out."

"No?" Aaron said. "Didn't you want to at least hear his side of the story?"

Lewis—who had been watching Owen—sighed. "You did your brick wall thing, didn't you?"

Owen blinked, taken aback by that. Even more taken aback when he caught a look on Aaron's face that suggested he knew exactly what Lewis meant. This was something they'd talked about, Owen realised. Something about him.

Feeling stupidly hurt, he said, "What do you mean by that?"

Lewis eyed him for a moment, as though deciding whether to continue. "I'm talking about that thing you do, Owen. You know."

"What thing?" Owen blurted defensively.

Lewis looked away. "Okay, fine. Whatever."

"No, it's *not* fine. What are you talking about?"

Lewis was scowling now. "That thing you do when you switch off and there's no reaching you. You started doing it after Mum died."

"Started doing *what*?"

Lewis scowled harder. "You *know*. I'd get angry about some stupid thing, like us not being able to afford breakfast cereal that week or having to be home for the social worker coming round, and you'd just get that closed-up look on your face, and I'd know there was no point saying any more."

Owen stared at him, feeling faintly sick—this was a reference to the Stoic Owen routine, as Mac had called it.

"Oh God," he breathed. "I'm sorry, Lew. That's—that's really bad."

Lewis shook his head dismissively. "I'm only saying it now because"—he paused, eyeing Owen—"you still do that, you know? When bad stuff happens. You shut down, and I just have to wait till you're ready to talk. Like when Michelle left. I was really worried about you—I knew you weren't okay, but you kept putting me off, and even when you finally let me come and see you, it was like she'd never lived at your place. You didn't even mention her."

Owen's stomach clenched painfully. He didn't like the picture Lewis was painting of him. In his mind, he was the

323

grounded one, comfortable in his caring, nurturing role. He was the man who could tell his younger brother *"I love you"* without embarrassment. Who could freely hug and show affection. *Lewis* was the one who was emotionally stunted and unable to share his feelings. Fuck, was that all *Owen's fault*? Had he *damaged* his brother with his behaviour?

Lewis leaned over the table and gripped Owen's wrist. "Hey!" he said sharply. "Don't you start beating yourself up." He glanced at Aaron, a panicky look on his face. "I knew I shouldn't have said anything. Look at him."

Aaron looked thoughtful. "You know, I used to think you two were chalk and cheese, but I'm beginning to think you're not so different after all." He turned to Owen. "Listen, you did an amazing job looking after Lewis when you were kids. And honestly? Yeah, you probably have a few communication issues, but don't we all? Nobody's perfect—not even you, though to hear Lewis, you'd think you were a canonised saint."

"Maybe not a *saint*," Lewis murmured, looking embarrassed.

"But right now, the point is this," Aaron continued, as though Lewis hadn't spoken. "Yes, Mason fucked up, no question about that. But did you actually give him a chance to explain himself? I mean, maybe you won't feel any different once you hear him out, but doesn't he at least deserve to be heard? It is *possible*, right, that the footage was edited in a way he didn't expect?"

Owen rubbed his hands over his face. "Maybe, but why was he even filming that stuff in the first place? He's not stupid. It's obvious that the reason Misty wanted more footage was because what she'd already shot with me didn't suit her narrative." He shook his head. "He *must* have known."

"Except," Lewis put in hesitantly, "you don't actually *know* what Misty said to him or what he claims was edited out by her. Aren't you at least curious to know what he has to say about all this?"

Owen groaned. "I don't know. The simple truth is, he did what he did for the show and his own career. And he'd probably do the same again because creating content is how he earns his living. He always needs new content. Hell, his life is his content. But I"—he paused before admitting the embarrassing truth—"I want to be more to him than that."

The pity in his brother's gaze was too painful to look at. Owen let out a long breath and pushed himself up from his chair. "Listen, thanks for tonight. For everything. You've both been incredible. I'm really grateful that you've got my back with this." He offered a tiny smile. "I promise I'll be on that call with Kushal tomorrow, but right now, I'm beat, and I need to crash. So I'm going to head off, okay?"

Lewis eyed him warily for a few moments; then he rose to his feet. "Okay. You know where we are if you need anything."

"I do," Owen said. "Thanks."

Later, as he drove back to his little house in Beckenham, he thought about all the stuff they'd talked about that night, not just Mason and the fucking pineapple thing, but their own family history. He thought about the way Lewis had opened up about his feelings, maybe for the first time ever. The way he'd made himself vulnerable. Was it strange that, somehow, that made Owen believe Lewis had his back in a way that a show of unassailable strength could never have done?

And that made him think about Mason again. He wondered who had Mason's back right now.

Did anyone?

Did anyone else even see past the glittering armour of Mason's beauty? The seeming perfection of his much-photographed life?

Owen thought about all those selfies with glamorous people at parties. All those friends that Mason didn't really know all that well. All those plates of beautiful food he didn't really eat.

All those perfect smiles.

All of it neatly labelled. #happy, #me, #livingmybestlife #love

CHAPTER TWENTY-SIX

Mason

Mason dressed down for his *Weekend Wellness* appearance. Even now, a week on, the online conversation was furiously judgmental. The situation called for, if not quite sackcloth and ashes, something fairly sober.

He opted for dark blue jeans, a white shirt and a pale-grey, fine-knit sweater. When he checked himself in the mirror, he saw a serious young man with an innocent, concerned expression.

Innocent. Hell, looks really could be deceiving.

He took a cab to the RPP studios and was met at reception by one of the production crew, Rowan. She was older than Adam, obviously more senior, and looked beyond irritated to have to fetch him. She made no attempt at small talk as she sorted him out with his security pass.

"You're late," she said irritably, leading him towards the lifts. "You were supposed to be here at eight."

"I'm not on till eleven," Mason pointed out. "I'd just have been kicking my heels for hours in the green room." Hours during which Misty could be badgering him when he wanted to avoid her as much as possible.

Rowan sent him an aggravated look. "Yeah, well, it's a pain for us—the show's started, and it's busy this morning. I've got better things to be doing than escorting you around the place."

"Sorry," Mason said meekly. "Don't let me delay you. I don't need Wardrobe, and I know the way to Make-up—room 3.09, right? I can find my own way to the green room after that."

Rowan looked undecided for a moment; then she nodded. "Okay. Third floor, yeah?"

"Yeah," Mason agreed.

"And *straight* to the green room after Make-up," she added firmly.

He held up three fingers. "Scout's honour."

She sighed, her hostility ebbing. "Okay, thanks. Sorry to be grumpy, but Misty—" She broke off, then began again, a note of weariness in her voice. "This morning's been a bitch."

"It's okay," Mason said. "My fault entirely."

The lift pinged, the doors opened, and he stepped inside, hitting the button for the third floor.

He found room 3.09 easily, but it was empty. The man in the next room, who was busy straightening a woman's hair, told him to try room 3.14.

Room 3.14 turned out to be hidden away on the other side of the third floor. When he finally found it, he knocked on the door softly, relaxing when Carmen's cheerful voice called out, "Come in."

Today, her kaftan was black with gold stripes, and she was rocking a black geometric wig and some serious eye make-up.

"Nice outfit," Mason said as he dropped into the chair. "Very Elizabeth Taylor."

She winked at him and whipped out one of her little plastic shoulder capes, a canary-yellow one this time.

"I thought you were in 3.09," he said.

"I am, usually, but the bloody lights have blown again," she grumbled as she fastened the cape ties at the back of his neck. "I've told them a hundred times there must be something wrong with the fuses, but they just keep putting in new bulbs. Still takes them all day to get around to it, mind." She shook her head irritably and turned away to rummage in her trolley.

"Anyway, this won't take long," she said. "You just need a smidge of foundation to even you out and some definition around the eyes."

She dotted his face with foundation and began blending it in with a sponge.

"Is your friend coming in today again?" she asked after a while.

"My friend?" Mason echoed faintly, though he knew who she meant.

"The fella from last week. Oooh, he's lush, that one! No offence to you, love—you're gorgeous, of course—but he's more my type, if you know what I mean." She waggled her dramatically painted eyebrows at him.

Mason swallowed. "Didn't you watch last week?" he said. "Or see any of the social media stuff after?"

She set down her sponge and picked up a mascara tube, pushing the wand in and out a few times before pulling it out entirely and inspecting the bristles.

"Oh, I don't watch the show, love," she said, tipping his chin back with her hand and leaning in. "Not my cup of tea."

A wave of some emotion washed over Mason, and he realised it was relief. There was, at least, one person on the planet who didn't know what had happened.

"It's not really my cup of tea either," he said, once he had himself back under control. "And, no, Owen's not on this week, just me. It was… rather a last-minute thing."

She brushed the wand over his lashes, right eye, then left.

"Yeah, well, you've got to be able to pick up last-minute opportunities when they come along in this business, haven't you?" Letting go of his chin, she returned the wand to the tube, screwing it in tight. "It's a tough old game."

"Yeah," Mason said softly. "It is."

She canted her head to one side, looking at him. "I'm wondering whether to give you a touch of eyeliner," she said, but before she could come to any decision, there was a frantic knocking at the door.

"Come in," Carmen called again, and when the door opened, there stood Misty's intern, Naomi. She was wearing her usual black-and-white ensemble, a pinafore dress today with a crisp white shirt underneath and flat Mary-Jane shoes, which made her look schoolgirlish. She was clutching her iPad and a sheaf of papers tightly, her expression harassed, a sheen of perspiration on her face. A few wisps of hair had escaped from her ponytail and were sticking to her forehead.

"Thank God, Mason. There you are!" she exclaimed breathlessly. "Misty wants you urgently. She's only got a few minutes, and she needs to speak to you before your segment." She glanced at Carmen and said tightly, "Aren't you supposed to be in 3.09?"

Carmen bristled and opened her mouth to retort, but Mason said quickly, "I'd better leave the eyeliner, thanks, Carmen. Am I good to go?"

She glanced at him, distracted. "Yes. You better get off if Misty wants you. God knows you'll be in trouble if you keep Her Highness waiting." She deftly untied the canary-yellow cape and pulled it off his shoulders. "Break a leg, kiddo."

～

Naomi race-walked down the corridor with Mason at her heels. Her colour was high, and she was practically vibrating with anxious energy.

"Are you okay?" Mason asked her, quickening his own pace to keep up. "You look really stressed."

Naomi gave a jerky nod. "I'm fine. It's just been a rough morning. Our main guest pulled out at the last minute, and we've been running around like mad sorting it out. When Misty heard you were late, she was *not* happy, and when she called Carmen's room and no one answered, she went off her head at Rowan for not escorting you up here..." She trailed off, letting out a huge sigh. "And now she'll bawl me out for taking so long to find you."

Mason frowned. "She treats you like crap. You shouldn't have to put up with that."

Naomi sent him an incredulous look. And yeah, they both knew this industry was full of people like Misty. But it shouldn't be.

"I suppose things have been pretty full-on this week with the whole #pineapplegate thing as well," he added.

"Yeah," she agreed wearily. "It's been intense."

"You look pretty tired," Mason said bluntly, noting the shadows under her eyes. "You been working late?"

She nodded grimly. "Twelve-hour days all this week."

Shit. And she wasn't even fucking *paid*.

They took the lift down to the ground floor where the studio was located. Crew members were rushing around, talking into headsets, carrying gear, everyone wearing matching harassed expressions.

Clearly, it was a bad day on the *Weekend Wellness* set, but even on his previous visits, when things had been calmer, it hadn't seemed to Mason that this was a happy crew.

It certainly didn't have an ounce of the 'family' vibe that Misty insisted she so carefully cultivated.

"I hold myself responsible for failing to protect my WW *family from Hunter's bullying and lies."*

The outrageousness of that lie hit Mason all over again, filling his belly with pure, white-hot rage. But he couldn't give in to that rage. Not now. He was here to do a job. He had to grit his teeth, sit himself back down on the *Weekend Wellness* sofa, and make himself say the words he needed to say. No matter how much those words might hurt him.

Finally, they reached the green room.

Naomi opened the door, holding it open for Mason to go in ahead of her.

It looked exactly the same as the last time Mason had been in here. The same institutional rows of seats, the same depressing array of tired refreshments on the table underneath the widescreen TV mounted on the wall where *Weekend Wellness* played silently, the dialogue showing up as captions on the screen. The only difference was that Owen wasn't here. Instead, there were two other occupants: a minor soap actor who Mason recognised but whose name he couldn't remember—and Misty, who was pacing the floor impatiently.

She looked up when they entered, her expression furious. "Jesus Christ, Naomi! Did you go via fucking Scotland?"

Naomi flushed scarlet. "Sorry," she muttered. "Carmen had moved to 3.14."

Misty made a noise of disbelief. "You've been gone seventeen fucking minutes!"

Naomi didn't say anything, her shoulders rounded, her whole mien defeated.

"Well, I'm here now," Mason said calmly, "so what did you want to talk about?"

Misty turned to him. Then her gaze shifted to the soap actor who was considering a plate of limp pastries at the refreshment table and probably pretending not to listen.

"Come and sit down," she hissed, grabbing Mason's sleeve and tugging him over to the end of the row of seating, as far away from the actor as possible. Over her shoulder, she said to Naomi, "Make yourself useful and get me a skinny cap. No fucking sprinkles this time."

Naomi nodded and slipped away, the door closing softly behind her.

Mason lowered himself onto the seat next to Misty, trying to maintain a sliver of space between them, hating the way she crowded in against him.

"Bloody hell, Mason, what were you thinking, swanning in here two hours late, today of all days?" she began in a low voice, her eyes hard with fury. She shot another glance at the actor, then said, even more quietly, "Forget it. We don't have time to talk about that now. Did you get the notes Naomi sent through last night?"

"Yeah, I did."

"And you're clear about how your segment is going to go?"

Mason nodded. "The notes were very straightforward," he said, keeping his voice calm and measured. "It doesn't look like it's going to take long."

"We were aiming for five minutes," Misty said, "but Gregor Peterson cancelled on us, so we're extending to ten. We'll cover the key points from the notes first, then show a short VT, and then Leah will do some follow-up questions. I've emailed them to you—check your phone."

"Okay."

Misty let out a sigh. "Look, I know it's been a rough week for you—it's been rough for all of us—but this has actually turned into a great opportunity. And I don't just mean for you to grow your followers and me to increase our viewers—it's an opportunity for us to say something *important* about how we treat other people, you know?"

Mason stared at her, utterly flabbergasted. Had she actually convinced herself of her own lies somehow?

But he didn't say that out loud or any of the other furious words that had been percolating inside him all week. Even though it felt like those words were poisoning him and he hated that he had to push them down, leave them unsaid.

"Okay, key messages," Misty said briskly. "Be regretful about what's happened but not defensive. We're not to blame here. We need to put clear blue water between us and Hunter on that front. Got it?"

He nodded. "Got it."

"Good." Some of the tension in Misty's lean frame seemed to go out of her. After a pause, she added, "And what about your socials? Have you posted anything yet?"

"Yeah, last night—just saying I'd be on the show today talking about #pineapplegate. Nothing more."

He'd wondered, as he'd posted the unfiltered picture of himself, whether Owen would see it—and if so, what he'd think. The worst, probably.

"Good stuff," Misty said. "And you saw what we've got lined up for socials after?"

"Yeah. It was all in Naomi's notes. I've lined up my own posts, ready to go after the show. I just used the suggested wording she sent."

Finally Misty smiled, clearly pleased with his efficient obedience. "This is why I like working with you, Mason. Other than today's tardiness snafu, you've been very professional, and I want to get you back on the show as soon as I can. I've been batting around some ideas with the team, and, in the run-up to summer, we think a segment on top-secret supermodel eating plans would play really well with our audience. Help getting beach-body-ready is like catnip for our pudgy demographic." She laughed. "Which, let's face it, is about 99 per cent of our viewers!"

Mason didn't have a top-secret supermodel eating plan, but he didn't bother to point that out. Just smiled and said, "That sounds great. I appreciate it, Misty."

She patted his arm. The slightly frantic look she'd been wearing when he first arrived had melted away now. "Okay, I better go," she said, her voice rising to its normal volume. "I need to get back to the control room. I daren't leave Cam and

Simon too long on their own. I could really do without any more disasters today!" She rolled her eyes and got to her feet. "Oh, and Naomi's put Austin Coburn's PA in touch with your agent for that article, like I promised." She gave him an exaggerated wink and said archly, "You're welcome!"

He smiled again. "Thanks."

"Always happy to spread the love," she said airily. "Right, you're up at eleven, so you've got half an hour or so in here to look over the extra questions." She glanced at the refreshment table and grimaced. "The green room coffee is awful, but if Naomi ever gets back with my skinny cap, I'll send her out to get you a decent one. Black Americano, right?"

"I don't need a coffee," Mason said, thinking of poor, harried Naomi.

"It's no bother," Misty protested.

Jesus.

"Honestly? I try to avoid too much coffee. Caffeine ages your skin so badly, don't you find?" Mason smiled sweetly. "All part of the top-secret supermodel eating plan!"

Misty laughed uneasily, touching her cheek. "Yes, well. Just make sure you've looked at those new questions and know what you're telling our audience. I can't afford any more fuck-ups today."

"Don't worry," Mason assured her solemnly. "I'll be very professional, just like always."

CHAPTER TWENTY-SEVEN

Owen was up early on Saturday. It was a gorgeous day, with the sun strong and the air cool. He'd decided to spend the morning in the garden, catching up on some of the jobs he'd neglected because he'd been so busy working. And spending time with Mason.

The air was full of the sounds of his neighbours—kids playing, someone cutting their grass, music from a distant radio.

Just the usual weekend sounds.

Unfortunately, his early start, combined with the furious pace he maintained in order to keep himself distracted, meant that he'd finished everything by quarter to eleven. Which was exactly the time when he most needed to be doing something else.

Lewis had phoned last night to break the news that Mason would be doing another live slot on *Weekend Wellness* this morning. And apparently, he'd said on Instagram that he'd be talking about #pineapplegate.

The thought turned Owen's stomach. So much so that

he'd had to force himself to go into his greenhouse to water his actual bloody pineapples. The idea that Mason would publicly go along with this whole #pineapplegate crap was just so fucking *painful*.

A part of Owen hadn't actually believed it until he'd seen the post on Instagram himself. Even that had pinched his stupid heart. In the picture Mason had posted, he looked sad and unkempt. Like a man not sleeping well at night. But then Owen had remembered how meticulously Mason curated the pictures he posted. No doubt this one had been used to produce exactly that effect: sad, regretful, wistful.

Mason the victim.

Even so, it had prompted an instinctive rush of concern in Owen that he hadn't been able to reason away. Apparently, whatever else had happened this week, Mason was still under his skin. Owen still… loved him. That was something he was going to have to get over, but that didn't mean it didn't hurt like hell.

By eleven o'clock, Owen found himself standing on the patio with nothing to do, staring through the glass doors of his kitchen at the blank television screen.

He told himself he didn't want to watch.

He'd told himself he wouldn't watch, but the idea of everyone *except* him knowing what Mason said was somehow worse than hearing it himself. Lewis and Aaron would certainly be watching, and then they'd phone him afterwards. Try to kindly tell him how badly Mason had screwed him over.

It wasn't that *bad…* he could hear Aaron saying, like a man dancing on eggshells.

Owen's stomach churned anxiously, fizzing with dread and anticipation.

Any minute now, Mason would be speaking, would be talking about Owen, maybe repeating Misty's lies…

Was Owen really going to hide from that? Be the only

person not to have heard what Mason had to say about him? No. He wasn't that much of a coward. If Mason was going to trash his reputation, Owen wanted to see it for himself, so he could refute each and every lie when he next spoke to Kushal.

Toeing off his work boots at the door, he strode through the kitchen and into the living room in his socked feet, switching on the TV without sitting down. His shorts were grubby from the garden, and he didn't want to muck up the sofa, so he stood as he flicked through the channels and found *Weekend Wellness*.

Butterflies, angry ones, were dive-bombing in his stomach.

On the telly, they were running a segment on geocaching with a young guy Owen didn't recognise charging about the countryside. Owen didn't listen to what was going on, just stood staring, waiting. Dreading.

He didn't have to wait long.

As the film came to an end, the screen switched back to Marc and Leah sitting on the familiar sofa. "Well, I don't know about you," Leah said, "but I have a hard time keeping track of my car keys, let alone finding a geocache!"

"Isn't that the truth?" Marc said, laughing unconvincingly. And then, more seriously, he added, "Talking about telling the truth, if you've been on social media this week, you might have seen quite the controversy raging about a segment we ran last Saturday."

"That's right," Leah added, her expression now very grave. "Last week, we ran a story about how to grow your own pineapples, but it turns out that everything was not as it appeared. To get to the bottom of the whole controversy, we're joined again today by one of our gardening team, Mason Nash, who's talking for the first time about what's being called '#pineapplegate'."

Owen's heart raced, beating so hard he could feel it in his chest. He was breathing fast, too, his fingers locked rigid around the remote control.

The camera pulled back to reveal Mason sitting on the same sofa he and Owen had occupied last week. He was dressed casually, in dark jeans and a grey jumper, still as beautiful as always. Tense, though. Owen could see that immediately. His smile looked brittle, and his fingers were knotted together in his lap.

"It's been quite a week," Leah said to Mason. "Thanks for coming in to see us again so soon."

"No, thank *you*," Mason said, and that voice... Its familiarity brought a lump to Owen's throat. "Thanks for having me back to talk about all this."

"Let's cut to the chase," said Marc. "At what point did you realise the pineapple plants you thought were Owen's had actually been bought from a plant nursery?"

For a long, tense moment, Mason was silent, Marc and Leah both watching him with matching looks of concerned interest. He wet his lips, looked down at his hands, and then out past the camera towards, Owen knew, the production control room.

Mason cleared his throat. "That's a difficult question."

Marc nodded sympathetically. "I'm sure this whole thing has been difficult for you."

"It has, yes. It's put me in a very awkward position. I've been doing a lot of thinking, but in the end it comes down to a simple choice: tell the truth or don't. And the truth is..."

Owen's chest squeezed, his lungs paralysed, incapable of drawing breath.

"...the truth is," Mason said again, his voice shaking, "I knew those pineapple plants had come from a nursery from the start."

Marc's face fell. "Uh, really?" He shifted uneasily. "That's not what—"

Mason spoke over him, his words tumbling out in a rush. "The producer of this show, Misty Watson-King, brought the plants onto the set and told us to pretend they were Owen's.

Owen refused, so she asked me to film a piece to camera without him. Owen had no idea."

Something clattered to the ground, and Owen realised he'd dropped the TV remote. "Oh my God," he breathed, lowering himself shakily to the sofa, his attention riveted on the screen.

Leah was laughing nervously. "Well, Mason, Misty Watson-King isn't actually here to speak for herself, so—"

"Yes, she is," Mason said, gesturing past the camera. "She's right there in the control room. Ask her. Or ask Lucy, the director. She was there when we filmed that extra segment without Owen."

"All right, I think we should—" Marc cut in, but Mason ignored him and kept talking.

"I shouldn't have done it," he said bitterly. "I regret it more than anything, but Misty made it clear that I had to do what she said if I wanted to stay on the show, and I thought—"

"Okay, well, that's just a wild allegation," Marc said, this time getting to his feet. The camera tracked him as he hurriedly crossed the set, cutting away from Mason. "And we're going to leave it there and move, to, er..." He glanced off screen again, and there were scuffling noises and voices hissing.

Owen could hardly believe what he was seeing. His stupid, broken heart was bounding with a hot, fierce sensation he only belatedly realised was pride. Pride in Mason. Pride, and love, and fear for him.

On the telly, Marc was saying, "Our next guest is—" Only to break off when Mason suddenly stumbled back into shot, his blond hair mussed and his clothes slightly disordered.

"Okay, sorry..." he said breathlessly. "I really don't want to mess this up for you, Marc. I know Misty is unforgiving and will probably give you hell for this even though it's not your fault, but I have to tell the truth."

He was looking straight down the barrel of the camera now, and to Owen, it felt as though he was looking right into Owen's eyes, into his heart and soul.

"Owen Hunter did nothing wrong," Mason said, speaking rapidly. "He didn't claim those pineapples were his, and he definitely didn't bully *anyone*. Misty Watson-King, the executive producer of *Weekend Wellness,* is using him as a scapegoat to cover up her own mistakes. Worse than that, she's lying about him and stoking outrage against him online. She's using #pineapplegate to boost her profile and the profile of her show, feeding off all the hatred and outrage and self-righteous indignation she's stirred up. And Owen Hunter doesn't deserve any of it. He's a..." Mason's voice broke, and Owen, heart thundering, pressed a hand to his mouth. "He's a good man. A kind, loving, hardworking man who I... I was proud to call my friend. He doesn't deserve any of the crap that —"

Abruptly, disorientatingly, the feed switched to a perky young woman dressed in exercise clothes standing in a park. "Well, you've heard of yoga," she said brightly, "but have you heard of *naked* yoga? I'm here in Holland Park with..."

"Oh my God," Owen breathed, slumping back on the sofa, dazed.

What the hell had Mason just done? Had he just ended his career live on TV? Had he ended it over a bloody *pineapple*?

From somewhere in the kitchen, Owen's phone started ringing. He almost tripped over his own feet in his haste to reach it, thinking—hoping—it might be Mason.

It was Lewis. "Fuck, Owen, you won't believe what just happened on—"

"I saw it."

"You were watching? Did you see what he did?"

"Yeah..."

Suddenly, Lewis laughed, a deep full-bellied chuckle.

"Misty is going to be *so* fucking pissed off. She must be going off her head right now."

Owen couldn't care less about Misty when his mind was conjuring up visions of Mason being turfed physically out of the studio. "They won't hurt him, will they?"

"Hurt him?" Lewis snorted. "No. Well, Misty's probably tearing him a new one as we speak. He'll be escorted off set, but they're not going to punch him, if that's what you mean. He can kiss goodbye to working on any of Misty's projects, though, but he must have known that before he started." Lewis went silent for a moment, then, in a more hesitant voice, said, "You know he did that for you, right? They must have thought he was going to toe the line, or they wouldn't have let him near the studio, but... well, who knew Mason Nash had a fucking backbone?"

Owen swallowed hard. *He* should have known.

A better friend—a better *boy*friend—would have had Mason's back from the start, would have trusted him, not stormed off like a bloody diva.

Not turned into a blank wall.

Owen squeezed his eyes shut, wincing at the stab of shame. And all the time he'd been thinking he was the one wronged ....

"They're back," Lewis said sharply. "Shit, who's that?"

Owen opened his eyes, and across the kitchen counter, he saw Naomi, Misty's long-suffering intern, perching on the edge of that bloody sofa looking like a rabbit in the headlights. Leah was introducing her, oozing plastic sympathy as she did so.

"So, Naomi," Leah said at last. "I understand you're the junior member of staff Misty referred to in her statement last week? The person who said they were bullied by Owen Hunter?"

Naomi stared at her in silence for a moment. Then she whispered, "Yes."

Owen's heart dropped through the floor. What the *hell*?

"Can you tell us what happened?" Leah said, gently.

Naomi stared at her. Her eyes were shadowed, and she seemed much less put together than usual.

There was a long, uncomfortable silence. Owen was scarcely breathing.

"Naomi?" Leah prompted.

Naomi cleared her throat. "After what Mason Nash just said, Misty asked me to come on camera to talk about this."

"And we *so* appreciate your bravery," Leah said, leaning forward to touch her knee.

Naomi closed her eyes. She looked genuinely distressed, and Owen's heart went out to her even though he didn't understand what was happening.

"Take your time," Leah murmured.

Naomi shook her head, her eyes still closed. "I didn't want any of this," she whispered.

Leah made a soothing noise, her perfect brows drawn together in concern. "I know," she said softly. "No one would. But sometimes we have to step up and speak our truth." She laid a hand over her heart.

"This is fucking bullshit!" Lewis cursed—Owen had forgotten he was still holding his phone to his ear till that outburst.

"*Sshhh*," he said, his gaze still fixed on Naomi, sitting there looking about sixteen, her eyes screwed closed.

"I just wanted a chance to work in TV," she whispered. "I never expected any of this."

"I know," Leah said. "But you're speaking out now, Naomi. And that *matters*. To so many people."

Slowly, Naomi opened her eyes.

For a moment, she was silent. Then she took a deep breath and said, very clearly, "Owen Hunter has never bullied me... But Misty Watson-King has. Since the moment I started working for her as an unpaid intern."

343

Leah gaped at her.

Naomi plunged on grimly.

"It's true what Mason said. When Owen refused to lie about the pineapples, Misty made Mason shoot extra footage and then edited it to make it look like the plants in the green-house were Owen's. She said it didn't matter whether it was real or not because the *Weekend Wellness* audience was too stupid to know the difference."

"Now, hang on," Marc said.

Suddenly, a security guard blundered onto the set. He stepped towards the sofa, and Naomi quickly stood up and took several paces back. The security guard followed, grabbing for her and taking hold of her arm.

Naomi blinked big, frightened eyes at him. She looked very young in her pinafore dress and ponytail, and the security guard's hand looked massive curled around her slender arm.

"Oh my God," Lewis said in Owen's ear and began laughing. "This just keeps getting better!"

Owen watched in astonishment as the security guard tugged at Naomi, trying to pull her off-screen—and bloody hell, Naomi *resisted* him! She pulled back as the guard tried to haul her away, looking straight at Leah as she said, "Misty Watson-King is a *bully*. You know it, Leah. She bullies every-one, no matter how hard they work. She makes unreasonable demands because she knows that if we want to work in this industry—"

The screen went blank. After a moment, the velvet tones of a continuity announcer came on. "We seem to be having some technical issues with *Weekend Wellness* this week. So, instead, let's see what's happening on tonight's episode of *Celebrity Cook-Off…*"

"Holy shit!" Lewis crowed down the phone line. "They actually pulled the plug!" His voice sounded tinny and distant because Owen had let his hand fall to his side as he'd watched the chaos unfold in utter disbelief. He lifted the phone back to his ear just as Lewis said, "What a fucking shit-show. That was *brilliant*!"

All Owen could think about, though, was Mason. Where he was, what they might have done to him, how he might be feeling.

And how Owen had treated him.

Instead of listening to Mason, he'd let the banshee wails of social media frighten him. Instead of believing in him, he'd assumed the very worst. And instead of loving him, he'd turned his back and walked away.

To Lewis he said, "What do I do now?"

With surprising gentleness, Lewis said, "Do you really need me to tell you?"

And of course, Owen didn't. His heart knew exactly what to do, and he was already reaching for the keys to his van when his brother added, "Go and get him, you idiot."

He was on the road before he even knew where he was going.

He considered driving up to the RPP studio, but Mason would probably be long gone by the time he got there, so in the end, he drove to Mason's flat in Clapham, parking a couple of streets away and feeding all his spare change into the meter.

He jogged down the steps to the front door of Mason's garden flat and rang the bell, then knocked on the door for good measure. No answer. For a few beats, he stood there, unsure what to do. Maybe he should have gone to the studio after all? But no, he was pretty sure Misty would have had Mason chucked off the set by now. Might he have gone some-where else? To a friend's? His family? Owen wasn't sure that either of his parents were likely to be sympathetic about what Mason had just done...

Stop being a fucking coward—you have his number.

Sitting down on the bottom step, Owen pulled out his

phone and navigated to the long thread of messages they'd exchanged over the last weeks and months. The last twenty or more were all from Mason, all of them unanswered—message after message begging Owen to just let him explain.

Owen's gut squirmed with guilt and regret as he thumbed through them, reflecting on some of the uncomfortable truths he'd had to face over the last few days. Like the fact that he was, apparently, a control freak.

Provided he was in control of a situation, he had no problem putting others' needs first—in fact, that was his natural reaction. If he looked back over his life, he could see that he had indeed taken on the role of knight in shining armour on more than a few occasions. And yeah, it was a role he'd quickly fallen into with Mason when he'd agreed to do *Weekend Wellness*.

But Owen's problem wasn't when he was playing the saviour role. It was when he was the one who needed help. When he had to trust someone else, *rely* on someone else. When that happened—well, that was when he brought down the shutters. Did his *"brick wall thing"* as Lewis had called it, shutting out even the people who meant most to him in the world.

Sitting there, at the bottom of Mason's steps, Owen faced a truth that made his heart pound and his palms sweat: maybe he wasn't as strong as he'd always believed himself to be. Because being strong wasn't always about galloping in on a white horse to save the day. Sometimes, it was about making yourself vulnerable. Sometimes, the strongest thing you could do was admit that you'd been wrong, that you'd made a mistake, knowing that all you'd get for your pains was criticism and public humiliation.

Owen's eyes stung with sudden tears as he thought of Mason on TV this morning, sitting alone in the RPP studio on that huge sofa with no one to look out for him. No one to cheer him on. In fact, pretty much everyone had tried to close him down, but he'd kept on going, exposing his own flaws in the process.

Wiping his eyes, Owen began typing a message to Mason.

I'm so sorry. I need to see you. Please tell me where you—

And right then, he heard it—the unmistakable sound of a black cab pulling up outside the flat.

He shoved to his feet, cramming his phone back in his pocket and raced up the steps. And when he reached the top, there was Mason.

Mason looking exhausted and dejected as the cab pulled away, only to freeze at the sight of Owen standing there, gripping the iron railing.

"Owen—" he breathed.

He looked so fragile, so uncertain and wary. His eyes were red-rimmed and smudged with traces of TV makeup, as though he'd been crying, and the shadows under them hinted at too many nights of lost sleep, but to Owen, he'd never looked more beautiful.

"I saw you on the show," Owen said, walking slowly towards him. "I couldn't believe it—what you said."

Mason's face crumpled. "I know," he said, "I'm so fucking sorry. I've been a selfish idiot." He swallowed visibly, his eyes gleaming with unshed tears. "You must hate me."

They were very close now. Owen reached out to touch Mason, his thumb stroking gently over one of his ridiculously gorgeous cheekbones. "Hate you?" he said shakily. "I don't hate you, Mason. I fucking *love* you."

Mason's mouth dropped open in an expression so unexpectedly gormless that Owen couldn't help but laugh, but it was a strangled sort of laugh, more desperate than amused.

"You—y-you said—" Mason stuttered, staring at him, wide-eyed.

Be strong.

"I love you," Owen confirmed again. He tried to smile

reassuringly, but his own throat bobbed with emotion, and his voice was hoarse as he added, "So fucking much."

Mason didn't try to talk again. Instead, he let out a choked sob and slammed into Owen, burying his face in Owen's neck as Owen's arms came around him and pulled him in close.

Kissing the top of Mason's bent head, he whispered. "I'm sorry I didn't listen to you."

"You—you don't have to be—" Mason tried, but he couldn't seem to get a full sentence out, and eventually, he gave up, settling for clutching Owen closer instead.

Owen rocked him, nuzzling his hair, glad for now just to have Mason back in his arms again.

After a minute, when Mason seemed calmer, Owen whispered, "Shall we go inside?"

Mason nodded his head against Owen's neck, but he didn't move right away. Eventually, though, he pulled back, straightening up to his full height to meet Owen's gaze. His eyes were wet, and there were tear tracks on his face, but he wore a tremulous smile that filled Owen with wary, hopeful joy.

"I love you too," he croaked. "I meant it when I said it the first time—and I still mean it."

"I was such a dick to you," Owen said, closing his eyes, trying to blot out the memory of their argument. "I'm sorry. You said you loved me, and I just shut you out and walked away."

"It's okay—"

"It's *not* okay. I was being a fucking coward, and I hurt you and—"

"And I hurt you too," Mason interrupted. "But that's over now, isn't it?"

"Yes," Owen said, reaching for him. "We're not going to hurt each other any more."

CHAPTER TWENTY-EIGHT

MASON

When they got inside, Owen hung back. He still looked a little uncertain, as though he was waiting for Mason to make the first move. So Mason did, stepping in close, loving the warmth of Owen's big body and the way he smelled and how he looked at Mason. As though Mason was amazing, instead of being a fuck-up who'd just about managed to avert total disaster after a long period of being very, very stupid.

Mason's hands were shaking with nerves as he lifted them to unzip Owen's jacket, but it was impossible not to relax as soon as he touched Owen's familiar body. Mason slid his hands over the solid roundness of Owen's shoulder muscles as he pushed his jacket off, relishing his size and strength, while Owen pressed a soft kiss to Mason's cheek. Such a shy, boyish kiss. Mason's heart squeezed.

"Mason," Owen murmured in his ear. "God, Mason."

Mason turned his head, catching Owen's lips with his own as his hands slipped up under Owen's shirt, stroking the smooth, warm skin beneath. Owen groaned, parting his lips to give Mason access, groaning again when Mason slid his tongue inside. And that quickly, everything turned very carnal. Owen's hands reached for the hem of Mason's shirt, and before Mason knew where he was, Owen had whipped it off over his head and was thumbing one of his sensitive nipples, while his other hand gripped Mason's hip and rocked against him, his sizeable, clothed prick rubbing obscenely against Mason's.

"Fuck," Mason gasped. He bucked against Owen, nipping at his earlobe as he muttered, "Take me to bed. *Please*."

Owen shuddered and kissed him again, then began muscling him towards the bedroom, and God, but Mason loved that. Loved the uncompromising thrust of Owen's body shoving him down the corridor, using his sheer bulk to move Mason along.

When they reached the bedroom, they practically tore each other's clothes off, then crashed down onto the bed, Owen's brawny body caging Mason in. He pressed his whole length against Mason so that they lay chest to chest, hip to hip, toe to toe, matched in height, if not in mass. Their faces were aligned too, Owen staring down at Mason, their noses brushing, their mouths just a whisper apart so that when Owen spoke, Mason felt the movement of his lips against his own.

"You're so perfect for me," Owen breathed.

The lump that appeared in Mason's throat was huge and achy. He blinked. "Am I?"

"Yeah," Owen breathed, his eyes soft with affection. "Brave and bright and funny… and a fucking amazing cook."

He hadn't even mentioned Mason's looks, and somehow, that made Mason happier than anything.

He opened his mouth to point out how perfect Owen was too, but Owen was quicker, already swooping in for another kiss, and then they were moaning into each other's mouths, their bodies shifting and realigning as their hips sought, then found, a perfect driving rhythm.

Mason toyed with tearing his mouth from Owen's and demanding to be fucked, but he couldn't bring himself to break that perfect kiss, and anyway, this felt too incredible to stop. So, when Owen's big hand slid down between their bodies and took hold of both their cocks together, he only choked out a sob of pleasure and hooked an arm around Owen's neck, holding on for the ride.

And Christ, but it was a beautiful ride.

Owen's kiss was hard and consuming, his hand firm and demanding at once. He forced Mason to observe the pace he wanted, his steady, relentless strokes dragging from Mason a sudden and shuddering orgasm, one that broke over him just as Owen's own cock erupted. Chests heaving, they spilled together, their spunk mingling between their bellies, sticky and warm.

Gradually, they stilled, their kisses growing soft and affectionate.

"That was fantastic," Mason murmured against Owen's lips. "But I'm going need you to fuck me too."

Owen's blue gaze was warm, the gorgeous crinkles at the corners of his eyes deepening with amusement. "You might still be in your twenties, angel, but I'm not. I'll need a recovery period first." Then he grinned wickedly. "But in the meantime, if you want me to eat you out till you come again, I can totally do that."

Mason whimpered, and Owen laughed softly, kissing an affectionate path from Mason's ear, down his jawline to his lips.

They kissed for a while longer, tender, laughing kisses, punctuated with nonsense love words. Then Owen sighed contentedly and rose from the bed, padding through to the bathroom to clean up.

"You stay there," he said over his shoulder. "I'll bring you a cloth."

"Now, that's what I call love," Mason called after him. His grin felt so huge his face ached.

Once they were all cleaned up, and lying side by side in bed, facing each other, Owen said softly, "No one's ever done anything for me like you did today."

Mason quirked a half-smile. "You're giving me too much credit. I should have come to my senses sooner than I did. I was so fixated on building my following, landing bigger brand deals, getting more work as though, if I finally got enough of those things, that would magically sort out all my problems and make me happy."

"Yeah, well, I get why you thought that. Landing those big contracts and getting on TV would have meant a lot more money." Owen's expression was apologetic. "Do you think you'll lose followers over this?"

"By the time the taxi dropped me off here, I'd already lost over a thousand," Mason said, then chuckled at the horrified look on Owen's face. "Oh, it'll be *way* more than that by now. God only knows. Frankly, I don't care." He really didn't. Nor did he care about the hundreds of other notifications and comments that had been piling up, or even the messages and voicemails he'd ignored from Frankie and his family.

Fuck it. All of that could wait. The only thing that mattered right now was him and Owen. Because, over the last week, Mason had discovered that what he wanted—more than a TV career or a million devoted followers, more than anything else—was a future with Owen.

"Shit, I'm sorry," Owen said, his brows stitched together with worry. "I feel responsible. Is there anything I can do? I'm not much good at this stuff, but I'll post anything you need, or even"—he grimaced—"make a video if you want."

Mason laughed softly, but he shook his head. "No, I don't want you to do any of that—I know you hate it, and besides, that stuff I said on TV today was only really for one person: you."

"Yeah?" Owen whispered, his gaze very soft.

"Yeah," Mason said. "And the fact that you heard me? That's everything, Owen. It's all that matters to me. So, no, I'm not going to try to mitigate the online damage or find some way of getting my side of the story out there." He smiled. "No more feeding the sharks."

Owen reached out to brush Mason's hair back from his forehead. "Okay, so long as you understand that I don't need or want you to change for me. I love you just the way you are, Mason. Hell, it's not *my* business what you choose to do with your life. If it ever seemed like that, it's just because I worried about how anxious you sometimes got about stuff that didn't seem to me to really matter." He smiled gently. "But I know that came from the pressure you felt to keep supporting your family financially." He shook his head. "I never meant to make you feel like I look down on what you do."

Mason smiled ruefully. "Yeah, well, as much as I appreciate you saying that, the truth is, you were right about a lot of what you said. After that shitshow last week, and our argument, I realised how unhappy I was making myself, constantly presenting this fake version of myself to the world."

"Mason—" Owen stroked his hair again, his dark brows creased with concern.

"That's not the person I want to be," Mason said hoarsely. "I don't want to keep compromising on who I am. I want to be myself."

Owen leaned in and kissed him tenderly. When he pulled back, he said, "You're already yourself, Mason. What you did today was so fucking brave and beautiful." He paused, then added, "For what it's worth, I'll be one hundred percent behind you, whatever path you choose. And that stands, regardless of what happens between us in the future."

Mason frowned. "Sorry, *what*? What do you mean by that?"

Owen flushed a dull red and shrugged, glancing away. "Just… you're a lot younger than me, and the way you feel right now may not be how—"

Mason pressed his hand over Owen's mouth to stop him saying another single word. His heart was racing with something that felt like anger and fear together. "Hey!" he said. "Don't—just don't—"

Gently, Owen's fingers encircled his wrist and tugged his hand away. "All I'm saying is that I need you to know that I'll have your back, whether we're together or not."

"But—but you just said you *loved* me," Mason croaked.

Owen's expression grew anguished. "I *do* love you," he said. "I love you so fucking much, Mason, and that's not going to change for me. But it might change for *you*, and—"

"No, it fucking won't!" Mason cried.

Owen blinked.

"It's not going to change for me either," Mason said, glaring at him. "So bad luck, you're stuck with me!"

"But how do you *know* it won't change?"

"How do *you*?" Mason retorted.

Owen's blue gaze searched his face. At last he whispered, "I just do."

"Yeah? Well, same here," Mason replied. "Guess we're just going to have to trust each other on that one."

Owen was quiet for a long time, considering that. Then he smiled, a crooked sort of smile. Tentative and hopeful.

"I guess we are," he said.

~

"Don't get me wrong," Owen said, much later, as they sat at the kitchen table eating spaghetti al limone, "I think you've done absolutely the right thing, but how do you think your mum will deal with it?"

Mason, who had just told Owen about Min's intervention

with Frieda a few days before, swirled the same few strands of spaghetti around his fork, over and over, as he considered that. "I'm not sure," he said at last. "But like I told her, I'm not going to cut her off tomorrow. I want to give up modelling, but I won't stop taking jobs until I've got a plan sorted out for what I'm going to do next." He felt a surge of excitement, the stretching of wings too long clipped. "You've made me realise that it's *my* life, and that it's okay to make plans without considering what Frieda or Kurt might think about them. It's helped that the girls have been so supportive."

Across the table, Owen beamed, his eyes so bright and fond that Mason couldn't help but smile too. "Any ideas on what you might want to do?"

"It'll be something with food, I know that much, but I'm going to think it through carefully. I'm not making any sudden decisions. Besides, the lease on this place has another six months to run, and I need to cover the rent."

Owen shot him a glance. "You're giving this flat up?"

Mason shrugged. "I'll have to get somewhere cheaper. This is… expensive."

"London's expensive," Owen pointed out.

Mason chuckled without much humour. "Yeah."

Owen shifted in his seat. "I know it's probably too soon but"—he stopped and cleared his throat—"maybe when you get to the end of your lease, you could move in with me? Beckenham's not as trendy as Clapham, but it's nice."

Mason's heart began to race. It *was* too soon, no doubt about it, but the thought of moving in with Owen, of sharing his well-loved house and garden, filled Mason with sudden fierce happiness.

Before he could reply, Owen looked up and said, "Don't say yes or no right away. Just—put it in your pocket for now, okay?"

"Okay," Mason breathed, though he suspected his helpless smile probably gave away his true feelings on the subject.

After a bit, Owen said, "What about your dad? Have you spoken to him about your plans?"

Mason shook his head. "I will, though. I need to tell him that he's going to have to step up more—and that I'm done being an intermediary between him and Frieda." He gave a careless shrug, though the thought of the conversation to come made him feel anything but nonchalant. "He's not going to like it, but he's going to have to deal. Besides, Mel and Min are going to back me up." He laughed softly. "Min's pretty fierce these days."

Owen grinned. "Sibling solidarity?"

"Yeah," Mason said, grinning back. "It's very new but kind of awesome."

They went back to their spaghetti.

"This is so good," Owen said after another mouthful. "How do you make plain old pasta and lemon taste so incredible?"

"Best-quality olive oil and parmesan," Mason replied. "My top store cupboard standbys."

Owen slurped up the last forkful from his dish, then leaned happily back in his chair, patting his stomach. "If this is what you do with a bit of oil and cheese, I can't wait to see how you handle my homegrown tomatoes."

Mason waggled his eyebrows. "I'm happy to handle your tomatoes any day, but I thought they needed some recovery time?"

Owen laughed, and so did Mason, the pair of them giggling helplessly across the kitchen table at each other. At which point, Mason's phone—abandoned in his jacket, somewhere near the front door—started to ring, the shrill sound tipping a bucket of ice water over their good mood.

"That's probably Frankie," Mason said, grimacing. "Or Frieda."

All of a sudden, his optimistic thoughts about making

decisions without reference to his parents' wishes felt hollow, punctured by a familiar stab of anxious guilt.

Across the table, Owen's lips pressed together. "Want me to answer it for you?" Then he frowned, shaking his head. "No, sorry, that's stupid. You don't need me to fight your battles."

"I don't," Mason said, resolved, "but it's nice to know you've got my back."

The phone stopped ringing and went to voicemail. Into the sudden silence, Owen said softly, "I'll always have your back, angel."

"I know." With a sigh, Mason pushed away from the table and stood up, holding out his hand to Owen. He took it and let Mason lead him into the hall to retrieve his jacket, which still lay on the floor where he'd abandoned it during their frenzied make-up sex.

The memory made Mason smile.

He dug his phone out of the pocket, saw a gazillion notifications, and dismissed them all. There were messages from Misty, too, which he ignored, and from Frankie—lots of ALL CAPS!—as well as from his mum. But there were also messages from Min and Mel. Plenty of hearts and thumbs up emojis in those ones, which made him smile again.

"Come on," Owen said, one hand on Mason's shoulder as he guided him into the living room to sit down.

Owen took his favourite corner of the sofa, and Mason snuggled in next to him, his back against Owen's chest as Owen looped his arms lightly around Mason's waist and propped his chin on Mason's shoulder. It felt good, to be held like that, to be supported.

First, he sent a message to Frieda.

I'm taking a few days off, but I'll come and see you next week. We'll have lunch. Everything will be ok. xx

Then, to his sisters.

Hiding out with Owen for the weekend :) Will sort things with Frieda and Kurt next week… Love you both!! <3

Finally, to Frankie.

Taking a few days to think about my future. Tell Misty whatever you want, but I won't apologise for telling the truth. Sorry for dumping this on you. Will call you in the week.

Then he swiped back to his home screen, hesitated only for a second before holding his finger on the Instagram icon until it began to tremble. It took moments to delete the app and to do the same to all his other social channels. Not quite as significant as deleting his accounts—he *did* need to talk to Frankie about how to handle his withdrawal from social media—but nevertheless, it felt good to remove the buggers from his phone, for now at least.

With that done, he hit the power button, switched off his phone entirely, and slung it onto the coffee table. It slid into a pile of books and stopped, its blank gaze fixed on the ceiling.

"Well," Owen said after a moment, tightening his arms around Mason's waist, "looks like we've got the rest of the weekend to ourselves."

Mason smiled, snuggling back into him. "Looks like we do."

"Any ideas on how to pass the time?"

Squirming around so he could graze his lips against Owen's scruffy jaw, Mason murmured, "Well, you *were* talking about me handling your tomatoes…"

Owen chuckled, shifting them both until Mason was straddling his lap and their lips met in an unhurried kiss. After a while, Owen said, "Apparently, my tomatoes are… recovering nicely."

"I noticed." Mason gave a suggestive wiggle, feeling Owen's growing arousal beneath him. "So how about we go and, er, juice them?"

Owen grimaced, laughing. "Oh my God…"

Mason laughed too, helplessly, collapsing against Owen's

chest, his head on his shoulder as Owen wrapped both arms around him. After the misery of the morning, Mason's laughter, his sheer happiness, fizzed through him like freshly poured champagne and washed everything else away. He felt dizzy with joy, delirious. Euphoric.

Still chuckling, Owen nuzzled the side of his head, brushing the top of his ear with his lips. "I love you, you nut."

"I love you, too." Lifting his head, Mason met Owen's sunny blue eyes, sparkling in his honest, loving face. It was, without question, Mason's favourite face in the whole world. "I'll love you forever," he said seriously and knew it to be true.

Owen grinned up at him, and, with his heart overspilling, Mason leaned in to kiss that lovely, joyful smile.

EPILOGUE

6 months later — October

Owen blinked his eyes open. He could tell it was early from the gentle quality of the light that glowed around the edges of the blind—and by the birdsong in the garden.

Yawning contentedly, he turned his head to gaze at the occupant of the neighbouring pillow, his heart squeezing with happiness to see Mason lying curled up on his side facing Owen, his features half-obscured by his rumpled hair, his shoulder gently moving up and down with his deep, quiet breaths. He was still sound asleep.

Mason had spent a lot of nights in this bed over the last six months, but last night was special: his first night sleeping here after officially moving in. The bedroom was littered with bags and boxes still to be unpacked—as was the kitchen and living room—but Owen didn't care about the mess. Over the next few days, they'd find places for everything. He was looking forward to intermingling their books and music and kitchenware.

For a while, Owen lay there, idly watching Mason sleep as he tried to isolate the different garden birds singing. He'd been listening to their songs online recently and trying to remember them—mostly because it made him feel accomplished when he told Mason new stuff about nature. He was getting addicted to the expression Mason wore when Owen impressed him, which was pretty pathetic, he supposed, even as he grinned at the thought.

There were fewer birds in the autumn than at the height of summer, which should probably have made it easier to identify them. But other than the robin's song, with its distinctive watery trickles, Owen wasn't able to hone in on any others in the general song-babble, so he decided to get up.

He rose slowly, careful not to disturb Mason, pulling on a pair of loose flannel PJ bottoms and a long-sleeved t-shirt before tip-toeing out of the room.

He smiled as he wandered through the house and saw all the new signs of Mason's occupancy. He smiled at Mason's toothbrush in the bathroom and the pile of cookery books on the coffee table. He smiled at the state-of-the-art espresso machine with its proper steam wand which now sat on the kitchen counter—even though, by force of habit, Owen still made his usual jug of filter coffee in his ancient Morphy Richards coffee maker. He even smiled at the heavy box of crockery on the kitchen floor that he stubbed his toe on.

When the coffee was ready, he took it out into the garden, padding down the winding path in his bare feet to the two-seater swing seat at the far end. The swing seat was a new addition, along with the sturdy pergola frame it hung from. Owen had planted rambling rose and honeysuckle at the base of the pillars, and, in a year or two, the bare timbers of the pergola would be covered in green, not to mention a riot of flowers from early summer right through to autumn.

Owen sighed happily and sipped his coffee as his gaze

moved over the garden. The courgettes and runner beans were almost done now, just one last small crop to collect, and there was a myriad of other jobs to do—the raspberry plants to be transplanted to a new location, the beds mulched, the faded sweet peas and perennials cleared out. He had a load of colourful spring bulbs to be planted and plans to put in some more crops for Mason to cook with—and write about, since he now had his own food blog, *Ground Up*. It had started as a hobby, a way for Mason to record the steps he was taking to simplify his life and resume his passion for cooking. But with encouragement from Aaron and Tag, he'd begun—very cautiously—to cross-post the content on his by-then-quite-neglected social media accounts.

They'd all been surprised at the level of engagement he'd got from his remaining followers. And yeah, okay, those followers had dwindled by about half, some having dramatically unfollowed Mason at the beginning of the #pineapple-gate hoo-ha, while others had just lost interest in him when he stopped posting so often. But despite going dark for several months, he had retained a good number of followers, a healthy segment of whom actually seemed to be interested in his new food-related content. Now he was even picking up new followers and, in the last couple of weeks, a few media queries, an approach from a small cookware brand and a tentative email about a possible book deal. It was all very new, but it looked… promising. And as wary as both of them were about Mason going back to social media after every-thing that had happened, the fact was he was good at it. He understood it, and he knew how to make it work commer-cially. And this time, he was determined not to make the same mistakes.

"I'm not letting it take over my life again," he'd said last night as they cuddled on the sofa—their sofa—with a celebra-tory bottle of champagne. "And as for you and me, our personal life will be just that—personal. Private."

"Yeah, you best keep me off," Owen had agreed, grinning. "It'll fuck with your ratio. I'm probably still public enemy number one on Insta."

That wasn't exactly true. In fact, so far as Owen and Mason were concerned, #pineapplegate had blown over remarkably quickly. Once the live exposé of Misty had happened, the social media mob had lost interest in them, the story morphing into the fall of Mistletoe Watson-King, then morphing again when similar complaints surfaced about the host of a popular talk show. By the time the pipeline of stories had finally dried up, Owen and Mason had been pretty much forgotten. Thankfully, Owen's online trade listings had recovered, thanks to a concerted campaign by a small bunch of hard-core *Owson* fans who had flooded the sites with enough five-star reviews to balance out the one-star ones. Owen would have preferred that any reviews that were not from people he'd actually done work for could be removed, but he supposed he was grateful. Sort of.

Just then, the glass door onto the garden slid open, and Mason stepped out of the house. He was wearing his favourite tatty grey shorts and one of Owen's hoodies and carrying his own mug of coffee. He ambled down the path to join Owen.

"Morning," he said when he reached the swing. "How long have you been up?"

Owen grinned at him, his heart light and happy. "Not long. I didn't want to wake you. Yesterday was tiring."

"Too true," Mason said, his tone heartfelt. "My arms are aching from carrying all those boxes. Here. Budge up."

Owen shifted to make room for Mason on the swing, stretching his arm out along the back of it, and Mason snuggled in beside him, leaning back against Owen's shoulder and lifting his feet up onto the seat. He felt warm and relaxed, and when Owen kissed his head, he caught a lingering trace of the tea tree scent of his shampoo. Glancing at Mason's coffee, he saw it was topped with a fat pillow of milk foam and dark chocolate flakes.

"Still with the cappuccinos?" he said in disbelief.

"Yup," Mason replied. 'I'm making up for all those years I spent yearning for them while I made do with black, sugar-free coffee."

"Ugh, milky coffee," Owen said in mock-disgust, sipping his own resolutely black brew. He smiled, though, happy that Mason didn't have to deny himself life's little luxuries any more. Over the last few months, he'd even put a little weight on. It wasn't much, just a few pounds—Mason was naturally slim, and his appetite was pretty moderate—but it made a difference. Somehow, it softened his edges, easing a subtle tension he'd carried when having to consider his calorie consumption and exercise regime every single day.

Owen rubbed his cheek affectionately over Mason's head, smiling at the indulgent chuckle this provoked.

"You're very friendly this morning."

"I'm very friendly every morning," Owen pointed out.

"That you are," Mason said and gave a happy sigh.

For a few minutes, they sat quietly, sipping their coffee, Owen keeping the swing gently rocking with his foot. It was a sunny autumn day, and though not particularly warm, this part of the garden was nicely sheltered and got the best of the morning sun, so it was pleasant to just sit there and rock.

"So," Owen said at last. "What do you want to do on your first weekend in your new home?"

For a moment, Mason was silent; then he sighed and shifted, turning himself around till they were facing one another. "If I'm honest," he said, "I just want to chill with you, but..." He trailed off.

"What is it?" Owen asked, frowning.

"I got a text from Frieda." He made a face. "She asked if she and Kurt could come round tomorrow to see the place."

Frieda and Kurt were—to everyone's astonishment except, apparently, themselves—back together. Regan had chucked Kurt out unceremoniously back in July. Luckily, Mason had been doing one of his last shoots at the time, in some remote part of the Scottish Highlands with horrendous midges... and terrible network connections. That piece of good luck had prevented Kurt from being able to crash at Mason's—and thereby becoming Mason's problem. Eventually, with nowhere else to go, he'd turned up on Frieda's doorstep with his tail between his legs, and amazingly, she'd agreed to let him sleep on the sofa for a few days. According to Mason's sisters, it had taken him less than a week to find his way back into the bedroom.

Now they were acting like newlyweds, both of them claiming that breaking up in the first place had been a huge mistake, and they'd known they'd end up back together one day.

On the plus side, Frieda was blissfully happy—and honestly, Kurt seemed happy too. After all, Frieda adored Kurt, and Kurt adored Kurt, so they had that in common, and after the last few difficult months with Regan, Kurt appeared to be enjoying the uncritical adoration of a woman who, despite being of the view that he was spawn of the devil for the last decade, now appeared to believed he could do no wrong. More importantly, it had certainly helped on the financial side. Now that Kurt and Frieda's expenses were combined in one household, the main financial stresses around Mason's decision to quit modelling were more or less eliminated.

Even so, Mason was understandably sceptical about the whole thing. He didn't trust Kurt not to stray again, and he was worried about Frieda getting badly hurt. But, as Min had said when he'd discussed it with his sisters, this was the happiest Frieda had been in years, and it was, ultimately her decision to make. Mel had added, more practically, that Frieda and Kurt would probably last as a couple at least until Mel and Min had left home, and Mason had established his new path in life. And that was good for everyone since, if they broke up again in future, the break up wouldn't involve any of the siblings—Frieda and Kurt would have to work out how to fund their new single lives for themselves.

Owen knew that Mason would never leave his mother in the lurch and was resigned to the fact that she would probably always lean on Mason, but that conversation with his sisters really had seemed to help him get more comfortable with his parents' new situation. And honestly, it was impossible not to feel a little pleased for Frieda when she was undeniably so much happier. And hey—maybe she and Kurt would make it this time. After all, they had been together for fourteen years the first time around, which was ten years longer than Kurt had managed with anyone else.

Owen reached out to smooth Mason's rumpled hair back from his face. "I'm taking it from your expression that you don't want them to come round tomorrow?"

Mason sighed. "No, but you know how Frieda gets."

"Okay, why don't you text her and say we do really want to have them round once you're properly moved in, but the place is a mess, and we need a little bit of time to sort things out? If you give her a firm invite for an actual date, that should keep her on side. We can invite them all over—Frieda, Kurt and the girls—and cook a fancy lunch."

Mason's tense expression softened. "That's a good idea. She'll like that."

Owen shrugged modestly. "I'm full of good ideas."

Mason leaned forward and kissed him. "You are," he agreed, his lips grazing Owen's. "And you're lovely. I know my parents are a pain."

Owen quirked a smile against Mason's lips. "They're not so bad. I mean, they're part of the deal, aren't they?"

"The deal?"

"You," Owen said simply.

Mason pulled back, frowning a little. "You don't have to put up with them just because we're together."

Owen just shrugged. "We don't exist in isolation," he said. He lifted a brow. "I mean, you have to cope with my insufferably rude little brother."

Mason chuckled at that. "I *like* Lewis—but we make way better brothers-in-law than boyfriends."

"*Brothers-in-law?*" Owen echoed, raising his brows.

Mason's face flushed scarlet as he realised what he'd said.

Owen put a hand to his chest and whispered, "Oh my God, did you just propose?"

Mason punched his arm. "Shut up."

"If you want to get down on one knee…"

Mason laughed. "Oh my God, shut *up*. If and when I ask, you'll know about it, okay?"

Owen clasped his hands over his heart. "He wants to *marry* me," he gasped dramatically.

Mason was laughing in earnest now, his green eyes bright with humour and happiness. And right then, in that moment, Owen felt a stab of such perfect joy that he didn't even know what to do with the feeling. So he just let it fill him up and, grinning like an idiot, leaned forward to kiss his love.

Mason's lips were soft and warm. He murmured Owen's name and slid his arms around him, pulling him closer. Owen thought, *This is happiness. This is joy.* And in that moment, he understood, perfectly and profoundly, what led people to blurt out those old hackneyed words. *Will you marry me?*

He almost said them then, but he didn't want to do it when they were joking around, when Mason mightn't think he meant it. He'd save that for another day.

And besides, now he had other things on his mind.

"Since we're having a lazy weekend," he murmured between kisses, "shall we go back to bed?"

He felt Mason's lips curve up against his own. "Yeah," Mason breathed. "Let's do that."

The End

THANK YOU, DEAR READER

Thank you for reading this book!
We hope you enjoyed pouty Mason and good-guy Owen's
story. You may not be surprised to hear that the third book in
the series will focus on actors Jay Warren and Tag O'Rourke…

We love hearing from our readers. You can find all the
different ways to connect with each (or both!) of us below.

If you have time, we'd be very grateful if you'd consider
leaving a review on an online review site.
Reviews are so helpful for book visibility and we appreciate
every one.

Joanna & Sally

CONNECT WITH JOANNA

Email: authorjoannachambers@gmail.com

Website: www.joannachambers.com

Newsletter: visit my website to subscribe for up to date
information about my books, freebies
and special deals.

Connect with me on Facebook, Twitter, Instagram, Goodreads
and Bookbub.

Joanna

CONNECT WITH SALLY

Email: sally@stargatenovels.com

Website: www.sallymalcolm.com

Newsletter: visit my website for news, book recs, and giveaways. All new subscribers get a free copy of *Rebel: An Outlawed Story*..

Connect with me on Facebook, Twitter, Instagram, Goodreads and Bookbub.

Sally

ALSO BY SALLY MALCOLM

Read on for an excerpt of **Rebel**

Rebel

Saturday came and found Sam feeling unaccountably anxious—or, rather, not anxious but nervous, or, rather, not nervous but excited. He had May build up the fire and Peggy prepare a good dinner. It was the first time since the typhus that his house had been filled with the warmth of another person, and from the smile Peggy gave him, she approved.

He and Tanner talked over dinner, and late into the night, until the candle had burned to a stub and there wasn't enough light to carry on. They talked of Rousseau and his radical ideas, of the brewing trouble in Boston, of poetry and novels—The Castle of Otranto, which Sam loved, and Nate disparaged—and of nonsense, such as the best honey bread in Rosemont and John Reed's son (also John) and his vain attempts to pass himself off as a dandy.

After Tanner left, Sam hardly slept. His restless mind turned the evening over and over, dwelling on certain moments: the way Tanner leaned forward as he spoke, elbows on knees, almost brushing Sam's leg; the way his face softened when Sam was talking, his dark eyes bright; the way he'd dawdled in the hall as he left, holding Sam's hand in a lingering farewell handshake.

From that night onward, every Saturday evening was spent before his fire with Tanner—sometimes reading a novel or poetry, always discussing what they'd read, but increasingly reading Tanner's political philosophy. Pamphlets and books with startling ideas that Sam found interesting, but that set Tanner alight. Sam loved to listen to him talk. He loved the way his eyes flashed when he was excited, the way the skin over his cheekbones flushed with fervor. Sam loved that zeal, admired it more than he could express. He didn't agree with all Tanner's wild ideas about America's future, but seeing him burn with passion made Sam burn too. He could feel the heat smoldering down deep, ready to set the world on fire if he let it escape. But he didn't let it; he knew he couldn't.

"My father? He calls me a 'free thinker'," Tanner said when Sam asked what he thought of Tanner's philosophies. "It isn't a compliment."

"Isn't it? Why would anyone want to be an unfree thinker?"

"An unfree thinker!" Tanner laughed. "Quite. Conformity of thought is simply recitation." He sobered, favoring Sam with a warm smile that could only be called pretty.

Tanner had a pretty mouth. "I like how you think, Hutch. It's uncluttered."

Sam raised his eyebrows. "Is that a compliment?"

"Of course! You see things clearly. You cut to the point and stay there. You're not battered about by other men's opinions once you know your own."

"My father used to call me stubborn."

"You're constant. I admire that."

Sam felt himself glow at the praise. "I do like to think I know my own mind. But Mr. Reed's taught me a lot about thinking clearly; the credit for that is probably his. The law's a black and white business, isn't it?"

"Reed?" Tanner shook his head, smiling. "You're loyal, Hutch, and to a fault. But Reed, a thinker? No."

"What do you mean?"

"He's a good man—he's the best of men!—but a thinker he's not. No don't protest; you know I'm right. At best, Reed is a walking aphorism. If I hear 'A lie has one leg, the truth has two' one more time I won't be held responsible for my actions!"

Sam grinned, scandalized and delighted in equal measure. Tanner wasn't wrong. He was never wrong—brilliant, quick, clever. Dazzling. Sam had come to admire him so much over the past few months. He wished he had some of Tanner's brilliance himself, but he wasn't envious; he enjoyed basking in Tanner's radiance too much for resentment. Yet it made him restless, eager for something he couldn't quite name.

"It can't be left unchallenged," Nate said another night, in different humor, clutching a new pamphlet from Boston. "We have a voice, and we must be heard. We have the same rights as any Englishman, and they can't take them away."

"I'm not arguing with you," Sam assured him. "We should have representatives in parliament. Maybe even elect our own governors, too. American men, not crown placemen. Men who understand the colonies."

"Or better—elect our own parliament."

Sam laughed. "That is a radical thought, Tanner. A colonial parliament?"

"Well, why not? Are we less able to run our own affairs than the king's other subjects?"

"Perhaps it could work here, or in Massachusetts, but surely not everywhere? What about Carolina? It's wild country down there, Tanner."

"Wild country?" Tanner flung himself back in his seat, his anger dissipating as he smiled at Sam. It was such a beautiful smile, warm and…fond? "My dear Hutch, you're a Rosemont man to your roots."

My dear Hutch. Sam flushed, laughed, and shook his head.

When he looked up again, Tanner wasn't smiling. He was regarding Sam with that appraising look, the one Sam usually couldn't decipher. But this time he felt blood rushing under his skin, felt his breathing catch and burn—this time he felt his admiration unfurl to reveal its true colors. His body flooded with a thick, syrupy desire it was impossible to misunderstand. And in that moment, he knew it wasn't admi-

ration making his heart race, but something different. Something far more dangerous.

He didn't want to be like Nate—he simply wanted him.
He wanted him in the most forbidden of ways. He was
drenched in desire for him.

God only knew what showed on his face, because Tanner
abruptly looked away, biting his lower lip so hard it turned
white.

∼

ALSO BY JOANNA CHAMBERS

Enemies Like You

PORTHKENNACK SERIES (RIPTIDE)

A Gathering Storm

Tribute Act

OTHER NOVELS

The Dream Alchemist

Unforgivable

NOVELLAS

Merry & Bright (festive anthology)

Humbug

Rest and Be Thankful

You can start the **Winterbourne series** for **free** today by signing up to my newsletter at my website.

Tormented by his forbidden desires for other men and the painful memories of the childhood friend he once loved, lawyer David Lauriston tries to maintain a celibate existence while he forges his reputation in Edinburgh's privileged legal world.

But then, into his repressed and orderly life, bursts Lord Murdo Balfour.

Cynical, hedonistic and utterly unapologetic, Murdo could not be less like David. And as appalled as David is by Murdo's unrepentant self-interest, he cannot resist the man's sway. Murdo tempts and provokes David in equal measure, forcing him to acknowledge his physical desires.

But Murdo is not the only man distracting David from his work. Euan MacLennan, the brother of a convicted radical David once represented, approaches David to beg him for help. Euan is searching for the government agent who sent his brother to Australia on a convict ship, and other radicals to the gallows. Despite knowing it may damage his career, David cannot turn Euan away.

As their search progresses, it begins to look as though the trail may lead to none other than Lord Murdo Balfour, and David has to wonder whether it's possible Murdo could be more than he seems. Is he really just a bored aristocrat, amusing himself at David's expense, or could he be the agent provocateur responsible for the fate of Peter MacLennan and the other radicals?

∼

READ ON FOR A TASTER OF PROVOKED...

～

"Come away in, sir," the landlady said as the maidservant scuttled past them. "Make yourself comfortable. This gentleman is Mr. Lauriston, my other guest."

The man turned towards David with a polite smile. His dark gaze moved over David with candid interest, and it seemed to David that his smile grew as he took in what he saw, becoming faintly predatory. David's heartbeat quickened in response, rising to struggle like a trapped bird at the base of his throat. Discomfited, and annoyed at himself for his reaction, he nodded more curtly than he ordinarily would.

"Pleased to meet you, Mr. Lauriston," the man said. "Do you mind if I join you for dinner?" His accent was the accent of the very rich Scot. Cut-glass English with just the slightest lilt. Over six feet in height, almost a full head taller than David, and far broader.

"No, of course not, Mr.—?"

"Balfour. Murdo Balfour."

They shook hands. Balfour had removed his gloves, and the brief, icy clasp of his fingers chilled David's own. He could still feel the ghost of their grasp once Balfour had released him.

Balfour turned away to hang his coat and hat on a stand in the corner of the room while Mrs. Fairbairn readied the table. Lifting the tallow candle stub, she set it aside and fetched a white bundle from the sideboard. With a shake of her arms, the bundle opened up like the sail of a ship catching the wind and settled over the dark wood in soft folds. She finished the table with a branch of beeswax candles, lighting them with a flame borrowed from the crackling fire.

David glanced surreptitiously at Balfour as he settled himself into a chair. He was perhaps thirty or so. Not classically handsome, but arresting, with bold, startling features. His thick hair looked black but might be very dark brown—

difficult to tell in this light—and his complexion was fashionably pale. It was a startling combination with all that height and a pair of shoulders on him that had surely brushed the sides of the doorway when he walked in here. Straight nose, dark brows, a wide, sardonic mouth with a twist to it that suggested the man spent his life laughing at his fellow man. Not a particularly friendly face but a compelling one. And right now, David realised—dismayed to notice Balfour had just caught him cataloguing his features—one that was animated with what appeared to be veiled amusement.

The man's dark gaze was very direct. Meeting it, David felt a surge of something that was part excitement, part alarm. *Could he be…?* David damned the question even as it arose in his mind. He wasn't looking for company tonight. He wasn't. It had been many months since his last lapse.

"What is your direction, Mr. Lauriston?" Balfour's tone was neutral, but his gaze seemed to linger a little on David's mouth. Or was David imagining things?

"I am due to return to the capital tomorrow. And you?" David kept his voice cool.

"It appears we are taking different roads. I am bound for Argyllshire."

A boy entered the dining room. He placed a jug of ale and two pewter cups on the table and hurried off again, leaving the men to help themselves.

Balfour poured ale for them both and offered his cup in a toast. "To safe journeys."

David echoed his words obligingly.

The ale was surprisingly decent. A pale ale, the colour of weak tea, hoppy and cool. They both drank deeply, and Balfour filled their cups again.

"Did you see the hanging today?" Balfour asked as he poured, eyes on the jug.

David managed to repress his urge to shudder, though only just. "Yes," he said. "Though it wasn't just a hanging."

"No, they were beheaded too, I heard. Treason, wasn't it? A pair of radicals?"

David nodded and drank again. "You were not there?" he asked when he placed his cup back on the table.

Balfour shook his head. "I've only just arrived in town."

David took the opportunity to change the subject. "And where have you come from, Mr. Balfour?"

"London."

"A long journey," David observed. Odd, he thought, to come through Stirling on the way to Argyllshire, but he made no comment on that.

"I'm used to it. I've lived in London for a number of years now, but my family home is in Argyllshire, and I'm back at least once a year."

"I guessed you were a Scot," David admitted, "though your accent is difficult to place."

"So I'm told." Balfour gave a thin smile. "Most of my own countrymen think I'm English."

Most of them would. But David came across men like this all the time—wealthy Scots who preferred to spend their time in London, where the real political power was. He'd wager that the home in Argyllshire was a large estate. Balfour seemed like the sort of man used to having his own way, and the carelessly confident way he'd looked David over fitted with that.

The boy returned, carrying two heaped plates of meat pie and a dish of roasted vegetables. He set the dishes down before them wordlessly and hurried off to his next task. David stared down at the golden pie crust and pool of thick brown gravy and wondered why he'd ordered the meal. His already poor appetite had deserted him entirely now.

"This smells good," Balfour said conversationally. He tucked in with gusto. He probably had to eat a lot with that big, brawny body.

They made civil conversation while they ate, enquiring

after one another's journeys and commenting on weather, which they agreed looked like imminent rain. The topics they chose were safe and bland, and gradually David's edginess began to ebb a little.

Once he'd forced down half of his dinner, David pushed his plate aside.

"Aren't you hungry?" Balfour asked.

"Not really." David took a long draught of ale, wishing he'd asked for some whisky as well. The ale was too light—it didn't even touch him. He felt raw and too sober. He kept seeing Baird's and Hardie's linked hands, their bodies jerking against the rope. The moment he realised they were gone.

A wave of intense sadness and loneliness swamped him. Was this all there was? A few brief moments of connection— the grasp of another's hand on the scaffold—and then you were cast out, alone, into the great universe?

Balfour's voice, rising in a question, drew him back to the world.

"I'm sorry, I didn't catch that," David admitted, mortified by the heat he felt creeping into his cheeks.

"I was asking how you occupy yourself day to day, Mr. Lauriston." Balfour looked David in the eye as he spoke, his gaze disconcertingly direct. He didn't seem to obey the normal rules of social conversation. Wasn't it terribly unusual to stare so? Or was David seeing things that weren't there?

"I am a member of the Faculty of Advocates," David said. Even now, that announcement gave him a small, prideful thrill, though something about Balfour's answering smile took away a little of David's pleasure.

"Ah, a lawyer," Balfour said with a raised brow. "A noble profession."

Why did David get the sense that Balfour meant the exact opposite of what he said? He considered pointing that out, but at the last moment decided not to and took another mouthful of ale to swallow the words down with. Balfour grinned, and for some reason, David had the unsettling feeling the man had followed his train of thought.

"I practice mainly civil law," David said after a moment, aware of the tightness in his voice, "Though I have recently been involved in some criminal cases."

"Is that so? I may look you up when I am next in Edinburgh. I have a few legal matters that I need attended to."

"I am an advocate, Mr. Balfour. I only deal with court cases. If you need a will or some property deeds drawn up, you will need to engage a solicitor, though I would be happy to recommend someone."

Balfour gave him a long, unsmiling look. "I know what an advocate is, Mr. Lauriston."

Again, David felt discomfited. "I apologise," he said stiffly, "it's just that people often confuse the two professions." Now he sounded pompous.

"No need to apologise," Balfour replied easily, returning his attention to his plate. "This is an excellent pie," he added, changing the subject. He glanced at David's half-eaten effort. "It's a crime to leave so much uneaten."

"I'm afraid I'm not especially hungry."

"With the greatest respect, you look as though you could use a bit of feeding up."

"You sound like my mother," David replied before he could think better of it.

Balfour laughed at David's waspish tone, his mouth curving, a deep dimple flashing in his cheek. "Well, mothers are usually right about these things." The laughter lines at the corners of his dark eyes crinkled when he laughed, making him look suddenly much less cynical and worldly.

That infinitesimal change in expression inexplicably lightened David's mood; he gave a reluctant laugh of his own. "She gets annoyed with me when I forget to eat," he admitted.

"You forget to *eat*?"

Balfour sounded so horrified that David couldn't help but laugh again. "Not for long, but I do miss the odd meal. I'm not married, you see. It's easily done when I'm working—I lose track of the time."

Balfour gave him another of those direct, amused looks. "Now, why am I not surprised to hear that you're a bachelor, Mr. Lauriston?"

Made in United States
Troutdale, OR
11/15/2023

14594502R00219